BOUNDARY LINES

By Melissa F. Olson

Boundary Magic series

Boundary Crossed
Boundary Lines

Scarlett Bernard novels

Dead Spots
Trail of Dead
Hunter's Trail

Short Fiction

Sell-By Date: An Old World Short Story
Bloodsick: An Old World Tale
Malediction: An Old World Story

Lena Dane mysteries

The Big Keep

BOUNDARY LINES

BOUNDARY MAGIC, BOOK 2

MELISSA F. OLSON

47N⬤RTH

Published by 47North, Seattle

www.apub.com

Amazon, the Amazon logo, and 47North are trademarks of Amazon.com, Inc., or its affiliates.

ISBN-13: 9781503947061
ISBN-10: 1503947068

Cover design by Jason Blackburn
Cover Image by Mae I Design

Printed in the United States of America

For Paul, Jake, John, Brieta, Anna, and all the rest of my cousins:
these characters may not resemble you guys,
but Lex's love for them is my love for you.

Chapter 1

By nine o'clock on Halloween night, I had decided that something was definitely off with the witches of Boulder.

If I hadn't been leaning against a wall watching the crowd, I probably wouldn't have noticed it, or maybe I would have written it off as their discomfort with my presence. Hazel Pellar, the witch leader of all of Colorado, had invited me to her farm to attend her clan's Samhain festivities—a cocktail party followed by some kind of outdoor ceremony—as a PR move, to prove to the other witches that I wasn't really as scary as my abilities might imply.

It was a nice thought, I guess, but the night was turning into a minor disaster. The other witches didn't want anything to do with me, since my magic deals exclusively with the boundary between life and death. In their defense, witches with my bloodline have been accused of some pretty horrific things over the years: child sacrifices, raising armies of the dead, killing people with our minds. Not to mention fairly large chapters of the Inquisition. I wish I could say it was all slander, but really, that list was probably just what boundary witches had gotten *caught* doing.

As for me, well, I had only found out about all of this a couple of months ago, but that didn't seem to matter to the women chatting in tight clusters on the other side of Hazel Pellar's living room. If anything, my ignorance only made me *more* dangerous in their eyes. I did have a couple of allies in Clan Pellar, but Hazel's son, Simon, was still at home recovering from injuries he'd sustained while helping me, and his sister Lily had been pressed into service as co-host: putting away coats, checking on refreshments, that kind of thing.

So I stood alone, nursing a glass of white wine and trying to keep my own social anxiety off my face. All the isolation gave me plenty of time to notice a certain uneasiness in the air, a miasma that seemed to spread from person to person like an airborne electric shock. It wasn't just my presence, because the witches arriving at the party seemed ill at ease before they even spotted me.

I reached out and snagged Lily as she rushed through the room with a stack of napkins. "Hey, Lex!" she said brightly, wheeling around to face me. Lily was dressed like most of the women at the party, in a long skirt and knit top with little holes punched through the sleeves for her thumbs, a modest silver nose ring in one nostril. On everyone else, the look seemed like an amusingly outdated attempt at hippie chic. But with her flawless dark skin and inherent grace, Lily could have just stepped off a bohemian runway. "Sorry I haven't been by yet. I want to hear all about your trip." I winced, not really ready to discuss the unfortunate few days I'd spent in Los Angeles. Luckily Lily trailed off, looking around me with annoyance. "No one's talking to you?" she demanded.

"No, but—"

Her pretty face clouded over with irritation. "Goddamned witches," she spat. "They shouldn't be ostracizing you; acceptance is supposed to be their whole thing." She set a fistful of napkins down on a nearby table and turned around to face the room. "Let me just have a word with a few of these nice . . . *ladies.*"

"Whoa." I grabbed her elbow as she stepped forward, steering her back to me with her own momentum. "Leave it, Lily. Yelling at them isn't going to get me anywhere."

"But they're treating you like a leper because of your frickin' *blood,*" she protested, getting worked up. "This is such archaic bullshit! Not to mention total hypocrisy—"

"Maybe," I interrupted her, keeping my own voice low. "But the last time these people saw me, I was drunk on magic and about to flick your mother into the next county. Give them some time." Lily's face softened a little, and I pressed my advantage. "Time in which I appear to be calm, normal, and harmless. Not like a kid throwing a tantrum because she can't make friends."

She held up her hands. "Okay, okay. I'll play nice."

"Thank you." I took a deep breath. "Listen, is something else going on tonight?"

"What do you mean?"

"There's a weird vibe here. At first I thought it was just . . . you know, *me*, but everyone seems really antsy."

Lily frowned and looked around, her gaze taking in the tight body language of the guests. Then she squeezed her eyes shut, a look of fierce concentration on her face. When she opened them again, she surveyed the crowd critically, and I knew she had tuned in to the magical spectrum to check their auras. I couldn't do that. Nor could I access most of the other magic available to these witches. I could tune in to a magical spectrum of my own, but it was pretty much limited to seeing life essences, the spirits or souls that inhabited living creatures. "You're right," she murmured. "Their auras are weird, like they're churning or something. Well, not *yours*, of course—"

"Lily," said a steely voice behind us. I turned and saw Hazel Pellar approaching. She was a Caucasian woman in her midfifties, dressed in simple black slacks and a bronze-colored sweater that set off the silver in her long braid. She looked stern, but to be fair I don't think I'd ever seen Hazel when she *didn't* look stern. "Where are those napkins? That wine spill is starting to set."

"Mom, are you seeing these auras?" Lily asked. "They're all shifty tonight."

I watched Hazel's reaction carefully. I knew from experience that unlike most witches, Hazel Pellar couldn't turn off her view of the magical plane. She saw auras all the time, which was why she'd thrown me into the side of my own car the first time we met. Boundary witches have very telling black auras, a fact I'd learned when I regained consciousness.

"It's been happening for days, on and off," Hazel said briskly. "I'm sure it's just the sabbat on everyone's mind. Napkins, please."

Lily hesitated, looking like she wanted to argue, but after a moment she just shrugged, shot me an apologetic look, and hurried toward the living room with the napkins in hand.

Hazel turned to face me, and I tried not to squirm. I did *not* like having Hazel Pellar's full attention. "How has it been going?" she asked, her voice brisk and businesslike. Just to make sure I knew this wasn't actual small talk. "Is your niece okay? The tattoos are working?"

I nodded, automatically reaching down to rub my forearm under my sweater. "The tattoos are working. Lily's going to start teaching me about channeling, now that Simon's doing a little better," I said. "And Charlie is fine. My brother-in-law had her checked out just to be safe, but the doctor said her health is perfect."

Hazel nodded and turned to face the room. The witches nearest us were talking in low, frightened tones, their arms wrapped around themselves.

"What's really going on with them?" I said quietly. "It's not just the holiday, or me being here, is it?"

"No, I don't think so," Hazel admitted. "Word has spread that you're working for the *vampires* now"—her voice hardened with distaste—"and no one's happy about it. But they were like this before you arrived tonight." I opened my mouth, but she added tiredly, "I don't know what it is, Lex. I really don't."

Whoa—Hazel Pellar was admitting she didn't know what was happening? I actually considered teasing her for a second, but Hazel looked genuinely troubled, and it occurred to me how much our positions differed: I was still stumbling through all this magic stuff, which meant I was allowed to make mistakes. The other witches may have disliked me, but none of them expected me to know anything. Hazel, on the other hand, was supposed to have all the answers. It must have felt pretty awful for her to suddenly have no idea what was going on. "Do *you* feel different?" I asked.

The older witch frowned, and I could see her eyes lose focus as she considered the question. "That's the interesting part," she said. "It's almost . . . power-based."

"Power-based," I echoed, just to keep her talking.

"Think of witches as batteries for a moment, with varying degrees of power left in them," she lectured, and for a moment she sounded exactly like her son, the professor. "In our clan, I would be at the high end, and someone like Tracy"—she nodded toward a petite Asian woman in the corner, Simon's long-term girlfriend—"would be at the low end. But look at her."

Tracy was huddled with her arms wrapped around herself, rocking back and forth on her heels just a bit. She was trying to listen to the woman in front of her, but her eyes kept jerking around like she was being hunted. "That could be anything," I pointed out. "A bad day at work, an argument with family. Maybe she has a cold."

"True. But you yourself noticed how many people seem affected. Something just seems a bit unsettled, that's all." She shrugged, then seemed to remember who she was talking to. "Wait, are *you* feeling different?" Hazel demanded. My powers could be dangerous, and she was already more or less convinced that I was going to go off the deep end at any moment.

In her defense, she had already seen me do it once.

So I thought about her question carefully, using the techniques Simon had taught me in my training to examine my own feelings and mood. I was definitely uncomfortable, but I didn't think it had anything to do with magic, just being at this party. It was unusual for me to be in a room with this many people who weren't my own family, and like many veterans, crowds made me nervous. Especially borderline-hostile crowds of judgmental witches.

It didn't seem like a great idea to say any of that to Hazel, though. "Nah," I said finally. "Nothing out of the ordinary. Lily seemed okay too."

"And Lily's more powerful than most of them," she muttered, but I didn't think she was talking to me. I had been the one to point out the weird mood in the air, but now I found myself not wanting to discuss it. I just wanted to get out of there.

Hazel saw my discomfort and glanced at the clock on the wall. "Lex, I appreciate you coming here tonight, that you're trying," she said, without looking at me. "But we're about to start our sabbat rituals, and they're agitated enough without adding a—" her voice faltered for a moment, and I could almost see her effort to avoid the term "boundary witch," "—new person," she finished instead. "It's up to you, but it might be best if you ducked out before we begin the ceremony."

I set my wineglass down on the nearest hard surface. Didn't have to tell me twice.

To my surprise, Hazel abruptly stepped forward and enveloped me in a warm hug. "It was great that you could join us," she said brightly, which is when I realized we were putting on a show. "Take care, now." I hugged her back, forcing myself to smile.

I reminded myself that I should be grateful to Hazel for making an effort to assimilate me into her clan at all. Boundary witches had a reputation for being truly evil, an aberration. Judging by the looks we were getting, there were plenty of members who'd just as soon have me burned at a stake, like so many of my ancestors. But while I didn't entirely blame them, I didn't have to stand there and take it, either. As soon as Hazel stepped away, I practically sprinted for my car.

Chapter 2

The Pellar farmhouse was northeast of Boulder, almost all the way to Longmont. As I sped away from the farm, I rolled down my window for a moment, taking a few gulps of the crisp mountain air, which smelled pleasantly of bonfires and leaf piles. Trick-or-treating had ended hours ago, but as I maneuvered through the suburban area that led to Diagonal Highway, I saw that many of the residents had left out fat bowls of candy for late arrivals. I smiled. Earlier that day I'd had a stream of trick-or-treaters myself, mostly my local cousins and their kids. My cabin east of Boulder is fairly remote, so I gave out king-sized candy bars to make up for the trouble. It had been nice to do something as normal as hand out candy and chat with my family. I'd come to really crave the parts of my life from before I'd found out about the death magic in my blood. Before I'd learned that my niece, the only child of my deceased sister, was a valuable commodity in the Old World, the supernatural community.

As I thought of Charlie, my spirits sank again. My brother-in-law, John, had brought her over tonight too, her wiggly little body encased in a bright yellow bumblebee costume. John had stayed for coffee so I could take pictures and Charlie could play with a couple of my rescue dogs. She was just so adorable, like any human toddler. You'd never guess from looking at her that Charlie is a null, a human being who cancels out all kinds of magic: witch spells, vampirism, even werewolf magic. If you put the most powerful vampire in the world close enough to harmless little Charlie, he or she would become human again, complete with human vulnerabilities and strengths.

Nulls are very useful, very dangerous, and very rare in the Old World. Discovering nulls when they're young and emotionally pliable is rarer still. Charlie had already survived two kidnapping attempts, and I was determined that there wouldn't be a third. It was why I'd made the deal with the cardinal vampire of Colorado to keep her protected. In exchange, I had to do whatever she wanted short of killing people, an arrangement that only made the witches of Boulder hate me more.

I realized that my thoughts were just tangling into knots again, so I tried pushing them away, looking for something else to focus on. The radio station in my car was playing "Thriller" in honor of Halloween, and I tapped my fingers on the wheel, feeling restless. For some reason I didn't feel like being alone, which was unlike me. I sort of wanted to go downtown to see Quinn, my . . . friend? Coworker? The vampire for whom I had a thing? There really wasn't an easy label for him, but of everyone I'd met so far in the Old World, he knew me best, and although we both worked for Maven, he didn't seem to want anything from me, or worry that I might accidentally kill him.

Then again, things were awkward with Quinn. We had kissed less than two weeks ago. Then I'd left for Los Angeles to look for new information about my sister's death, and when I returned I'd been upset, not wanting to talk about it. I had been . . . well, not *avoiding* Quinn, exactly, but I wasn't going out of my way to resume our slow momentum toward each other.

It's Halloween. He's probably busy anyway, I told myself, trying not to feel like a coward. The vampires hung out at Magic Beans, a coffee shop in the heart of the touristy Pearl Street district. That area was also where the CU students went to drink, and if the past hundred years were any indication, they would be getting rather rowdy on Halloween night. I'd come to realize that rowdy college kids equaled a free buffet for vampires. They could always press their victims to forget being an involuntary blood donor, but it was probably easier to do when the victim in question was drunk and prone to blackouts.

There were lots of cars on the road now, adults on their way to and from their own Halloween celebrations. Time to make a choice. I had already passed the exit that led to the cabin. Now I could either turn around and go home or fight traffic to awkwardly face my crush.

I didn't really love either option, so I was clamoring for an alternative as I passed the thick hedge that had been planted around Mountain View Memorial Cemetery, ostensibly to protect mourners from the busy highway noise. I glanced over just in time to see a break in the shrubbery, giving me a perfect view into the cemetery . . . which was full of people. They stood in front of the graves, staring down at the in-ground markers. Absolutely, inhumanly still.

That in itself seemed unusual at ten p.m., but it *was* Halloween. I could dismiss the gathering as part of some organized college prank or protest . . . except for the fact that each and every one of them was emitting an eerie, continuous glow.

Adrenaline surged through me and I wrenched the wheel sideways across the median, spraying cedar chips and bits of shrubbery in my wake. I barely heard the honks and shouts behind me as I stomped on the brake and pulled into one of the entrance turnoffs. Breathing hard, I put the car in park and checked my rearview mirror for cops.

That was so stupid, I berated myself. Why hadn't I just pulled off at the next exit and circled back? I could get arrested for that little stunt, and what the hell did I care if . . .

Then I got a good look at the figures glowing against the darkness, and my thoughts seemed to drift away like an untethered helium balloon. They weren't at every grave—or even every fourth grave—but there were still hundreds of them, maybe more. If they had heard my tires squeal or the other cars honking when I crossed the median, they weren't showing it now. They were just standing there, each one staring down at a headstone.

It wasn't cold in the car, but there were chills crawling up my back underneath my heavy sweater. Despite everything I'd seen in the last two months, it still took me a long moment to realize that I was looking at ghosts. Actual *ghosts*. That word didn't seem to fit them, though. It was too silly, too whimsical. "Ghost" was a construction-paper decoration or an amoeba-like cartoon character. But what I was looking at now was connected to the human souls or spirits that I could see with my magic.

Then I remembered that weeks ago Simon had warned me I might be able to see . . . what had he called them? Remnants. At the time, I'd been so preoccupied with protecting my niece and learning to use my other abilities that I'd completely forgotten. And I had no idea why there were so many of them in this place.

I found myself shutting off the car, opening the door. I had no real plan, but I was unbearably curious. More than that: I was *pulled* to them, the same way I was pulled to Maven, the powerful cardinal vampire of Colorado. Cautiously, I walked toward the closest one, a short, round Caucasian woman with long silvery hair. She was wearing a simple violet cotton dress with a blue apron tied around it in a drooping bow. She didn't look up as I approached, so I slowly began to circle her, intent on seeing her eyes.

Before I made it all the way around her, however, I saw the blood.

It had welled out of a grisly dark slice at her throat, then spilled forward to saturate her dress and apron. It streaked all the way down to pool in her sensible shoes, a red waterfall that still looked wet. For a moment I was tempted to touch it to see if it *was* wet, but I curled my fingers into a fist to restrain myself. I looked up at the woman's face. She was around fifty, with empty eyes and wispy bangs that had started to curl away from her forehead, exactly as if she'd started to sweat and pressed them away with a damp palm. Her eyes were cast down at her gravestone, like all the others.

"What happened to you?" I said softly, without thinking. The woman's gaze seemed to flicker for an instant, like something buried deep inside her had reacted to me, but then she continued to stare down.

"Are you okay?" I asked, and my hand automatically rose to touch her shoulder.

Stupid, *stupid* Lex.

A bolt of condensed emotion jolted through my arm, driving me to my knees as the wave of feelings crashed into me. Bright purple flashes of pain, peppery anguish, and oh, such horrible fear. *Nononono no why do I have to die I'm still so young what about Jody no I can't leave her why is he doing this I don't even know him it isn't fair please don't please no—*

As I fell, my fingers lost contact with the woman, and I let out a ragged wail, my butt hitting the dead grass hard. I looked up and saw all of the figures turn their heads sharply, like a coordinated movement. They weren't staring at the graves anymore. They were all staring at me.

And their eyes were hungry.

Chapter 3

Not daring to breathe, I began inching backward on my hands, wanting to get enough distance from the bloody woman to stand up and run. Now that they were facing me, I could see that many of them had visible injuries: a splash of blood over a teenager's heart, a missing piece of an old man's head. One woman had no obvious wounds, but she appeared to be soaking wet, though nothing dripped off her. Her face was bloodless, her eyes bulging, desperate.

Except for the eyes, all of their faces were completely slack—not like a human at rest or asleep, more like a human with no muscle control at all. Dead. I had seen horrible things when I was in the army, and I'd done some pretty horrible things too. But these people, each in their isolated, timeless, bloodied space, were like grotesque action figures under bell jars. They were gruesome in a way I'd never imagined.

Their gazes were fixed hungrily in my direction, and I got the sense that they wanted something from me. Something that would consume me, use me up until I was nothing, not even a soul. A few of the closest ones even swayed a little, as if shifting their weight to come after me. I was too overwhelmed to move away. A whimper escaped my lips, and I hated myself for it. At the sound, the ghost nearest me took a slow, laborious step, like his foot had grown roots he had to snap. The next step was much swifter. I braced myself for . . . something.

Then a short, girlish figure stepped in between them and me. "Go back, go back," she said softly. "She cannot help you. Not now." The voice was accentless, in that very particular way of someone who has worked at not having an accent. It was low and gentle and extremely familiar. It pulled at me too, a different kind of glow.

"Maven," I gasped.

"You shouldn't be here, little witch," she said over her shoulder to me. "Go back to your car, slowly."

I rose to my feet and began to obey, forcing myself to inch backward as slowly as I could manage. I didn't want to turn my back on those things. Maven started moving backward too, but she kept herself angled between me and the dead. When they could no longer see me, they began to lose interest, and one by one their heads swiveled slowly, unnaturally, back toward their gravestones.

When I lost sight of them around the hedge, I finally turned and rushed back to my car, knowing Maven would follow. I opened the door and climbed in—only to find her already waiting in the passenger seat next to me.

I jumped. Goddamned vampires. "Quinn does that too," I grumbled.

Maven gave me a slightly confused look, and I realized she hadn't been trying to startle me. She was just that fast. The cardinal vampire of all Colorado appeared to be a girl of nineteen or twenty, with a fringe of bright orange hair, chunky glasses, and lots of necklaces and rings. Tonight, like every other time I'd seen her, she was dressed in layers and layers of baggy cotton and flannel, like a homeless flower child. I had long since concluded that she was trying to disguise her beauty and immortal poise behind all that junk, but it only partially worked. If you looked past the glasses and unflattering layers and bad haircut, she was still breathtaking.

I shook my head. "Never mind. What just happened? What were those . . ." I took a breath. "They were ghosts, right? Um, remnants?"

"Not exactly. Ordinary remnants are like short recordings of a death event. Common enough, and they fade away by themselves eventually. These were . . ." Maven twisted one hand in the air, a human gesture for when you can't find a word. *"Gjenganger,"* she said at last. "Restless, unhappy spirits whose deaths were violent enough to leave a psychic impact. I turned them away, but we should still leave. Take me to the coffee shop." I nodded and started the car, pulling us back onto the highway.

I wanted more information, but when I glanced at Maven, I saw that she was frowning slightly. Unlike most vampires I'd met, Maven actually did a pretty good job of remembering to practice human mannerisms—she used contractions, laughed, and I'd even seen her flirt with customers at the coffee shop she manages. But she often dropped it when there were no humans nearby. The worried expression suggested she was too distracted to drop her own act.

"What's wrong?" I asked.

There was a heavy silence, in which I could practically feel her trying to decide whether to trust me with information. I can never just get a goddamned straight answer from vampires. They have to think eight moves ahead to make sure telling me something won't hurt them down the road.

"They should not have been so vibrant," she said at last. *"Gjenganger* appear every Samhain, but I have *never* seen them in such detail."

I felt goose bumps prickle my arms under my jacket. Maven was a gajillion years old, so anytime she said she'd never seen or done something, it was significant. "For a moment, I wasn't sure I could turn them away," she admitted, and that scared me even more.

I wondered if I should tell her about the strange vibe I'd felt at the witches' Samhain celebration. Could the two things be related? It seemed possible, but it also didn't feel right to expose a potential weakness in the witch clan to the cardinal vampire, even if the two groups *were* technically allied. When push came to shove, I'd sworn my loyalty to Maven, but that didn't mean push was all the way to shove right now. *It's probably just Samhain throwing everyone off, like Hazel said,* I told myself.

"Why would angry ghosts listen to you at all?" I asked.

"They recognize me," she said simply. "I am death."

Her tone was so matter-of-fact, especially from her girlish, teenage-looking mouth, that her words sent chills across my shoulder blades. Then she added, "They recognize you too, boundary witch. You should not be in a graveyard on Samhain."

I blinked. I'd looked up Samhain on Wikipedia. It was a pagan celebration for the end of the harvest season, loosely connected to the modern Halloween. It didn't seem like it had anything to do with boundary magic. "Why not?"

She gave me a confused look again, as if she thought I was putting her on. "Three hundred and sixty-four days of the year, the *gjenganger* are tethered," she explained. "But on Samhain, the barrier between the living and the dead is at its thinnest. That's why they must return to their . . ." she gestured toward the ground, reminding me of the figures' downcast eyes. "Their remains."

"Oh."

Maven gave me a curious look. "I've never known a boundary witch with so little understanding of death. Didn't Hazel Pellar tell you any of this?"

I shook my head. "She doesn't . . . well, she *says* she doesn't know anything about boundary magic." Then the implications of Maven's statement sunk in. "Wait, you know other boundary witches?" I said eagerly, peering over at her impassive face. I still knew so little about what I could do. "Living ones? Where are they? Can I meet them?"

She sighed. "No, not living. Look, we're getting off track. I'm here to speak to you about a job."

I had about thirty follow-up questions, but I tried to focus. I hadn't been working for Maven long, and so far she'd required very little of me: I'd really just run a few daytime errands, things Maven and her vampires couldn't do after business hours. But the way she'd said "job" just now was not the way you talked about picking up dry cleaning or running to the bank—and she'd come to see me herself, which had never happened before. "You didn't just run into me at the cemetery, then."

"No. When you didn't answer my call, I tracked your phone."

Oh. Right. I'd agreed to let Maven keep tabs on me when I'd sworn my oath of loyalty. "What's the job?" I asked.

"Two of my people have gone missing," she replied. "I want you and Quinn to investigate. He's getting supplies together now." Her voice was calm, almost dismissive, as though we were discussing her misplaced keys instead of two of her *vampires*.

"What kind of supplies?" I asked, wary. Weapons? Was she expecting a fight?

She turned her head to study me, and I tried not to squirm. "Quinn explained that there are no werewolves in the state of Colorado, yes? And why?"

I blinked at the abrupt change in topic. "Um, yes. He said that a crazy alpha werewolf started a war here years ago, and you and Itachi destroyed him and scattered the pack."

She nodded. "My covenant with the witches is to keep the werewolves out of Colorado for twenty years. In return, they must serve my interests, should I call upon them."

"Right . . ."

"Every full moon, when the werewolf magic forces them to change, I dispatch vampires to the state border to hunt for signs of pack behavior. The last full moon was four nights ago, on the twenty-seventh," she explained. "My representative at the northeast border was supposed to return to Boulder on the twenty-eighth, but I didn't hear from her. One of my representatives at the western edge of the state did not report back either."

"You think werewolves got them," I said, fury building in my chest. In Los Angeles, I'd learned that my sister had been killed by a mad werewolf. The idea of getting to hunt and kill some was disturbingly appealing.

But for the first time that night, Maven hesitated. "It's possible," she said at last. "But after what happened with Itachi . . ." She trailed off, leaving me to fill in the blanks. Itachi had been the leader of all things supernatural in Colorado up until a few weeks ago. Maven had assisted him as a sort of advisor, a lieutenant. But Itachi hadn't liked having a lieutenant who was so much more powerful than himself, so he had tried to have my niece kidnapped in order to increase his long-term power base. Quinn and I had helped Maven bring him down for good.

"You think they might have fled the state because they were loyal to Itachi," I surmised.

Maven nodded. "There has been some . . . unrest over the last few weeks." There was a sudden hardness in her tone that I recognized. Someone else in her organization had recently deserted, or threatened to mutiny, something like that. Which explained why she'd taken the time to come talk to me herself, instead of sending a minion. She needed to keep the whole thing quiet until we knew for sure there was a problem. The power structure of the Old World, I'd discovered, depended heavily on perception. The more it seemed like Maven didn't have control of her territory, the less control she'd have over her territory.

But she knew Quinn and I could be trusted—well, at least as much as she could trust anyone. After all, Quinn had been publicly outed as Maven's mole in Itachi's old organization, and Maven had made sure every vampire within a thousand miles both hated and feared me. If she ever lost control of Colorado, we were both toast—and Charlie would be fair game.

You chose this, I reminded myself. *You made a deal; now honor it.* "I'm supposed to work tomorrow morning; should I get someone to cover my shift?" I was still technically employed as a register monkey at the Flatiron Depot, a 24-hour convenience store, though

I had cut my hours to part-time and switched to day shifts. Maven gave me a stipend, but she didn't use me often enough to fill my time, and I needed to have a job I could explain to my family.

"I don't think that will be necessary," Maven answered. "One way or the other, we should know before sunrise."

Well, that sounded ominous.

Chapter 4

Magic Beans was located on Pine Street, in between a cutesy store that sold overpriced jewelry and a restaurant that made its own cheese. It was near the Boulderado, a popular tourist hotel, and only a few blocks away from my parents' mini mansion in Mapleton. I cut across Iris Ave and down Highway 7, hoping to avoid the majority of drunk college students who were likely still roaming Pearl Street, bouncing between bars like balls on a pool table. Despite my efforts, the closer we got to Magic Beans, the more crowded the sidewalks became, and the costumed college kids seemed to have some kind of jaywalking death wish. I came very close to running down three young women dressed as a sexy nurse, sexy doctor, and sexy dolphin (!), respectively, after they decided to run diagonally through an intersection in a drunken, zigzag fashion.

When the sexy dolphin's tail flared up to reveal shapely thighs, Maven looked over at me, cocking a questioning eyebrow. I just shrugged. "Don't look at me. When I was twenty-two my costume was desert camo."

Finally I pulled into the tiny parking lot behind Magic Beans. I spotted Quinn coming out the back door, headed toward a new-looking Jeep Wrangler Unlimited. He was dressed for fieldwork in dark-washed jeans and an all-weather jacket, and he carried a duffel bag.

He paused as he saw my car, squinting against the glare of headlights, and my heart did a happy little leap, which annoyed me. I'm in my thirties. I should not get *butterflies*.

As we climbed out of the car, Quinn nodded respectfully at Maven, then shot me a quick, private smile that burned through my resolve. I couldn't help but grin back. "You have everything you need?" Maven said brightly. The perkiness surprised me, but then I realized that she'd dropped into her spacey barista persona, the one she used when she worked the front counter.

"I think so," Quinn replied. "I'll call if we're not going to be back before sunrise. Hey, Lex."

"Hi," I said. "Where are we going?"

"Julesburg," he said, naming a town in the northeast corner of the state. "That's the closest disappearance." He tossed the duffel bag into the back of the Jeep and opened the passenger-side door. "Shall we?"

I looked back and forth between him and the massive vehicle. When the two of us went looking for Charlie's kidnappers, we'd taken his car or my old Subaru. But I just shrugged and climbed in.

As Quinn took his turn navigating through the drunken coeds, I looked around the interior of the fancy car, half afraid to touch anything. The Jeep's dashboard and floor mats were spotless, and when I peeked over my shoulder I saw that the back had been tricked out to include some kind of concealed compartment in the floor that took up the whole width of the Jeep. "What's with the wheels?" I asked Quinn.

"Maven's answer to Air Force One," he explained. "She bought it shortly after she took over, and lends it to her people when we might need to be out after dawn."

Ah. "The compartment in the back is lightproof?"

He nodded. "Lightproof, armored, and climate controlled. Cost a fortune." He shook his head a little. "Maven doesn't put on airs or throw around money, but she invests where it counts." His tone was admiring, and I wondered if things had gotten easier or harder for him now that we'd taken Itachi off the board.

"How will she get home?" I asked.

A faint smile crossed his lips. "She'll ride her bike."

Ah, Boulder.

When the last lights of the city were behind us, Quinn glanced over at me. "The thing in LA," he said. "Did you find out what you needed to know?"

"Yes," I said shortly. "She was eaten by werewolves. I don't really want to talk about it."

Quinn nodded, his face falling into its usual implacable expression. I regretted my curt tone. There had been a time when that dispassionate look was the only one I ever got from Quinn, and I'd hoped we were past that. But I just couldn't talk about Sam right now. "Tell me about the vampires who disappeared," I prompted instead.

He nodded. "Every full moon, ten of us take a shift patrolling the state borders, watching for any signs of werewolf activity," he began. "We've found natural wolves a couple of times, but never any weres, at least for as long as I've been in Colorado. But on the last full moon, two people didn't report in."

"Maven told me that much. Who are they?"

"Travis disappeared from Dove Creek, and Allegra went missing out of Julesburg."

I raised my eyebrows. "Just Travis and Allegra? Don't vampires *ever* have last names?"

A brief smile twitched across his face, and I felt like I'd scored a point. "Of course we do, on all our legal paperwork. But those change every few decades, or so I'm told. We typically just use our first names within our own territories. It's easier to remember—and easier not to expose someone by mistake, like if you were to refer to me as Quinn Adams after I'd already changed my name to Quinn . . . Merlin." He lifted his hand off the wheel long enough to wave it dismissively. "Or whatever."

I laughed. "Merlin? Your example of a fake last name is *Merlin*?" He glared at me, but the smile was obvious in his eyes. "Oh shit," I blurted. "Don't tell me that's your last name *now*."

Quinn laughed out loud, a sound I'd heard only a few times. It made something in my chest loosen. "No, Quinn is currently my *last* name."

"So what's your current first name?"

"Arthur," he said airily. I laughed, unable to tell if he was kidding or not.

"Back to Allegra and Travis," I prompted. "Maven brought up the possibility that they might have just . . . defected."

He considered that for a moment. "It's possible," he allowed.

I tried to think through the implications of that. "Hypothetically," I said in a careful voice, "if Allegra or Travis, or anyone else, for that matter, decided they wanted to leave Maven's enclave, would there be consequences?"

His brow furrowed. "You mean like, would Maven hunt them down and kill them for leaving?"

"Well . . . yeah."

"Technically, vampires are not supposed to jump territories without permission," he told me. "We have to be careful with things like population control and population density, and if everyone starts crossing borders willy-nilly, it increases the chance of all of us getting discovered by the foundings." That was the Old World term for ordinary humans, and it was always used dismissively, the way you would say "cattle."

"But Maven's still trying to lock in control after the takeover," Quinn continued, "and frankly I don't think she has the resources to hunt down defectors right now. That's part of why she waited this long before sending us after Allegra and Travis—she's been spread too thin to deal with it. Most likely, if someone leaves, they'll make Maven's permanent shit list, to be punished later. *I* sure as hell wouldn't want to be on her shit list, but leaving the state isn't like an instant death sentence or anything."

"Hmm." This was enough to give me a headache. There were too many possibilities, too many suspects, including Travis and Allegra themselves. Once again, I felt like it was my first day at a new job. Everyone else could think faster and clearer than I could because they had decades or even centuries of experience with the Old World, and I had known about it for less than two months. I sighed. "So is it safe to assume Maven didn't kill them herself? I mean, if she had, there'd be no reason to send us on this little quest."

"True," he conceded. "I think that's a pretty safe assumption, yes."

Great. So that was *one* person who probably didn't kill them. "Did Travis and Allegra . . . er . . . know each other?"

He shot me a wry smile. "You mean like, biblically?"

"Well, yeah."

"No. Travis was a bit of a dandy, and Allegra was really down-to-earth. I can't see her spending more than two minutes with him."

There was something in his tone—admiration, maybe? He glanced over at me, and discomfort crossed his face. "Listen, Lex, there's something else you should know. Allegra and I, we used to . . . date. Years ago."

"Date," I repeated.

He sighed. Vampires, I had discovered, don't technically *need* to breathe, but most of them do out of habit, and to blend in. "We used to sleep together. Recreationally."

"Oh." I mulled that over for a moment. Quinn was a relatively new vampire—we had never discussed the specifics of his turn, but I knew it happened between five and ten years ago, in Chicago. I also knew that he had been sold to Maven against his will . . . and that sometime in between getting changed and coming to Boulder, he had attacked his human wife. In that context, it made sense that he'd want to sleep with another vampire: he was wary of hurting humans. Which was pretty ironic given his job as Maven's fixer.

But then, I knew better than anyone that there was a big difference between hurting someone on orders and hurting someone because you couldn't make yourself stop.

Still, it was hard to picture Quinn—or any of the other vampires I'd met—craving sex or intimacy at all. They seemed so remote, so detached from their emotions. Yeah, Quinn had shown a little interest in me, and we had kissed, but in that moment, I realized I wasn't sure how far that interest extended.

I groped for something to say, but what came out of my mouth was, "I wasn't sure you guys . . . did that." *Oh, great recovery, Lex.*

"What, have sex?" He rolled his eyes. "I'm a vampire, Lex, I'm not dead."

"Well—"

"You know what I mean," he replied, a little irritated. "Our bodies can do all the same things human bodies can; we just choose whether to prioritize them. It takes energy—blood—to turn on biological functions, but it can be done."

I thought that over. "So you get to decide whether or not you'll . . . um . . . crave intimacy?"

"Yes. Just like I can devote energy to having a heartbeat, sweating, or even eating, although I can't digest food the way you can," he said matter-of-factly. "Our bodies adapted to power our basic functions first—hunter instincts, feeding capabilities. Everything else depends on how much blood we drink, how often."

"Huh." Science was never my particular interest, but that made a lot of sense, in terms of how vampires had managed to stay hidden within the human race for so long. It also said something about Quinn that he'd chosen to devote energy to human emotions when he didn't have to.

We rode along in silence for a few minutes, and then I couldn't help but ask, "Did you love her?"

"No." His voice was weary. "We got along okay, and we both needed somebody. I care about what happens to her, but I mostly just thought you should know about it since you and I are . . . you know."

"Interested in each other?" I suggested. It made my heart pound hard in my chest, but I was too goddamned old to play games.

"Yes," Quinn said simply.

I didn't know quite what to say after that, so we rode in peaceable silence for quite a while. I was just starting to doze off in my seat when we saw the sign for Julesburg.

"Where exactly are we going?" I finally asked.

"Maven keeps these little chambers buried underground for us to hide in if we get caught away from home," he explained. "They're safer than a hotel. We'll start there, see if we can pick up Allegra's trail."

"I don't suppose it's a *gigantic* underground chamber?" I said hopefully. "Like the size of a building, with lots of great ventilation and maybe some skylights?"

He smiled. "Nope, sorry. I know you're claustrophobic, so you can stay on top and guard the entrance."

"Guard duty?" I said, brightening. "I *love* that plan. I crush it at guard duty."

We drove all the way through Julesburg, a former stagecoach station whose only real claim to fame was its connection to corruption and torture. The town was named after Jules Beni, a station manager who was guilty of *helping* the horse thieves instead of stopping them. According to legend, Beni was killed by his former boss, Jack Slade, a gunslinger who shot off each one of Beni's fingers and sliced off his ears to keep as trophies.

Unlike many former Wild West towns, for some reason Julesburg never really caught on as a tourist destination. Today, the population still hovered at a little over a thousand people.

We followed Highway 138 past Julesburg and were nearly to the Nebraska border before Quinn turned off onto an unmarked road headed east into fields of . . . well, something. It was too dark to make out the crops, but eventually the field terminated next to some scrubby woodlands. Quinn pulled off onto a little one-lane offshoot of the road and turned off the Jeep.

"Who owns this property?" I asked him.

He shrugged. "This one's been tied up in will probate for years and years. I don't think anyone's ever discovered one of Maven's vaults, but if someone did, the foundings would just write it off as some weird construction error."

"What do you mean, construction error?"

"Come see." He hopped out of the Jeep, and I grabbed my flashlight and followed him. We walked about fifty feet into the grass, nearly to the edge of the woods, before Quinn found the spot he wanted and dropped his duffel bag next to it. I played my flashlight over the overgrown grass as he leaned down and dug his fingers in, like he was feeling around for something. I was about to ask what he was doing, but by then he was pulling up a four-by-four piece of sod, revealing a green metal circle underneath. It was flat and smooth like an oversized sewer cover, but larger and raised about four inches above the ground, with concrete underneath. Obviously a lid. I crouched down to tug at it, but Quinn grabbed my arm. "Let me," he urged. "The edges on these things can be sharp."

I nodded, understanding. There was death magic in my blood, and Quinn was afraid he wouldn't be able to keep himself from attacking me if I started bleeding. I had more faith in him, but this wasn't the time to get into it. I gestured toward the lid. "Be my guest."

Quinn reached down with one hand and easily lifted the steel cover, which came up with a sucking *pop*. There was a cavernous hole underneath, the interior so dark that my flashlight beam barely penetrated it, even when I crouched down. It smelled like concrete and earth, but the air wasn't particularly stale.

Directly below us I could just make out a small metal stepladder, but there was nothing around it except for gray concrete. "Uh, Quinn?" I said. "Is this a *septic tank*?"

"We prefer to think of them as 'portable emergency storage chambers,'" he deadpanned.

Well, that explained the "construction error" concept—if anyone ever found this, they'd just figure a tank had been installed and then the homeowners had changed their minds. "That's . . . kind of brilliant," I admitted.

Quinn nodded, then frowned. "I smell blood."

Before I could respond, he abruptly planted one foot on the concrete rim and dropped into the hole, landing without a sound. If I hadn't seen the little stepladder, I might have worried he'd just drop down forever, like in *Looney Tunes* cartoons.

I leaned down as far as I could before fear enveloped me. Septic tanks were what, eight feet by twelve feet? Something like that? I shivered. Not that different from the inside of a Humvee. "Quinn?" I called. "Um, is she down there?"

"No, but there's something written on the wall." His grim voice wafted up out of the darkness. He sounded far away now, and I wondered just how deep the tank was. "It's too dark, even for me. Can you pass down the lantern?"

"Yeah." I pulled the camp-style lantern out of his duffel bag, switched it on, and put one hand on the rim of the concrete lip to steady myself so I could lean forward and lower it down by its long cord.

The concrete was old, or maybe I just put my hand on exactly the wrong spot, but the palm-sized piece directly under my hand crumbled off, and my fingers slipped off the lip. I tried to jerk backward to right myself, but my center of gravity was too far over the chasm by then. I tumbled forward into the hole, and the next thing I felt was the impact of concrete on my skull.

Chapter 5

"Lex!"

To my surprise, I did not wind up as a skin-bag of shattered bones on the floor of the concrete tank. Instead I found myself awkwardly positioned in Quinn's arms, as though we were dancing and he'd led me into an elaborate dip. Only my head was about three inches above the floor of the concrete tank.

I was disoriented from my head smacking into the concrete opening on my way down, so it took me a few moments to get my bearings and realize he had caught me. It didn't help that the heavy-duty lantern was rolling away from us, sending light spinning across the walls. It finally came to rest against the wall of the tank, leaving my left side bathed in light, the right side in darkness. "Thanks," I said, my voice coming out dazed and thick. "Think I hit my head."

Quinn didn't answer or even move to help me up. He just froze in place, his arms locked around my back, our faces less than a foot apart. I heard a miniscule *tap . . . tap . . . tap . . .* on the concrete just below me. Like something dripping. My fingers rose to touch my temple where it had hit the concrete, and came away bloody. Only then did I finally register the long, warm trickle of hot liquid that ran down the side of my head into my hair.

I didn't think I was seriously hurt, but head wounds bleed like a son of a bitch—and Quinn was captivated by the magic in my blood.

"Hey—" I squirmed to get away from him, but his body was locked in place. I could only see one of his eyes in the half-light, but his pupil was dilated to the edge of the iris, his nostrils flaring. *"Quinn!"* I yelped, wriggling harder. His weight finally shifted, but it was in the wrong direction, pressing me to the floor. Holding me down.

Talk to him, commanded a voice in my head. *Make him see you.*

"Quinn, you have to push past it," I whispered. "You have to get over this if we're going to work together. *Be* together." I felt like I was babbling, and the words didn't seem to have any effect on him. "Please, I know you can do it."

He showed no sign that he'd even heard me, just relaxed his own weight down on top of mine, leaning against my body, smothering my options. For a moment I had that specific, explosive sense of terror that's familiar to so many women—but Quinn had no interest in raping me, and my fear dissolved as he began nuzzling the side of my head, straining toward the blood. I didn't fight him as he licked at the wound, instinctively understanding that it would only make him use more strength, trap me further. He pulled back to meet my eyes, and a flare of new pain ignited in my head. He was on vampire autopilot now, trying to press his victim into submission.

But I do not press. And I am no one's fucking victim.

His hand came up and brushed against my cheek, intending to turn my face sideways for better access. But that freed up my arm, and for just a moment, I could move.

I could have clocked him. I almost did: Violence was the time-tested Lex reaction, after all. But I knew that if I hit Quinn, the best-case scenario was that it would bring him back to his senses. Once he was in control again, he would hate himself for attacking me, even though he wasn't really causing me any harm just yet. No, what I really wanted was to show him he could stop *himself.* So without thinking much about it, I grabbed his face hard, turned it toward me, and pressed my lips against his.

His body went completely rigid for a moment, frozen again. I could probably have stopped there, but instead I traced my fingers along his cheek and slid them into his hair. I nipped lightly at his lips, then more urgently, and at last he relaxed, his mouth softening against mine. And before I knew it, he was kissing me back, tentatively, as though he'd just woken up. As our lips opened I tasted blood in his mouth, *my* blood, but it was no more than if I'd bitten my own lip, and by then I was too caught up in the kiss to be bothered. When I didn't pull away, Quinn's arms went to my hips, firmly flipping us over so that I was on top of him, in control, and I smiled into his mouth. He was back.

Still kissing him, I scooted down his body until I was more or less in his lap, and then sat up so he was forced to either follow me or break the kiss. He propelled himself upward, his mouth moving from my lips down the line of my jaw and down my neck. I shuddered with pleasure, opening my eyes to see stars. A tiny hole of stars. Anyone could come along and put the lid back on the septic tank, and then we'd be trapped in here forever, buried alive.

The claustrophobia slammed down on me, and I forgot all about my hormones. Terror raced through my body, crushing my chest, and Quinn went still as he sensed, or maybe smelled, the change in me. I scrambled off his body and stood up unsteadily, lunging for the stepladder. But in my haste, I somehow managed to kick it farther away. The ladder crashed into the lantern, sending the light swinging wildly around the small space, and I was sobbing for breath now, convinced I couldn't get enough air.

"Lex!" Quinn had realized what was happening. I got a quick glimpse of the wall behind him before he wrapped his arms around me. "Close your eyes," he whispered. "You can breathe, I promise. Just close your eyes and you'll see."

I squeezed my eyes shut, trying to trust him. But even without being able to see the concrete walls, I knew they were there, and it felt like they were closing in. I couldn't get my breathing to slow down.

"Hang on, I'm gonna boost you out," Quinn said as he pulled away from me. I opened my eyes and stared into his face. "Put your foot in my hand," he instructed. "On three. One, two, *three!*"

Without even a grunt of effort, he lifted me up, and for a second I flew like the girl at the top of a cheerleader pyramid, not that I'd ever been a cheerleader. I hit the grass and tumbled, but he'd judged the distance well, and I managed to turn it into a sort of dizzying roll, coming up on one knee. When I found my balance, I let my body sag back down so I was lying on my back, staring at the sky, my breath finally slowing down.

Quinn popped up through the hole a moment later. He didn't try to touch me, just collapsed next to me on the cold, dying grass. We stayed that way for a moment, side by side on the ground, neither of us quite sure what to say.

"Honestly," I panted, "we have the *most* fun."

He laughed, a startled, sonorous sound that I could see myself getting addicted to. "How's your head?" he asked.

I touched it gingerly. I had a mild headache, and would probably have a bump the next morning, but the bleeding had already stopped. "Fine, I think. I'll have Lily look at it when I get back to town, but I don't think it'll even need stitches."

I heard his head nodding against the dry grass. There was a silent moment where we could have discussed the kiss, but I watched it come and go without working up the nerve.

"Did you see the message?" he asked at last.

The message. Right. The whole reason we were in the septic tank in the first place. "Yeah." I'd noticed the rust-colored words painted on the wall of the tank, but my gaze had only touched on them briefly given all the . . . distractions. The picture surfaced in my memory, the words finally registering. "Was that her hand-writing?"

"I think so. And definitely her blood."

I didn't ask how he could tell. I didn't really want to know. I was getting cold, so I sat up and wrapped my arms around my knees. "So she was wounded?"

"Not necessarily." Quinn sat up next to me and draped an arm around my shoulders. His body gave off very little heat—probably another conservation of energy thing—but I appreciated the gesture anyway. "There's no blood spatter anywhere else, and I can't smell any up here either. More likely she wanted to leave a note, but there wasn't time for her to find a paper and pen. She probably bit her finger, wrote the message, and went to investigate."

Allegra had left just five words, painted in her own blood: *Quinn—howling to the north.*

Chapter 6

"This means she didn't just defect, right?" I asked Quinn.

He was silent for a moment, thinking it over. "With anyone else—hell, even with Travis—I'd argue it doesn't prove anything," he said slowly. "If a vampire hated Maven's leadership, the best way to escape her grasp unscathed would be to skip town and blame it on the werewolves. It'd create a lot of confusion and distraction, giving them the chance to get far enough away that Maven couldn't find them."

"But . . ." I prompted.

"But Allegra doesn't play games," he stated. "It's one of the reasons why I liked her. If she didn't want to be under Maven's rule, she'd either ask for her freedom or quietly leave the country."

"So we think it's werewolves," I concluded.

"Yeah," he said heavily. "We think it's werewolves."

Quinn got out his phone and paced a little ways away to check in with Maven and get instructions. Wanting to help somehow, I found his spare flashlight in the duffel bag and began pulling out cleaning supplies, figuring she'd at least want us to clean up the blood. I was also hoping Maven would send us after the werewolves. Nothing sounded better to me at that moment than looking a werewolf in the eyes before I killed it.

If that sounds harsh, well, I had my reasons. When, less than a year ago, my twin sister, Sam, was murdered in Los Angeles, the police had told us that she was the victim of a serial killer and that we would probably never find her remains. But being a boundary witch allowed me to talk to Sam, now on the other side of that life/death border, in my dreams. During our last conversation, she'd urged me to talk to Detective Jesse Cruz of the LAPD and find out how she had *really* died. Hence my trip to LA to find him.

After I managed to convince Cruz that I already knew about the Old World—that I was now a *part* of it—he and his friend, Scarlett Bernard, finally told me the truth about my sister's murderer: he was a werewolf, trying to make himself a mate. I'd heard from Simon and Lily that magic had been fading in the world for generations, and apparently this made changing someone into a werewolf far from a sure thing. The werewolf in LA had killed three women, including Sam, before successfully changing the fourth, Lizzy. I'd met her briefly, and she was a mess from the werewolf magic. She called herself a monster, and I couldn't exactly disagree.

Any doubts I'd entertained about whether Sam was actually dead had vanished the first time she reached out to me from the other side. But my parents . . . I was pretty sure they were holding on to a tiny bit of hope that she was still alive somewhere. I had asked Scarlett if I could take her body back to my family, for closure. But as it turned out, she had tossed my sister's corpse in a furnace—like she was *garbage*—to hide any supernatural evidence. And now my parents and Sam's husband had nothing to bury, and they never would.

The worst part was that I was now a member of a team that did the exact same thing: covered up crimes, destroyed bodies. I'd signed on before I'd really felt the impact of what it would mean, what I might be doing to other families, and I'd done it to save Sam's own daughter.

I flopped back in the grass, which made my head ache even more. Everything in my life had become so *complicated*.

"Lex? You okay?"

I snapped back to attention, sitting up again. "Yeah. What did Maven say?"

Even in the flashlight's dim beam, I could see Quinn eyeing me. "She wants us to come back. Allegra's note is too vague for us to go after the wolves tonight. We need more intelligence."

There was a weight to his voice, enough to make me forget my own problems. "What's wrong?"

He shook his head. "Werewolves sneaking into Colorado is bad enough. It means they're not afraid of Maven like they should be. More importantly, though, this means Maven has technically broken her covenant with the witches. If they find out, all hell could break loose. We're gonna need to hit back hard and fast."

"A war," I said softly.

We cleaned up the writing in the septic tank—well, Quinn did. I stayed up top and checked the area for footprints or other telling signs of our presence—and left for Boulder just before two in the morning. On the way, I called the Flatiron Depot to tell them I'd be too sick to come in for my shift late that morning. If there was going to be a war, I would be needed, which meant I had to get a few hours of sleep before night fell again. I wasn't twenty anymore; lack of sleep was like a toxin to my body.

Quinn was subdued and quiet on the three-hour trip back to Boulder, and I wasn't sure what to say to him. Our second kiss had happened right next to the damning evidence that his friend was probably dead. *I* didn't know how to process that, and I'd never even met Allegra. Was he feeling guilty? Grieving? Or—and this was somehow scarier—had it not affected him at all? When I glanced over, Quinn was as unreadable as ever.

On top of all that, I really wanted to know how hard it was to kill a werewolf, and how the wolves had managed to take down a vampire, but it didn't seem like the right moment to ask him if were-wolves ate vampire bodies—a thought that sounded so ridiculous in my brain that I had to bite down on a laugh.

Maybe I'd hit my head harder than I'd thought.

When we finally arrived back at Magic Beans, Maven was waiting for us in her office, a cramped little space attached to the big concrete-floored room in the back of the building. I struggled not to yawn as Quinn filled her in on the night's events. When he was finished, Maven stared thoughtfully into space as if she were reading through a list of her options. After a few minutes of her silence, I had to make a conscious effort not to jiggle my knee up and down.

"What troubles me," she said at last, and I nearly started in my chair, "is that there were two attacks, from two sides."

Quinn nodded. "I was thinking the same thing. I know I haven't been around that long, but I've never heard of werewolf packs joining forces against a common enemy."

Maven shook her head. "They're too territorial for that, too competitive."

I spoke up. "Do we know for sure that's what happened?" They both looked at me with polite interest, like I had performed a card trick rather badly. "I mean, isn't it still possible that Allegra was attacked, but Travis . . . defected?"

"No," Maven said, without a hint of uncertainty in her tone. "After speaking with Quinn, I called one of my vampires in Grand Junction and had him check out the storage chamber Travis was using. He found Travis's wallet, car keys, and car still there." She gave a little shake of her head. "There was a thousand dollars in that wallet, just sitting there."

Quinn nodded as if that was particularly significant, and I raised my eyebrows at him. "Travis has . . . *had* . . . expensive tastes," he explained. "Burberry, Saint Laurent, Dior Homme, that kind of thing."

I gave him a slow blink. "I have heard *one* of those words before."

"The point is, he wouldn't have left cash behind. Or his car," Maven cut in. "We need to assume that he's dead, as well."

"So what now?" I asked. "Do we go hunting?" I tried not to sound hopeful, but I'm not completely sure I succeeded.

Quinn frowned. "Unless they're still in Colorado, it'll be difficult to identify the specific werewolves who did this."

"They won't be," Maven replied. "A pack in wolf form may be able to take out a vampire, but they wouldn't dare face us as humans, not when we're expecting it. They'll stay over the border, out of my territory."

I must have looked as confused as I felt, because she added, "With the exception of the pack's alpha, and perhaps beta, werewolves can't change form very often. They *have* to shift on the full moon when their magic is strongest, but other than that"—she shrugged—"maybe once, twice a month, at the most. We should have at least a week after the full moon before they can manage another attack."

"So three days from now," I said, just to clarify.

Quinn frowned. "There's another thing that doesn't make sense. If they were really trying to attack us, why linger on the border? Why not sneak into the state as humans, change on the full moon, when they're most powerful, and come after us en masse?"

I nodded, picking up on his line of thought. "And if this wasn't their big attack, why warn us by taking out two of your scouts? No one was expecting two packs to work together. If they were going to do that, why give up the element of surprise?"

The three of us looked at one another, but no one had a good answer. "We need more information on the werewolf packs," Maven said simply.

Well, *that* seemed easier said than done. I had no idea how to get more intel on werewolves. Quinn gave me a quick glance that said he was just as much in the dark as I was on this subject.

"After the conflict with Trask," he began, naming the werewolf who had caused the original war, "did you keep tabs on any of the packs in the area?"

Something hardened in Maven's eyes. "Itachi had that responsibility," she said in a brittle voice. "But he kept the information to himself. As I was only an advisor, it was not my place to question him. And since his passing"—which was a really nice way to say *since I ripped his heart out of his chest cavity*—"I have found no records of any kind on the werewolves."

I opened my mouth to ask if she'd learned anything else since she'd taken over, but I stopped myself just in time. Quinn had implied that Maven was barely holding her territory together at the moment. There was too much confusion and unrest over Itachi's death, not to mention the discovery of both a boundary witch and a null within her enclave. When would she have had time to spy on werewolves in other states?

"However," Maven continued, possibly noticing my dismay, "I do know of one werewolf you can ask, just over the border in Wyoming." Her eyes fixed on me. "You'll need to introduce yourself during the day, however."

"Why?" Quinn asked.

I could have been imagining things, but for a moment I thought Maven's eyebrow quirked with amusement. "Because that's when the nature preserve is open."

Chapter 7

We spent a few more minutes making plans before I finally trudged out to my car. Maven and Quinn would need to go to ground for the night anyway, and I was so exhausted I was almost nauseous from it. It was hard to believe that only a few hours earlier, I had balked at going home after Hazel's party. Now I was ready to cry with relief at the sight of my own driveway.

My home was a modest three-bedroom fishing cabin near the Sawmill Ponds, about twenty minutes outside of Boulder proper. After I had returned from Iraq, my parents had insisted on giving it to me outright. I tried to refuse, but Sam had eventually made me see that I would be doing them a kindness if I accepted: The rest of my squad had been killed in an IED explosion in Iraq, and my parents were so stupendously grateful to have me home and alive; they'd been desperate to do *something* to take care of me. So I let them give me the cabin, and in return, they didn't bat an eye when I more or less let my rescue animals half destroy it.

I was aching for sleep—and from the bump on my head—but I made myself stay awake long enough to carefully wash the dried bloodstains off my skin from where I'd hit my head. There was probably still a bit of dried blood in my dark red hair, but you couldn't see it, and I decided a shower could wait until the morning. Before I could collapse, I took ten more minutes to feed everybody, let the dogs out, and scoop the cats' litter boxes. My usual herd of three cats and four dogs had recently grown by one: I was currently fostering a one-year-old pit bull named Lady, and she was so happy to see me I thought she might tip her crate over before I could get it open. I felt guilty for being gone so long, and eventually fell into bed with three of the five dogs crowded around me.

Before I could do more than wiggle into a comfortable position, my phone began to chirp where I'd left it on the bedside table. I groaned and rolled over to check the caller ID, figuring it was Old-World related. Who else would call me before six in the morning?

But to my surprise, the caller was my cousin Elise, a patrol officer for the Boulder Police Department. I knew she was working watch three this week, the night shift, but that still didn't explain why she'd call me before six in the morning. For some reason my thoughts leaped to Charlie, and my heart skipped a beat before I answered.

"Lex?" Her voice was breathless with excitement. "Hey, sorry to call so early, but random question: Are you still in touch with that biologist from CU?"

I blanched, thrown off by the whole idea of a connection between my personal life and the Old World, but after a moment I remembered: a few weeks earlier Elise had invited me to coffee on a day I had a magic lesson with Simon. I try to lie to my family as little as possible, so I'd said I was meeting up with a CU professor, the brother of a friend, to talk about auditing one of his classes. "Uh, yeah, we're still in touch. Why, what's up?"

"We got a call from an early-morning hiker who found a sort of bundle of something slimy on one of the Chautauqua trails," she explained, the words tumbling out of her mouth so fast that the meaning seemed to appear in my brain a full second later. "My commander thinks it's just garbage, but it looks animal to me. I thought it might be worth having a scientist look at it *before* our criminologist takes it apart."

"A bundle of something slimy," I repeated, trying not to sound as skeptical as I felt. The Old World was facing a serious threat from the same monsters who had killed Sam, and Elise was worried about some gooey clump of trash?

"Yeah, I know it sounds crazy. But I'm trying to go the extra mile here, Lex," she wheedled. Elise wanted to be a detective someday. "I can go through the university, of course, but they won't be open for a couple of hours, and the watch commander is humoring me by waiting *this* long. You said your friend's brother was a biologist, right?"

"Uh, evolutionary biologist, yeah."

"What's the difference?"

Hmm, good question. "I honestly have no idea."

"Well, can he come take a look?" she pleaded. "Please? As a favor to me?"

I rubbed my eyes with the heel of one hand, trying to think. Elise was pushing awfully hard, and she was family, so I couldn't say no. At the same time, I wasn't sure Simon would be up for this kind of adventure—the last time I'd seen him he'd needed crutches to walk—but I couldn't actually *tell* Elise that Simon was too hurt, since I had no idea what story he'd told the university.

"Let me call him," I said finally. "I'm not sure he's the guy, but he should know who is." Elise thanked me profusely, and I promised to call her right back.

I was half expecting Simon's phone to go to voicemail, since it was So. Very. Early. But Simon was sort of like Quinn's counterpart in the witch clan: He was a general problem solver, a fixer for the lady in charge—in his case, his mother, Hazel. And fixers have to answer their phones, even if they sound very groggy and possibly on painkillers.

"Lex?" he mumbled. "What's up?"

"Sorry to wake you," I began, because that's just good manners. I told him about Elise's call, ending with, "Everyone else at the station thinks it's nothing, but maybe you could get Elise a phone number for the right person at CU?"

"Actually, *I'm* the right person," he replied. "One of them, anyway. The biology department gets requests to identify specimens all the time, from hunters or new property owners or whatever, and we all take turns. I think this is the first time it's come from the actual police department, though."

"Okay . . . but you're probably not at full strength, right? So maybe you could call one of your colleagues?"

There was a long, very loaded pause. "I'm perfectly capable of doing my job," he retorted, and I winced at the sharp edge in his voice.

"I wasn't trying to—"

"Besides," Simon interrupted, "one of my duties within the clan is to keep an eye out for weird shit that might be traced back to the Old World. If the cops are calling, it's probably pretty weird. So I'm going, Lex."

"Okay," I said, as mildly as I could.

There was a pause, and Simon cleared his throat. With great dignity, he added, "But, um . . . I'm not cleared to drive yet. Can you give me a ride?"

I grinned, glad he couldn't see it. "Pick you up in twenty."

Chapter 8

I called Elise to say we were on the way, and threw on the nearest outfit at hand, jeans and a T-shirt with the name of a local radio station. Boulder is really expensive, and I don't make much money, so roughly half of my tops began life as free swag somewhere. The other half were birthday and Christmas gifts, usually from Sam or my mom.

Simon and his girlfriend were renting a bland townhouse in Lafayette, about fifteen minutes away if I didn't hit any traffic. I'd stopped by the townhouse a few times right after Simon got out of the hospital, but Tracy had never exactly warmed up to me. It was possible that she was just a shy or introverted person, but there was also a good chance that she disliked me because of the boundary magic thing. Or, you know, because I'd gotten her long-term boyfriend critically injured. Either way, I couldn't really blame her. It made my visits to Simon awkward, though.

I went as fast as I dared, trying to make it before the early-morning commuter traffic. By six forty I was parking in the townhouse's narrow driveway, just behind Simon's Chevy. There was no sign of Tracy's VW Beetle, which surprised me a little. None of my business, though.

Simon opened the door before I'd finished knocking, dressed in a blue flannel button-down and jeans, his trademark messenger bag clutched in his teeth. The crutches were gone, but he was leaning on a simple wooden cane. "Can you . . ." he said through his teeth, and I reached out and snagged the messenger bag, looping it over my own shoulder. "Thanks," he said. "Hurts to lift my arms that high."

"No worries." I looked him over carefully. The search for my niece a couple of weeks earlier had ended at the farm of a hillbilly named Atwood, in a decrepit barn full of rusty junk. Simon had climbed a ladder to the hayloft where Atwood was keeping Charlie, not realizing that the "shitkicker witch" had sabotaged the ladder to collapse when he was halfway up. My friend had landed on top of a pile of rusty junk, including some metal-and-glass lanterns, and wound up with torn-up back muscles and a lacerated kidney. The metal shards had also nicked the iliac artery in his lower back, which had caused him to bleed out and, technically, die.

Because Atwood was a witch, Simon would have been responsible for tracking him down regardless of my involvement. During the rescue, though, *I* was the one who'd told Simon to go into that barn to get Charlie. I used to be a soldier; I knew that you have to make decisions in the heat of the moment. And even when I look back now, I'm not sure I could have done anything differently with the information I had at the time. But there was still a voice at the back of my mind that insisted it was my fault Simon was hurt.

All things considered, though, he didn't look too bad. He'd dropped weight from his lean frame, but his hair was clean, and his olive skin—Hazel and her late husband were a mixed-race couple—was no longer sickly. He looked tired, though. "Stop examining me," Simon snapped.

My mouth dropped open, just a tiny bit. That wasn't like Simon. He was always kind and even tempered—sometimes almost *too* laid-back.

Without waiting for me to respond, he hobbled past me onto the front steps. "Let's go."

I scrambled to follow, trying to spot him on the steps without looking like I was spotting him on the steps. Could whatever was bothering the other witches also be getting to Simon? Or was he just cranky from dealing with his injuries?

"Everything okay?" I ventured, when we were buckled in my car and on the road toward Boulder.

"Fine."

"How have you been feeling?"

"Good. Much better."

Yeah, right. I'd heard that tone of voice before. Like out of my own mouth. "Uh-huh," I said, keeping my voice playful. "And how are you *really* feeling?"

"I'm *fine*, Lex," he snapped, and then sighed. "Sorry. I know you mean well."

There was a pause, and I didn't think he was planning to finish the thought anytime soon. "*But . . .*" I prompted.

"But you don't really know what it's like for me now."

I'm not sure what I'd expected him to say, but it wasn't that. "Actually," I pointed out, "I may be the only one who does."

His whole face creased into a frown. "What do you mean?"

"You *died*, Simon," I said, trying to keep my voice light. "And I've . . . you know . . . died a bunch of times." As a boundary witch, my body had a natural resistance to crossing the line from living to dead. I had drowned as a teenager and I'd bled out after surviving the IED in Iraq. I'd also been stabbed to death by a crazed vampire only a few weeks earlier. My body wouldn't let me die—and now I had refused to let Simon's.

"I guess you're right. Do you . . ." he started, but had to pause and take a breath. "Do you have nightmares?"

I smiled sadly. "On and off. When I was a kid, I dreamed about drowning a lot, and death. Dead people. And after Iraq . . . yeah. But it fades. For what it's worth."

Another long moment of silence passed between us, and I could feel him working up to something. "You haven't asked me where Tracy is," he said at last.

I shrugged. "None of my business."

"She's been sleeping at her mother's. She says it's because of the nightmares, but things have been tense."

I didn't know how to respond to that. Simon and I had always enjoyed a very casual student-teacher relationship, so it felt strange for him to share something so personal. Then again, I was the one who'd encouraged him to share, wasn't I? "I'm sorry, man," I finally said.

"I remember, you know," he said abruptly. "I remember disconnecting. Floating. Seeing you." I glanced over at him. He was staring it me intently, curiously. "You were crying."

There wasn't much I could say about that. Simon squirmed in the seat, trying to find a comfortable position despite the bandages he probably had on under his clothes. I changed the subject. "So in case someone asks me, what kind of biology do you do?"

Some of the tension smoothed off his face. Back on familiar territory. "Officially, I'm an associate curator at the Natural History museum on campus, and I teach undergraduate classes in biology. My specialty is mammalian vertebrate systemics."

When I had untangled that particular phrase in my mind, I asked, "And unofficially?"

"I've spent most of my career trying to understand Old World systemics," he explained with a little shrug. "Why we evolved the way we did. But the police don't need to know that, obviously."

"Got it."

I knew the way to the massive, concrete-and-glass Public Safety building that housed the police department in Boulder—not because of my arrests, after which I was sent straight to the county jail, but because I stopped by every now and then to bring Elise some lunch or shoot with her in the basement firing range. The range wasn't technically open to civilians, but sometimes Elise talked them into letting her ex-military cousin help her train for the firearms qualification.

When we arrived I parked in the small visitors' lot in front of the main doors and showed Simon to the marble-floored lobby, where the receptionist called Elise for us. My cousin rushed through the security door a moment later, dressed in her street clothes: slim-fitting dark khakis and a lavender button-down. Her shift must have ended at six, which meant she was here on her own time now. Stifling a yawn, I made the introductions, and Elise shook Simon's hand with enthusiasm. "Thank you so much for coming, Dr. Pellar."

Simon shook back, subtly cocking an eyebrow at me to say *See, she treats me with respect.* I tried not to chortle. Teacher or not, it was too weird to think of Simon as a doctor of anything. He was only a couple of years older than me.

Elise used her ID card to swipe us through the security doors and led us down a long, narrow corridor. I looked around with interest. Though I'd been downstairs to the shooting range and upstairs to the dining area, I hadn't spent much time on the ground floor. I had to admit, I didn't hate the decor: some brave and optimistic interior designer had dared to pair the usual institutional beige with accent walls of a gorgeous deep teal. The hallway was lined with photos of cops: men and women who'd earned medals or other accolades, or who'd been killed in the line of duty. I wanted to stop and read some of the placards, but Elise was hurrying us along at a pace Simon could barely match.

We turned a few corners, enough for me to know I'd need help to find my way back out again, when I began to notice the smell, like vomit that had been left out in the sun for days. The deeper we got into the building, the worse it was. "What *is* that?" I asked Elise. "Did something die in the ventilation system?"

She smiled wryly. "I wish."

Finally we turned one last corner and entered a small room dominated by an enormous table. A teeny cubicle office was attached, and Elise poked her head in. "Natalie? The expert's here."

There was a mumble, and then the sound of chair wheels squeaking. Elise backed up to make way for a Caucasian woman of around forty, with a cropped haircut and smile lines in her golden tan. I had been expecting a lab coat, like in the movies, but she was dressed in neat charcoal trousers and a boatneck sweater that flattered her figure. "This is our criminologist, Dr. Natalie Lafferty," Elise introduced. "Natalie, this is Dr. Simon Pellar, and my cousin Lex, who's sort of serving as his assistant today."

That was a nice way of putting it. "It's nice to meet you," she said, her words turning into a giant yawn. "Sorry, haven't had my coffee yet."

"Right there with you," I muttered.

"Where is the object?" Simon asked, ignoring me.

The woman gestured at the table. "Ordinarily I'd have it out already, but under the circumstances we didn't want to stink up the building more than we absolutely have to." She gave us a wry smile. "I did try to pawn it off on the CBI—that's the Colorado Bureau of Investigation—but they won't accept it until we take it apart. And Elise here"—she glanced at my cousin with a faint smile—"*insisted* that we couldn't do that without a biologist present."

I realized that Elise was very pointedly not looking at me. Wait a minute . . . was she *blushing*? I hadn't even known she *could* blush, but there was definitely a little chemistry going on between her and the criminologist, no pun intended. I worked to keep the grin off my face.

Then Dr. Lafferty took a deep breath and stepped toward a closed door. "Breathe through your mouth," she advised. She opened the cupboard, and I forgot all about teasing Elise.

The smell hit us like a concussion wave, violent and foul and revolting. Elise had already experienced the stench, so she just locked her fingers around her nose without comment. Simon gagged and covered his mouth and nose with both hands, but I got that sense that this was less to keep the smell out and more to keep his stomach contents *in*. I had smelled worse in Iraq and managed to keep my hurried breakfast down, but my eyes were watering. "Yeah," said Lafferty, as though the word explained everything. "There's that."

She turned around, struggling under the weight of a metal tray, and we finally got a good look at the bundle. "Whoa," Simon breathed. It looked like a number of wet objects had been compressed together into a brown, lumpy sphere, then covered in some kind of translucent liquid. It was much larger than I'd imagined, like someone had taken one of those big stuffed medicine balls and dipped it in snot.

"The hiker smelled it first," Elise explained, her plugged nose subduing the words. "She thought maybe something had died near the trail, went to look."

"The working theory is that some kids from the university got hold of a bundle of clothes," Lafferty went on, "maybe from a homeless man, and decided to dump a chemistry experiment all over it. We already took photos, so I'm ready when you are."

I glanced at Simon. I'd nearly forgotten he was here to do a job. My friend had straightened up a bit, lowering his hands and breathing hard out of his mouth. I recognized his expression, because it was the same one he'd worn all the time when we were first experimenting with my abilities. Simon was fascinated.

He stepped forward and handed me his cane without taking his eyes off the bundle. Lafferty gave him a pair of latex gloves, and while he put them on, she opened another cupboard and pulled out a pan full of sterile instruments. She set it on the table near the tray.

"Do you know what it is?" Elise asked Simon, her tone a little more demanding than the situation required.

"It's the strangest thing," he murmured, and from his distracted tone I wasn't sure he'd even heard the question or if he was just thinking out loud. He had bent over to get a closer look at the mound of slime, so I did too, trying to breathe as slowly as possible. On closer inspection, I could make out some bits of clothing and what might have been the sole of a shoe.

Simon murmured, "It almost looks like a—"

"Gastric pellet?" Elise interrupted, excitement in her voice.

To my surprise, Simon nodded. "Exactly," he said. For the first time his eyes lifted from the bundle, to fall on Elise. He and Lafferty both stared at her.

She ducked her head, embarrassed but pleased. "I saw a thing about Komodo dragons on the Discovery Channel."

Lafferty looked impressed, but Simon just nodded, his attention moving back to the thing on the table. "Gastric pellet?" I asked no one in particular.

"When birds and lizards swallow insects and small animals," Simon explained, spinning the tray slowly so he could study the thing from all angles, "they regurgitate a little pellet of undigestible materials—bones, fur, claws, and so on." He selected a large set of tweezers from the tray and looked at Lafferty. "May I?"

She shrugged in a "be my guest" kind of way, and Simon gently probed the edges of the sphere, looking for a weak point. While he was doing that, he continued, "But the largest living animal that produces gastric pellets is probably the Komodo, and those are maybe the size of a softball." He found a spot he liked and inserted the tip of the tweezers, the tongs tightly closed. Then he slowly released pressure on the handle, and the tweezers opened, cracking the pellet open like an egg. Although it seemed impossible, the smell somehow intensified. The two halves of the bundle fell apart with a disgusting wet sucking noise, exposing more scraps of fabric, the sole of a sneaker, and a large piece of rounded bone. The table was big enough to hold both halves, but only just.

Frowning, Lafferty and Elise both leaned in for a closer look. Simon used the tweezers to gently lift the bone and turn it to the side, revealing two serrated metal pins. His eyes met mine, and now I could see the horror behind them.

"It's the ilium," he said softly. "Hip bone. It's human."

Chapter 9

As soon as Lafferty realized that the pellet contained human remains, I was hustled out of the room and delivered to a patrol officer, who escorted me back to the lobby. They were polite about it, and besides, I couldn't really blame them: I was a civilian with a record. I wouldn't want me anywhere near evidence, either.

I wandered over to a black leather bench and closed my eyes, trying to slow my whirling thoughts. In the last twelve hours, two vampires had been killed, probably by werewolves, and something had killed—or at least, eaten—some or all of a human body and spit it out again. I supposed it was still possible that the gastric pellet had been faked; that it really *had* been the brainchild of a bunch of CU students with too much free time and a key to wherever the university stored their research cadavers. But it seemed too coincidental that this would happen right when a different animal threat was intruding on Colorado.

At the same time, I couldn't see a connection between the werewolves and the gigantic regurgitated pellet. I didn't know a lot about how birds or lizards digested their food, but I was certainly familiar with canine digestive tracts, and they didn't spit out *hairballs*, much less swallow clothes and bones. Just for my peace of mind, I did a quick Internet search on my phone and confirmed that wolves don't regurgitate gastric pellets.

Then again, I thought as I pocketed the phone again, werewolf digestion could be different from that of natural wolves, couldn't it? Was it possible that werewolves, I don't know, spat out their undigested food when they changed back into human form? I had no idea. I was still learning about the magic in my *own* blood, much less werewolf physiology.

I ran out of ideas after that, and the exhaustion began to catch up with me. I even dozed off for a little while on the black leather bench, but I woke up in a hurry when I heard a familiar voice barking out my name.

"Allison Luther," said Detective Keller's snide voice, "shouldn't you be in handcuffs?"

My eyes flew open. Keller hovered over me on the bench, holding a paper coffee cup with "Espresso Roma" printed on the side. He was a balding, tight-lipped man on the wrong side of forty, and he'd had the misfortune of being the officer in charge both times I was arrested. He'd also been on the receiving end of my father's unasked-for lawyer. Twice. To say he had it in for me would be a hilarious understatement.

I was too disoriented to process his question properly, so I grunted something along the lines of, "Huh?"

"You're in the police station; I can only assume you're under arrest for something." Keller made a show of looking around. "What happened? You get a rookie who had to go back for his cuffs?"

I stood up and stretched to my full height, forcing Keller to take a step backward. I was mostly using the movement to wake up, but his eyes narrowed as though I had physically threatened him. "My friend is consulting with your criminologist," I said calmly, tilting my head back so I could meet his eyes. Keller was average height, a few inches taller than my five feet five inches, but he acted like a short guy who was overcompensating. Maybe he'd been a late bloomer. "I gave him a ride."

"Uh-huh," Keller said. "You sure it's not the other way around?

Your friend's bailing you out after you got arrested for—what would it be this time? More bar fighting? Maybe some light prostitution?"

I gritted my teeth so the words *watch your mouth* didn't spill through them. Keller was just trying to get a rise out of me, and this time he was being particularly clumsy about it. I could handle this. "Nope, just waiting on my friend. But hey, maybe next time."

His mouth twisted into a smirk, and he lowered his voice so only I would hear. "I get it, I get it—you think you're on the straight and narrow, don't you? That you're all rehabilitated? But you and I both know you came back broken. You've gotten a taste for hurting people."

My stomach turned to acid, and I wanted to punch him and laugh it off and burst into tears, all at once. Keller saw that he'd gotten to me, and shot me another triumphant little smile.

Then I was back to just wanting to punch him.

"Lex?" Elise's voice was worried, and I turned to see her coming toward us. I hadn't even heard the security door open. "Is there a problem?"

"No problem at all," drawled Keller, taking a leisurely sip from his cup. He outranked Elise by quite a bit, and now that she'd jumped to my defense he was going to draw out her discomfort. "I was just catching up with your cousin here."

Elise looked at me worriedly, but I just gave a little headshake, the tension broken. "How's it going in there?" I asked, turning my back on Keller. If I couldn't get rid of him, at least I could completely ignore him.

"Dr. Pellar is almost done," she promised.

Disappointed with the general lack of fear or rancor, Keller grunted and turned to go. "Remember what I said, Luther," he called over his shoulder as he disappeared into the secure area.

"He's a dick," Elise grumbled as he disappeared through the door. She was wearing her jacket, carrying her bag. Done for the day. "You gonna tell me what he said?"

"Nah, it was nothing." I wanted to dismiss Keller's words, but in truth they had shaken me to the core. What if he was right? What if I *was* a time bomb, just not in the way he thought? I glanced down at my forearms, where the new tattoos were covered by my jacket sleeves. What if I couldn't control the boundary magic? A few months earlier, I might not have given a damn what happened to me, but now Charlie needed me to keep the Old World away from her, at least long enough for her to grow up. If something happened to me, my nineteen-month-old niece would be fair game. I shuddered and forced myself to return my attention to my cousin, changing the subject. "So was the commander impressed with your quick thinking?"

Elise flushed with pride, then glanced over to make sure the receptionist was out of earshot. "Well . . . yeah. Kinda."

I bumped her with my hip. "And was it just me, or was there a little something-something happening between you and the good Dr. Lafferty?"

She looked scandalized, but at exactly that moment the security door opened again and Simon hobbled out. Elise shot me a smug look because it meant she didn't have to answer me.

There were a few minutes of handshaking and polite good-byes, and at last I was accompanying Simon back to the car. I managed to wait until both of our doors were shut before I said conversationally, "So. What the fuck was that thing?"

"Drive, Lex," he told me. "There are cameras."

Reluctantly, I started the car and began backing away. "I think your cousin was right," Simon began. "I believe it was a gastric pellet. The smell, the contents, the way it was shaped . . . yeah. Elise was smart to recognize it."

I shot him a wary glance. Simon's eyes were bright, his cheeks flushed. He was *thrilled*. "I thought it was too big," I remarked.

"That's the thing—it's *way* too big," he blurted. "And there have been no other signs of an animal like that, so I looked at it in the magical spectrum, and the thing was *buzzing*." Damn. I wished I'd thought to look at it in the magical spectrum, although unless the thing was actually *alive*, I probably wouldn't have seen anything. Simon pointed toward the next turnoff. "Can you drop me off on campus? I need to look through some of the collections, maybe check out the journals . . ."

I eyed him. I didn't want to burst his bubble, especially since this was the most positive I'd seen him since his fall. But under the bright expression, he still looked exhausted. I hadn't seen dark circles that big since Charlie was a newborn, keeping Sam up all night. "Just to be clear," I said, "your hypothesis is that there is a giant lizard monster running amok in Boulder, and it *ate* a human being and spat out the parts it didn't like?"

Simon deflated a little bit then, and he had the grace to at least look embarrassed. "Well . . . yeah. Although it's also possible that the creature ate a body that was already dead," he pointed out. "But you don't get it, Lex. I've been studying Old World systemics for years, but there's just never been enough data to make the connections I need. Whatever made that pellet, if it's real, could be the Rosetta stone for everything I've been working on since I was twenty. Why some species intermingled with magic, and most didn't."

Anxiety burned in my stomach, but I wasn't sure what was causing it. Something about that pellet felt *wrong* to me, but Simon was so excited . . . I was probably just exhausted. I'd been up for nearly thirty hours without real sleep, and I wasn't a kid anymore. If I didn't get some rest soon, my vision was going to double.

I dropped Simon off at CU as requested, and finally headed back toward the cabin. After a moment of indecision, I called Lily on the way and filled her in on the morning's events. I didn't explicitly say I was worried about Simon, but she read between the lines and promised to check on him after her yoga class. Lily had bounded around from job to job after leaving med school, and at the moment she was cobbling together a living by teaching yoga, selling her photography, and who knew what else. She also served as the de facto doctor for a lot of the witches, myself included. She would check on whether Simon was pushing his body too hard. She offered to come take a look at my head wound, but by now it was just a bump and a small cut that I could hide behind my hair. I thanked her and said I was fine.

I went back to the cabin, showered, minding the bump on my head, and managed to grab a couple of hours of sleep. When my alarm went off I made hasty arrangements for my cousin Brie to check on the herd if I wasn't back by evening. I spent a fair amount of my spare time babysitting for free, which allowed me to call in such favors when necessary. I grabbed a big to-go cup of coffee at Magic Beans and was on the road to Wyoming by one.

I had a date with a werewolf.

Chapter 10

I've spent so much of my life in Boulder—pretty much all of it, minus my time overseas—that sometimes I forget that there are other places. That sounds childish, I know, but I love Colorado, and the hour and a half drive up to Wyoming was a nice, scenic reminder of why. I hadn't had much sleep, and I'd spent most of the previous night in the car too, but damn if I didn't have a large delicious coffee, a padded seat, and Brandi Carlile on the old car's sound system. It was weirdly relaxing. By the time I reached Cheyenne, I had shed most of the anxiety and sense of wrongness that the gastric pellet had stirred up in me.

And also I really had to pee.

Pit stop accomplished, I followed directions on my phone until I pulled into the gate of the Southern Wyoming Sanctuary for Wolves. It was a large wooded property spread out over a series of small hills, and the whole thing was divided into multiple fenced-in paddocks. As I parked the car and walked up the muddy driveway to the welcome center, I could see a pair of wolves peering at me through one of the massive chain-link fences, about twenty feet away.

I stopped in my tracks, gaping at them for a moment. I'd expected them to be big, of course, but I realized in that moment that I had imagined big *dogs*, like Chip and Cody. The wolves just *felt* different from any of my dogs. They didn't bark when a stranger approached, for one thing, and they gave off an air of detached assessment, like I was being sized up as a food source. Which I probably was. I kept my eyes on the ground and hurried forward to the sanctuary building.

Just inside the door was an enormous wooden receptionist desk, which formed a sort of gateway to the rest of the main room. There was a big cash register on the desk, and most of the room beyond appeared to be devoted to selling wolf-themed objects.

"Good afternoon!" chirped the receptionist, a pretty teenager with a dark curly ponytail spilling out of a khaki hat. The letters "SWSW" were embroidered on both the hat and her polar fleece jacket. She had an ID badge on a lanyard around her neck that read "Christy." "Welcome to the Sanctuary for Wolves! Are you here for the feeding tour?"

Excessively cheerful people unnerve me. "Um, yeah," I said awkwardly. "Am I early?"

"Just a bit! Your tour guide will be taking you guys out in about ten minutes," she promised. I nodded my thanks and wandered around the small gift shop area, examining the wolf-themed trinkets and posters, from "dog tag" necklaces (cute) to mugs to posters and T-shirts. Behind the merchandise, the walls were decorated with newspaper articles about wolves and signs directing the reader to call their congressman about wolf protection laws.

I raised my phone and snapped a picture of the instructions, thinking I might do that when the current crisis was over. I had nothing against wolves, per se. If anything, I felt a little sorry for them, because a long time ago some shapeshifting conduits—the ancestors of all Old World creatures, myself included—had decided to limit their magic to one animal transformation, and they'd chosen wolves as their alternate form. Wolves hadn't asked to be infiltrated by magical human hybrids who would go on to commit terrible acts, any more than regular red blood cells ask to be infiltrated by cancer.

The rest of the tour group arrived: half a dozen high school kids and a chaperone, some sort of after-school nature club. The kids were jocular and teasing, bumping around the crowded retail space like so many overgrown pups. After one of them sent a display of necklaces crashing to the ground, the middle-aged chaperone lost her patience and threatened to donate the lot of them as the wolves' next meal. The kids sobered up fast after that—they'd seen the two wolves at the entrance too.

Our guide was a college-aged kid named Phil, tall and lanky, with a habit of speaking very, very fast. He didn't waste a lot of time with introductions, just picked up a bucket of frozen meat chunks and led our group outside to the first enclosure, which housed the two wolves we'd seen at the entrance. Phil introduced them as Nina and Shikoba, a mated pair who'd been rescued together from a "photo farm," where animals are raised to be models and discarded as soon as their looks begin to fray.

His wolf activism speech was just getting started, but after a moment I tuned him out, fascinated by the wolves themselves. Shikoba in particular was enormous, over a hundred pounds, with inky black fur and playful amber eyes that danced as they followed Phil's every move. Nina, a classic gray wolf, seemed more somber, but she focused just as attentively on Phil's arm as it threw chunks of frozen meat over the fence.

The group moved on, and I had to scramble to keep up. We visited two more paddocks that were similar to the first, each containing two wolves that stood eagerly at attention, ready for their supper. At each enclosure, Phil gave us background on the specific animals, plus more information about the species and a few ways we could help protect them in the wild. I learned that wolves' life spans are similar to many dogs, at least in captivity, and that they prefer meat but will eat just about anything when they're hungry. I also learned that captive wolves were kept in twos because it meant there could only be an alpha and a beta, first and second command. If a third wolf were enclosed with them, one of the three would become the omega—a term used to describe the wolf that is bullied and picked on in every pack.

That sounded awfully familiar. I had been sent here to find a wolf who had once been the weakest member of the Colorado pack, according to Maven. In werewolf packs, this position was usually referred to as the sigma for some reason. Maven had explained that while werewolves tended to be very protective of their sigma, Trask had preferred to treat his more like wild wolves treat their omegas: lots of bullying, physical torture, mind games. Eventually Trask had broken his sigma's mind.

I found the werewolf in question when we reached the fourth and largest pen. Like the others, this one had a sign attached to the chain-link fence with a name burned into the wood, but this sign only had one name instead of two: "Tobias." The wolf in this pen peered at us from behind a tree, revealing a coat of sandy-brown hair skimming the top of a white undercoat, like several of the other wolves. Then he stepped all the way out, toward the fence, and most of the teenagers gasped.

I'd gotten used to the size of the six previous wolves, but even compared to them, Tobias was monstrously large. But it was his attention that was the most unsettling: Unlike the other wolves, who were only interested in Phil and the meat, Tobias eyed every single one of us with a wary intensity that said he *saw us,* not as background noise or distractions, but as real and present threats. He had a sharp intelligence that was so unnatural, I wondered how anyone, even humans, could miss it. I would have known exactly who this was, even if Maven hadn't given me his name.

"Our next wolf's arrival is something of a mystery," Phil said, with exaggerated wide eyes and a professional smile. "Tobias was found tied to a tree at the front gate more than ten years ago, with his name written on the leash with a marker. Our staff has never been able to determine where he came from, though we did make inquiries."

I could have solved the mystery for him right then and there. After the war, Tobias Leine was so traumatized that he wouldn't even shift out of his wolf form without hours of coaxing or threats. Even Maven could see that the sigma had been Trask's victim, not his co-conspirator. Leine was still dangerous, though, and since werewolves couldn't be contained by psychiatric institutes or prisons, he had to either be killed or go native, staying permanently in wolf form. It was decided that the sanctuary was the safest and most merciful place for him.

Phil threw the meat, and Tobias trotted forward to pick it up. Out of the corner of my eye, I saw nearly all of the students take an unconscious step backward. Even Phil, who hadn't blinked an eye earlier when one of the Arctic wolves stuck a muzzle through the fence and nipped playfully at his jacket, shot an uneasy glance at Tobias. "As you can see," he said, gesturing at the attentive wolf, "Tobias is quite large, nearly two hundred pounds. He may be one of the largest wolves in the world. He'd be a record breaker, except for the fact that he's undoubtedly a dog-wolf hybrid."

"How do you know?" asked one of the teenagers.

Phil gave him a little frown—he'd obviously been *just* about to explain—but said in the same professional tone, "Full-blooded wolves are usually born with blue eyes, which then lighten to that amber color we've seen in all the other wolves today. Tobias, on the other hand, has bright blue eyes." I stepped closer to see, and sure enough, the werewolf's eyes were blue, kind of like a husky's. Or, more accurately, like a human being's. It was spooky.

Phil began to back away, and I heard myself speak up. "Have you had any problems with him?"

Phil shot me a surprised look—I'd been silent throughout the tour—so I added hastily, "Because of his size, I mean. And he's the first wolf we've seen who's in a pen by himself."

Phil nodded. "Good question. Yes, Tobias prefers to be solitary, although he'll sometimes play with a companion for a few hours. Despite his size, he's been extremely docile and well-behaved for us. The only exceptions are when we've tried to sedate him for routine medical examinations." He gave a nervous little laugh. "Tobias here will evade the darts, and he always seems to know if we put

medication in his food. So we leave him be, and he behaves himself."
One of the teens shot up a hand, but Phil was already backing away,
moving on to the next enclosure. "Let's move on to Juana and Rafael,
our pair of Mexican wolves. They're unique for several reasons . . ."

I tuned Phil out, lagging after the group. When the lopsided
mass of teens had all moved away from Tobias, I went to the exterior
fence directly in front of the big wolf and crouched down, making
it harder for Phil to see me behind the other people.

Tobias cocked his head with innocent curiosity. "I'm here as
Maven's representative," I said quietly. "Show me that you understand."

The enormous wolf didn't respond right away, and after a
moment I started to feel ridiculous. But then Tobias thrust his muzzle up quickly before moving it down and up again, and I realized
it was a parody of a human nod. "Good. An hour after sunset, I'll
be by your back fence with a vampire. We have some questions.
You will be there, and you will be in human form." I reached into
my pocket and pulled out the small metal object Maven had given
me, making sure he saw the .45 caliber bullet that had been hand-
poured out of silver. *Some of the legends are true,* Maven had said,
sounding bemused. All of the Old World species came with their little vulnerabilities. The vampires were allergic to daylight, the werewolves to silver. And of course it was painfully easy to kill witches.

Well, most of us.

"Do you understand?" I asked. Another pause, and then Tobias
shook himself, showing me a long, slow yawn. I had five dogs at home;
I recognized this as *Maybe I will, maybe I won't. I do what I want.*

"Try me," I told him fiercely, hearing the hatred in my voice.
"I'd love that."

"Miss?" Phil called, hurrying back toward me. I quickly shoved
the bullet back into my pocket. "Please step away from Tobias. He
is *not* a pet . . ."

"You don't know the half of it," I muttered under my breath.

Chapter 11

The sky was already darkening as the tour wrapped up at five. I spent a few minutes nonchalantly buying postcards in the gift shop—paying with cash, of course. I thanked Christy the receptionist and Phil the tour guide, and strolled out to the car like I didn't have a care in the world. If anything happened tonight, I wanted to look like any other tourist visiting the wolf sanctuary. The place closed in a half an hour, so we were cutting the timing pretty close, but it was a necessary risk: We needed to figure out what was happening with the werewolves and resolve it quickly, before Hazel found out something was up. And we didn't want to give Tobias any time to contact the other werewolves, just in case he had some way of doing so.

I drove back down the dirt road that led to the sanctuary, taking a few extra turns before I pulled over on a long stretch of road with no people or cars. I twisted around in my seat, knocked on the long, flat compartment where the backseat was supposed to be, and stepped out of Maven's Jeep with my cell phone in hand. For some reason, I didn't want to see Quinn climbing out of the vampire box. Assuring myself that I was just giving him some privacy, I leaned against my door and dialed Simon's number. If anyone drove by, they'd assume I had a flat tire and was calling AAA.

When he answered, I could hear talking and music in the background, which implied he was still on campus. "Hey," I said loudly. "How's the hairball research?"

"Gastric pellet," he said reflexively. "Hang on, let me get somewhere quieter."

There was a pause, and I turned around to peek at Quinn. He was sitting calmly in the driver's seat, *right* behind me, and I jumped, startled. He smirked and gave me a little wave. I stuck my tongue out at him, then circled the Jeep to climb into the passenger seat. Simon still hadn't returned to the phone. "Early this morning, the police found a bundle of slimy clothes with a human hip bone buried inside," I explained to Quinn. "Simon thinks it's a gastric pellet from an enormous reptile that's also the Rosetta Stone for magical systemics."

Quinn's face remained as inscrutable as ever, but he did give me one long, slow blink. "You have a *serious* gift for summary," he deadpanned.

I grinned. "Thank you."

Simon got back on the phone. "Okay, I'm here."

"Did you find anything?" I asked him, holding up a finger to Quinn. Which was stupid, because he could probably hear Simon as well as I could.

"Yes and no." Simon sounded exhausted, and I wondered if Lily had stopped to check on him. "There haven't been any reports about giant lizards anywhere in Colorado, and I went back ten years. I've been checking records for fossil finds around here too, but the results are inconclusive."

"Inconclusive how?"

He sighed. "There are *thousands* of dinosaur finds in Colorado, Lex. Not all of the remains have been identified. Plus there are things like preserved footprints and coprolites with no identified source."

I had taken some of my cousin's kids to the Dinosaur Resource Center in Colorado Springs; I knew coprolites were fossilized poop. "Hang on, you're saying you think this thing is a *dinosaur*?" I didn't bother keeping the skepticism out of my voice.

"No, not really. Its behavior doesn't match our knowledge about any previously identified species." There was a pause. "And I'm not convinced it has legs."

Quinn's eyebrow arched with curiosity. "Wait, *what?*" I said.

"This afternoon I went over to Chautauqua, where they found the pellet," Simon explained hurriedly. "There wasn't much to see, but I did notice some displaced dirt and loose soil, like something had dug a big hole that had caved back in on itself. The police barely noticed it, but I think this thing could be a burrower, a big one. It would explain why there weren't any tracks."

"Huh." I looked at Quinn, but he shrugged, as baffled as I was. I needed to think that over for a while, so I changed tack. "Did the police make any progress on identifying bones?"

"Not that I know of," Simon said wryly. "Since it's obviously magic related, we can't give them too much information. I backed up their hypothesis about it being a science cadaver from the college, so there's no reason for them to keep me in the loop at this point."

Quinn motioned for me to put the phone on speaker. "Simon? Quinn's here with me. You're on speaker."

"Oh," Simon said, a little surprised. "How's it going, Tall, Dark, and Undead?"

Quinn, whose hair was as blond as Daniel Craig's, rolled his eyes. "Can it, Dungeon Master. Listen, do you need some assistance with getting information from the police?"

A pause. "Not at this point, but it may come to that."

I winced. Quinn was talking about pressing the cops to believe whatever Simon told them about the pellet. I didn't like that, not the least because my cousin would be one of them. Despite my two arrests, I felt a little protective of the Boulder Police. With the exception of Keller, all of them had been decent to me.

Quinn must have seen me flinch, because he gave me a little "it is what it is" shrug. I didn't like that, either, but we both knew this was what I had signed on for. "Okay, one other thing," Quinn said to Simon. "You said you checked fossil finds. What about local folklore?"

There was a long pause while both Simon and I were impressed with Quinn. "That's a good idea, thanks. I'll get into it."

When I hung up with Simon, Quinn raised his eyebrows at me. "Hi," he said, smiling.

For some reason the fact that he smiled, instead of giving me his usual unreadable expression, made me flush. "Hi."

"Ready to go question a werewolf?"

The smile faded from my face.

We parked a half mile away from the sanctuary and hiked back down the road until we reached the outer fence, the same one I'd driven past on the way up the driveway. It was still light enough for me to see eyeshine reflected back at us, as the penned wolves silently watched our approach through the fencing. They still didn't bark or whine, but this time when I walked up, every single one of them was pacing back and forth in their individual spaces, agitated and skittish. I watched their body language and realized they weren't hoping to attack us. They were hoping to flee.

"What's got them all riled up?" I murmured.

I caught Quinn's sidelong glance. "How would you feel if your neighbor suddenly and rather violently changed into another animal in front of you?"

"Good point." I counted paddocks as we walked, and stopped when we reached the back fence of the fourth enclosure. "This is it."

I peered past the double fence, looking for a glimpse of Tobias. I had brought a flashlight, but I didn't want to turn it on until absolutely necessary. I didn't see any cars, and the building lights were off, but the sanctuary employees could still be around. There were five or six large trees in Tobias's space, and between the growing darkness and the trees' shade, I saw nothing. Quinn reared an arm back and threw a rough blanket from the back of the Jeep over both of the fences. It fluttered a bit but landed true, well within Tobias's enclosure. I was hoping it would be enough to tempt him to come out, but nothing stirred in the enclosure.

"Do you see him?" I said under my breath, hoping Quinn's vampire eyesight would serve us better than mine.

"No. Wait . . ." Out of the corner of my eye I saw Quinn's head tilting up. "Look in the—"

There was a tremendous crash, and a skinny, naked form dropped out of the nearest tree, no more than six feet away.

I jumped, but managed to suppress the shriek that threatened to erupt from my throat. He'd annoyed me, though, and I rather vindictively clicked on the flashlight and shone it right at his face.

"Owwwwww," Tobias complained, dropping instinctively into a crouch. He held up one hand to shield his eyes. In his human form, the werewolf was average height, slender, with ropy limbs and dun-colored hair that stood up in angry tufts like he'd been pulling on it. His blue eyes glared at me. "Just funny," he sputtered, and then more carefully, he said, "Joke-telling, I was joke-telling." His face creased into a frown. "Joke-being, maybe."

Quinn gave me a questioning look, but I just shrugged. I'd met a crazy werewolf in Los Angeles who made Tobias look downright coherent. As far as I was concerned, werewolf magic was called a curse for a reason.

Tobias went over to the horse blanket, wobbling a little on his two legs. He scooped it up carelessly and wrapped it around his belly, tucking it in like a towel. I moved the beam of the light toward his chest, and he relaxed, his fingers reaching up to casually grip the fence near his face. Taking charge, Quinn stepped forward so he was right up against our side of the fence. "My name is Quinn," he said in the same cool, distant tone he'd used when we first met, when *I* was the one being questioned. "I work for Maven."

Tobias glared at me. "Silver girl," he growled.

Aw. He remembered me. "Lex," I corrected him. "I work for Maven too." It still felt weird saying it out loud.

"In charge now Maven in charge now," Tobias said in the same odd, jarring cadence, like he was having a hard time modulating his volume and tone.

Quinn and I exchanged another look in the light leaking from my flashlight. Maven had only usurped Itachi a couple of weeks ago. "So they visit you," I said casually. "The other werewolves."

Tobias's tongue snaked out, swiping the air in front of his face. Then he seemed to remember himself, his form. "Yes, visit," he agreed. "Brothers-sisters too."

"When?" Quinn asked. "When were they here last?"

Still gripping the fence with his fingers, Tobias leaned backward, swaying back and forth. "Moons and suns ago," he sang.

I rolled my eyes. Of course the idiot had no concept of time. "Who, Tobias?" I asked. "Who comes to visit?"

The werewolf gave me a perfectly human look that clearly suggested I might be daft. "Brothers and sisters," he said again, more loudly this time.

"Names? You must know their names."

Tobias nodded. "Mary-Cammie-Ryan-Matt-Alex-Jamie," he said happily.

"Last names?" Quinn asked. "You know, surnames?"

Tobias shrugged, humming to himself.

Quinn made a frustrated sound at the back of his throat, but I pushed on. I wanted to get this over with and get the hell away from this thing. "Do they all come at once?" I asked. "Many brothers and sisters? Or only one at a time?"

He cocked his head, as if it took him a moment to translate the meaning of my question. "One, two to talk," he said, his voice maintaining at least an even volume now. "Talk to Tobias, 'cause Tobias won't talk back."

"They come to see you when they need someone to talk to?" I translated.

He nodded, looking relieved that I understood.

"Tobias, the last full moon was five nights ago," Quinn said in a patient voice. "Has anyone visited you since then?"

The werewolf cocked his head again, untangling Quinn's words, and then he giggled. "Five nights . . . moon lines called. Call me still." The mirth left his face and he looked almost solemn. Reverent, even. "Call me *now*."

I had no idea what that meant, but before either of us could ask, Tobias leaped backward, his makeshift skirt slipping off his waist, and threw himself against the fence in the adjacent corner of his cage. We raced along our side of the fence in time to see Tobias's body crash into the chain link with a sickening screech of metal. The werewolf stumbled backward, blood streaming from his nose, which must have hit the chain link wrong. As soon as he recovered his footing he ran at the fence again. "Stop!" I cried, but he ignored me. This time he bounced off and fell flat on his back on the ground, writhing with pain. The blood from his nose had already stopped— werewolves could heal even faster than vampires—but he whimpered with pain anyway.

Quinn shot me a horrified look. Maven had warned us that Leine was unstable, but this was way past "a little off" and well into *Cuckoo's Nest* territory. I jogged along the fence until I was right in front of Tobias and crouched down. "Tobias, are you okay?"

"Don't want to we don't want to," he moaned.

"Tobias, what happened on the full moon?" I asked desperately.

"Don't want to we don't want to," he sang again, lifting his throat to turn the words into a howl.

The sound of answering howls rose from the dark enclosures all around us. I looked nervously at Quinn. Would other people hear that? Did the sanctuary wolves often howl at night, or was this exceptional? The noise went on for several minutes in long, fluted sounds that rose and fell discordantly. When it finally died down, I tried again. "Tobias? What is it you don't want to do?"

The look he gave me was filled with desperate frustration, and it struck me as eerily familiar—it was the same expression Charlie had when she was trying to communicate what she wanted, but couldn't make her mouth form the right words yet. "Don't. Want. To." he said blearily, and then he staggered to his feet and ran at the fence a third time.

"Stop it!" I shouted, but he didn't stop. When he fell to the ground this time he was bleeding from several gashes on his chest. He lifted his throat and howled again, and once again the wolves around us joined in.

"Let's go," Quinn urged, tugging at my elbow. "This isn't getting us anywhere, and someone's going to hear them."

I allowed him to pull me to my feet, and we began hurrying along the fence. "The blanket!" I remembered, turning back.

"It's fine, they'll assume some tourist threw it in," Quinn replied, but I'd already paused, my light pointing back at Tobias. Quinn stopped too.

"What is it?" he asked when I didn't move.

I watched the werewolf, who had crawled to his feet and was now standing inches from that same corner of the fence, letting his body fall against it over and over again. I turned my own body so I was facing the same direction, then squinted toward my right, where the dying sun had disappeared. "Quinn," I breathed. "The direction."

"What about it?"

"He's facing south." I stopped mimicking Tobias and turned back to my partner. "Toward Colorado."

Chapter 12

"Moon lines."

Maven's voice was thoughtful, like she was sampling the way the words tasted in her mouth. Tonight she was wearing purple leggings and an orange corduroy jumper that didn't *quite* match her orange hair. I was pretty sure she'd purchased the whole ensemble in 1995. "That phrase sounds familiar, but I can't place it. What else did he say?"

We were crammed into her tiny office, having driven straight to Magic Beans from Wyoming. I didn't love being in a space this small, but I sat near the door and kept an eye on the little window that looked out on the large event room. "Not much, really," Quinn replied. "He kept saying 'we' didn't want to, and then he'd run at the fence. Toward the south."

"I think he was trying to say they didn't *want* to invade Colorado, but they didn't have a choice," I added. "Something is forcing them. Witches can't use magic on werewolves, so maybe it's their alpha?" I thought of the demented wannabe alpha who'd killed my sister. What was forcing one werewolf to run into a fence, compared to *that*?

"If it were just one pack, just one attack, that might be it," Maven mused. "But I still can't see the Wyoming werewolves and the eastern Utah pack working together. It goes against their basic territorial instinct."

"I don't know, then," Quinn said, and if I hadn't been looking, I would have missed the frustration on his face.

"Neither do I." Maven's voice was contemplative. Her eyes unfocused for a moment as she dug through her memory, but then shook her head, not catching it. I wondered what it was like, trying to remember things that had happened tens or even hundreds of years ago. I barely remembered high school.

There was a knock on Maven's office door, and a heavyset young man poked his head in, pushing trendy thick-rimmed glasses up on his nose. "Hey, Maven. Oh hi, Lex, Quinn." I lifted one hand in a wave, and Quinn gave the kid a stony nod. We'd both met Maven's most recent hire, a twenty-five-year-old human named Ryan. He was the daytime manager of the coffee shop, and Maven's all-around errand boy, who had to give the occasional unwitting blood donation. That was my suspicion, anyway—the kid was always pale—but he seemed content enough, and it was none of my business.

"Maven, I'm gonna take off now, if that's all right," he said. "I think the rush is pretty much over. Adrian can handle it from here."

"Awesome, thanks, Ryan," she chirped, using her teenage hippie accent. It sounded so strange coming from the same voice that had often frightened the crap out of me. They exchanged a couple of words about the next day's schedule, and as soon as the door closed behind Ryan, Maven's eyes came to rest on me. "I'll need to get out there in a moment, so let's move on, for now. Lex, tell me more about this hairball business."

I went through the whole story about the phone call from Elise and driving Simon to the police station, and told her his theory about the creature that'd left the gastric pellet. Maven didn't jump up and say "Ah ha, I know exactly what that is," like I'd kind of been hoping, but when I was done, she leaned forward and pointed at me. "I want you to stay on that. Keep in touch with Simon, assist him however you can, and let me know everything he learns about the pellet."

A rock formed in my stomach, tumbling around unhappily. I had known in theory that I would need to report on the witches to Maven, but that didn't mean I liked it. Then again, as long as they didn't know about werewolves in Colorado, the witches technically worked for Maven too. So I could probably at least be upfront with Simon about the fact that I would report back to Maven. I just couldn't be upfront with him about the werewolf attack.

I resisted the urge to thunk my head into Maven's desk, but just barely.

"Do you think they're connected?" I asked her instead. "The werewolf attack and the pellet?"

"I think we need to proceed as if they are," she said somberly. "As if they're two parts of a threat to Colorado."

"What do you want to do about the werewolves?" Quinn asked.

"We need more information. Specifically about the history of magic in this state." Maven stood up and began to pace the short width of her cramped office. I'd never seen her do that before. Quinn and I sat in silence as five long minutes ticked by on the wall clock. Finally, Maven turned back to us. "When I came to this state twelve years ago, to break up the war," she said at last, "it wasn't my first trip to Colorado."

Quinn and I exchanged a look, and he gave me a little shrug. Neither of us had been expecting a lesson in Maven's personal history. "I was here in 1892, newly arrived from Europe to explore the burgeoning businesses of mining and prostitution. Both professions were particularly lucrative for vampires, for different reasons." I felt a little flutter of fear, just based on her tone. "At any rate, I spent some time with one of Colorado's madams in Denver, Nellie Evans, who just happened to be a witch. She was very close to the native peoples, and became something of an expert on the natural magic in this lovely state. I could swear she used the phrase 'moon lines' before. "

I was hoping Maven would say something like "And she taught me everything she knew," but instead she paused and studied her fingernails. It was a surprisingly human gesture. "Unfortunately, Nellie and I experienced something of a falling out, over money. She killed me . . . or at least she thought she did." Her smile was cold and barbaric. "As I am a vampire, and *not* a helpless soiled dove, I killed her right back."

There was a pause, as both Quinn and I struggled for something to say.

"That's . . . quite a falling out," I remarked finally.

Maven nodded, unperturbed. "At any rate, after her death, Nellie's spirit did not move on to the next plane. Her remnants are still right where I left them. But although she and I are both old and strong enough to see each other, we are not exactly on speaking terms. So Lex," she said, nodding at me, "will go to see Nellie tonight, and question her about Tobias Leine's story."

Quinn was already nodding obediently in the chair beside me, but I hesitated. "One problem," I said. "I can't actually see ghosts." Maven's eyebrows shot up. "I figured I was just sort of missing that part of the boundary witch thing," I added lamely.

"That's not how it works," she informed me, looking puzzled. "I have been dead long enough to make out the strongest remnants, but as a boundary witch you should be able to see them each night, wherever they are. Besides," she added, "you saw the *gjenganger.*"

"True, but assuming those aren't the only ghosts in all of Boulder, they seem to be the exception," I admitted. "I haven't seen a ghost, before or since."

"Hmm." Maven stared at me some more, making me squirm in my seat. I was really starting to wish she'd fidget like everyone else. "Then you will go to Clan Pellar tonight," she declared. "Find out if Hazel can help repair or restore that part of your magic. As soon as you are able to see remnants, go visit Nellie."

"Pardon me," Quinn interjected, "I thought remnants were only bits and pieces of a person's memory. Like playing a little bit of a home movie over and over. Will Lex even be able to communicate with the spirit?"

Maven gave him an indulgent smile. "There are as many kinds of remnants as there are kinds of witches, Quinn. Their degree of coherency depends a lot on how they died, under what conditions, and whether or not they had any access to magic while alive."

"The remnants of witches are more sentient?" I said in confusion.

Maven's sudden smile was the most human expression I'd seen from her: sly and a little wicked. "Indeed. In fact, this remnant should be particularly sentient. In life, Nellie was a boundary witch."

Chapter 13

There was silence as my head spun with the new information. A boundary witch left a functioning and aware ghost. If I died, that could happen to me. I *really* didn't want to become like those things at the cemetery.

Then my brain caught up to the meaning behind her words. Boundary witches could die. *I* could die. For some reason, this came as a great relief.

Maven must have read my thoughts on my face, because she nodded. "Yes, boundary witches can be killed. It's easy for your magic to close wounds or briefly ignore internal damage to keep your body from crossing the line. But there are things you can't come back from."

"Like what?" I said in a small voice, aware that I was talking to a woman who had killed one of my kind. "How did Nellie die?"

Maven's eyes seemed to puncture me, leaving me empty and cold. "I cut off her head."

There wasn't a lot to say after "I cut off her head." Maven told me to check in with her at Magic Beans the next afternoon at sunset, and waved a hand to dismiss me. Still a little unnerved, I got out of there as fast as I could.

My car was parked at the Randolph Center, and parking at CU is a bitch, so I began walking toward the CU campus, where I was pretty sure Simon would still be working. I had every intention of obeying Maven's order to talk to Clan Pellar. But why take the problem straight to Hazel when her children were much more welcoming? Besides, Maven *had* told me to check in with Simon about the pellet-leaving creature. I was really just killing two birds.

I called Simon on the way, and he confessed that he hadn't eaten since breakfast. We arranged to meet at a calzone shop just off campus. I texted Lily to join us too, both because I wanted her opinion on this remnant business, and because I wanted another pair of eyes on Simon. I didn't mean to fuss over him, but I had been a little worried about him *before* he'd spent an entire day working without food.

The calzone shop was located in a tiny building on Broadway, part of a row of fast-food and delivery places that catered to the students. It was a nice enough location, decorated in bold shades of red and black, but it was obvious that their main business was delivery. The four employees behind the counter were bustling back and forth, calling out to each other, but aside from Simon, there was only one occupied table in the whole place: two college girls with textbooks spread under their calzone boxes. I ordered a veggie calzone at the counter and went to sit by Simon, who was so entranced by something on his laptop that he hadn't even seen me coming. He looked genuinely surprised when I sat down.

"Oh, hey," he said, closing his laptop and setting it on the bench seat next to him, where his cane was propped. I winced as I got a good look at his sunken features and pale skin. He looked worse than he had early that morning . . . Good God, had it been just this morning that we'd seen the gastric pellet?

"Hey. Did you order something to eat too?" I asked, pointing at the fountain soda near his elbow. "Otherwise I can go up for you."

"No, I ordered. They're just a little slow tonight." He took off his wire-framed glasses to rub his face. "You want an update on the pellet for Maven." It wasn't really a question.

"Yes, but first I need to talk about another problem." Before I could continue, Lily came breezing through the front door. She grabbed the chair next to me and flipped it around so she could straddle it backward. She was wearing black leather pants and a buttoned jean jacket that should have looked ridiculous together, but somehow it worked perfectly.

"Hey, Lex. What's up, big brother?" she said casually, reaching over to steal a swig from Simon's soda.

"Dammit, Lily, get your own," Simon complained, but without any heat to it.

Ignoring him, Lily looked at me. "What's up, Lex? Why have you assembled the Scooby gang?"

I missed most of Lily's pop-culture references, but I had seen *Scooby-Doo*, so I shot her a quick smile. Before I could answer her, Simon contended, "Technically, a complete Scooby gang meeting would have to include Quinn."

Lily rolled her eyes. "Your boyfriend doesn't get to be in our Scooby gang," she told her brother. Lily and Quinn couldn't stand each other, although I'd never found out why. It made me a little uneasy. "We're not accepting douche-nozzles."

"Then how are *you* here?" Simon countered.

"Guys!" I interrupted. "Can we?"

They both looked appropriately shamed, so I started explaining how Maven wanted me to get in touch with the remnant of Nellie Evans, who had also been a boundary witch. I left out everything about the werewolves. As I spoke, I realized that it made sense that I'd want to talk to Nellie anyway—not only was she someone like me, but she might know something about whatever strange creature had coughed up that gastric pellet.

While I was talking, both Simon's calzone order and mine were called, and Lily got up to fetch them. When she sat back down she pulled a plastic baggie of mini carrots out of her jacket pocket and began crunching on them. "Paleo," she said by way of explanation.

Simon rolled his eyes, beginning to cut up the cheesy calzone with his plastic silverware. "*Anyway*, Lex, I understand that Maven wants you to communicate with this person, but if you can't see her, you can't see her. I'm not sure what we can do to help."

"Maven said it doesn't work like that. All boundary witches can see ghosts, period." I bit my lip. "Also . . . I saw some last night."

"*What*?" Lily was shocked. She blurted, "Why didn't you say anything?" at the exact same moment Simon exclaimed, "You were with me *all morning* and you never mentioned this?"

I held up my hands defensively. That had been right before Quinn and I had taken on the missing vampire case. "Honestly, I kind of just forgot." I told them about the *gjenganger*, only stumbling a little when I used the word. I'd be damned if I could spell it, though.

"Yeah, Mom calls them wraiths," Lily said, nodding her understanding. "They died particularly horrifying deaths, and they have to return to their bones on Samhain. But why would you be able to see *those* remnants, but not everyday remnants? Makes no sense."

Simon was staring at me, showing no sign that he'd heard his sister's question. He'd stopped eating his calzone, and his right hand hovered over the cardboard box as if it had gotten lost on the way to his food.

"*What*?" I finally asked.

"You said you had nightmares," he began, "right after you drowned. When you activated your witchblood."

I stared blankly at him for a moment as I tried to switch gears back to our conversation about nightmares. "Yeah, so? Lots of people have bad dreams." I said, pointedly not reminding him that he was having them too.

"But you said you dreamed about dead people," Simon persisted. "What did you mean?"

I shrugged. "You know, dead people. I dreamed that they were everywhere—in my parents' house, at the grocery store, library, whatever. But lots of people have night terrors," I said again, a little more desperately. "My parents had me talk to a shrink, and Sam slept with me for a while. Eventually they went away." It had been a big deal to me at the time, but it was the same way everything is a big deal to you when you're a kid: a softball game, a snubbing in the cafeteria, losing your favorite backpack. Honestly, once I was past the night terrors, I'd nearly forgotten about them.

"What if they weren't dreams at all?" Simon said quietly.

Now it was my turn to stare at him. "You . . . you think I was seeing ghosts? That makes no sense." I spread my hands out in front of me. "If I saw ghosts when I was thirteen, where the hell did they go?"

Lily was looking back and forth between her brother and me as though she were watching a particularly interesting game of Ping-Pong. Simon studied me, and I knew from his expression that he was examining me in the magical spectrum. Again. "I think . . . I think maybe you *made* them go away."

I just stared at him. "When your magic first comes in," he explained, "it's a little bit . . . malleable."

"Sort of like how a newborn's head is all soft and squishy," Lily interjected, munching on another carrot stick.

Simon rolled his eyes at his sister. "I was gonna go with parents who take the pen away from their left-handed kid and make him write with the other hand, but okay. Squishy newborn head." Lily stuck her tongue out at him. "Anyway, your specialization develops in that malleable time, if you have one. But I think you did more than develop a specialty. I think you blocked part of it off."

Lily gave him a skeptical look. "I've never heard of that."

He shrugged. "I haven't either, but we don't know much about boundary magic. And we don't know many witches with bloodlines as strong as Lex's."

"Hang on," I objected. "If I blocked out my ability to see ghosts, how come I saw the remnants last night?"

Simon's brow furrowed, and I could practically see him fitting pieces against each other in his mind, trying to get them to fall into place. "Wraiths happen when someone's death leaves a *serious* imprint on the magical spectrum, like a psychic scar. Halloween is when that echo is the strongest," he said. "It's so strong, in fact, that a lot of foundings who have just a hint of witchblood, but have never activated their powers, can see the wraiths on Halloween."

"That's where all the stories come from," Lily supplied. She was still noshing on carrot sticks, as though we were discussing a favorite sitcom instead of freaking *ghosts*. "Why humans fear graveyards at night."

I tried to process all of that. "So you're suggesting that because wraiths are stronger than ordinary ghosts, they were able to penetrate the magical . . . *fence*, or whatever, that I built in my mind when I was thirteen. Does that pretty much sum things up?" Simon nodded, and Lily rolled her eyes toward her brother, shrugging as if to say *It's his theory, not mine.*

"No offense, Simon," I said, "but that sounds goddamned ridiculous."

His face clouded over with annoyance. "More ridiculous than chatting with your dead sister?" he asked, his voice rising. "Or sucking the life out of all the fish in a lake? How about bringing the dead back to life?"

I flinched, and Lily elbowed her brother hard. "Ow," he protested. I glanced at the young restaurant staff, but they were all preoccupied with their headsets. "What was that for?" Simon complained.

"That was not tactful."

He gave her a wide-eyed look. "*You're* lecturing *me* on tact?"

"No, he's right," I murmured. Much as I didn't like to think about it, I *had* done those things, and the idea that I'd built my own psychic wall wasn't any less likely.

There was an awkward pause. Simon got up laboriously to refill his soda, and Lily went to fill her own plastic Nalgene bottle. Either one of them could have gotten both drinks, but I understood that they were giving me a moment to process Simon's theory.

And I needed it. Every time I thought I had a handle on what I could do, the rules seemed to change. It was driving me nuts. I couldn't get a grip on *what* I was, much less who that made me.

Charlie, I told myself firmly. The most important thing in my life was protecting Charlie, which meant doing whatever Maven wanted. And right now, she wanted me to tear down a wall I'd built in my mind. That wasn't so bad, right?

When Simon and Lily sat back down, I glanced around the restaurant. The two students had departed, so we were alone except for a pack of busy, distracted employees. "Okay," I said quietly, "if you're right, and I built a mental wall when I was a kid, how do I take it down now?"

"I don't think it's a wall," Simon contended. "I think it's more like scar tissue. You were a kid; you thought remnants were scary, so you . . . well, *deadened* part of your boundary powers, no pun intended, so you wouldn't see them anymore. I don't mean you did it consciously or intentionally—more like your mind did it to protect you."

I considered that for a moment. I'd had to see a VA shrink after my return from Iraq, and he'd used more or less the same words to explain why I couldn't remember my last couple of days in Iraq. My brain had built a barrier to protect me. "Okay," I said, accepting the idea, "assuming you're right, how do I get rid of the scar tissue?"

Simon and Lily looked at each other thoughtfully, and I could practically see them doing sibling telepathy. Whenever they did that, I felt a new pang of grief for my sister.

"Check with Mom?" Lily suggested.

Simon nodded and pulled out his phone. I worked on my calzone as he ran the situation past Hazel. There was some nodding and a few uh-huhs before he finally hung up. "She has one idea, but it's kind of a long shot."

Something on his face must have tipped off his sister, because Lily said doubtfully, "She didn't suggest Sybil's friend?"

"Sybil doesn't have *friends*," he replied. "But if you mean Sybil's thaumaturge acquaintance, then yeah, that's what Mom's thinking."

Lily chewed her lower lip. "It's probably not going to work, though."

"Guys?" I waved my hand. "Right here. What are you talking about?"

"Sorry," they said in unison. Simon went on, "Our older sister Sybil knows a thaumaturge witch in Las Vegas . . ."

"A witch who specializes in healing, the way you specialize in death," Lily added helpfully.

I winced at the phrasing, but it wasn't like she was wrong. "So you're thinking she can heal the scar tissue?" I asked.

"If you were human, *maybe*," Lily answered, shooting her brother a look. "But her magic shouldn't work against your magic."

"She might not be able to *heal* the scar tissue," Simon reasoned, "but she can probably communicate with it." Lily and I both gave him wide-eyed looks. He shrugged. "From what I understand, she doesn't just give you a potion or do a spell, like some witches—"

"Sybil included," Lily put in.

"She sort of communicates with your body on a subconscious level," Simon went on, starting to look a little excited. "Honestly, I think it's fascinating, and I've been hoping to meet her. This could be just the reason."

My skepticism must have shown on my face, because he shot me a pleading look. "Please? It could help. It certainly wouldn't hurt."

I sighed. "Fine," I said, giving his cane a pointed look. "But only if she takes a look at you, too."

Lily crowed, and Simon flushed a little. "In the interest of science," he said with elaborate graciousness, "I'd love to experience what she does. Lily," he added, turning to his sister. "Can you call Sybil and get the number?"

Lily made a face. "Ew. Like, right now? Why don't you do it?"

I hadn't actually met Sybil or Morgan, the two elder Pellar siblings, but from what Simon and Lily had said, Morgan was the heir-apparent golden child and Sybil was fussy and cold. Although to be fair, that could just be part of Simon and Lily's schtick.

They squabbled for a few more minutes before Lily agreed to make the call. She stood up, grabbed Simon's soda spitefully, and skulked toward the back door.

"Is Sybil really that bad?" I asked, watching Lily go.

"Honestly, she's become a lot more tolerable since Morgan started having problems with her husband," Simon said absently. I raised my eyebrows and he winced, as if just realizing what he'd said. "Sorry, that was an overshare. Let's just say the Pellar family dynamic is complicated. Especially since my dad died."

I didn't think I'd ever heard Simon mention his father. "What was his name?" I asked.

Simon's eyes, which had gone distant for a moment, focused back on me. "Nero. Nero Carter. He was from Louisiana. Why do you ask?"

I shrugged. "Just wanted to know what to call him when I think of him."

Simon's face softened. "It's funny," he said in a sad voice, "I hardly ever think of him anymore. It used to be every day, all the time."

"How old were you?" I asked. "When you lost your dad, I mean."

"Nineteen. Lily was fifteen."

I had just asked out of curiosity, but it suddenly occurred to me that Simon was in his early thirties. He would have been nineteen maybe twelve or thirteen years ago . . . right about when the werewolf packs were warring in Colorado.

Had Simon and Lily's dad been killed by werewolves?

Simon must have seen the spark of understanding in my eyes, because he gave me one slow nod. Before I could get the question out, he added, "You needed me to fill you in on the pellet too, right?"

For a moment I floundered. "Uh, yes," I managed, feeling incredibly guilty. Werewolves had invaded Colorado, and I hadn't told him. I pushed it aside to think about later. "Any word on our mystery creature?" I asked, composing myself.

Simon raised his eyes to meet mine. His voice was completely casual as he said, "Yes and no. Since we talked this afternoon, I did learn that another pellet was found in Golden Gate Canyon Park."

Chapter 14

"Whoa," I exclaimed, barely resisting the urge to smack my injured friend. "Way to bury the lead, Simon!"

He held up a hand. "Hang on, it's not the same situation. The park rangers found a pellet on the twenty-eighth, probably dumped either that day or the day before, since it rained two days earlier. But this one had no human parts or clothes inside."

"What was it, then?"

"Antlers," he replied. "And hooves, and a little bit of fur."

"A deer?"

Simon nodded. "The parts it couldn't digest, anyway. That's why the rangers didn't pursue it much. It was odd, but not threatening. They sent a sample on to the CBI, but figured it'd be weeks before they got results."

"So it ate a deer on the twenty-seventh-ish," I said slowly, "and then it ate a person . . . do you know when?"

"Hard to determine. I called your cousin Elise and fished for more information. The cops are done with the CU prank theory, because they've tentatively identified the remains we found. The clothes matched descriptions of a homeless guy who hung out between Broadway and Chautauqua, panhandling the tourists. No one remembers seeing him since the twenty-ninth. Which could be when he was taken, or just when he went off-grid."

I winced. It was one thing to find an anonymous hip bone, and quite another to know where it came from. I'd volunteered at a couple of local soup kitchens with my mother; I knew some of those guys. A lot of them were veterans. "So this animal, whatever it is, ate on the twenty-seventh and the thirtieth, spitting out gastric pellets both times. When will it need to eat again?"

He shrugged helplessly. "There's no way I could determine that with the data we have now."

"Best guess, then."

Simon cracked his knuckles, thinking. "Best guess, the thing needs two days to digest a deer, maybe a day to digest a person, with its smaller mass. That's approximate, Lex."

"So it could be taking its new victim as we speak." I grunted with frustration and rose to pace back and forth a little near our table. I kind of understood how to hunt down vampires, and even werewolves thanks to the silver allergy, but how the hell were we supposed to track a magical monster that lived underground? "What about the folklore?" I said, sounding a little desperate even to my own ears. "Quinn suggested you look into that."

Simon leaned forward, excitement brightening his eyes again. I went over and sat down so we wouldn't be overheard. "Now, *that* was interesting. Folklore isn't my specialty, but when I started digging into it, I found that a number of cultures around the world believe in an enormous wormlike cryptid."

"Yeah, I don't know what that is."

"A cryptid is a plant or animal that people believe exists despite the fact that there's no definitive proof," he lectured. "Bigfoot, the chupacabra, the Loch Ness Monster, that kind of thing."

"I don't believe in any of those things."

"Well, that's all right. I don't either." He waved a hand. "The thing is, belief in a specific cryptid is usually regional—the people of Loch Ness believed in Nessie, so it became a local legend. That's standard. What's interesting is when there are *multiple* cultures across the world that develop a belief in the same thing."

I finished my calzone and pushed the cardboard box aside. "Gimme an example."

Simon smirked. "Vampires. Hundreds of different cultures around the world have developed a myth about a parasitic creature that could pass as human and is intricately linked to the dead."

I made a face at him. "I walked right into that one, didn't I?"

"Yep. Anyway, when you look at the folklore about a carnivorous worm- or snakelike creature that dwells underground, you run into the same widespread legends." He began ticking off numbers on his fingers. "There are a number of Central American myths about the Minhocão—a giant snakelike earthworm that was theorized to be part of the caecilian family. Which are amphibians that look like snakes," he hurried to add, before I could ask. "In the Gobi Desert there is supposedly a creature called the Mongolian Death Worm—seriously—that spits a paralyzing venom before dragging its prey underground to be consumed. It can also electrocute people from several feet away. Then there's the lamia—half woman, half enormous snake body. And European bestiaries tell of the basilisk, the king of snakes that can kill with a single glance—"

I held up a hand to stop him. "I read Harry Potter with my cousin's kids. I've heard of a basilisk."

Quick nod. "Anyway, you have to realize that South America, China, and Europe are thousands of miles apart, and when these legends originated, the natives had no way of traveling those distances," he said excitedly. "Then you add on the creatures we know to be real—Komodo dragons, anacondas, and the other members of the genus *Eunectes*, and of course the many appearances in science fiction of the sandworm—"

"Science *fiction*?" I interrupted him. "Simon. You are a *scientist*, for crying out loud. Get your shit together."

He deflated, but only a little. "You're right, I am a scientist. But remember, when we look at the fossil record and make all the connections, there are always bits and pieces of evidence left over: footprints or tail prints or coprolites that we can't conclusively say came from any certain creature. All I'm suggesting is that perhaps there is, or at least there *was*, some kind of snakelike creature that inspired some of these myths."

"But where has it *been*?" I demanded. "Even if this cryptid thingy once existed right around here, how could something that big disappear for a thousand years and then pop right back up?"

Simon grinned. "Magic." My face must have indicated that I was ready to punch him, because he hurried to add, "No, seriously. Remember, that gastric pellet was drenched in magic. It's possible that magic allows it to slumber for centuries, or move around the tectonic plates from place to place so it's never spotted. And now it's here."

"And it's gonna need to eat again soon," I said grimly. I didn't love how excited he was getting about something that was literally eating people.

"Well, there's that, yeah. But if I could study this thing, or even autopsy it once we find it, I could learn so much about magic, about where we came from."

It was hard to give a shit about that, considering John took Charlie to the playground at Chautauqua. Seeing that I wasn't invested, Simon pressed, "Look, Lex, you asked me to find a connection between nulls and boundary witches, remember? Well, it's entirely possible that this thing could provide us with some clues."

I fell silent, considering that. I did want to know if there was a connection between boundary magic and nulls, but was I willing to risk more lives in order to find out?

No. I was not. "Can't the witches help?" I asked him. "Put up a barrier or ward or something?"

"We can try," he said, looking uncomfortable. "But deflection spells don't work that far underground. All that earth, well, *grounds* them." He gave a helpless shrug, not meeting my eyes. I was pretty sure there was something Simon wasn't telling me about the witch clan. It stung a little, but I wasn't really in a position to push him on it. I did sort of work for the oppressor.

Moving on. "You're not gonna like this," I said, "but I think we better talk to Maven about pressing someone to close down the park for a couple of days, until we can figure out what this thing is."

"You're right, I don't like it," he said immediately. "That's the most popular park in Boulder, Lex. Shutting it down is gonna bring up a lot of questions." He drummed his fingers on the table for a moment, and I let him think it over. "But yeah, I agree," he said at last. "It has to be done. We just gotta move faster." I saw him shoot a venomous glare toward his cane. "The snakelike creature . . . God, I don't even know what to call it." For a second his eyes gleamed, and I could see the words "*Eunectes pellaricus*" practically glowing off him.

"*I* wanted to call it a graboid," Lily said, returning to the table. I'd been so focused on the conversation I hadn't even heard her come back in. "But Simon wouldn't let me."

"Why graboid?" I asked.

They shot me identical disbelieving stares, which I recognized as *Lex is missing a pop-culture reference*. I held up my hands. "Forget I asked. Let's go with 'sandworm,'" I decided. "It's a lot less terrifying than 'Mongolian Death Worm.'"

"Plus, very *Beetlejuice*," Lily said agreeably.

Simon looked up at his sister. "Did you get a hold of Sybil?"

"Yes, and I called the thaumaturge," she reported. "She said she's worked with psychic trauma before, like repressed memories, but never on a witch. She'll come if you want to give it a try, but only if we pay her expenses and a fee, and she wants to bring her daughter along."

"How much?" I asked.

Lily winced. "I did a quick look at last-minute flights on my phone. It's not going to be cheap."

She named a figure so high I nearly fell off my chair. "What? I could buy a car and go pick her up for that much."

Lily shrugged. "She gets top dollar for what she does, Lex. That's already with a friends-and-family discount." She looked at me hesitantly. "Don't you have, like, mad hazard pay from being in the army?"

"Not anymore," I said shortly. I *had* made good money as a soldier, and hadn't blown through it the moment I got home, the way a lot of us did. But Sam had died so young, without much life insurance, and John had wiped out a lot of their savings to pay for the memorial and moving back to Boulder, not to mention the empty grave with Sam's headstone. My parents had money, but it was all tied up in Luther Shoes, which had taken a hit during the recession that they still hadn't bounced back from. So I'd quietly shoved all of my leftover army pay into a savings account for Charlie's college.

I was making a bit more money now that I had the stipend from Maven, but my checking account barely had a comma, much less the money I'd need to bring the Las Vegas witch to Boulder. Especially after my recent last-minute trip to LA.

"You want me to call it off?" Lily asked, seeing my expression.

"No." I stood up. "Gimme the info. I'll call Maven and ask for the money."

Lily handed me a scrap of paper with a name and number written on the back. "Better you than me, lady."

Chapter 15

Simon promised to call me as soon as he had more information, and I said I would let both of them know when I had the travel plans for the thaumaturge witch. Lily offered to walk me part of the way back to the coffee shop to get my car, and I accepted, suspecting that she wanted to talk about something without her brother present.

Sure enough, as soon as we were in the parking lot, Lily blurted, "He looked bad, didn't he?"

I glanced over at her worried expression. Lily was a sunny person, cheerful, animated, with very little interest in filtering. I was starting to feel like everyone in my life had done some sort of bizarre personality flip-flop. "He looked tired," I said cautiously. "This sandworm thing . . ."

She shook her head. "It's not just that. He's been different since . . . well, since you brought him back."

Oh. That's what this was about. I had never actually told Lily what I'd done to Simon, preferring to let him decide, but he must have told her. Or, more likely, she'd pried it out of him. "He was only gone for a couple of minutes," I offered. "That happens to people all the time, with no lasting damage."

A big group of CU students threaded through the two of us, talking and laughing. When they had passed, Lily said, "Yeah, but it's not like Simon was brought back with a defibrillator and kept alive with an IV. That, he could accept."

"Well, *that's* kind of hypocritical," I pointed out. "You guys are witches, and you're suggesting Simon could only tolerate being brought back to life by science?"

She shook her head. "Simon doesn't see science and magic as mutually exclusive, but that's not really the point. There are things that we . . ." She struggled for the right words, finally sighing. "Look, Lex, how much do you know about the witches' deal with Maven?"

That got my attention. I looked over at her. Lily had jammed her hands into the pockets of her jean jacket, and there was something like anger on her face. "Quinn told me that when the werewolves were going crazy under Trask, some of the clans got caught in the crossfire. Your mom went to Maven and asked for her help," I said carefully. "Maven got Itachi to ride into the state and kill the bad guys."

"That's all true," Lily allowed. "But how much did he tell you about what we gave up in exchange?"

My brow furrowed. I wasn't sure what she was getting at. "He said the witches had to agree to Maven and Itachi's leadership in Colorado for a period of twenty years. You guys basically have to do what Maven says. And that was, what, thirteen years ago?"

Lily nodded. "Also true. But there's something Quinn left out, or maybe he doesn't even know. He's only been a vampire for a few years. Hey, stop a second." She led me to a nearby wrought-iron bench, scrunching herself into the far corner and glancing around to make sure no one was paying attention to us.

Ignoring the cold coming off the metal bars, I turned sideways on the seat to face her. "There are some big-league spells out there, for things like violence, healing, and protection," Lily explained. "We call that upper-tier stuff apex magic, and even when you have good intentions, it's very powerful. Things can go wrong. In Clan Pellar, we stopped teaching it a couple generations ago. My ancestors decided to focus on Wicca, using our magic to do good rather than as a tool for getting what we wanted." She winced. "But we aren't the only clan in Colorado. When Maven cut her deal with the witches, she ordered all the clans in the state to bind their abilities. None of us can use apex magic during that twenty-year window."

I suddenly remembered Simon's expression, how he seemed to be holding something back from me about the witches. "Why would she do that?" I asked. "What does she care if witches are using witch magic?"

Lily sighed. "Her argument was that if witches were using combat magic, they could use it against *her*, or each other, and restart the Old World war all over again. My mother thought it was a valid point. More importantly, she didn't think the other witches should be using magic for violence anyway. That catapult spell she used on you? That's as violent as we get. Mom hoped that weaning the other clans off apex magic would be a good thing in the long run. But there were plenty of witches who didn't agree with her."

She was leading me toward a connection. I tried to push my thoughts ahead to see it. "Was Simon one of those witches?"

Bingo. Lily's face went stony. "He wasn't then. At the time, he threw his full support behind Mom. We all did."

"And now he's changed his mind," I summed up. I was struggling to see why this was relevant right now, with everything else going on. I was worried about Simon, too, but unlike the sandworm, his problems didn't seem all that time-sensitive.

"*You* were the one who changed his mind, Lex. When you brought him back, it wasn't just that you used magic to do something that he only expected from science. You also reminded him that there are dangerous things out there, and that our people are no longer equipped to handle them. And *we did it to ourselves*."

"Oh," I said softly.

She nodded. "It's weighing on him. And creating a lot of tension between him and Tracy, who basically worships the ground my mother walks on."

I winced, unsure how to react to that. Oops? "Is this why the clan doesn't like me? Because I represent all the violent magic you guys stopped using?" A new thought occurred to me. "Or because I'm not a clan witch, so *I* don't have to abide by Maven's agreement with you?"

"Yes. To all of the above." She sighed. "Look, from their perspective, you came along, proved that you have power over life and death, and immediately threw in with our evil overlord."

She was trying to keep her tone light, but failing miserably, and it was obvious from her expression that she felt the same way. I wanted to ask her why no one had told *me* any of this, but the answer was too obvious: I was an outsider, a threat, and that put me on a need-to-know basis.

Pressure built in my chest as my temper rose. "Let me show you something," I said, pulling out my cell phone. I scrolled through the functions until I found what I wanted, a message my mother had sent me that morning while I was napping. I held it up so Lily could see: A picture of my nineteen-month-old niece standing on top of my mom's kitchen table, holding a giant stack of graham crackers she'd swiped while Mom was in the bathroom. Rather than looking guilty, Charlie's whole face had erupted into a gleeful, euphoric smile. Everything was right in her world.

Lily looked at it, then at my face, not getting it. She shrugged. "Cute."

"She *is* cute," I said evenly, because, well, she was. "And she's also the only part of my sister that's left in this world. I would do anything, *anything* to protect her, just like you're trying to protect your brother right now."

Lily crossed her arms over her chest. "I get that."

"No, Lily, you don't. I don't really give a shit if Clan Pellar feels hamstrung. I want a good relationship with the witches, but you've *all* made it clear that I'm not actually one of you. And I'm sure as hell not one of the vampires, either, boundary blood or not. All the witches in your clan—even you and Simon—act like I happily signed up to be some vampire hench-slave because I'm an evil boundary witch who doesn't know any better. But it's not like that. I didn't pick Hazel's side or Maven's side. I picked *Charlie's*."

Her lovely face hardened. "You walked into this situation that has all these years of history, and you can *bring people back to life*," she hissed. "And you just signed right up with the big bad; you didn't even give us a *chance*—"

I couldn't help it; I started laughing. I was physically exhausted, and so sick of Old World politics that I could scream. "A chance to what? Have the clan adopt me? Pull me into the fold? We both know that's never going to happen, Lily. You saw how those witches looked at me last night. I'm never going to be anything to them but a black aura and a bad attitude. An *atrocity*. You and Simon are my friends, and I'll help you however I can, but your clan's subservience to Maven is not my concern. Charlie is."

Lily's lips compressed into a single thin line. "I see," she said curtly. "Good to know where we stand." She stood up, turned on her heel and strode away without another word.

I sat there on the bench for a long time, staring into space and absently rubbing my tattoos under my sleeves. I could have handled that better, I knew. Without Simon and Lily, I would never have gained enough control of my magic to earn the deal with Maven. But what exactly did Lily want from me? It wasn't my fault that the witches had made a deal with their perceived devil. And it wasn't my fault that I could use magic that existed more or less outside of that deal. Besides, I wasn't exactly going to apologize for bringing Simon back.

But you could have been more understanding of Lily's position, said Sam's voice in my head. *You know what it's like to be stuck in a deal with Maven, and you didn't show much sympathy.*

I no longer knew if this really was Sam, talking to me from across the line and through our bond, or just what my imagination told me she would say. It didn't really matter, I supposed. Either way, she was right.

I jumped as my phone began vibrating in my hand. I checked the screen. To my surprise, it was Maven, whom I'd just left less than two hours ago. She couldn't, like, sense when I was thinking about her, could she? Yesterday I would have said no, but it was becoming clear that I had no idea what Old World creatures could do. And also no idea what I was doing.

I answered the phone. "Lex, you need to get to the Walrus," came her voice, crisp and tense. There was loud music in the background, so I could barely make out her words. "I need you."

"Walrus . . . ? Oh, the bar?"

"Now!" she hollered, and the line went dead. I shoved the phone in my pocket and started running.

Chapter 16

I didn't actually attend CU, so my personal knowledge of the downtown bars is limited to the ones I explored right after being discharged from the army. I'd poked my head in at the Walrus only once, took a look around, and made an immediate retreat. The place existed to service those reasonably attractive suburban kids who spent high school being athletic, well-groomed, and popular B students, the same kids who got drunk every weekend and cared more about lettering in volleyball than about a war on the other side of the world. Not that I'm bitter.

Anyway, the place has a reputation for a few things: great DJs, despite a small dance floor; regular reggae nights; and being a welcoming home for douchebaggy behavior. It's also loud, dark, and below ground—I could instantly understand the attraction for hungry vampires.

The Walrus was on the corner of 11th and Walnut—literally on the corner; it was one of those businesses where the front door was located precisely where the building's edges met, like in Times Square. I ran straight up Broadway to 11th Street, ignoring the students and tourists who paused to stare at me. As I got closer, I realized the bar was too quiet: there was no music, no bouncer, no lit neon signs. When I finally reached the door, beginning to pant a little, I saw that someone had taped a piece of ordinary printer paper to the front door. The words "Closed for Inventory" were written on it in sloppy black marker.

I'd seen stuff like this at Magic Beans before, and recognized it as one of the vampires' tactics. This is America; we love obeying signs, even if they look like they were written by middle-school students. I knocked hard on the front door, and when that produced no results, shouted, "It's Lex!" as loud as I could. A middle-aged dog walker gave me a funny look as he went past. "Supposed to help with inventory," I explained. He shrugged and moved on.

I heard the sound of a lock being undone, and the door opened just far enough for me to slip into the building. The entryway was dark, and my eyes hadn't yet adjusted from the glow of the streetlights when a scared-looking girl of about twenty stepped out of the shadows. I jumped.

"Sorry! Didn't mean to scare you. You're the boundary witch, right?" She raised the back of her hand to her mouth, and I realized she was wiping a smear of blood off her chin. I automatically shifted my weight to fight, wishing I'd brought a shredder stake with me.

Sensing my wariness, the girl raised the other hand, too, and took a step backward. "Easy, there. I'm Opal," she said, trying to mollify me, "one of Maven's vampires. I'm supposed to bring you to her." The girl took a couple of steps deeper into the bar, gesturing for me to follow. I did, slowly.

The dance floor was, as promised, especially tiny. It was also covered in blood, which showed up well against the wood floor. The blood was bright red, still wet, and smeared around in puddles like someone had tried to make a snow angel in finger paint.

There were a number of people in the back of the bar, but my eyes shot straight to Maven, partly because her power drew me in, and partly because everyone else was staring at her too. She looked like the poster for a horror movie, standing on top of the bar in a tight black miniskirt and the remains of a torn tank top. I couldn't tell what color it had once been, but now it could best be described as bloodred. Her feet were bare, and long ribbons of blood ran down her legs, but I didn't see anything that looked like an injury.

Some of the blood probably belonged to the two vampires she was restraining. In one hand, Maven was holding a broken pool stick to the heart of a vampire who was splayed on his back on top of the bar, hands held defensively near his shoulders. The wood had already pierced his shirt and drawn blood, but it must not have gone deep enough to reach the heart yet. In the other hand Maven clenched a handful of black curly hair belonging to a second vamp, a man who had to weigh well over two hundred pounds. She held him at a strange angle—on his knees with his face tilted up—and from the expression of agony on his face, I was pretty sure she could snap his neck with a simple twist. I'd seen a vampire do that before.

It was obvious that I'd *just* missed a fight, but something felt wrong to me, too still. Then I realized that no one was breathing hard, because they didn't have to. I swallowed, my mouth suddenly dry. "Hello, Lex," Maven said pleasantly. "Thank you for coming." She looked up at me, and I almost gasped. Gone were the enormous soda-bottle glasses, and her orange hair was slicked back against her skull, possibly with blood. She was stunning, probably the most beautiful person I had ever seen. Her power was practically pulsing out of her, and I had to resist the urge to fall to my knees.

"Hi, Maven," I managed to say. "I like the new look."

In a sublimely human gesture, Maven looked down at herself. "Oh, thanks," she said, giving me a little *what, this old thing?* shrug. "When in Rome."

"Uh-huh." There were bodies on the floor, at least five of them, mostly close to the bar area. Blood was sloshed over the walls and tables, and I heard whispers coming from the far side of the room, behind Maven. I circled slowly into the center of the space, and saw that Quinn was crouched in the corner next to the bar with a dozen or so terrified-looking college kids. Judging by their wide eyes, and a few urine stains on their clothes, they were human. Quinn gave me a quick nod, and turned back to the group, keeping them calm. He was obviously awaiting further instructions.

So was I. "What exactly can I do for you, Maven?" I asked.

"These two," she said, tilting her head at the two male vampires she was restraining, "broke the peace in my territory. They started a *bar fight*"—she spat the words distastefully—"and killed humans, revealing themselves to the human world. Their punishment is death." Her fingers must have tightened on the bigger vamp's scalp, because his face twisted into an agonized grimace.

"Oh-kay," I said cautiously. I had no problem with putting down vampires who'd killed humans, but it kind of seemed like she had all this under control. Why was I here?

"Before they die," Maven went on, "I want you to press their minds and find out who compelled them to do this."

Oh. "But . . . they're vampires. Isn't this kind of what they do?"

Across the room, I could see Quinn wince. Maven hissed, "*No.* Week-old vampires have better control than this. Someone put them up to it, in an effort to further destabilize my territory. I *will* have that name."

Her voice chilled me, and I found myself glancing at Opal for some reason. Vampire expressions were usually pretty impassive, but her face flooded with pure fear as she looked at Maven. Oh, good. It wasn't just me then. "Yes, ma'am," I said, stepping forward.

As I moved closer, the kneeling vampire gave an anguished cry and twisted out of Maven's grasp. I heard the sound of his hair ripping out by its roots as he did a neat roll onto the floor and charged straight for me.

Quinn's voice rang out, screaming my name, but I ignored it and shifted my weight. Vampires were fast, much faster than humans, but I'd had years of combat training, and this guy clearly hadn't. He just raced straight toward me, intending a simple tackle, so I stepped aside and thrust out my right arm, clotheslining him with my forearm. It nearly dislocated my shoulder, but he crashed to the floor. Curly shook his head hard and popped back up within seconds, faster than I could see.

Luckily I'd already picked up a high-legged bar stool, and before he rushed me again I wielded it toward him like a lion tamer, throwing all my weight against it. Three of the four metal legs drove into Curly's torso, drawing blood and forcing him back a few steps, but I'd come nowhere near the heart. I clenched the seat and twisted as hard as I could, but with a scream of pain he tugged the stool legs out of his torso and threw *his* weight back against it, sending the seat straight into my chest.

I flew backward, my back hitting the edge of a table as my feet lost purchase. *Ow.* While I was still struggling to get back up, the vampire spun to my right, apparently deciding to cut his losses and flee.

I may not have had a stake, but that didn't mean I was unarmed. I dropped to the floor and pulled the Springfield subcompact out of the ankle holster on my right foot. There's no point in threatening werewolves with silver bullets unless you have the means to back it up.

I'm fast, but by the time I stood Curly was throwing Opal aside—the female vamp had apparently tried to slow him down. As soon as she was out of my line of fire, I raised my weapon and put three shots into his spine.

Curly went tumbling to the floor, and I came after him, sticking the Springfield in my jacket pocket as I walked. "Lex!" Quinn called out from the other end of the room. I turned my head to look at him, and just managed to catch the spelled stake he'd thrown in a soft underhand toss. I nodded my thanks and glanced quickly at Maven, who was watching me with widened eyes. She hadn't moved from her position on the bar, except to lean a little harder on the pool cue—the prone vampire's eyes were bulging with pain.

Maven gave me a curt nod—permission—and I stalked over to Curly, who was writhing on the floor, on his stomach. Only his arms seemed to be working at the moment—I'd severed his spine. Good. My back hurt too. I kicked him over and plopped down on his chest, pressing my hands against his face so the tips of my griffin tattoos made contact. "Hi. What's your name?" I said conversationally.

Glaring and cursing at me, he tried to shove me off with his arms, but his body was so busy trying to heal the bullet wounds, he didn't have the strength. I fended him off easily and put my hands back. "Name?" I asked again.

"Tony," he growled.

"Hey, Tony!" I shouted, leaning forward, and for a second the vampire was so startled that he forgot he was fighting me and looked right into my eyes. Which was exactly what I wanted. Keeping the eye contact, I dropped into the mindset that allowed me to create a mental connection between the two of us. It was sort of like opening your eyes inside a tunnel, and focusing on the light at the far end. Then I sort of *willed* myself into that light.

And just like that, I had him.

"Tony," I said softly. There was no reason to yell at him now. He'd do anything I wanted. "Who sent you?"

Confusion erupted on his face. I knew the look—he wasn't refusing to answer; he just didn't understand my phrasing. Belatedly, I remembered that commands got better results than questions. "Tell me what happened at the Walrus tonight," I said, pressing the demand into him.

"Darren and I came to hunt. We just wanted to feed." His voice wasn't defensive; it was toneless, as if he were talking in his sleep. "Then we couldn't stop."

Cold fear sparked in the back of my mind, but I had to stay focused or I would lose control of him. "Tell me who wanted you to come here tonight."

Confusion again. "No one. We met at Darren's apartment and decided where to go."

I risked a quick glance at Maven. From past experience I knew I could look away without breaking the connection, but I didn't dare do it for long. Maven was giving me nothing, just a slight furrow of her eyebrows that said she was as confused as I was.

Turning my attention back to Tony, I tried, "Explain why you couldn't stop. Explain why you lost control."

Tony's eyes went distant for a moment, but the connection between us hadn't broken. I could feel it. He just didn't know how to respond. "I'm not sure what happened," he said slowly, as though he were watching a video of the events and couldn't quite interpret it. "Everything was intense tonight, deeper. Like I had a motor, and it'd just been souped-up."

That sounded unpleasantly familiar. "Hang on for a second, Tony," I said, though I kept my eyes on him. To Maven, I called out, "I'm not sure it was their fault. Something is driving them. Maybe the same thing that's been causing . . . other events."

"Kill him."

Her voice was so cold and hard, I had to look up again. When I did, she was sitting on the edge of the bar, her bloodied bare legs dangling below her. The pool cue was now jutting up at an odd angle, and I realized it was sticking out of a desiccated corpse dressed in Darren's clothes. She'd gotten the answer she needed. "They broke my laws. I can't afford to be soft now," Maven said coldly. "Kill him, Lex."

"I can't just—" I began, but I'd broken eye contact for too long. Tony began to buck and holler underneath me, trying to throw me off. I tried to open another connection, but he wasn't having it, his eyes rolling wildly as he fought for leverage. Then all of a sudden his fingers shot up and planted themselves around my throat like it was magnetized.

"What did you do?" he whispered, horrified. "Get out of my brain, you stupid bi—"

The rest of the word was lost, as my shredder found his heart.

Chapter 17

When a vampire dies, the body rapidly decays, like time-lapse photography, until it catches up to where it would be if the vampire magic had never infected it. So a two hundred-year-old vampire would become brittle two hundred-year-old bones, and a three-month-old vampire would become a disgusting still-rotting corpse. I knew all that in theory, and I'd even seen it happen—but not while I was sitting on top of the corpse.

Right underneath me, Tony's body immediately began to desiccate, growing softer and sort of slippery, like his skin was loose underneath his clothes. I scrambled to get off, but I slipped on the bloated skin, catching myself about two inches away from his rotting face. I screeched and leaped to my feet, and for a few seconds I turned into a complete and total girl, shuddering and squirming around while I chanted "Ew, ew, ew!"

Finally the revulsion passed, and I collapsed into a nearby chair, desperately wanting to shower in antibacterial gel. By the time Maven had hopped off the bar and sauntered over, Tony's body looked like a weathered skeleton. She dropped into the chair next to mine, and we sat there silently for a long moment.

"You didn't have to kill them," I said softly. I knew exactly how she'd respond, but I also needed to hear myself say those words out loud.

"Yes, I did."

Behind us, I could hear Quinn pressing the minds of the human bar patrons one by one and sending them out the back door. He was telling each of them they'd witnessed an ugly bar fight and just wanted to go home now.

"What about the bodies?" I mumbled, gesturing to the dead humans scattered around the bar.

"Oh, we'll make up a story," Maven replied. She sounded utterly unconcerned with covering her tracks. "One of them went on a killing spree, or maybe we'll just start a fire. We've done it before."

I just nodded, too numb to be outraged. "Could you make it an accident?" I implored, feeling like a child. "So none of them have to be remembered as a killer?"

Her face didn't change. "Sure."

"Thank you." We sat quietly for a moment. I looked at my hands. There was blood on them, from when I'd rolled around during the fight. It wasn't just my hands, though: my leather jacket. My jeans. My sneakers. Nothing was really saturated, but the red stains were all over me, like I'd rolled against a freshly painted wall. There was probably still a little dried blood in my hair from the night before, too. My back hurt where I'd hit the table, and my shoulder from when I'd clotheslined the guy. Mostly, though, I wanted a shower *so bad*.

"You used a gun," Maven said abruptly.

I raised my eyebrows at her. "Was I not supposed to?"

She shook her head, hesitated, and shrugged. "I'd prefer that you didn't use firearms in highly populated areas, because of the noise. But it's more that we—that I—never even really think of using guns. I know Quinn has some, of course, but that's because he's such a recent vampire." She smiled faintly. "For us old ones, it's considered very . . . tacky."

I snorted. I'd watched Maven reach into Itachi's chest cavity and literally yank out his heart. Of course she didn't need a gun. "Yeah, well, every one of you is faster, stronger, and has better reflexes than I do. I'm happy to be tacky if it means staying alive." A new thought occurred to me. "Why didn't you help me? When Tony almost had me, or when he was running away?"

"I wanted to see what you'd do," she said frankly. "How you'd handle it."

Ouch. It was the answer I'd expected, but it still kind of stung. Sensing my thoughts, Maven added, not unkindly, "I'm not running a charity, Lex. If you can't handle one vampire I need you to press, you're not much good to me."

I didn't let myself react to that; I also didn't give myself any time to question the wisdom of what I was about to say. "Speaking of handling things, I need to borrow some money."

That surprised her. As quickly as I could, I explained about the Las Vegas witch I needed to consult. "It might not even work, honestly, given that she would be using her magic on mine. But Simon and Hazel think there's a chance," I finished.

Maven took in all the information, motionless as she listened to me. "Okay," she said eventually. "Call Ryan first thing and have him set up her travel. On me. I'll leave a note so he knows you have my approval." Before I could thank her, she rose in her seat so she could watch Quinn press a witness. My eyes followed hers. He was talking to the last person. I checked my watch. Almost ten. It felt like about four in the morning.

"Do you need me to help with . . ." I gestured at the bloody bar around us. "Cleanup?"

Maven chuckled. "Go home, Lex. I know you've had a busy day, and tomorrow may shape up to be similar. Get some rest while you can."

I began to stand, but there was something else that needed to be said aloud. "It's related, isn't it?" I ventured. "To the werewolves, and maybe even Simon's pellet thing."

"That," Maven said in a strange, hollow voice, "is exactly what I'm afraid of."

I retrieved my car from the lot and started toward the cabin, but after a moment of thought, I texted John and asked if I could drop by for a minute. I was really asking if he was alone—John had recently indicated that he was seeing someone, although I had no idea if it was serious. But he texted *Yes* back almost immediately.

I drove straight to John's suburban house off Kings Ridge Boulevard, one of the nicer areas in Boulder.

He was waiting by his front door, so I didn't even have to ring the bell before he swung it open. John was half Native American, with strong features and lustrous black hair that stood up in tufts whenever he was tired, like he was now. Working all day and being a single parent all night had to be exhausting. "I know this is weird," I said by way of hello. "But I just kind of wanted to see Charlie."

A smile broke over his face, and I felt a familiar twinge in my chest. John and I had been in love with each other for about five minutes in high school, back when everyone called me Allie, before I'd decided that I needed to serve my country. That girl had died a long time ago, though, and I'd come home from the war a different person, with a new name. While I was gone, John and Sam had grown toward each other, building something between them that eventually turned into a marriage.

I didn't think I would ever see John without feeling a tiny sting of what-could-have-been, but he and I had missed our chance, and that was that. Neither of us would ever let our history or any other awkwardness keep me from having a relationship with Sam's daughter.

"It's not weird at all," he assured me, stepping aside so I could come in. Then he frowned down at my clothes. "Were you painting something?"

I glanced down. I'd left the jacket in the car and zipped on a hooded sweatshirt, but you could still see a few dark stains on my jeans. "Uh, yeah, the back room at work."

He nodded, accepting my explanation without question, and I felt another stab of guilt for lying to one of the few people in the world who trusted me completely. "You know the way," he said, gesturing for me to go ahead of him.

John's house was always messy, mostly due to Charlie's burgeoning sideline in destruction, but we were family, so he didn't bother apologizing for it. I removed my shoes, picked through the minefield of toys on the staircase, and tiptoed into Charlie's bedroom, opening the door slowly so it wouldn't creak. A pink mushroom-shaped nightlight shone above the crib, and I smiled down at my niece. She had kicked off her covers again, but she was dressed warmly in little polar-fleece pajamas with ladybugs on them. I leaned my forearms on the rail of the crib, drinking in the sight of her. I felt a great peace inside myself, which I knew came partly from knowing she was safe, and partly from the fact that my proximity to her was canceling out my connection to death magic. Around Charlie, I actually was the normal human woman I'd always thought myself to be.

John came in and leaned over the other side of the crib, smiling down at his daughter. We'd been quiet, but Charlie stirred suddenly, stretching her limbs out as far as they would go before relaxing back into a starfish shape. "Sam used to sleep just like that," I whispered, delighted.

"I remember," John said wryly. Then: "She looks more like Sam every day."

His expression was so complicated: sad, pleased, longing. I felt a sharp rush of grief. "I miss her," I said simply.

"Me too."

We stood there silently for a few minutes, just watching the baby sleep. *She's perfect, Sam.* I sent the words toward my sister, hoping she'd somehow hear them. *And even more precious than you knew.* I couldn't help but feel a touch of apprehension with that last thought. When she was alive, Sam hadn't known that Charlie was a null. John *still* didn't know, a blissful ignorance that was getting harder and harder for me to maintain. The Old World had an iron-clad rule about never letting humans know about the supernatural. It was essential to their survival. Quinn had implied once that occasional exceptions were made, and I'd met one of those exceptions: an ex-Homicide cop in LA.

But although I was hoping Maven would eventually let me explain the truth to John, I wasn't looking forward to that conversation. Every parent worries about their kid. Telling John that he also needed to worry about vampires or werewolves kidnapping his daughter wasn't going to be fun for anyone. But he deserved to know.

Even if I got permission, however, I didn't think I'd tell John how Sam had really died. He didn't need to know that my sister, his wife, had died after a werewolf ate chunks out of her. I would go to my grave making sure no one else who loved Sam ever had to know.

John sighed suddenly. "I can't believe it'll be a year next month. Sometimes it seems like I just talked to her."

"Yeah, I know the feeling," I said honestly. Of course, I *had* talked to Sam recently. I knew for sure that her spirit was alive somewhere, thinking of us. I could take comfort in that.

I wondered if there was any way I could give some of that comfort to John. Surely it couldn't hurt to tell him a *little* bit of the truth. "I've been dreaming about her," I ventured. "In the dream, she's okay. She's watching us, and she's really proud of how you're taking care of Charlie."

John's eyes welled up, and he turned away so I wouldn't see. I pushed on, careful to keep the tears out of my own voice. "So, you know, if you believe in twin ESP or whatever, maybe it's true. *I'm* sure it is."

John nodded fiercely, and without looking at me, he reached across the crib and clasped my hand. I squeezed it and let go.

I wanted to linger, to pull up a chair and stay there all night watching Charlie sleep contentedly, but Maven was right: I needed sleep. I got up on my tiptoes and leaned way over the crib wall so I could kiss my niece in her fuzzy pajamas. Charlie didn't stir, her little face lost in whatever babies dream of.

"Goodnight, babe," I whispered. "Love you."

Chapter 18

When I woke up at seven the next morning, I saw I'd missed a text from Simon, which had come in three hours earlier: *drunk college student went missing at Chautauqua last night.* Sitting up in bed, I called him immediately.

"I don't know much else, really," he said by way of a greeting. He didn't sound like he'd slept, which meant he was pushing himself harder than ever. "The missing kid's name is Dave Banort. He and his two buddies were out partying last night, and Dave decided he had to take a walk in the park to sober up before class this morning. The park was closed, but his friends said he went in anyway. They reported him missing this morning when he didn't show up to class."

"So he could still just be asleep behind a bush somewhere?" I said hopefully.

"Maybe. BPD is searching the park now, but it's a bit of a cluster-fuck because the county sheriff has jurisdiction over part of the park, too, so now they're getting involved. And the park rangers. And I guess a bunch of the kid's friends showed up wanting to help too." He sighed. "Needless to say, the park will be closed until further notice."

Oh, fuck me. I'd forgotten all about talking to Maven about closing the park. I tried to comfort myself with the fact that the college kid had gone in there when it was supposed to be closed anyway, but it didn't really help. I knew I'd dropped the ball.

"If I'm right about this thing's digestive cycle," Simon continued, "he'll spit out another pellet tonight, or maybe sometime tomorrow. Then he'll go hunting again tomorrow night."

Simon no longer sounded excited about the prospect of a new creature. He sounded . . . defeated. "You don't think they're going to find him," I stated.

"Just the parts it didn't like," he said heavily.

"Why nighttime?" I asked. "Is it nocturnal?"

There was a pause. "Good question. It might be nocturnal, or it might sense that the best way to remain out of sight of its prey is to only hunt at night. Or it could be a supernatural thing. Most Old World creatures operate at night."

I blew out a breath. "Well, shit."

"Yeah. The only *sort of* good news is that Dave was a pretty big guy. It's possible we'll get a full forty-eight hours before it needs to feed again."

Dopey began dancing around on my outstretched legs, disrupting Raja, who was asleep on the other side of me. From the other room I heard Cody and Chip crashing around, and the puppy begin to whine. If I was awake, they assumed it was playtime. Still hanging on to the phone, I swung my legs over the side of the bed and went to let everybody outside, wearing panties and an oversized army T-shirt. There are benefits to living out in the middle of nowhere.

"There's something else you need to know," I told Simon. "There was an incident last night with the vampires. It could be related to your sandworm." I briefly sketched out the events from the night before. It was a risk, since Maven hadn't given me explicit permission to involve Simon, but fuck it. People were being eaten, and I figured Simon was the best daytime resource we had. As long as I kept quiet about the werewolf case, surely Maven couldn't get *too* upset. "So anyway, the guys seemed unnecessarily stirred up," I concluded. "It could definitely be related to the sandworm's sudden appearance."

"*That's* what happened to the Walrus?" Simon said disbelievingly. "Damn. I saw the thing on the news about the fire, but I thought it was just, you know, a *fire.*"

"Did the whole place burn down?" I asked. I had no love for the Walrus, but it was kind of weird to imagine it being gone.

"No, just the room with the dance floor. They found five dead, and a broken back window. The current theory is that the victims broke in to steal booze and passed out with cigarettes burning."

Probably not the most airtight story, but I supposed it would work. Meanwhile, there wasn't much I could do for Maven or the vampires until nightfall, and the werewolf situation was at a dead end: If we were right, and the attacks were more of a symptom than a calculated attack, the best way to restore Maven's authority was to figure out what was stirring up magic. It's just that I had no idea how to do that.

This investigation was getting complicated, and I was starting to feel flat-out useless. Simon was a biologist, and Quinn a trained investigator—he'd been a cop before he was turned. Aside from pressing one vampire for basically no information, I wasn't helping much. "What can I do?" I asked Simon.

"Not sure yet," he admitted. "I'm not entirely sure what *I* can do, at this point, other than more research. What does your day look like?"

I wandered over to the fridge to check my calendar. "I'm supposed to work a midday shift at the Depot, magical crises permitting. And I need to call Magic Beans this morning to pull the trigger on getting that Las Vegas witch up here."

"The only other thing I can think of doing is going to Chautauqua to look around for evidence," Simon offered, not sounding very convinced, "but the cops will be crawling all over the park until nightfall."

"We *could* go back tonight, and stake the fucker out," I said, mostly just thinking out loud. I probably had a little bit of time to kill before the thaumaturge would arrive; it'd be nice to do something useful. "Except that Chautauqua has like fifty miles of trails, and we don't know where it will go, let alone how to stop it."

"No, that's a great idea!" Simon said enthusiastically. "I know where the first pellet was found; we could wait there and see if it reappears."

"Simon, this thing is hostile," I objected. "And we don't know how to kill it."

"Maybe not, but at least we can learn more about it," he argued. "And technically, we don't *know* that it's hostile. It could just be unaware of humans as a sentient species."

That wasn't possible . . . right? Killing and eating a human being didn't seem like the kind of thing you could do by mistake, but then again, Simon was the biologist, not me. "I don't know," I said dubiously. "No offense, Simon, but you can't even run yet."

There was a long pause before Simon spat, "I'm still a goddamned witch, Lex. I've got a few other tricks up my sleeve before I'd resort to *running away*."

Whoops. I'd hit a soft spot. "Sorry," I mumbled.

"Look, you can call Quinn, get him to come, too. Best-case scenario, you guys get a shot at the thing. Worst-case scenario, I get some more information we can use to track it."

I thought it over. I *was* getting really sick of playing defense on this case. I was more than ready for some action. "Okay, I'm in. You bring the coffee, I'll bring the weapons."

"Why do I feel like you've said that before?" he teased.

We arranged to meet half an hour after sunset, to give Quinn enough time to arrive. Then I hung up with Simon and called Ryan, Maven's human errand boy, at Magic Beans. He promised to start working on the Las Vegas witch's travel plans, and swore up and down that he would have Maven and/or Quinn call me the second they "arrived" at the coffee shop that night.

It was an unseasonably warm day for early November, so when

I was done on the phone I took Chip and Lady for a run outside, enjoying the sunshine. I had learned (the hard way) that it was difficult to run with more than two dogs at once, so poor Cody was stuck at home this time. As usual, we took the path that veered the hell away from the small fishing pond where I'd accidentally sucked the life out of all the fish the month before. When we got home, I waded through the jealous animals weaving around my ankles and headed for the shower.

By the time I got out and dressed in khaki pants and my work polo, Ryan had called back: the Las Vegas thaumaturge was booked on the first flight the next morning. I'd kind of hoped she'd arrive sooner so we could get started, but I couldn't exactly blame the woman for needing a day to get her affairs in order. At least she was coming. And at least Maven was paying for it.

At ten, I drove into town, to the Flatiron Depot. I used to be the full-time night shift manager, and the store manager, Big Scott, liked me enough to keep me on despite the sudden unpredictability of my schedule now that I was working for Maven. It was a paycheck job, but I'd come to kind of appreciate the mind-numbing customer-service drudgery after all the supernatural drama that had tangled up my life over the last few weeks. I did miss the night shift, though, where my main responsibility had been organizing displays and straightening up the store. Customer interaction wasn't my strongest suit.

A couple of hours into my shift, I was just returning from the back room, where I had organized the list for our next greeting card shipment—so fun—when I was paged over the intercom. I sped up to the front, expecting to see a sudden long line of customers, but instead, my cashier was staring with nervous awe at a single person. Lily.

She was wearing a skintight white tank top that set off the intricate tattoos on her brown arms, and a dark green skirt that clung to her skin at the top and flared out at her knees like a mermaid tail.

When she saw me her eyes flicked over to my cashier, saying *Can you get rid of this guy?*

"Thanks, Random Todd," I told the cashier. "Would you go check on the photo printer? The overnight manager said it was making spitting noises."

He nodded and wandered off. "Hey," Lily said to me. "Did you just say that guy's name is *Random Todd*?"

I shrugged. "That's what it says on his name tag."

Lily just arched an eyebrow, demanding more information. "He rushed a frat," I explained, "and there were three Todds in his pledge class: Gay Todd, German Todd, who is actually from the country of Germany, and him. And now he insists on using the full name."

"Couldn't he just have called himself Todd?" she demanded. "And isn't he like, twenty-five? He can't still be in the frat."

"Don't get me started."

Lily's face broke out in a sudden grin, and I couldn't help but smile back—until I remembered our fight the night before. "What can I do for you, Lily? Or are you here for toiletries?"

She glanced toward the aisles. "Now that you mention it, I could use a new eyelash curler . . . but no, I'm here because I wasn't happy about how we left things last night."

"Neither was I." I realized that I had planted my feet, a defensive stance, and made a conscious effort to look more relaxed.

Lily took a deep breath. "Look, I'm sorry. At the Samhain party I told you that the witches' bad opinion of boundary witches was archaic bullshit, which it *is*, but I let it get in my head too. I know you're just looking out for your niece."

I shrugged. "I'm sorry that I upset you, and that bringing Simon back has created problems for him. You guys have been really good to me, and I don't want to create problems for you . . . but I won't apologize for my oath to Maven. I'd do it again in a heartbeat."

"I know. And I know protecting Charlie is your way of honoring your sister." I remembered the conversation I'd had with John the night before, and felt unexpected tears spring to my eyes. It irritated the hell out of me. I was at *work*, dammit. "I can't imagine losing any of my siblings," Lily went on. "I know we complain about Morgan and Sybil, but they mean well. Mostly."

"Lily—" I began, but just then the bell over the door rang, and she had to step back so I could deal with the customers who'd entered. I knew from experience that business was about to pick up, as people came in for their lunchtime errands.

When we were alone again, Lily said in a rush, "Listen, speaking of my sisters, we're having tea this afternoon. Bonding and shit. I think you should come. They said it was okay."

That caught me off guard. "Uhhhh . . ." All three Pellar sisters at once? "It definitely sounds like I'd be intruding."

She waved a hand dismissively. "Nah. Really you'd be saving me from the horrors of facing the two of them on my own." Seeing the look on my face, Lily rushed to add, "Listen, I heard what you said about how the clan hasn't exactly welcomed you with open arms. Mom's tried a little, but I thought if Morgan and Sybil could get on board . . ." She trailed off with a little shrug.

"I don't know, Lil," I said, still dubious.

"Look," she said, "maybe it doesn't have to be like this us-versus-them thing, with you stuck in the middle. Maybe you could be, like, an ambassador in a hostile country."

I couldn't help but smile at that, even though I wasn't sure which group represented the hostile country. "I get off at three," I said reluctantly.

Her face broke out in a grin. "Great. Four o'clock at the Teahouse. I'll change the reservation to four people. Wear something nice."

"Wait, the Teahouse? Goddammit—Lily!" But she was already pirouetting away, throwing a smug grin over her shoulder on the way out.

Chapter 19

The idea of "town-twinning," or creating a sort of cultural friendship between two cities that are often thousands of miles apart, has been around for a while—in fact, by now most decent-sized US towns have at least one "sister city" somewhere else in the world. It's often just a kind of ceremonial/paperwork thing, with maybe the occasional push to send postcards or raise donations after a tragedy. In Boulder, however, we take our sister cities *very* seriously. We have seven of them, with murals and landmarks scattered around town in their honor. The city even built a special Sister Cities Plaza a few years ago to commemorate how awesome we are at international friendship.

But our largest monument to town-twinning has got to be the Boulder Dushanbe Teahouse, which was a gift from the people of Dushanbe, Tajikistan, back in 1987. The idea is that the Teahouse represents a really, really expensive version of Tajikistan traditions, with gorgeous hand-carved and hand-painted art, a central pool with copper sculptures, delicate china, and the kind of menu where the waitstaff knows the exact humane method used to kill every animal that died for your meal.

Basically, the moment you walk in there you have to start throwing around the word "artisanal" a lot.

I had to admit, from a thematic standpoint, the Teahouse was an appropriate place for me to mend some fences with the ladies of

Clan Pellar. It was also, however, pretty damned swanky. Oh, you could get away with dressing casually, although Lily had specifically requested that I dress up, but the *atmosphere* was upscale and sophisticated. Which meant I'd be uncomfortable the whole time I was in there. I'm not a particularly clumsy person, but whenever my mother or Sam managed to drag me to the Teahouse in the past, I always ended up feeling like the proverbial bull in a china shop.

After my shift, I raced home, let the dogs out, and unearthed a cocktail dress from the back of my closet: a sapphire-blue silk dress with a kicky skirt, small pockets, and a deep V-neck. I'd had it so long I couldn't remember how I'd originally acquired it, but it was both flattering and comfortable. It would show off my large, intricate tattoos, which I wasn't crazy about, but this was Boulder: it wasn't like I'd be the only tattooed person on the block.

The sports bra I was wearing actually had a low V-neck, so I was good there, and I put on some lipstick and a pair of simple hoop earrings. After a moment of hesitation, I tugged my hair out of its ponytail and shook it out, ignoring the slight wrinkle left by the elastic band. Then I stepped into a pair of flats—I wanted to make a good impression, but it took a lot more than tea to get me into heels—and even had the foresight to toss some street clothes into a gym bag for later, in case there wasn't time to come home before my stakeout with Simon. Then, I headed into the spare bedroom where I kept both a cranky iguana and my firearms safe.

I said hello to Mushu, dialed the combination, and swung open the safe door, looking over the contents. If we managed to find the creature and I had an actual shot at it, I would need stopping power and accuracy a hell of a lot more than I'd need to conceal my weapon, so I skipped over the Springfield in favor of the .357 Smith & Wesson revolver I'd bought at an estate sale shortly after returning from Iraq. I wanted a shotgun too, so I took out my favorite, an Ithaca Model 37 I'd inherited from my grandfather. Well, okay— my grandfather, a prolific hunter, had left it to my hippie father, who was extremely squeamish about firearms. He'd given me the Model 37 "and good riddance" in between my two tours. I owned a newer shotgun, but like my grandfather, I had a soft spot for the John Browning-designed weapon. This shotgun and I had done our part to combat the scourge of clay pigeons invading the skies of Boulder.

Picking out weapons to kill the sandworm, I decided, was way more fun than picking out clothes to impress Lily's sisters.

I put the new pup back in her crate and carried both weapons out to the car. I locked the revolver in the glove box and circled around the car to stow the shotgun in the back. I had a permit to carry concealed, but I didn't like to leave weapons in the car where someone could get them. I've had nightmares about punk kids stealing my car and using my weapons to shoot up a school or something. I couldn't exactly bring them to the table with me, though, for so many, many reasons.

When I opened the back, however, I was surprised to see a Post-it Note stuck to the spare-tire container. I picked it up.

I took the liberty of installing this when you were in LA. Thought it might come in handy. —Q

Underneath the note was a small key, which fit into a new lock that had been affixed to the spare-tire compartment. Puzzled, I unlocked it and pulled up the top, which is when I discovered that I no longer had a spare tire in there. Instead, the space had been enlarged and refitted with soft foam, the kind that's cut in small squares you can remove so that something nestles perfectly inside. It was big enough for the shotgun I'd packed, and about four more weapons, if I'd felt so inclined.

Quinn had built a weapons safe into my car for me.

He'd also left another gift: the soft leather quick-draw holster I'd borrowed before we stormed Billy Atwood's house looking for Charlie. It was a custom job that could be worn either right- or left-handed, and I suspected he'd bought it with me in mind. He'd even punched a new hole in the belt, so it would fit around my hips better. The Springfield would be too short for it, but the revolver fit perfectly. I grinned. Quinn was such a romantic.

I loaded my shotgun into soft foam, relocked the little cabinet, and took off for downtown Boulder.

The Teahouse itself is a brightly colored building just off Arapahoe Ave, a breathtaking oasis of color and exoticism that always takes me by surprise when I drive by it. I parked on the street, paid the meter, and walked through the front door at exactly 4:02. The hostess took me straight to the Pellars' table, where Lily and her sisters were already waiting.

As I approached I could pretty easily guess which Pellar sister was which: One of the two women was pleasantly plump, with glossy straightened hair, an easy smile, and a warm earth-mother confidence that exuded from her in waves. This could only be Morgan, the heir apparent. The other was a painfully thin woman with angular cheekbones, a pinched expression, and eyes that flicked around, suspicious and hungry at the same time. Obviously Sybil, and obviously unhappy.

Lily, who was sitting on the near right of the four-person table, spotted me approaching and rose from her seat to give me a hug. She was still wearing the shirt and skirt from earlier, but she'd added a cropped fuchsia jacket. "Hi, Lex. Meet my sisters, Morgan and Sybil."

Morgan stood up to shake my hand. Lily stepped aside so Sybil could reach me, but the other woman gave me a cool nod instead, making no move to rise. Lily shrugged imperceptibly and motioned for me to sit in the empty chair next to Morgan.

"Nice to meet you guys," I said. "Sorry I'm late."

"It's nothing," Morgan said.

"Nice dress," Sybil observed, her first words to me. "Is it vintage?"

"I—No, I don't think so," I said, taken off guard. Was that a dig at how old the dress was, or a sincere compliment that I was overthinking?

Before I could decide, Morgan said, "I'm so glad we could do this, Lex. I saw you at the party, of course, but we didn't get a chance to visit. Have you come here for tea before?"

"Yes, my mother is a fan," I replied, trying to force myself to relax. "She's probably here every other week."

"I brought my eldest daughter here for the first time last week," Morgan began.

We continued to make small talk through our tea order and the first wave of food: tiny sandwiches. Morgan was almost artificially warm and chatty, like she'd been trained on interpersonal relationships by a Southern debutante. Sybil was cool and unyielding, but she did ask a few questions about my niece that seemed genuine. I responded to as many as I felt comfortable answering. There was no point in trying to hide that Charlie was a null, and I couldn't really blame Sybil for her curiosity. Nulls were very rare in the Old World.

By the time the waiter served a second round of tea, I was more or less relaxed, and Lily seemed satisfied with how it was going. Then Morgan said in her warm, pleasant voice, "So, Lex. It sounds like you've been spending a lot of time with Simon and Lily these days."

I glanced at Lily, who shrugged. "Yes, they've been training me," I replied. "I believe that's what Maven wanted."

Sybil's face hardened at the mention of Maven's name, but Morgan just smiled. "Of course. But I swear, every time I talk to one of them, they've either just finished visiting you or are on their way to see you. It's putting a serious cramp in my free babysitting options." She said the last part with exaggerated good humor, but I could feel Lily tense beside me. Where was this going?

"I suppose that's true. It's really great to have friends in the new"—I glanced up at the waiter, who was setting out tiny pastries—"community," I finished. "I don't know how I would have handled everything without them."

"Well," Sybil said, in a cool, knowing tone, like a teacher calling on a habitually poor student, "you didn't *entirely* handle things, did you? Or we wouldn't have needed to bail you out last month."

"*Sybil,*" Lily said under her breath. The waiter seemed relieved to scurry away.

"You were there?" I asked both of them. "When I was . . . um . . . when Lily tattooed me?" I subconsciously pulled my arms into my lap, hiding the griffins.

"We were." Morgan blew across the surface of her tea, though if the temperature of my own cup was any indication, it hadn't been hot in a while. "I'm not surprised that you don't remember. You were pretty out of it."

Lily was looking back and forth between her sisters, apparently as confused about the subtext as I was. But she was also a lot more tolerant. "Is there something you two would like to say to me?" I said, keeping my tone level but firm. "Because I feel like there's maybe some air that needs clearing."

"I don't know what you mean," Morgan said innocently, but Sybil broke in before she could finish.

"You used to have a sister, right?" she said. "Wouldn't *you* be a little anxious if she started hanging out with a boundary witch? The same person, in fact, who nearly got her killed?"

I sat back as though she'd slapped me. *You used to have a sister, right?*

Next to me, Lily was obviously about ready to snap at the two of them, but I reached out and touched her wrist to let her know I was fine. I'd spent ten years serving Uncle Sam with a bunch of clumsy teenage horndogs who'd eventually become a second family to me. I could handle this. "I understand you may be feeling anxious," I said, keeping my voice level, "but I'd prefer that we keep my sister out of this conversation. She died before I knew anything about boundary magic."

Sybil raised her eyebrows a little smugly, as if I'd only proven her point. "Is that why you've glommed onto *our* siblings?" she asked.

"Sybil!" Lily broke in, but Morgan spoke up before she could continue.

"We're just not sure you understand the impact you've caused," the eldest sister said in her warm, cordial voice. "Mom's been on edge since the day she met you, Lily's attention span has gotten even shorter, and Simon, well. He and Tracy are having problems for the first time ever."

"Which began shortly after he started training you," Sybil added. "Spending all that time alone together."

Whoa. Before I could even process the fact that I'd been accused of being a home wrecker, Lily lost her temper. "What the hell is wrong with you two?" she hissed. "I invited my friend here so you could get to *know* her. I thought both of you were open-minded enough to have a civil goddamned conversation with her before you wrote her off because of some label. Was I wrong?"

Morgan had the grace to look a little embarrassed, but Sybil's eyes just narrowed. "You were naive, as usual," she said, keeping her voice low. "You think magic is all rainbows and kittens and braiding friendship bracelets, but we are fighting to protect our way of life after Mother shackled us to a vampire, and this *person*"—she didn't bother trying to hide her disgust—"is as dangerous as she is unstable."

Both Morgan and Lily opened their mouths to speak, but I beat them to it. "Oh, I assure you, I'm far more dangerous than I am unstable," I said to Sybil.

That must have come out more threatening than I'd intended, because all three of them went silent, staring at me with wide eyes. I took my napkin off my lap and put it on the table, taking a long look at Morgan and then Sybil. "Your sister and brother are the best friends I've made since I came home from Iraq," I said, in as calm a voice as I could manage. "I'm so grateful they're in my life. Now Lily is trying to find a way for us all to coexist together, and maybe that *is* naive, but I'm still proud of her. You should be too." Sybil started to roll her eyes, and I went on, "And if you can't be proud, you should at least be grateful to have her. I'd give anything to have *my* sister."

The three of them all started to speak at the same time—Lily to apologize to me, and, well, I didn't care what the other two were saying. Loudly, intentionally, I slammed my fist down on the table, causing the silverware to rattle, the three women at my table to jump, and most of the restaurant to turn and stare at me.

I ignored all of them. "Since that's not an option, or at least, not an option I'm willing to take, I'll settle for doing anything I can for her daughter. If that means working for Maven, I'll do it, and if it means playing nice with you stuck-up *witches*, well, I can do that too." I picked up my purse, dug out a twenty and a ten, and dropped them by my plate. "Thanks for tea. Gotta go meet Simon." I kissed Lily's cheek and marched out without looking back.

Chapter 20

I called Magic Beans to check in with Maven, as instructed, but she wasn't in yet. It was a little early, but I drove straight to the meeting spot I'd arranged with Simon, feeling simultaneously angry, embarrassed, and maybe a little wistful. It had been stupid of me to try and make nice with Morgan and Sybil; I shouldn't have let Lily talk me into it.

At the same time, in a weird way, the whole nasty scene at the Teahouse had made me miss Sam even more. Morgan and Sybil might have been assholes, but they were also trying to protect their little brother and sister. It reminded me of what I'd lost—and, somewhat ridiculously, got me thinking about the few times Sam and I had fought, *really* fought. It had always been over stuff like this—one of us wanting to keep the other safe, certain we knew the best way to do it. I hadn't wanted her to go out drinking the night before the SATs. She hadn't wanted me to join the girl's hockey team because she thought I would get hurt, and it would scare boys away from me.

Okay, she'd been right on both counts. The point was, I could kind of see where Morgan and Sybil were coming from, even if I didn't like it. But I had no idea how to show them I wasn't dangerous.

Yeah, it would probably be a little easier if I was more confident about that last part.

But setting all of that aside, there was still the matter of Sybil's suggestion that I was ruining Simon's relationship with his girlfriend. That hurt me, in a way that pierced my usual defensive anger and shot straight to a place of real anxiety. Had this come from them, or from Tracy? Could any part of it be true? Quinn was the person in my heart, I was sure of that. He was the one I thought about, the one I wanted to go to when I felt upset. But at the same time . . . hadn't I been thinking more about Simon since Atwood's barn? Didn't I worry about him more?

Was I just more invested in his welfare because I'd saved his life? Or could it be that my magic was drawing me to him, or him to me, now that he'd crossed the line and come back? For about the fortieth time, the enormity of what I'd done to Simon struck me. I'd brought him back from the dead, and I had no idea what that might mean for either of us long-term.

Unfortunately, I reached the rendezvous point long before coming up with any answers. Simon's Chevy was already parked at the curb when I pulled up, so I pulled in behind him. I'd intended to go straight to his door so he wouldn't have to do any unnecessary walking, but he'd already gotten out of his car and was limping toward me when I climbed out. He wore a slightly beat-up-looking backpack, the kind with a cross-strap over the chest to secure the weight for long hikes. He seemed to be leaning a little heavier on his cane, though that might have been my imagination.

"Whoa," Simon said when I stepped out of the car. "Where are *you* coming from?"

I looked down at myself, remembering the dress. Right. "Tea with your sisters," I said sweetly. Simon's mouth dropped open, which made me laugh. "Did the doctor give you the okay to drive?"

"Only when I'm not on the painkillers," he explained. Ah. That might explain why he looked in rougher shape than before.

He was obviously about to ask me questions, so I held up a finger. "Hang on a second, I'm gonna change."

"Where—oh." Simon turned his back as I climbed into the backseat with my bag of clothes. I heard him whistling purposefully, to protect my modesty, and laughed again. The sports bra and panties I was wearing provided more coverage than most bikinis, but who was I to stop Simon from being a gentleman?

When I climbed out of the car, it was in jeans, a T-shirt, and low hiking boots that were flexible enough for running. Simon was leaning against the hood, still whistling. "Did you hear from Quinn?" I asked him, heading to the back of the Subaru. Simon followed me.

"No, I figured he'd call you first," he answered.

"I left a message at Magic Beans, but he hasn't called back. Maybe he just hasn't gotten it yet."

I glanced over at Simon in time to see an uneasy look flicker across his face. "Quinn's usually pretty good about returning messages right after sunset," he said hesitantly. "Do you think he's still cleaning up the mess from the thing at the Walrus?"

I hadn't thought of that, but I supposed it made sense. "That's probably it."

"Did you really have tea with my sisters?" he said disbelievingly. "All of them?"

"I really did. Hold this for a second." I handed him the light knee-length jacket I'd packed with my clothes—although the day had been warm, the temperature was dropping with the sun. After looking around for cameras or witnesses, I unlocked my new safe, loaded the Smith & Wesson revolver, and secured the weapon in the quick-draw holster, which I strapped around my waist. Then I picked up the Ithaca shotgun, loaded it, and attached the three-point sling to the mounts at the bottom of the grip. I slipped the sling over my shoulder and took my jacket from Simon. After shrugging it on, I shoved extra rounds into all the pockets and tied the strap closed at my waist. There were buttons on the jacket too, but if I secured them, I wouldn't be able to get the shotgun out quickly. Finally, I tugged out my earrings, tossed them into the trunk, and snapped the trunk shut. I looked at Simon and held out my arms. "Well?"

"Um, you look really good?"

I rolled my eyes. He obviously had a lot of sisters. "No, dummy. How obvious are the guns?"

"Oh." He studied my jacket. "Everything's covered. You've got some suspicious lumps, but I'm sure it'll be fine from a distance."

"Cool. Ready to go?"

He nodded. "I stopped by the ranger cottage today while you were at work, talked to some of the cops," he said. "They didn't want to let me into the park while they were investigating, but given my previous involvement they were willing to talk to me." He dug a map out of his jacket pocket, unfolding it on the trunk. I used the flashlight function on my phone to illuminate the map, which turned out to be a satellite view of the park. I knew the trails, of course, but it was good to see the bird's-eye view.

"Based on the dogs' reactions, they think the kid disappeared about here," he said, pointing to where the Flatirons Loop intersected with the Royal Arch Trail. "And the pellet was found over here"—his finger slid down close to the trailhead, just off the Bluebell Mesa Trail—"which is also where I found the displaced dirt when I stopped by yesterday."

I studied the map. The two spots were relatively close together, which was good for us. "So you just want to kind of hang out in between the two?"

"More or less. The police have the parking lot and the trailhead closed off, but there's not much they can do about us walking into Chautauqua itself. If we go in south of the trailhead, through this neighborhood, we'll end up at Bluebell. If I'm remembering right, there's an outcropping of rocks where we could wait."

I nodded absently. Chautauqua is right on the edge of the busiest part of the city. This whole stakeout idea had seemed like a smart move on the phone, but now that I was standing next to a heavily populated area, running around at night wearing lipstick and two guns, well, I felt more than a little ridiculous.

On the other hand, what was the harm? If we got caught by the police, I'd say I was there to protect Simon, who was investigating the sandworm. If there really was a sandworm.

Then I realized I was thinking about using the word "sandworm" with regular humans, and decided we better get moving before I came to my senses.

We had to go slowly because of Simon's cane, but I tried to keep my body language relaxed so he wouldn't think I was impatient. Still, I couldn't help checking on him out of the corner of my eye. It was getting darker every second, but there was still a little light from the setting sun, and the glow in the sky from Boulder kept the area around us more or less visible as we hiked in. As soon as we got farther from the main roads, I switched on the red-lens flashlight I'd stuffed into my jeans pocket, illuminating the path in front of us. I also opened up my jacket to make the shotgun more accessible.

After about half a mile, Simon caught me looking at him and grunted with frustration. "I know, I know. I'm slow."

"It's not that, I just . . . I worry about you doing more damage to your nerves."

Simon snorted. "Don't be. I've got enough people fussing over me already. I was counting on you to be the one who just had my back."

"If I'd had your back two weeks ago, it might not have gotten messed up in the first place," I muttered, but he didn't hear me.

We walked a little farther, and then I checked my phone for the thirtieth time since sunset. I was getting reception, even up here, but there were no missed calls from Quinn or Maven. "I'm gonna try the coffee shop again quick," I told Simon.

He nodded, and I listened to the phone ringing at Magic Beans. After half a dozen rings, a recording of Maven's voice kicked in. "Thank you for calling Magic Beans, located in Boulder's historic Pearl Street district. We are either closed for a private party or unable to come to the phone . . ."

I left a message there, too, just in case, and jammed the phone back in my pocket.

Simon offered, "We could go back, if you want. Check on him. Them."

I blushed, glad that the darkness would hide it. "I'm sure he's fine."

Simon made a noncommittal noise, and then said, "There. That's the spot I had in mind." He nodded forward.

I panned the flashlight and spotted an outcropping of flat rocks, big enough to sit on. Simon had chosen well. "Looks good to me."

As soon as we reached the rocks, Simon sank gratefully down onto the biggest one and peeled off his jacket. He was sweating from the exertion of walking with a cane, which I could sympathize with. I'd had my share of sprained ankles and broken toes as a kid. After taking off the pack, he unzipped it and pulled out a heavy-duty camp lantern. It looked familiar, and I couldn't hold back a little smile. "Did you and Quinn go shopping for those together?" I teased.

"You mean that vampire scum? Hardly." Simon sniffed imperiously. "One of us *may* have called the other to inform him about a sale," he said airily.

I laughed. He switched on the light and set it a few feet out from the rocks, so it lit up the whole immediate area. I glanced around a little anxiously, but I was pretty sure the tree line hid us from any cops patrolling the trailhead. Either way, I figured it was worth the risk to be able to see the sandworm coming.

Simon also pulled out the promised thermos of coffee, took a sip, and offered me some. I turned off my flashlight and put it back in my pocket to preserve the batteries. And to keep my hands free for coffee and my shotgun, which I cradled across my lap.

"I swear I could fall asleep on these rocks," Simon muttered. I took a closer look at him. Underneath his wire-frame glasses, Simon's eyes were red with fatigue.

He'd texted me at four in the morning to tell me about the missing CU student, I remembered. He obviously wasn't sleeping.

"Nightmares getting any better?" I said nonchalantly. Simon just shook his head. "Can you tell me what happens in them?" I tried.

He was silent for a long moment, surveying the landscape in the dimming light, and I didn't think he was going to respond. Then abruptly, he began, "There are a couple of different recurring dreams, but in the one that really gets to me, I'm on my way home and I'm hurrying, because something important is happening. I don't know what it is, but there's this sense of *urgency*, like when you're running late and you know you're gonna miss an appointment, but there's nothing you can do except go through the motions of trying to make it there in time."

I nodded. I had certainly done that. Hell, I'd done it this afternoon on the way to the Teahouse.

"Anyway, I'm running to get there, and I'm excited, because something big is happening. Then I start to remember that I've had this dream before, and I realize what's coming, but by then I can't stop running. And there's suddenly this *ripping*." He shuddered. "It's like I'm being torn in half. Maybe I get hit by a bus or something? It's always really vague."

I considered that for a moment. "You said you're going home in the dream. Do you mean to the townhouse? Or to your mom's farm?"

Simon's eyes went distant as he thought about that for a moment. "I . . . I'm not sure," he admitted. "It's not so much that I'm picturing a destination. It's more like I'm picturing the sense of safety I'll have when I get there. Home."

Oh, God. My heart sank into my stomach. I had never put much stock in dream theory, but that was before I started using them as a rendezvous with my dead sister. And even a simple analysis of Simon's nightmare was pretty telling.

"I'm so sorry," I whispered.

His brow furrowed. "Why?"

"Because I ripped you back," I said softly, and Simon went very, very still, his eyes going wide as he put together what I was saying.

"You think it's a memory," he said disbelievingly. "That I'm remembering my *death*?" Letting his cane fall to the ground, he scrubbed his palms through his shaggy hair, as though he could scrape the idea out of his brain. "Is that what it was like for you, when you died?"

"No, but . . ." I held up my hands helplessly. "Each time I died, there was never really the possibility of moving on to another place, you know? My magic wouldn't let me cross the line. But maybe those dreams are your mind replaying the trauma of crossing the line and being dragged back." I felt tears sting my eyes. "I'm so sorry."

"Oh. Hey." Awkwardly, he scooted off his rock to mine and enveloped me in a hug. His lean swimmer's body was warm, and I allowed myself to accept the comfort despite the way one of the weapons was now digging into my side. "In case it wasn't obvious, I'm glad you brought me back." He moved back and pushed up his glasses, giving me a slightly crooked smile. "I wasn't ready to die, Lex."

"But maybe there was a cost," I whispered. "The things that have been happening—the sandworm, the vampires—is there any way they're related to me bringing you back? Like I threw magic out of balance, or something?" During the hunt for Charlie's kidnappers, I'd accidentally pulled too much magic into myself, throwing my whole body out of whack, threatening my life. It was the reason Lily had given me the tattoos, to help me channel my magic. Could all the strange things that had happened lately be a larger-scale version of that?

But Simon shook his head resolutely. "I've thought about it," he said. "The timing does seem strange. But, look, after the nightmares started, I actually increased my research into boundary magic. It was something to do while I lay around recovering."

"You didn't tell me that!" I interrupted. It came out more accusatory than I'd intended.

Simon just arched an eyebrow. "You were in LA," he pointed out, his voice mild. "You only just got back."

Right. Duh, Lex. "Sorry," I mumbled. "Did you find anything?"

"I still haven't found a connection between nulls and boundary magic," he said. "I confirmed that for trades witches like us, trying to do boundary magic is almost guaranteed to fail. It's dangerous, unstable. But it's totally different for you. You can manipulate line magic because you are *of* the line magic." He reached for my hands, gently turning them over to expose the griffin tattoos peeking out from under my sleeves. "And these help keep you steady. Anyway, everything I've read suggests that what you can do is self-contained. You followed the rules: traded a life for a life. There's no reason why bringing me back would affect vampires or witches."

I felt my shoulder sag with relief. "Thanks, Simon."

"Thank *you*." He gave me a wan smile. "I can handle some nightmares, if it means more time with my family. With my work. With Tracy."

"Right." I realized he was still holding my hands, so I drew them back and jammed them into my pockets. "Are you—"

Then the ground began to rumble beneath us.

Chapter 21

I'd felt a small earthquake once, while I was visiting Sam in Los Angeles. It was just a tiny vibration, so minor at first that I wasn't even sure it was there. This was a lot like that—except this tremble didn't stop. It kept coming, kept building. Then the ground exploded twenty feet to our left.

I switched on the flashlight and swerved it in that direction just in time to see earth falling back down, looking for all the world like a mine had gone off. My flashlight beam trembled as the dark hole began to birth a writhing mass of shadows and mud. It emerged slowly, insidiously: first a pointy, rock-hard snout as big around as my biggest dog, then a head covered in those flat, hard scales you see on dinosaurs in movies. I stared, entranced. It was thin, only about as big around as my waist—no, wait, check that. As it surfaced, the elongated tube of snake seemed to fatten and swell, like a rat coming through a particularly tiny hole. Once it emerged, the coil thickened to an impossible girth—the thing had to be at least six feet in diameter. That was how it got around without leaving a wide tunnel behind, I realized.

It didn't even come all the way out of the ground, just rose and rose until it towered above us. The visible length of creature doubled over and opened its snout, displaying unbelievably sharp teeth. Its jaw unhinged, like a snake, and both Simon and I instinctively shrunk back, though I doubted it was even aware of us yet. It began to cough.

"That's impossible," I breathed. Simon and I had been talking about the sandworm for two days, yet my rational mind had never really believed in it. Now it was real, and all I could feel was . . . small. And infinitely fragile.

"Everything about this is impossible," Simon whispered back. "Got your gun?"

Right. I brought up the shotgun, taking the safety off in the same motion. The sandworm stopped regurgitating and swerved its enormous snout toward the noise. Two tiny fissures opened on what would sort of be its face, and then the fissures cracked open to reveal wet, slitted eyes. They were covered in clear mucus, like it had more than one set of eyelids.

My finger tightened on the trigger, but I hesitated. It felt wrong to just flat-out shoot this thing—what if Simon was right, and it wasn't a mindless killing machine? What if we were dealing with an intelligent being?

You dare.

Simon and I both dropped to our knees, clutching our hands to our ears. The words actually *hurt*, in a sharp, not-quite-real pain that was exactly like someone scraping nails down a chalkboard on the inside of my skull. As soon as those first words faded and I could think clearly again, I realized that the sound hadn't come from the creature's mouth, but from inside our own heads. *It can get inside our heads*. And it spoke English. For some reason that threw me almost as much as the telepathy.

The minds I consumed spoke this language and know your weapon, so I do as well. Why do you come to me with killing tools?

"Aargh," was all I managed to say. The concept of a talking telepathic snake monster had shorted out my brain.

I felt the creature sort of settle back, like it realized its speech was hurting us and was adjusting its frequency. Beside me, Simon was crouched defensively, and I could see his lips moving in a spell. Whatever he was doing, I figured it was up to me to distract the sandworm.

"You . . . are . . . killing . . . my . . . people," I said out loud. Each word was an effort, but dammit, there was no way I was just going to *think* at this thing.

It regarded me for a long moment. They are not yours.

The words didn't hurt this time, but I still felt like my brain had been scraped over a cheese grater. The creature's eyelids lowered farther, so we could barely see any evidence of its eyes. I clenched my teeth and pressed on, "This city belongs to my mistress, the vampire ruler of this territory. She does not approve of eating humans. Nor do I."

I could feel, rather than see or hear, the creature's baffled curiosity. Then why did she awaken me?

Huh? I almost said exactly that, but managed to scrape together the words, "She didn't."

The creature made a hacking sound, and I got the distinct impression I was being snorted at. Then she does not control the vestige, and I care not what she wants.

"What vestige?" I yelled. "What are you talking about?" It began to turn away, and in desperation I shouted, "Hey! I'm talking to you!" Without thinking, I bent down and picked up a rock the size of my fist, then threw it at the sandworm with all my strength. It glanced harmlessly off its scales, but the sandworm turned in annoyance, and skin flaps like a cobra's hood spread ominously from its skull.

You interfere. I do not suffer interference. Its head snapped with movement, backward, then forward again, and a luminescent ooze spattered from its jaws toward the two of us.

"Lex!" Simon yelled, and he limp-darted toward me, grabbing my arm and raising the palm of his free hand. The slime smacked into the naked air a foot in front of his fingers before dropping to the ground, where it began to hiss. A shield spell. He'd prepared a shield spell and gotten it over both of us.

My jaw dropped open. "Venom," he explained grimly. "Remember the Mongolian Death Worm?"

Fear hit me hard—a gripping, overwhelming terror that threatened to root me where I stood. But I would not give in to it, not before, not now.

"Is the shield one-way or two-way?" I asked Simon urgently, lifting the shotgun.

"Shoot it!"

With no further prompting, I squeezed the trigger, and the shotgun roared. I was expecting to blow a small crater in the sandworm's belly, but the shot just glanced harmlessly off its long, flat scales, whistling away into the dark. I cursed and dropped the shotgun back on its strap.

The sandworm paused, its mouth still open, its fangs displayed. A long, forked tongue as wide as my waist snaked quickly out of its mouth and back in. You smell of death. I know this smell, it thought at me. Chills crept across the back of my neck. You are a line-walker. Death-trader. Bridge-maker.

Boundary witch. The sandworm knew I was a boundary witch.

It slid a few feet to one side and turned back to regard me with curiosity. What is this word you call me in your mind? It is impudent.

"Sandworm?" It had picked that out of my brain? "Um, what would you prefer to be called?"

It paused, considering that, and I realized it hadn't once blinked those big stone-like eyelids since emerging from the ground. The people who once roamed here, they called me Unktehila, it said finally. They were not impudent, and I allowed many of them to live. I will allow you to live this night too, necromancer. Tell your mistress I obey none but the vestige. It is my sun, and I will not tolerate interference in my orbit. Faster than I would have imagined possible, the great face swiveled to Simon. You, wounded disruptor, I will eat, the next time I am hungry. With a careless, lazy motion, it slid higher out of the ground, its hood flattening against its neck as it bent double once more and coughed. A slimy, sucking noise told me that it had just hacked up another gastric pellet.

Without another word—thought or spoken—it turned its snout back toward the ground and began to burrow. I ran forward a few steps, but the thing was surprisingly fast, and I was suddenly convinced it was using some kind of magic to manipulate the earth above and below it. The ground seemed to seal shut beneath it, leaving only a tiny area of disturbed soil. Simon and I stared at each other, and I was pretty sure my own expression mirrored his.

What the hell just happened?

But before either one of us could remember how to speak, a different voice cut through the darkness behind me, from the other side of the rock cluster. "The fuck was *that*?"

Simon and I both spun around, and I lifted the shotgun unconsciously. Quinn stood up behind us and raised his hands when he saw the Ithaca. I lowered the shotgun and gaped at him. Blood had soaked his white shirt and was gleaming on his dark suit pants. There were small cuts and abrasions all over his face and hands, which meant his vampire magic had been too busy tending to other, greater injuries to heal the cosmetic ones. He swayed a little on his feet, and I realized with sudden fear how terribly pale he was. "Sorry'm late," he slurred. "We've got trouble."

With a hiccupping noise that was somewhere between a laugh and a sob, he collapsed onto the ground.

Chapter 22

Simon and I both darted toward Quinn, but Simon's leg slowed him down, and I got there first. "Quinn? Quinn! Open your eyes!" Slowly, the vampire obeyed me. "What do I do?" I asked desperately.

His lips moved, trying to say something, but he didn't have the strength to push air through his vocal chords. That scared me nearly as much as the sandworm had. I ripped at his once-white shirt, popping off the buttons. His flat chest was bloody, and a wide puncture mark an inch to the left of his heart oozed watery blood. Someone had tried to stake him, and they'd come damned close to succeeding. His eyes drifted shut again.

"He needs blood," Simon said grimly. I hadn't even seen him drop to his knees beside me. "Do you have a blade?"

I searched my pockets and found the small Swiss army knife I'd tucked in with the flashlight. "I can do it," I told him.

"You can fight," Simon replied. "I can't. And I've done this before." Simon and Quinn had worked together long before I knew the Old World existed. He picked up the knife, and without another word, made a careful slice across the back of his left hand near the wrist. I knew just enough about anatomy to know he'd purposefully nicked one of those minor veins doctors use to insert IVs. Blood spurted, and Simon held it up to the vampire's mouth. "Quinn," Simon said softly. "You gotta drink this, man."

No response. Crowding Simon aside for a second, I reared back and slapped Quinn hard across the face. "Quinn!"

His eyes opened. "Drink," Simon said again, and this time Quinn's lips parted to accept the blood. After maybe thirty seconds, he raised a shaky hand and pushed Simon's wrist away.

"Lex," he gasped. "Maven was challenged. Clara. She was smart. Came after resources first . . ." His voice faltered, and his eyes pleaded with me to understand something.

But I was lost. If one of the other vampires had challenged Maven for this territory, it made sense that she would go after Quinn, a powerful mind-presser and probably Maven's most loyal follower. Was I included as one of her resources? But I wasn't home; in fact, no one knew where I was except the two men before me. "They're coming after me? Is that what you're saying?"

He made a sound like the beginning of *no* and shook his head. He was fading again, but when Simon held out his dripping wrist, Quinn shook his head. "Charlie," he whispered. "They'll go after Charlie."

Oh, God.

Time stopped for me, the way it only can when you receive truly terrible news. For some reason, my brain started to shuffle through all the moments in my life when time had bent itself like that for me: When I'd drowned as a teenager. The day the towers fell. When I had stumbled out of the Iraqi desert, the only surviving member of my squad. When John had first called to say Sam was missing.

I shook myself violently and forced my mind to return to the present. My eyes met Simon's, and he tilted his head in the direction from which we'd come. "Go. I can handle this."

I looked helplessly at the fading vampire and the injured witch, hesitating. My friends were so vulnerable. "*I've got this,* Lex," Simon barked. "Go get Charlie!"

I sprinted for the car, pulling out my flashlight on the way.

With the beam bobbing ahead of me over the trails, I used my free hand to call Elise, figuring that of all the humans I knew, she had the best bet of slowing down a vampire. Shooting Tony had definitely slowed *him* down, and if she stayed close enough to Charlie, a gunshot would put any attackers down permanently. But Elise's cell phone went straight to voicemail. I tried John's cell, and then my mother's. No one was answering. I was trying to dial the police station when I tripped over something hard and went sprawling on my face.

The flashlight flew out of my hand, and the phone tumbled away into the darkness. *Ow.* I mumbled some colorful language and slowly picked myself up. With a groan, I flexed my limbs and managed to stagger over to the flashlight. Nothing was broken, but I would be stiff and bruised in the morning. Well, more stiff and bruised than I already was. I shone the light down on my legs and saw a tear in my jeans, a tiny smear of blood where I'd scraped my knee. Great. I looked for the phone for a moment, but it was nowhere to be seen. I patted my front pocket to make sure I still had the car keys and started running again in a mincing lope, cursing myself for trying to dial the phone and run at the same time.

I agonized over it for a moment, but reluctantly took the time to stow the shotgun in the trunk and the revolver in the glove box. Driving with them on the passenger seat wasn't safe.

John's house was only a couple of miles away, but it seemed to take me hours to get there. I was so focused on checking the mirrors and the windows for danger that I was practically in his cul-de-sac before I saw the flashing red and blue lights of the cruisers parked outside his house.

Chapter 23

I stomped on the brake, my breath freezing in my chest as I stared. Every window in John's house had been broken, and the front door was missing.

I don't remember putting the car in park or opening the door, but suddenly I was running, ignoring the pain from my stiff leg. I pelted across the cul-de-sac, past the cruisers and the shouts of several police officers. I could only see that yawning black hole where the front door was supposed to be.

"Allie!" Someone stopped me and grabbed me by the shoulders, pulling me to an awkward stop. "It's okay! We're okay!"

"John?" I panted, staring up at him. His face was pale, and his eyes were wild. I touched his face, his shoulders, unable to believe he was really in front of me. I'd thought they would kill him to get to his daughter. "Charlie, where's Charlie?"

"She's not here, but she's fine, I promise," John said fiercely. "The woman I've been seeing, Sarah, she took Charlie to the police station to wait with Elise. I just talked to her. They're fine. They're both fine."

I sagged, my whole body suddenly deflating from the relief. Then, to my surprise and horror, I burst into tears.

"Oh, hey . . ." John, who had always been a little uncomfortable with crying, pulled me into a hug. I wrapped my arms around him, holding on tight to make sure he didn't disappear. I knew intellectually that crying was a chemical-based reaction, that my body had built up adrenaline and had nowhere to put it, but in that moment it just felt like I was a sappy, weak little girl who cried all the time.

"I'm sorry," I sobbed into his chest. "I saw the lights and I just . . . I'm sorry."

"It's okay. It's okay, I promise." John patted my back again, and I couldn't bear it. I pulled away. "You're *sure* they made it to the station?" I demanded, smearing the tears off my face with my palms.

Someone else might have been offended, but John knew me well enough to smile, just a little. "I'm positive. I just talked to Elise and Sarah, and I heard the station noise in the background. Charlie was fussing because it's past her bedtime."

"Okay." I nodded, and said again, mostly to myself, "Okay. What happened?"

"Somebody broke in," he said, anger rising in his voice. "Charlie and I went to dinner with Sarah on the Hill, then took a walk with the stroller. When it got close to Charlie's bedtime, we came back and found the house like this. Nothing's missing, but everything is just . . . destroyed. They even trashed Charlie's crib."

"Everything okay here?" said a female voice. I looked up to see two detectives walking over. The speaker was a female detective I'd seen a few times at the station, a solidly built African-American woman. I couldn't remember her name, but she'd struck me as gruff and efficient. The other was, of course, Keller, who probably sat around all day hoping something bad would happen to someone I knew so he could blame me. But tonight I was too upset to even muster up any hostility toward him.

I nodded, and John said, "Yeah. Detective Stevens, this is my sister-in-law, Allison Luther. She's very close to Charlie."

Stevens held out her hand for me to shake, and Keller stepped forward to add, "And how did you know to come tonight, *Ms.* Luther?"

I looked at him, unable to keep the surprise off my face. I hadn't spent a single second of the car ride thinking about what I would say. I stammered, "I—I didn't. Know, I mean. I called John earlier just to say hi to Charlie, and when he didn't answer, and I couldn't reach my mom or Elise, I got worried."

"You got worried?" Keller said in a *perfectly* professional tone. "Just because he didn't answer the phone?"

"Yeah. I was hanging out with friends anyway, so I decided to stop by on the way home." That was more or less the truth.

Keller pulled his notebook out of his inner suit pocket. "I'd like the names of those friends, please."

"*What?*" I gaped at him, and so did John. "You think . . ." I sputtered, so angry with him that I momentarily lost the ability to form words. I should have seen the accusation coming, but I'd been too worried about John and Charlie's safety to give it a thought. "You think I trashed John's house? Where Charlie *lives*? Why would I do that?"

John came to my defense. "I can promise you that Lex—that Allison—had nothing to do with this. She would never hurt me or the baby."

"Of course not," Keller said. He had a controlled, everything-by-the-book expression that made me extremely nervous. "But this is the second time in—what, two months?—that Charlotte Wheaton has been the target of a crime. Ms. Luther was present for the kidnapping attempt, and as I'm sure you all know, that crime is still unsolved." Anger and self-satisfaction flickered across his face before it returned to a professional mask. "And now Ms. Luther has arrived at the scene of a serious vandalism only a few minutes after we did."

Stevens, who'd been quietly observing all of this, murmured to Keller, "Her reaction sure looked organic to me."

Keller ignored her. "Mr. Wheaton," he said formally, "isn't it true that you've recently begun a new romantic relationship?"

John winced, not answering, as I stood there with my mouth gaping open like a walleye. The implication that I had destroyed his house out of romantic jealousy lay thick and awkward on the air.

Stevens said pleasantly, "Ms. Luther, would you be willing to come down to the station for an interview? We would appreciate getting your take on events. You can follow us in your own car, of course," she added, like it was a great generosity she was bestowing on me.

John rolled his eyes. "This is complete bullshit, Lex, but it might be easier if you just went and explained."

They all looked at me expectantly. This was happening so fast. I opened my mouth to say fine, I would come answer stupid fucking Keller's stupid fucking questions, but then I realized that I couldn't. *Maven*. If this Clara had come after Quinn and Charlie, and possibly me, she had to make her move tonight. Right now. I had no idea how strong she was, especially in comparison to Maven, but if Maven fell, the other Colorado vampires would kill me and come after Charlie again. I couldn't let that happen.

Everyone was staring, and I said, "I'm sorry, there's somewhere I need to be right now." It sounded lame, even to my own ears.

Stevens raised her eyebrows. "I thought you said you were on your way home?"

Shit. "I was, but I've remembered something I need to do."

Keller snarled, "You do know how it looks, that you refuse to answer questions that could help us find this 'vandal'?" He didn't actually raise his hands and make air quotation marks, but he didn't have to.

"I'm sorry," I said more firmly. "I need to go."

"At least give us the names and numbers of the friends you were with tonight," Stevens said, giving me a hard look.

"I can't do that, either." I couldn't give him Simon or Quinn's names until we had a story for what we were doing tonight, something *other than* hunting an ancient snake monster. Besides, if he tried to track them down right now, he might find them in a pretty compromising position.

"Because you need time to get your story straight?" Keller suggested.

I saw his right hand drift to rest on the butt of his service weapon, and for some reason that made me furious. "I understand how this looks, Detectives, but unless you're arresting me for a crime, I am leaving now." Stevens's face clouded over, and I added through gritted teeth, "But I would be happy to come to the station first thing in the morning to answer all questions you have, in person."

Before he could say anything else, I said, "John, can I talk to you for a minute?" I took his arm and led him a few feet away.

"Lex," he said, puzzled, "what's going on? What do you have to do?"

"I can't tell you," I said apologetically. "I need to do something for a friend, and I promised not to say anything."

His brows were still furrowed, and although I was a tiny bit afraid of the answer, I had to ask. "You know I would *never* do anything like this to you, right?"

To my relief, he nodded at me, his face lit with perfect trust. "Lex, I've known you since you talked with a baby lisp. Of course I know you didn't do this. I just want you to clear things up so they can focus on finding the real bad guy."

"And I will, I promise. But I have to help a friend first." I took a deep breath. "Listen, where are you guys going tonight? You're not staying here."

He shook his head. "There's glass everywhere, and the beds are all torn up. I don't understand why anyone would . . . anyway. We'll probably go to your mom and dad's place."

I chewed on my lip for a second. "Do me a favor? Maybe go to your mom's instead?"

"What? Why?" John had a somewhat contentious relationship with his mother, which was why he'd spent most of his childhood at our house. Blossom Wheaton was a full-blooded Arapahoe Indian who had turned guilt and passive-aggression into scalpels she wielded mercilessly on her loved ones. She had hated Sam, and didn't like me much better. But Blossom's house was thirty miles away, as off the grid as you could get. She also had two defense-trained Dobermans and a hunting rifle.

"I'd just worry less if I knew you two were there. Please, just for the night?" *Until sunrise,* I thought, but didn't say.

John gestured at the house. "I know it looks bad, Lex, but I really think it was just some asshole high school kids, or maybe part of a frat hazing or something. They're not coming after us at your folks'."

"But what if they do? What if this was another attempt to take her?" I countered. I had to walk a fine line here: keep John afraid enough to get him to Blossom's, without making him ask too many questions. But I hated doing it. "Or what if this is some nut who hates Dad? He does get death threats now and then, and you *do* work for him."

I watched John's face change as the blow hit home, feeling like a monster. "You don't think . . ."

"No, I don't. But just indulge your crazy sister-in-law for a little while?" I pleaded, trying to smile. "Take her to Blossom's, just for the night. Please?" One way or the other, everything would be settled by dawn.

John thought it over for another moment, then shrugged. "Okay. I can do that, I guess."

"Thank you." I went on tiptoes to kiss his cheek. "I lost my phone, but I'll call you in the morning after I find it."

He nodded, still a little reluctant. "Be careful, Lex, okay?"

I gave him an innocent smile. "I'm *always* careful."

Chapter 24

As I drove toward Magic Beans, I cursed myself again for dropping my phone at Chautauqua—I was desperate to check on Quinn, but even if I got a new phone, I didn't have his or Simon's number memorized. Stupid, stupid.

I stopped in an empty parking lot to reload my weapons. For the second time in two days, I was desperately wishing I had a shredder stake. I'd packed for a confrontation with a giant worm monster, not a vampire fight. Quinn had once explained that to kill a vampire you needed to either cut off its head or thoroughly destroy its heart—hence the wooden stakes spelled to shred the heart tissue. From now on, I promised myself, I was going to carry them everywhere. In the meantime, I was hoping a direct shot to the heart with the Ithaca would do enough damage, since I wasn't convinced the shotgun could take a head off completely, even at close range. When this was over, I was definitely investing in a machete or something.

I parked illegally on 13th Street, and ran straight to the back door of the coffee shop, with my jacket belted over the firearms like it had been at Chautauqua. I ignored the "Closed for Private Party" sign and banged on the door.

A long pause, and then I heard bolts sliding back, and the door cracked open. I had a sudden moment of bizarre déjà-vu, reminded of a few weeks earlier when I'd been called to Magic Beans to witness Maven's execution of Itachi. To help her do it, really. Would I open the door on the same scene? Or was Maven already dead, and was I walking into my *own* execution? I unbelted the jacket and pulled out the big revolver before going inside. I wouldn't be going down without a fight, anyway.

The back door opened directly onto the big concrete-floored room at the back of Magic Beans, where they occasionally hosted open-mic night or acoustic musicians, the same room that led to Maven's little office. As I stepped inside, I almost slipped on the wet concrete, my foot bumping into something that didn't slide away at the contact. I looked down to see a hand.

I flinched back so hard I stumbled, my eyes adjusting to the dim light. The hand was stretched toward the door, attached to a bloody, half-rotted arm. The arm was attached to nothing, because it had been ripped off at the shoulder joint.

I tore my eyes away from it, because gaping too long at something like that is a great time for the enemy to ambush you. There was no movement in the room, though. Someone had stacked all the chairs against the back wall, leaving a single chair on the stage, lit by a spotlight. It was the only source of light in the whole room. Maven sat in the chair, her face resting on one palm, as she stared broodingly at a body that lay prone on the floor in front of her. There were streaks of blood all over the vampire leader, and more blood matted into her orange hair, but otherwise she looked fine. I surveyed the rest of the room and spotted the young-looking vampire from the Walrus—Opal, that was her name—standing near the door that led into the rest of the coffee shop, next to a body, this one missing a head. The body had deflated within its clothes, which marked it as a vampire's remains, but I didn't stop to stare at it. There was another vampire—I was assuming, since I couldn't see Maven willingly letting any humans into this little situation—curled up on the edge of the stage, hugging his middle. From the vacant expression on his face, I was pretty sure his body was healing a wound in his midsection. My eyes moved back toward the floor.

There was another body halfway in between me and the stage, and I realized I'd found the owner of the arm I'd nearly tripped over. Since there were no apparent, immediate threats, I stepped farther into the room, the revolver still in my hand.

"Maven?" I said cautiously.

She didn't stir, just continued to glare at the body in front of her. It had been flayed, I saw, its chest cavity ripped open and the rib bones snapped aside to display the heart. There were bruises and swelling around the female face and arms, and I realized that this must be Clara. Why had Maven left her in this grotesque position? I took another step closer, and the thing on the floor *moved*, the arm twitching as it struggled to rise toward the ravaged chest cavity.

Oh, God. She was still *alive*? That was too much, even for me. My gorge rose, and I turned my head and vomited up all of the tea and mini sandwiches I'd eaten with the Pellar sisters a few hours earlier.

"It is not an easy thing," Maven began, and her voice in the sudden silence was like a blast of cold air, "for a vampire to break troth. It's easier for humans, of course. The one area in which you are stronger than we are."

Oh, shit. I had absolutely no idea how to respond to her. Maybe she had lost her mind. What the hell was I going to do then? After a moment, she continued, "I see that you came to help, to keep your oath. I will not forget. Assuming we both survive this."

"What—What are you—"

"What am I doing?" she said with exaggerated patience, as though humoring a child. "I am contemplating how we got here." Her voice was formal, stiff, like she'd forgotten all her modern human mannerisms. She hadn't moved, hadn't even lifted her eyes from the mutilated mess in front of her. "I did not want to lead, you know." She glanced at me. "*You* know. The last time . . . ended badly." I honestly didn't know whose "last time" she was talking about—hers or mine—so I just nodded cautiously. Her gaze returned to the body. "I did not want . . . But then they asked for my help, and I could not refuse. Then Itachi . . . and I felt responsible. And now this." She sighed. "I can smell your fear, you know. We all can."

I didn't even know what to say to that. This whole situation was batshit fucking crazy, and I struggled against the urge to run. Or wet myself. I took a few deep breaths, trying to calm myself.

"Is Quinn dead?" she asked in a small voice, and I understood that she was scared of the answer—not just that he might be dead, but that he might have broken troth and run away too.

When I was certain of my voice, I said, "No. Another vampire came after him, and he was wounded pretty badly. Simon Pellar is helping him." Maven nodded, her shoulder relaxing just an inch. "What about her?" I asked, nodding at the mangled mess on the floor in front of her. "Will she die?"

"Who, Clara?" She sounded surprised. "Of course. The magic in her blood is still fighting, but there is too much damage. She'll succumb. But it will take hours."

"Who are the others?" It didn't really matter—I was certain I didn't know them—but for some reason it made me feel better to ask the question.

"The vampire who's healing over there is Stone; he just moved here, after Itachi. To support me." Her chuckle was dry and bitter. "I don't expect he thought it would come to this, much less so quickly."

"I meant the bodies," I said gently. "Who are the dead vampires?"

"Benton over there was a dominus, like Clara," Maven said, flicking a hand carelessly toward the headless body. "The armless one is Nels; he was Benton's newest villanus."

I pieced that together. Benton and Clara had been of the vampire ruling class, the domini. Nels had been one of Benton's subordinates. Check. "Why did they betray you?" I asked softly. "Why now?"

Maven's eyes finally lifted off Clara's body, looking at me with resignation. "Because their villani are dying," she replied. "Darren and Tony belonged to Clara, and Allegra was one of Benton's." She made a little sound that could have been a snort. "Or they just wanted an excuse to depose me, and saw their opportunity after three of their people were killed." Her face darkened, and she returned to her brooding stare.

Okay. Enough. I'd had enough.

"Maven." I circled the armless corpse and as much of the blood as possible, moving into Maven's line of sight. Unfortunately, this also put me uncomfortably close to what was left of Clara, but I tried not to look. "Maven, I'm going to speak to you as though you're an ordinary human for a moment, and I hope you'll forgive me later."

Detached interest bloomed on her face. I doubted anyone had ever said *that* to her. "You need to get your shit together," I said firmly.

Her face hardened. "Excuse me?"

"You heard me. Snap the fuck out of it. We need you. *I* need you. I met the sandworm tonight. It calls itself Unktehila"—I pronounced it carefully, thought I did an okay job—"and it is *terrifying*. It's going to keep eating people. It *got into my head* to tell me so. And in a couple of days, the werewolves will be able to change again, and all hell's gonna break loose, maybe literally. We have to figure out what's happening to the magic in Boulder before then, and we have to fix it. *You* have to fix it."

For a second I really thought she would dart forward and rip out my spinal cord, but she leaned back instead, regarding me. "How do you propose I do all that," she said, gesturing toward Clara, "when my own people won't even obey me? Are, in fact, actively working against me?"

"You start," I suggested, "by showing Clara mercy."

She gave me a shocked look, as if I'd just asked her to put on a clown outfit and perform at a children's party. "You're proposing that I let Clara *live*?"

"If I understand this situation correctly," I said very carefully, "she challenged you because she and Benton thought you let their people die. The assumption is false, but the response is somewhat understandable." I took a deep breath, giving her a moment to absorb that. "It's also possible that whatever has stirred up our magic is messing with Clara and Benton, too. This might not be their fault, just like what happened at the Walrus last night might not have been Darren and Tony's fault. I know you need to get your house in order, but I don't think killing Clara is the way to do it."

"What's to stop her from attacking again, with better support and more weapons?" Maven countered.

The words were out of my mouth before I even had time to consider them. "I'll press her."

She thought that over. "Even after she tried to take your niece?" In response to my surprised look, Maven added, "Yes, I know. Clara told me everything, of course. Nels was dispatched to collect the baby and return here. Since he came back empty-handed, I assumed he failed. Is Charlotte all right?"

I nodded. "They weren't home. And to answer your question, yes, I would let Clara live even though she came after Charlotte. Even though she destroyed my brother-in-law's home." I swallowed, remembering the fear and anger on John's face as he looked at his ruined house. I forced myself to look at what remained of Clara instead. "She has suffered enough. She doesn't deserve to die for wanting to avenge her people, and certainly not for busting up a house."

"Hmm." Maven looked at me. A full minute ticked by, during which Stone began to rock back and forth, and the thing that used to be Clara twitched several more times. "All right," she said finally. She hopped off the throne and did something with her teeth and arm too quickly for me to watch. When she was done, deep, glittering blood began to run down her arm in a long line, like water diverted from a river. Maven positioned the stream of blood to splash down first on Clara's ruined chest cavity, and then into her mouth.

After a few minutes, the . . . pieces . . . of Clara began stirring, seeking to reseal themselves inside her. I had to look away or risk vomiting again.

Out of the corner of my eye, I saw Maven put one palm on

either side of Clara's rib cage and squeeze the sides together. "There," she said a moment later. Her voice was satisfied, like she'd just finished installing a closet door. "She'll need more blood, and at least the rest of the night, to heal. But you can press her now."

I stepped forward. Maven's blood had simply stopped flowing out of her arm, and I wondered if her body had actually healed this quickly, or if she had some way of actually *controlling* it. "Make sure she does not challenge me again," Maven warned.

I crouched down beside Clara, whose head had lolled to the side, her eyes glazed with pain or shock, or maybe something else. I hadn't really looked at her face before—my eyes had been a little preoccupied—but she had broad Nordic features and pale blonde hair over a broad frame. There was no fat on her, but she was big, rawboned, like she was about to suit up for women's field hockey—or maybe men's rugby. Only her mouth was feminine, a delicate pink bow that was turned down in a grimace.

Her body was in one piece again, but blood and bits of torn cloth were smeared all over her chest, and I had a sudden flash to the moment in *The Wizard of Oz* when the Scarecrow's stuffing is spilling out of his chest. Disgusted, I put my hands on either side of her blood-smeared face so my tattoos touched her. "Clara," I said softly. "Look at me." Sluggishly, she raised her blue eyes to mine. I visualized a connection between us, pressing my will down the length of it until I felt Clara's spirit bend beneath mine. I had her.

"Tell me why you challenged Maven," I commanded, just in case we were wrong about the situation. She couldn't lie to me, and I would have felt it if she'd tried.

But Clara growled, "She killed my people and Benton's. She cannot hold this land. If someone strong doesn't take over, we will lose all we have built. Outsiders will come for this state."

I risked a quick glance at Maven, but the cardinal vampire was implacable. "Did something else push you? Did you feel anything urging you to attack?"

Clara's blank face registered surprise, but she didn't answer. I realized that I had phrased the command poorly. "Explain how you felt when you decided to challenge Maven," I tried instead.

"Righteous," Clara said at once. "Driven. No doubt."

"Tell me whose idea it was to attack Maven."

She blinked, confusion on her face. "My plan," she said slowly. "Attack was my plan."

"But not your idea?" I pressed. She just looked blankly at me, and I felt the *not-understanding* vibe coming off her. She'd personally come up with the plan, but it didn't feel like her idea.

"You will not challenge Maven again," I commanded. "You will be infinitely loyal to her. You will do everything you can to secure her possession of this state."

I put everything I had into the press: all my own anger and energy and frustration traveled down my tattoos and out through the ink, worming their way into Clara's soul. Her face hardened. "Yes," she whispered. "I will serve."

I released her, in both senses. To my surprise, I began to collapse too, but I managed to catch myself on my hands. I sat there for a long moment, panting.

Maven gave me a moment to collect myself, then said quietly, "Well done."

I lifted my head to look at her. She was still sitting on the makeshift throne, but her body language had changed: her arms were crossed under her breasts, and she just looked . . . tired. Had I ever seen Maven look tired? I didn't think so.

"There's something else," Maven went on, and I paused. "You asked for Clara's life, and I granted it—to you. She will need the rest of tonight to heal. Starting tomorrow, however, she belongs to you."

I just stared at her. "What does that mean?"

"Exactly as it sounds. You are responsible for her." Her smile was brittle, showing tiny sharp teeth. "Think of her like . . . a pet."

"What? Ew, no. I don't want that. And I'm sure *she* doesn't want that." I looked down at Clara, but her eyes were fixed worshipfully on Maven. "Whatever my mistress requires," she whispered.

"Lex is your mistress now," Maven told her. "Protect and obey her as you would me."

My breath caught. Oh, shit. Had I poured too much energy into pressing her? Was that why Maven wanted Clara to follow me around, as some sort of penance for insisting that her life be spared? I needed to think about that some more, and figure out how to undo what I'd just done, but in the meantime . . . I had an idea.

"As soon as you're well," I said to Clara, "I want you to keep watch over my niece, Charlotte Wheaton. Protect her at all costs."

Clara nodded, her eyes still vacant, and I winced. I had just destroyed another creature's free will, and I'd done it without a second thought. I paused, assessing my conscience, and decided I could live with it if it kept Charlie safe until this crisis was over.

I glanced back at Maven, but her expression was unreadable. "The thaumaturge witch will be here tomorrow morning," I said. "I'll go visit Nellie Evans as quickly as I can, and will hopefully have something to report by nightfall."

Maven shook her head slightly. "Ghosts are only out after twilight," she said dully, "so you won't be able to see Nellie until then. But please call me right after."

I nodded and got up to go. I was all the way to the doorway before I realized I wasn't sure where to go. Turning back to Maven, I asked, "Um, one other thing . . . can I borrow your phone?"

Chapter 25

I called Quinn's cell, but it was Simon who answered. I identified myself. "Hey, Lex," he said in a *very* heavy voice, like he was simultaneously drunk and asleep. "Is your niece okay?"

"She's fine. Maven's fine. We've . . . got it sorted. For now. How's Quinn?"

"He'll pull through. He's asking for you."

I swallowed hard. "Tell me where."

I stopped at home just long enough to take care of the herd, change clothes, and scrub the bloodstains off my skin. I put all of the clothes I'd been wearing over the last few days straight into the washing machine, because in some dim part of my hindbrain, I could just imagine Keller getting a search warrant for my house and finding bloody clothes. I threw on clean jeans and the next shirt in my dresser drawer, a scoop-necked deep red tee. I grabbed the leather jacket that Lily had insisted I keep, and tore off for Quinn's place.

I hadn't been to Quinn's apartment building before, but I knew Boulder well enough to find it without the aid of cell phone navigation. He lived in an upscale but rather generic apartment building off Walnut Street, next to a number of swanky single-family homes. Right away it reminded me of a vampire's apartment that we'd visited in Denver, and I suspected that more-established vampires looked for that particular "upscale but generic" vibe.

I started toward the little row of buzzers, but someone was waiting for me at the exterior door: Lily. "Hey," she said, sounding a little breathless. "The buzzer isn't working. I tried to call and warn you."

"Oh—I dropped my phone at Chautauqua," I explained. "What are you doing here?"

"Simon called me to come help." She held up her wrist, showing off a neon-pink Band-Aid with little skull-and-crossbones designs all over it. "Give blood, save a life," she said solemnly as she ushered me inside, leading the way to a carpeted stairway. "Quinn has a basement unit, obviously."

We started down the steps. "Kind of surprised to see you," I said lightly. "I thought you and Quinn hated each other."

She paused. "Did Quinn say that?"

I glanced around, but there was no one else in the hallway. "Um, no. That time you came over to take out my stitches, and Quinn showed up . . . lot of hostility there. I got the impression that maybe he did something to you, or maybe it was just a witch-vampire thing."

Lily stood there chewing her lip, not making any attempt to continue toward the apartment. "You guys are into each other, right?"

I should have expected something like that from Lily, but of course I was caught completely off guard. "What—I mean, we sort of, like . . ."

She waved it aside. "It's okay. You should probably know the truth, then. It's not a witch thing, and Quinn didn't do anything. It was me."

I just stood there, blinking stupidly, until she continued in a low voice, "A few years ago, shortly after we met, I made a pass at him."

"Okay . . ."

Wry smile. "All right, it was more like I threw myself at him. I was lonely, I'd been drinking, a casual hookup seemed like a good idea. Actually, most of us in the Old World don't get attracted to anyone outside our species, but there's something about Quinn that's just . . . yummy."

I blushed, mostly because I completely agreed. I didn't remember being attracted to any other vampires, but I hadn't met many male ones, and none of them . . . anyway. "Lily, you don't have to tell me—"

She blew out a breath. "I know. Anyway, he turned me down, nicely, and I've held it against him ever since. I just thought you should know it's not his fault. I've seen the way he looks at you. And the way you look at him." Her face softened. "There's real attraction there."

I drew a slightly shaky breath. "I'm not convinced that we're not just"—I gestured helplessly—"broken magnets."

"Oh—" She stepped in for an impulsive hug. "Don't overthink it," she advised.

We reached the door, which Lily had propped open with the deadbolt. It opened into a small entryway, which led to a kitchen with light blue walls and wood accents. I would have bet money the decor came with the apartment. The room was comfortable enough, but there was almost nothing in it: just a card table and a folding chair. Beyond it I could see a sparsely decorated living room with only a TV and a cheap IKEA couch.

Lily closed the door behind me. "The patients are in the bedroom in the back," she said, her voice surprisingly grave. "When you see them, try not to laugh. I think it's too soon."

Puzzled, I followed the hallway back to the single bedroom and peeked through the open door. Quinn and Simon were lying side by side in one queen-sized bed, on top of the covers. Simon still wore the clothes he'd had on at the park, dirty and splotched with blood. He looked worse than ever, but he was at least propped up with pillows, flipping channels with a remote control. A plastic bottle of orange juice rested on his stomach.

Next to him, Quinn was bare-chested, a bandage taped loosely over his chest wound, wearing clean athletic pants. He was still pale, and while his eyes were sunken, at least they were open. They crinkled happily when they saw me, but then he glanced at Simon, next to him on the bed, and shot me an alarmed, *it's not what it looks like* face.

I burst out laughing.

I couldn't help it. It wasn't just a quick snicker, either: I had to put one hand on the door frame and lean against it, supporting myself as I broke down into helpless giggles.

"Lily!" Simon cried out. "I told you to put his shirt back on!"

That just made me laugh harder. "I don't think . . . it would've . . . helped . . ." I choked out.

Lily came up behind me, hands on her hips. "I told *you*, his wound hasn't healed yet," she said severely. "It needs to get air."

"*Dammit*, Lily," Simon pouted.

I had to bend over with my butt pressed against the door frame. "Simon, stop talking," I said, shaking my head. "Everything you say makes it funnier." When the spasm of laughter finally worked its way out, I straightened up and wiped tears from my eyes. "Thanks, guys. I really needed that."

"I don't have to take this from you," Simon said with great dignity. "Especially when I went to so much trouble to bring you back a souvenir."

I raised my eyebrows, the laughter dying in my throat. "Oh?"

Slowly, he set the orange juice on the lone nightstand and picked up something that had been lying next to it, something flat and roughly the size of a dinner plate. It was thinner than that, though: when Simon lifted it up I could almost see through it.

"What is that?" I said, stepping closer.

"It's a scale," Simon explained. He offered it to me, but I shook my head. I felt no need to touch that thing. "When you shot the whatchamacallit, the Unk-teh-hi-la, you must have knocked it loose," he said, looking smug. "Now I can run all kinds of tests on the fucker."

"Nice." And it was. Hopefully the scale would give us some insight into the sandworm, because I was out of ideas.

"I'll let you know when I have more data." He began to swing his legs off the side of the bed. It was slow going, but I knew enough about men not to go over there and help him. "Lilith, take me home. I need a shower, and if I do it here, people will talk."

I slapped my hand over my mouth to keep more giggles from coming out. Now he was *trying* to be funny.

Lily rolled her eyes. "Yes, my liege." But she went to help him up. Even after he picked up his cane, he had to lean on her shoulders to move across the room. I couldn't help but feel worry cinch around me like a hunter's net. I shouldn't have let him donate blood when he was already so weak.

I picked up Quinn's keys and walked the two of them out. Simon was obviously feeling worse than he was letting on, because he allowed me to help him with his seat belt. "Thanks," I told him as I straightened up. "For saving me from the sandworm. And for what you did for Quinn."

The corner of his mouth turned up, pleased. "I told you I wasn't entirely useless." Then the smile faded. "Lex . . . see if he needs more blood. I'm not sure that what we gave him was enough."

I nodded. "I will." Then I remembered Keller and the police, and sighed. "We gotta get our stories straight, about tonight."

When I went back inside a few minutes later, I dropped my jacket on the folding chair in the kitchen and returned to the bedroom doorway, leaning against it again.

"Hi," Quinn said softly.

"Hi." I suddenly felt awkward. Quinn and I had barely kissed—hell, we hadn't even had a real date yet. I'd never even seen his place before tonight. And suddenly I was standing in his bedroom while he was half-naked and vulnerable. I smiled at him and crossed my arms over my chest, although I wasn't really cold. "I'm glad you're okay. For a second there . . ."

"I'm glad *Charlie's* okay," he broke in. "But what about you?"

I nodded, still feeling awkward. Grimacing, Quinn shifted on the bed, making more room on the side formerly known as Simon's. "Lex," he said, firm and certain, "come here."

Something long dormant stirred to life low in my stomach, but I still hesitated. Quinn tried to suppress a smile. "I'm not going to seduce you, I promise," he told me. I took a step forward, and then he added softly, "When I seduce you, I won't be injured, and you won't be afraid of hurting me."

I couldn't think of a thing to say to that, but I went over to the empty side of the bed and climbed on, leaving a foot of space between us. "The bed's still warm from your last visitor," I commented toward the ceiling.

"Please visualize me hitting you with a pillow," Quinn grumbled, "as I currently lack the strength."

I smiled and rolled over sideways to face him. "Quinn . . . do you need more blood?"

He shook his head, firm. "No. Not from you. Never from you."

"But—"

"I'll be fine, I promise. I'll be well enough to go out later, if I need to. Simon told me things were okay with Maven. What happened?"

So I told him about the scene I'd found at the coffee shop, how Maven had killed Benton and Nels and turned Clara into a pile of viscera. "I know I haven't known you guys that long, but I've never seen her like that, Quinn. She was . . . uncontrolled."

Worry flashed across his face, and he shifted his arm, inviting me closer. Forcing aside any hesitation, I scooted over and curled my body against his side, being careful not to interfere with the bandage on his chest. He smelled of antiseptic, and his skin was cool, his body more focused on healing than blood circulation. I didn't care.

Quinn did, though: he picked up a blanket from the floor next to the bed, grunting a little with the pain, and tossed it over me with one arm. "What about you?" I said.

"The cold never bothered me anyway," he said airily.

That startled me into laughing out loud. I really hadn't been expecting a "Let It Go" joke from a vampire. He kissed the top of my head. "Tell me the rest."

So I did, finishing with the fact that Clara was now my personal property, according to Maven, and I'd positioned her as Charlie's bodyguard. "I still didn't know if Maven was trying to reward me for helping her, or punish me for opposing her will. Maybe a little of both."

He sensed my discomfort. "It bothers you," he observed. "That Maven gave her to you."

"She's a *person*," I said, painfully aware that I'd already put her to work despite my reservations.

"Who would be dead if you hadn't intervened," he pointed out.

"Yeah, I guess." That didn't mean I was comfortable with the situation. "What do you know about her?" I asked him.

"Clara? Not a whole lot. Remember back when we were tracking Nolan, and I told you that Boulder is where Maven and Itachi stuck the problem vampires?" I nodded. "Well, my impression of Clara is that she's kind of . . . um . . . violent."

"Aren't you *all* that way?" I said, then added more apologetically, "No offense."

"None taken. What I mean is that most of the vampires I know will try to solve problems with natural charm first, and if that doesn't work, they start pressing minds. If *that* doesn't solve the problem, they resort to violence. But Clara tends to jump straight to the third option."

"Wait, back up . . . *You* have natural charm?" I said, in mock surprise.

He grinned at me. "Touché. *I* start with pressing minds, then violence, and if that doesn't work, I turn on the charm."

"I hope I never see that day," I said solemnly.

Quinn laughed out loud, then winced at the way it jarred his wound. "Ow. Not cool." He hesitated for a moment before saying, "Listen, speaking of pressing minds, this cop who hates you—"

"Keller."

"I'll pay him a visit tonight. Two minutes to press him, and then you'll be off his radar for good." He smirked. "I could even make him nominate you for citizen of the year or something."

I shook my head, remembering Keller's accusation. That I was unstable. That he'd be watching me for signs of violence. "Thank you, but no. I don't need you to fight my battles for me."

His smile shifted, becoming just a little patronizing. "Come on, Lex, the guy's all over you, for no reason. It's really not a big—"

"*No*, Quinn," I interrupted. "I don't want to spend my life depending on mind control to make things run smoothly. It's too much power. Too seductive. No offense," I added.

"This from the woman who can press me, but not the other way around?"

"I've never pressed you," I said honestly. He sort of shrugged, but using only his head. He hadn't really said he'd stay away from Keller, so I pushed. "Promise me. Promise me you won't press Keller."

Quinn tilted his head to look me in the eyes, assessing what he saw there. I couldn't read his expression. "I promise I won't press Keller," he said finally.

"Thank you."

I suddenly felt exhausted. It was only ten o'clock at night, but my vision was starting to get hazy with fatigue. I hadn't really caught up from the missed night of sleep on Halloween. "I think I need some rest," I said thickly. "Busy day tomorrow." The police, the thaumaturge witch, and hopefully the ghost of Nellie Evans were all on my docket.

"I wish I could help you with all of this," Quinn said, sounding a little forlorn. He raised my hand and kissed the palm. "I never missed the daylight until I met you."

It was an offhand comment, but it touched me, and I raised my head to give him a gentle kiss on the lips.

"Will you stay here, with me?" he asked.

"Mmm-hmm." I settled back down and closed my eyes.

"Good." But then his body tensed a little. "Lex," he warned, "in the morning, I'll be . . . out."

I opened my eyes, but didn't look at him in case the fear showed on my face. We'd never really talked about what happened to him during the daylight hours. "Dead?" I asked.

"Not exactly. I won't rot . . . I won't even look dead. I'm told it looks sort of like sleeping, but I don't breathe or even have a heartbeat."

"Okay," I said, nodding against his chest. "I can handle that."

He kissed the top of my head again, and I began to drift away in earnest. "Quinn?" I mumbled before I was all the way out.

"Hmm?"

"Is your first name really Arthur?"

His quiet laughter followed me into sleep.

Chapter 26

I slept hard, but had to get up around four to pee. When I returned to bed and crawled in next to Quinn, I realized he was breathing again. I reached out and pressed my palm against his cheek. His skin was as warm as mine.

At my touch, his eyes opened. He turned his head and kissed my palm. "Hi."

We were face to face, inches apart, and in the dim light from the hallway I could see that his color had returned. As my eyes adjusted, I couldn't help but notice he was still shirtless, and his chest was no longer bandaged. I put my hand against it, feeling only a tiny ridge where the injury had been. "You're better."

He nodded. "I went out and got something to eat," he said lightly. "I hope you don't mind."

I thought about that for a moment. Did I mind? I didn't really care about him drinking someone else's blood, but in the movies vampire feeding was always about sex, and the idea of him sleeping with someone else definitely bothered me. Then again, he'd fed from Simon and Lily, and that hadn't been sexual.

Well, if I wanted to know, I was going to have to ask. "Did you, um . . ." I blushed, not sure how to phrase it.

His eyes narrowed in confusion, and then he made a sort of chuckling/snorting sound. "Sleep with her?"

"Well, yeah."

"No. I didn't even do that before I met you. It's true that feeding is intimate, but so is therapy or a prostate exam," he told me. "Sometimes we press people to think they had sex, because it explains the slight amount of bruising."

"Oh."

"What I usually do is press someone not to feel pain and then bite or cut their wrist and drink. When I'm finished, I press them again not to remember what happened." His voice was matter-of-fact, clinical, like he was explaining a root canal. "It's a transaction, more than anything else."

"Oh." I searched for the correct response to that, but all I could think of was, "Does it bother you?"

His hand drifted up to play with a lock of my hair that had spilled forward. He twisted it around his finger, thinking. "It used to. It used to really scare me."

That seemed like an odd word choice. "Why scare?"

"It's . . ." he paused for a moment, searching for words. "This sounds kind of weird, but have you ever been addicted to something? Cigarettes or whatever?"

I smiled ruefully. "I never smoked, but when I was overseas I got really into those horrible energy drinks, the ones that are all chemicals and caffeine. I won't say how many I was drinking a day, because the number shames me, but let's just say it was too many."

"Yeah, but remember how good that first one tasted in the morning? How much you looked forward to that?"

I remembered. "It has a kind of power over you," I said. "Not just physically—I would get withdrawal headaches—but emotionally, too. You think about it all the time, the next one, where it comes from, how good it'll be . . ."

He nodded. "That's what blood is like for vampires. An addiction that never goes away, never gets better. There's no twelve-step program for something you need to survive. And the fact that you have to victimize someone else to get your fix . . ." His eyes were troubled. "At the same time, it's impossible to keep *feeling* that, every single time you feed. You become numb to it. And, slowly, most of us become numb to everything else, too. But I don't want that to happen to me."

Without thinking about it, I inched forward and closed the gap between us, my lips meeting his. The kiss started out gentle, but then it was like a switch flipped for both of us. He shifted on top of me at the same time I shifted beneath him, like we had coordinated it beforehand. The skin on his chest was warm, but his fingers were cool as they traced the waistband of my jeans, tickling my sides. Effortlessly, Quinn scooted downward until his face was near my belly, and lifted the hem of my T-shirt just a few inches. He kissed my stomach, his fingers dancing at the buttons on my jeans. I writhed with pleasure as he opened the fly and kissed lower, his mouth heating up the fabric of my panties as he tugged the jeans off. His fingers brushed against the raised scar on my thigh, and I felt him pause for a moment, considering whether to stop and ask me. I really didn't want that conversation right now, so I decided to distract him instead. Squirming, I pulled my shirt over my head, and he made a little interested noise, his mouth moving higher to explore. I laughed breathlessly as his lips traced a straight line up between my breasts. I thought he'd stop there, but he kept going until our lips met again. This kiss was more urgent, forceful, and soon I was so lost in it that I gasped when his hands found my breasts, cupping them through the thin fabric of my bra. With a growl, I rolled Quinn over so that I was on top. He grunted appreciatively, and just to mess with him I scooted down his body until I was straddling his crotch, his erection pressing against me. Grinning wickedly, I wriggled my hips, and saw something new on his face: a very human, very urgent expression of lust. Moving vampire-fast, he rose to meet me, his fingers tearing at the front of my sports bra, and after that we lost ourselves.

I managed to set Quinn's alarm clock before I fell asleep again, lying on my stomach with Quinn half-draped over my back. When it went off at seven, I automatically reached over to hit the snooze, but by the time I opened my eyes enough to look for it, I had also realized that behind me, Quinn's body had just sort of hit pause: no breath, no heartbeat, no more warmth.

I wanted to be cool and well-adjusted about the whole sleeping-with-a-vampire thing, but in actuality it felt pretty icky now, like being covered by a corpse. I scooted quickly out from under him and off the bed, letting the blanket puddle on the floor, and backed up until my naked shoulder blades hit the wall. Then I made a surprised noise of pain and realized that my whole body ached from the fight with Tony and the fall in Chautauqua. Great.

I got up, my movements stiff, and threw the blanket back over Quinn—not because he was cold, but because he looked so vulnerable lying exposed in the bed. I looked around on the floor for my clothes, intending to take a quick shower. That was when I noticed that at some point in the night, Quinn had brought the folding chair in from the kitchen. My jacket was still slung on the back, but he'd added a folded towel. I went and picked it up, uncovering a little packet of paper that had been set out underneath. He'd written my name on it, and drawn a little bow. A present. Smiling, I picked up the towel and wrapped it around myself, then unfolded the sheets of paper.

The pages were newspaper clippings and bits of text culled from Wikipedia and Google books, all on the topic of Colorado madam Nellie Evans and her brothel, the semi-notorious House of Shadows. Quinn had used part of his night to do research for me, knowing I wouldn't have a lot of free time today.

I looked back over at where he lay on the bed, wishing I could thank him, but he was . . . damn, I didn't want to say "dead to the world," but the bad puns just kept popping into my head. I sat down and began to read.

The House of Shadows had been built nearly a hundred and thirty years ago as a lovely Victorian home in downtown Denver. When the city's red-light district began to spread, however, the owners found themselves alarmingly close to the ladies of the evening. They eventually gave in and sold the house to a woman named Nellie Evans, who turned it into one of the city's nicer brothels. Nellie never achieved the fame or success of noted Denver madams like Mattie Silks, but she had a reputation for mischief that the newspapers of the time adored. There were stories of her and her protégé, a younger woman named Pale Jennie, racing horses and buggies through Main Street and dressing up in nun habits to sneak into a society party.

Nellie's House of Shadows prospered until 1895, when both she and Pale Jennie abruptly vanished. There were rumors that they'd gone west to ply their trade in the California mines, but Nellie had left behind her beloved cat, which everyone said was out of character. The general consensus was foul play, but the police barely bothered to investigate. No one much cared when prostitutes disappeared out of the red-light district.

Huh. Reading between the lines, it was easy to draw a connection between Maven and this Pale Jennie. She had been great pals with Nellie for a while, which fit with Maven's story—not to mention the complicated connection between vampires and boundary witches. Then Nellie had "killed" Pale Jennie, only to learn she was a bloodthirsty vampire. It was interesting that Maven had gone to the trouble of cutting off her head rather than drinking her blood to kill her, which might not have worked very well on a boundary witch. That implied that Maven had known what Nellie was, but not the other way around.

After Nellie's disappearance, the House of Shadows changed hands over and over, more often than any other building in the neighborhood. It quickly gained a reputation for being creepy, even making a number of "Haunted Denver" lists over the decades. Go figure.

The house's history took another turn in 1972 when an entrepreneur named J. J. Parks decided to buy the former brothel and turn it into a mini museum dedicated to the history of prostitution in Colorado. Denver was already the home of the Molly Brown House Museum, and I guessed he figured history buffs would be interested. It seemed reasonable, but the House of Shadows Museum only ran for a couple of years before complaints started filtering in from visitors: drafts that had no origin, bad smells, mustiness that couldn't be aired out no matter how many windows were left open. Attendance plummeted.

In 1979, Parks closed his museum and put the building up for sale, but it remained on the market for years, sliding into decay. Every now and then, according to a "paranormal investigations" webpage about the location, Parks would get an offer from someone who wanted to buy the property, tear it down, and put in a commercial business. Somehow, these plans always fell through. Since then, the only real visitors to the House of Shadows had been ghost hunters, including several from reality television shows, who found the usual: EMPs, cold spots, creepy sounds. The same haunted-house stuff they found at any number of locations, except this time I knew they were dead on.

Damn. Stupid puns were everywhere.

I refolded the pages and set them on Quinn's dresser. I didn't want to bring them with me to the police station in case Keller decided to search me. I took a shower and dressed in the same red shirt and jeans, which were rumpled as hell, but reasonably clean. I had to go without a bra, though, because mine had been shredded down the middle. I couldn't help but smile a little when I saw it. No, I definitely didn't have a problem with attraction to Quinn.

As I swung my jacket on, I felt a weight shift in the left pocket of the jacket. I put my hand in slowly and pulled out my own cell phone, last seen skittering into the shadows at Chautauqua. He'd gone back to the park to find it for me. I smiled at it for a second. Quinn wasn't exactly a "chocolate and flowers" kind of guy, but he knew how to show feelings where and when it counted. And he knew *me*, at least well enough to guess what gestures would mean the most to me. "Thank you," I said to his still form, just in case he had some knowledge of what was happening. I was kind of glad he couldn't see the stupid sappy smile on my face.

As I walked over to the car, I called Elise, who owed me a favor, and got her to agree to look after the herd on the way home from her watch-three patrol shift. Then I set my jaw and drove to the Boulder Police Station, promising myself that *this* time, I would not let Keller get to me.

Yeah, I know. Keep dreaming, Lex.

Chapter 27

The police station was already bustling when I arrived just before eight. It was shift change, and cops were rushing in and out, hurrying to clock in on time or hustling home to see their families. I saw Elise leaving, but she was engrossed in a conversation with another patrol officer and I didn't interrupt them. If she knew I was there to talk to Keller, she'd just worry about me, or worse, try to get herself involved.

I gave the receptionist my name and went to wait on one of the black leather benches, keeping an eye on the people moving in and out of the room. A couple of the patrol officers recognized me as Elise's cousin and gave me cool professional nods, which is how cops greet all civilians who may or may not be at the station willingly. After a while, it appeared that Keller's plan was to make me cool my heels. Typical of him, but I needed to be in Denver at nine thirty to pick up the thaumaturge witch from the airport, so after fifteen minutes, I went back up to the receptionist and told her very politely that I couldn't wait, but I would return when my attorney was available to join me.

That got Keller's attention pretty fast. In short order, I was admitted to an interview room, which was just like the ones you see on television, but smaller, with nice walls made of that burlap-like wallpaper. There was no one-way glass, either, but a video camera was mounted in one corner, and other detectives monitored from another room. I sat down in one of the chairs, and Keller bustled in a moment later holding a stack of manila file folders. Stevens followed on his heels, carrying a small notebook. They took the chairs across from me.

"Good morning, Miss Luther," Stevens began. "We brought a little visual aid to show you this morning."

"All of these cases," Keller growled, holding up his short pile of file folders, "are the ones that are either unsolved, or were just opened recently." He held up the folders one at a time like a game-show host. "First we have a botched kidnapping, six weeks ago." He slapped a file folder down, out of my reach. It was well-thumbed, more than half an inch thick. "Then human bones turn up at Chautauqua"—he put down another file—"and, of course, a college student goes missing." Another file. "They found another one of them pellets last night, with bones and clothes inside. Meanwhile, I find myself needing to open up a vandalism case for one John Wheaton." He dropped the last file carelessly on top of the others. He didn't mention the death of Billy Atwood or Simon's injuries, but I figured that was because Quinn had pressed everyone at the scene into truly believing the whole thing was some kind of farm accident. "Funny thing is," Keller went on, "you're connected to all of them."

I raised my eyebrows. "How do you figure? I'm connected to John and Charlie, of course, but I had nothing to do with these . . . what did you call them? Pellets?"

He glowered at me. "You brought Dr. Pellar to the police station to examine the first pellet. I saw you myself."

I shrugged. "Simon's a friend. I gave him a ride."

"How did you meet Dr. Pellar?" Stevens spoke up.

I had gotten so sucked into Keller's bit with the folders, just as he'd intended, I'd almost forgotten she was there. "Ma'am?"

"You said you and Dr. Pellar are friends," she prompted. "How did you two first meet?"

Oh. I gave her the same story I'd told Elise—that I'd visited one of Simon's classes because I was thinking about auditing. "When was this?" she asked, pen poised over her notebook.

"Sorry, I can't remember. Early September sometime."

"What was the name of Dr. Pellar's class, the one you attended?" she pressed.

Damn. I had kind of hoped this woman would be my ally, but if this was her version of "good cop," her bad cop might be worse than Keller's. I spread my hands wide. "Sorry, I don't recall."

"Is the relationship romantic?" Stevens asked.

"No, ma'am," I replied. "Simon has a girlfriend. We're just friends."

"That doesn't make sense to me," Keller broke in. "Two people in their thirties with nothing in common, no romantic attachment, suddenly spending all this time together?"

I gave him a look. "So your theory is, what, that the two of us are forming a gang of local hooligans who break windows and eat people?"

"How *do* you explain your relationship with Dr. Pellar, Lex?" Stevens asked kindly. Ah, *there* was the good cop. Too late now, lady.

"How do you explain your partnership with Keller?" I countered, pointing a thumb at the other cop. "You lose a bet? Transfer in from somewhere else?"

They both ignored me, taking a moment to shuffle their papers and scribble notes I couldn't see. With her eyes glued to her notepad, Stevens said in a casual tone, "Dr. Pellar is a fairly well-respected professor. His supervisors say he's brilliant, but he has a little trouble with time management. Doesn't publish much."

"I wouldn't know."

"He also has a lot of contacts in other countries," Keller said pointedly. "Contacts who might be able to get him a big snake or even a Komodo dragon."

Now Keller was accusing *Simon*? "Maybe he does," I allowed. "But you guys came to him, not the other way around. Elise was the one who—" I cut myself off, but it was too late: Keller pounced.

"The one who wanted to call in Pellar? We know. We also know that *you* were the one who told her to do that." He gave me a thin smile. "So you see, Ms. Luther, once again a suspicious situation can be traced back to you."

"Are you ready to tell us who you were with last night?" Stevens said, her voice innocent.

"I was with Simon and his sister Lily," I said, but my voice didn't sound as strong as I'd have liked. We'd planned the alibi when I was walking them out to Lily's car, but that was before I knew the police considered the Pellars my co-conspirators.

There was nothing to do now but stick to the story. "Lily was really upset over a breakup, so she asked Simon and me to come over and spend time with her. When I left last night, I told her to call me if she needed me to come back, and shortly after I arrived at John's house, she did call." That much was true—she'd called my cell to let me know the buzzer on Quinn's apartment building wasn't working. "I was worried, so I headed back as soon as I could. We stayed up late talking and watching movies at Lily's house, and I ended up crashing on her couch." I tugged at the front of my wrinkled shirt. "I haven't even been home yet this morning."

Keller started to bark something, but Stevens subtly signaled for him to wait. "Why didn't you just tell us this last night?" she asked me.

"Because I didn't want to tell you my friend's secrets without her permission," I said, trying to sound casual. "But I spoke to her this morning and she said it was okay."

"And we can confirm all of this by checking your cell phone records?" Stevens asked mildly.

"No, you may not." Both of their eyes narrowed at the same time, but I just shrugged again. "You would need a warrant for that, and I have a right to my privacy."

Keller made a skeptical grunt in the back of his throat. "Riiiiiight," he drawled. "So you've got this flimsy story, and we have no way of proving that any of it is true. How convenient."

"You're welcome to speak to Simon and Lily," I said. I kept my tone even, because I am a grownup, and I wasn't about to give in to the tiny voice suggesting I give Keller the finger. "Although of course I'd prefer that you not waste your time on me when you could be finding the real vandal."

Keller and Stevens exchanged a look. She gave him a barely perceptible nod, and he turned to face me, looking angry. "Here's what we're thinking, Ms. Luther," he said. "You came home from Iraq a hero, but then a few years passed. Now you're in a dead-end job, no real friends, no romantic attachments because you're in love with your dead sister's husband."

"John and I aren't—" I began, but he cut me off.

"You act out a little bit, get arrested a couple of times, then finally, you get an idea: You'll stage a kidnapping. Get even more attention and glory for yourself, and your brother-in-law's gratitude, to boot."

Even though I'd figured it was coming, I still felt like I'd been slapped. I could tell by Keller's smirk that it showed on my face. "But eventually the hubbub from all *that* fades too," he went on, "and suddenly you're bored and alone again. So you and your new pal Pellar cook up another, more exciting plan, kind of a fun *Strangers on a Train* twist: You help him get some exotic snake-thing and let it loose in Chautauqua. You hook him up with Elise, making him look like a big important police consultant, which makes him look good to his bosses at the university and helps balance out his lack of publishing. And in return, he helps you trash your brother-in-law's house. Was it like a revenge thing, because he's with another woman?"

"Simon's walking with a cane," I pointed out. "His doctors can confirm that for you."

Stevens jumped in. "He doesn't actually have to be the one who destroyed the house," she remarked. "Maybe he stood watch, or kept an eye on John while he was on his date."

I felt my temper heat up. The worst part was that their whole theory had terrifying little bits of truth in it. I *had* acted out after the army, not to get attention, but because I was all twisted up with fury and frustration and had nowhere to put it. And there was a time when I'd been a little bit in love with John, but I was certain that was over now. I loved him, but it was because he was family. Because he was Charlie's dad. But how could I prove *that*?

One of my bigger problems here was that I couldn't point them toward Quinn as either my alibi or my "boyfriend," not that I'd use that term anyway. If they managed to find him before the sun set, he wouldn't exactly be a credible witness. In fact, that would just set off a giant pile of new and more dangerous problems.

On the other hand, I was starting to get a bit nervous that they were actually going to arrest me for vandalism and maybe manslaughter-by-giant-lizard.

They were both staring at me expectantly, and Keller had begun to tap a pen on the table, trying to unnerve me. Ignoring him, I took a slow breath, in and out. "Your theory is full of problems," I said, as calmly as I could. "If I had planned the whole kidnapping, do you really think I would have let myself get hurt enough to actually *die* several times in surgery? If my whole goal was to attract attention and hero worship, why did I turn down interviews from every newspaper and news blog within five hundred miles? Pick a major paper, and they called me the week after the thing at the Depot. You can verify that too."

Keller started to retort, but now it was my turn to talk over him. "You have absolutely no evidence connecting the break-ins to the kidnapping, and even if you did, there's no evidence connecting those crimes to the pellets, or the pellets to me. All you know is that I gave Simon a ride. You're just fishing."

I saw the glint in Keller's eyes, and knew the emotional attack was coming before he opened his mouth. "You tore up that little girl's room," he said softly, dangerously. "I saw her crib, after someone ripped it apart. It takes strength to do that, real strength." His eyes flickered down to the sleeves of my hand-me-down jacket, where my biceps strained against the leather. "It takes a messed-up brain, too."

"It's not your fault, Lex," Stevens put in, her voice dripping with sympathy. "A lot of people came home from the war with wires crossed. We can get you the help you need."

"Before you hurt anyone else," Keller added. "Like that little girl you claim to love so much."

For reasons I will never fully understand, I felt stinging tears flood into my eyes. I cursed myself inwardly. I was making everything worse by crying, goddammit. I had known he was going to take a cheap shot, so why did it sting this much?

Because I *was* afraid of getting Charlie hurt. That part was real. But it wasn't because I thought I would hurt her, not directly. I worried I wasn't going to be good enough, strong enough, to keep her safe from the whole Old World. And that terror suddenly flooded my body, sharp and crippling.

There was a long, terrible silence, while I struggled for control of myself. Stevens's and Keller were looking at me with expectant faces—Stevens's was kind, and Keller was obviously trying to mask his glee. Before I could speak, however, the interview room door flew open and a woman walked in. She was about fifty, with that silvering blonde hair that looks great on middle-aged women. Her strong, competent features gave her a commanding appearance, which was further emphasized by her blue tailored business suit and the thunderous look on her face.

"Chief!" Stevens jumped to her feet, with Keller right behind her. "What are you—I mean, how can we help you, ma'am?"

The woman ignored the both of them and beelined for me, holding out her right hand for me to shake. "Ms. Luther. So good to meet you. I'm Kim Bryant, the chief of police."

Uncertainly, I stood up and shook her outstretched hand. She had a strong grip. "Um, hello."

Only then did Bryant turn her attention to Keller and Stevens, who were busy exchanging identical mystified looks. I was guessing that the police chief probably didn't storm into interview rooms all that often. "Can one of you two please explain to me why in the hell you've brought this young woman in here?" Bryant demanded.

"Uh . . ." Keller hastily picked up the pile of case files from the table. "She's been linked to a number of recent crimes—"

"Because she's a *victim*," Bryant snapped. "Not to mention a decorated war veteran and the daughter of an extremely prominent local business owner." She gave me a sincere look. "Thank you for your service, Ms. Luther."

My jaw dropped open. I never know how to respond when people say that to me, but this moment was so bizarre that I just sort of nodded my head. She'd mentioned my father—had he set this up? Had he sent his eight hundred-pound gorilla of a lawyer in to . . . no, that didn't make any sense, either. My dad had a little pull, probably enough to get me some nice manners at a questioning, but he had no idea I was here. Even if John had told him, he wouldn't have called the chief of police; he would have sent the lawyer. I wasn't sure he'd ever had a conversation with Bryant, let alone an interaction that would give him this amount of sway.

"You are free to go, of course, with my apologies," Bryant was saying, reaching out an arm to gesture toward the door. "I would walk you out, but I need to have a word with my *detectives*." There was real fury in her voice, but I had stopped listening. As she raised her arm toward the door, I saw it: a heavy-duty Band-Aid stuck to her right wrist. Suddenly I understood everything.

Quinn.

Chapter 28

I seethed the whole way to Denver.

I couldn't *believe* Quinn. He'd made me a promise not to press Keller, and what did he do but go out and feed on the goddamned police chief instead, knowing damn well that he was ignoring the spirit of my argument in favor of obeying the letter of it.

And then, I realized, and *then* he'd come back to his place and had sex with me? I pounded a fist into the driver's-side window, hearing it creak a little under the pressure. How could he just go behind my back and fuck around with my life, and then come to bed with me? I was so angry . . . and so hurt, too. Although he'd kept his promise not to press Keller, he'd carelessly used someone just to arrange things for me. And he'd done it after I specifically requested he stand down, as though I were some simpering princess who needed a rescue and was too foolish to ask for it.

He also saved your ass, said Sam's voice in my head. She sounded amused. *Keller was gonna put you in a cell.*

"I am not talking to my dead sister right now," I said out loud. "And if I were, I know she would be on my side."

Silence from the voice in my head. Oh good.

It took some effort, but by the time I hit airport traffic I had more or less pushed away that line of thought. I didn't have time to meditate on the ethics of mind-control powers, and there was nothing I could do about it until Quinn woke up anyway. I tried to focus on the drive, and what I was going to say to the thaumaturge witch when I picked her up. I was eager for her to help—given the events of the last few days, it seemed more important than ever for me to talk to Nellie, Maven's old contact. The fact that the ghost in question was also a boundary witch had me practically salivating with the desire to speak to her.

I scrounged up a clean piece of notebook paper and a permanent marker from the backseat of my car, and made a tacky sign to hold up at the entrance to baggage claim. Probably not up to the thaumaturge witch's usual standards, considering her fee, but it worked: a few minutes after I arrived, an East Indian woman with a sleek rolling suitcase separated herself from the crowd and moved toward me with a relieved nod. She glanced over her shoulder every few seconds, which showed off a silky black fishtail braid. As she got closer, I realized she was probably a few years older than me, but had that youthful look of someone who took care of herself. And she was *gorgeous*. I'd sort of imagined she'd be glamorous in a cheap, Las-Vegas-on-TV kind of way, with fake boobs, sky-high heels, and a tight sheath dress, possibly red. Instead, Sashi Brighton looked like she should be on the cover of a catalog for an upscale women's boutique. She wore slim-cut jeans, a silk top the color of lemonade, and one of those thick draping cardigans, mahogany-colored and probably soft enough to cuddle at night.

"Hello," I said, holding out my hand. "I'm Allison Luther, but everyone calls me Lex."

For a moment her big brown eyes sparkled with surprised good humor. "Lex . . . Luther? Like the comic book character?" she asked, with a slight English accent. Of *course* she'd have an elegant accent to match the outfit. "Superman's archnemesis?"

"It started as an army nickname," I said with a shrug. "After a couple of years, it started to feel weird to be called anything else. I really appreciate you coming on such short notice, Ms. Brighton."

"Call me Sashi, please," she said, glancing behind her again. "My daughter was just in the restroom—oh, here she is." A gawky teenager came moseying over to us, wearing plastic-framed glasses and a pink Caesar's Palace sweatshirt over yoga pants. Her skin was a bit lighter than Sashi's, but her features were just like her mother's. She had a bright purple backpack that looked a little young for her. I could instantly imagine the conversation she and Sashi had probably had over getting a new one when the old one worked just fine. "This is Grace. Gracie, say hello to Lex."

"Hi," she said to the floor. I held out my hand, and the girl shook it, a little surprised that I'd bothered. Then she shrugged and stepped back in line with her mom.

"It's nice to meet you, Grace. I'll take you guys to your hotel first so you can get settled," I nodded toward Sashi's suitcase. "Can I get that for you?"

"No, quite all right. Shall we?"

On the way out to the car we made small talk about the weather in Las Vegas versus Colorado. I opened the back of the Subaru so Sashi could put in her suitcase, and we got Grace settled in the backseat. I made the mistake of asking her what she'd dressed up as for Halloween. "I'm four*teen*," Grace said with a scowl. "Halloween is for little kids."

"Grace," her mother warned.

"It's okay," I assured her. To Grace, I added, "I guess I'm used to younger kids. My cousins have kids who all still trick-or-treat. The oldest is Dani, and she's twelve."

Begrudgingly, Grace muttered, "Twelve was the last year I went."

"Gracie, why don't you listen to your headphones for a bit so Lex and I can talk business?" Sashi suggested gently.

Grace shrugged, which seemed to be kind of her default reaction to everything, and fished a pair of over-the-ear headphones out of her backpack. A moment later "Death or Glory" began blasting out loudly enough for us to hear it in the front seat. Sashi sighed. "Sorry about that. I'm pretty sure she's trying to fry out her eardrums so she doesn't have to listen to her mother."

"Doesn't bother me." I glanced sideways. "The Clash?"

Sashi smiled. "She and her friends think they're *such* originals for listening to them instead of Taylor Swift, or whoever's hot these days. I haven't the heart to tell her that teens have been thinking more or less the same thing for more than forty years." She rolled her eyes fondly.

"Is she, um . . . like you?"

"A witch?" Sashi shook her head. "Near as I can tell, she's in the middle of her window, where she has to activate her powers or lose them. But Grace doesn't know anything about magic."

And it didn't sound as though Sashi was planning to tell her, which seemed awfully complicated to me. Then again, what the hell did I know? I'd realized I was a witch all of six weeks ago. "Her father, is he a witch as well?" I asked lightly. I wasn't sure about the social protocol for asking a stranger a question like that, but . . . well, I was really curious.

If Sashi was offended, it didn't show. "No, I don't think so. At any rate, he's not in the picture," she said.

I considered saying "I'm sorry," but that seemed sort of presumptuous, like it implied Sashi wasn't a great parent by herself.

Luckily, she changed the subject for me. "Those mountains are just beautiful," Sashi commented, twisting in her seat to see how far around us they went. I glanced in the rearview mirror and saw Grace was now focused on a tablet screen. "It's like you live inside a picture frame."

I smiled. "I hadn't thought of it quite that way, but I suppose we do."

Sashi settled back into her seat. "So. Are you my patient? The witch with the mental scar tissue?"

"Boundary witch, yeah."

I glanced over to see her reaction. Sashi's eyes widened, and her knuckles went white on the door handle. *"Really,"* she breathed. I saw her shoot an instinctual protective look toward the backseat.

I suddenly felt like Dorothy herself might pop up and throw a bucket of water at me. "I don't live in a house made of gingerbread," I said pointedly. "Haven't eaten any children all year."

Sashi had the grace to blush. "Sorry," she said, still looking uncomfortable. "I've just never met a boundary witch in person before."

"I've never met a thaumaturge in person before either."

Sashi took in a deep breath and blew it out hard. "Right . . . right," she stammered. Her voice was still a little shaky. "Tell me about this scar tissue, then."

I explained about how I had most of the boundary witch powers—I could sense life, communicate with someone on the other side, and pull the spirits out of small animals. I didn't say anything about sucking the life out of humans, pressing vampires, or bringing Simon back from the dead. Even I thought those abilities were scary, and Sashi was already looking at me like I was the inconvenient byproduct of a mad scientist's experiment. "But I can't see remnants, except on Samhain, when they were really strong. And my friends think it's because I blocked off that part of my magic when I came into my powers."

Sashi cocked an eyebrow. "From what I know of boundary powers," she said slowly, "seeing remnants isn't something you can turn on and off, like the way you sense life. You'll see them every night, when they are visible. Why would you want that ability back? I mean," she added, "you must have blocked it off for a reason, yes?"

"Maybe, but I need it back now," I said. "It's important."

"Would you say it's a matter of life and death?" she asked, and now there was a little mischievous sparkle in her eyes.

"And I would know," I said wisely.

"Well, I volunteer at a children's hospital in Vegas, where I've done a bit of work with psychological trauma—kids are really good at building up the kind of scar tissue you're describing. I can't heal natural-born psychological problems like manic depression, but I can usually knead at the damage caused by trauma." She frowned. "I'm not sure it'll work on you, though, given that you're a witch as well."

"Have you worked on Old World individuals before?"

She hesitated for a moment, then shrugged. "Not much. I mostly work on humans who are injured in compromising situations at the casinos. A long time ago, I helped a few werewolves by working around their magic and talking directly to their bodies— their original cells. I'm not sure about a witch, though, given that you were born with your magic. I was upfront about that on the phone," she added in a hurry, in case I was about to demand my money back. Well, Maven's money.

"I know," I assured her. "I'm aware that it may not work at all. I just honestly don't have any other ideas about how to break through."

She nodded. "Well, let's cross that bridge when we come to it. Meanwhile we'll need a quiet place to work." She glanced over her shoulder. "And someplace where Grace can go."

"That shouldn't be a problem," I informed her. "Ryan, the man who spoke to you on the phone, booked two rooms for you and Grace."

"Excellent. She can veg out in front of the television. Where are we staying?"

I couldn't help but smile. "My employer, Maven, made the call on that one. I think you're gonna like it."

Despite the cheesy name, the Hotel Boulderado is one of my home-town's many historic treasures. In 1909, the residents of then-tiny Boulder decided that the only way to boost their town's prominence and importance was to add a grand hotel. They solicited stocks from local businesspeople, held a contest for architectural designs, and let the leader of the *Let's Build A Hotel!* movement come up with the name. He promised no one would ever forget it. And that part's still true—you can't exactly draw a blank when you see "Boulderado" on your credit card bill.

I led the Brightons through the heavy front door and over to the small concierge desk across from the original 1909 elevator, which still works but you couldn't pay me to ride. The moment we walked in, Sashi Brighton's face stretched into a gleeful smile.

"Oh, my *God,* it's the hotel from *Misery!*" she exclaimed, practically bouncing up and down with excitement. "Gracie, you seeing this?"

Even the teenager looked impressed. "So cool," she breathed.

When I raised my eyebrows, Sashi remembered herself and straightened up a little. "Big Stephen King fan here," she explained. "Grace just started reading some of them too. This is the hotel where Paul Sheldon stayed whenever he finished a book. I can't *believe* we get to stay here."

I smiled. "Boulder has plenty of nice modern places, of course, but we figured, being from Las Vegas . . ."

"No, this is perfect." She caught my eye and gave me a little nod, and I knew she'd picked up on the other, unspoken reason for this location. If there was anywhere in Boulder that was almost guaranteed to be haunted, it was a hotel that had seen its centennial nearly a decade ago.

"And hey, the hotel from *The Shining* is just an hour north of here, if you have time before your flight," I added. Sashi's eyes went *so big,* I couldn't help but smile again.

We got the keys and went through the center of the hotel, a beautiful, rectangular atrium topped by a stained-glass ceiling. Though small, the whole interior is done in gleaming oak, accented with marble pillars, which gives the place what Sam used to call "old-timey fanciness." We got Grace set up in her own room with the remote control and some snacks, and then Sashi and I headed into the other unit, where Sashi directed me to sit down at the small round table in the corner.

I was starting to feel a little weird about this—even though it'd taken over a day to set up, it suddenly seemed like this meeting was happening really fast. Consulting a magical healing witch was, at the very least, socially awkward, sort of like walking into a strip club, a therapist's office, or a Chinese grocery store for the first time—you just don't know what to *do*. Weirdly, it reminded me of being in Iraq, suddenly surrounded by customs for which you have no frame of reference. And yet, this was *my* world now too.

"All right?" Sashi asked, seeing my expression.

I nodded. "Um, what do you want me to do?"

In answer, she held out her hands across the table. Given the surroundings, I had the sudden impression that we were in some old movie, holding a séance. Which was actually kind of funny, because if anyone were going to lead a séance, it would probably be me. I copied her, holding out my arms. To my relief, she didn't take my hands, which would have felt intimate, but instead grasped my forearms and closed her eyes. "Just try to be quiet," she said. "It'll take a few minutes to assess, and then to see if I can actually—*oh*."

Her eyes popped open and she jerked her hands back, looking at me with confusion. "How did you . . ."

She trailed off, and I had to prompt, "How did I . . . what?"

Sashi blew out a sharp breath. "Sorry, let me just try that again." She took my arms and closed her eyes, and her brow furrowed almost instantly. When she opened her eyes a moment later, she withdrew her hands again, more slowly this time.

"Something . . . unusual is happening," she said finally. "I should be able to sort of listen to what's happening in your body, but I didn't think I'd actually be able to communicate with it."

"But you can?"

"Easily."

I opened my mouth to explain that something was off about the magic in Colorado right now, and this could be related, but I stopped myself. Here was a chance for independent confirmation of our theory about the magic going haywire in Colorado, and I didn't want to sway Sashi's opinion. "Hang on a moment," she said, standing up. "I'm gonna run next door and read Grace. I want to know if it's you, or if it's this place. Something's not right."

I nodded and waited where I was as Sashi used her key to enter Grace's room. She was back in seconds. "Well, it's not just you," she said. She was rubbing one hand with the other and then switching, as if they were injured or scarred. "I don't understand what's happening."

"Yeah, about that. One of the reasons I need to talk to this specific remnant is because we think something is . . . stirred up with the magic here," I explained. "I would love to get your impression of how it feels, since your power is a little more . . . um . . . family-friendly than my own."

"Oh." She nodded slowly, processing that. "Don't you have other witches who can give you that kind of feedback?" she asked. "Sybil and her sisters and brother?"

"That situation is complicated," I said honestly. "I'm trying to figure out exactly what's going on so I can put a stop to it. It's causing all kinds of problems."

Sashi just shrugged. "It's like a boost, really. Like I've suddenly got a bit more . . . juice. But it doesn't feel like it's fully under my control, either. It's . . . well, 'artificial' isn't quite the right word . . . but it feels forced."

"Huh." No one had actually put it like that before, but if whatever was messing with the magic in town was actually *boosting* power, that might explain why it was affecting less powerful witches more than those who already had strong magic, like Hazel—and, apparently, myself. I remembered Hazel's analogy about magical ability working like a battery. It was as if everyone had been given a charge.

Like it or not.

Sashi took a deep breath. "Are you sure you want me to work on you?"

I nodded. "I'm sure."

"All right." She took my hands again, and this time kept her eyes closed, cocking her head a bit as though she were listening to something. Maybe she was. Seconds passed, and then something began to spread through me: some kind of glow or warmth. It started in my center and undulated outward in small waves. It slowly faded, taking with it all the aches and pains from the fight with Tony. I suddenly felt my stiff muscles unknot and relax, felt the strength return to my limbs. It wasn't the same feeling you get from pain-killers—not a numbing. It was more like a cleansing. "Oh, *wow*," I breathed. "That's amazing."

"Thanks," Sashi whispered. "But I shouldn't have been able to do that." She frowned again, and opened her eyes to give me a puzzled look. "I shouldn't be able to help a witch this much. Even your magic is wide open for healing right now, Lex."

"That's good, right? Did you do it?"

"Not yet . . . listen, I found the psychic scar tissue. I haven't pried into it yet, but I can sense that you're right—it has to do with you blocking something when you were young."

"And?" I prompted.

"And . . . um . . ." She squirmed in her seat, looking suddenly uncomfortable. "I'm not quite sure how to say this, but that's not the only mental block your mind has built for you." I froze. "Did something happen to you a few years ago, in the desert?"

Chapter 29

Without meaning to, I jerked my hands away. I could feel the blood drain from my face, and my just-restored body tensed up all over again.

I could never remember exactly what happened to me during those final days in Iraq. The last thing I recalled was riding in the Humvee. We were guarding a supply line along the desert road, and my gunner was joking about his girlfriend's aversion to his new mustache. Then there was noise, heat, and a sensation of movement like we were being dragged.

The next thing I knew, I was staggering out of the desert outside the town, covered in dried blood with sand caked into it. My clothes were in shreds, and I had internal injuries, shrapnel wounds, and burns on my back that had been done with something like a hot poker. The doctors in Germany had called it torture, but I couldn't remember any of it.

I'd always been grateful for that. Despite the urging of the shrink I'd talked to at the VA, I'd never wasted a moment trying to bring those memories back. I'd recovered, come home, and attended the funerals of all of those who'd died around me.

But I still woke up sometimes with the taste of sand in my mouth.

Unable to bear Sashi's kind gaze, I jerked my chair back and paced over to the window, looking out on Spruce Street. "I was a soldier," I said to the window. My voice sounded brusque, though that hadn't been my intention. "I don't remember all of it."

There was a moment of silence, and then Sashi said carefully, "The human brain is incredibly complicated, Lex. I'm very good, but I can't promise you that I can heal one scar and leave the other. It may be an all-or-nothing prospect."

I nodded, understanding the weight of the decision before me. I stared through the window glass, not really seeing the street beneath me. I didn't know what having those memories back would do to me. I didn't even know if I'd be able to function. If I curled up in a catatonic ball underneath Sashi's hotel bed, I wouldn't be much good to Maven, or Charlie, or anyone else.

On the other hand, if I *didn't* do this, we had no way of contacting the one spirit who might be able to help us. The sandworm, the Unktehila, would keep killing people. The vampires would challenge Maven again, and more of them would die. And the werewolves . . . I shivered. The goddamned werewolves would come back into Colorado. And all of that was before I even took Charlie's future into account.

I went back and sat down at the table. "Do it," I said simply.

She nodded. "This will take a few more minutes," she warned me. "The brain is a very complex instrument, and even healing a simple clot or cut takes time. Healing the mind is a much more delicate endeavor."

"Got it."

She shot me a brief, sympathetic smile, and closed her eyes again. I closed mine too, trying to think of something else, trying *not* to concentrate on those last days in Iraq. I thought about Charlie, and what she was doing right then—it was one of my mother's days to take care of her, so she was probably giving my niece a midmorning snack right now. John and my father were both working at Luther Shoes. I pictured their offices, the route I would take to visit them. Elise would have finished caring for the herd by now, so she was probably already at home, recovering from her night shift. My cousin Jake, the vet, would be at his clinic, and his daughter Dani would be in—

The rush of images abruptly snapped over me, like a pile of sticks breaking over my head. Only it wasn't on the outside of my head, it was *inside*, and there was no stopping the memory of pain, such pain, and the thirst and tears. I tried to jerk my hands away from Sashi's, to make it stop, but she held me fast, and I was too overwhelmed by the burst dam of memory to fight her.

The night was overcast. So dark; a frightening, muggy blackness. We never even saw the IED. Cisco had died in the crash, and Myers and Randolph were shot as they crawled away from the ruins of the Humvee. They'd taken me, kept me alive, because I was female. Didn't remember some of that. I remembered being told that the army thought I was dead, thought I'd been vaporized in the explosion.

They didn't want information. That was the scariest part. I fought, hard, and they hurt me. Then they killed me: slashed my femoral artery. The blood exploded out of it. They'd videotaped this part, I thought—I still had nightmares about that video surfacing.

I woke up in a shallow grave at the edge of town. I was face-down, curled up; there was a little air . . . my eyes opened and I began screaming . . .

"No!"

I skittered backward until I reached the end of the little space between the wall and the bed, pulling my knees against my chest defensively. "No no no no no," I chanted.

"Lex . . ." Sashi's voice seemed to be coming from a great distance. She approached me, crouching down, and I flinched away. "I did my best," she murmured. "But I imagine some of the memory is bleeding through. What can I do to help?"

I shook my head, unable to form thoughts just then. It was too much, too overwhelming. I'd begun rocking back and forth, hitting my back against the wall on each rotation.

A moment later Sashi threw something around my shoulders. The bedspread. She set pillows on either side of me, building me a sort of fort. I nodded my gratitude, and the thaumaturge reached out to smooth my hair, but I flinched away from her.

"Lex . . ." Sashi said gently. "Why don't I take Grace sightseeing? You can just rest here for a little while."

She began to move away, but I reached out and grabbed her hand. "I didn't expect you to be so nice," I whispered.

Something passed over her face then, a shadow. A very old sadness. "I won't say I've been where you are," she said quietly, "but I do know how it feels to try to make something better, only to have the rug pulled out from beneath you at the moment you thought you had your footing." She squeezed my hand. "Is there someone I can call?"

It was daylight. Quinn wasn't available. "Simon," I mumbled. "Simon Pellar needs healing. My phone . . ."

She nodded. "I've got this. You just rest."

I found myself tipping sideways onto a pillow.

Chapter 30

When I opened my eyes, I was in the bedroom that Sam and I had shared when we were kids.

On previous visits I'd started out very disoriented, but this time I knew I was in the space my brain had created so I could visit my sister, sort of my psychological safe room. Sure enough, Sam was sitting cross-legged on her bed, watching me quietly. This was the adult Sam, as I'd last seen her.

"Sammy?"

"Hey, babe," she said quietly. "How are you feeling?"

"I hurt."

Sam just nodded. "I know."

"Why are you here?"

"Because you called for me." She wrinkled her nose good-naturedly above her grin. "You screamed at me, actually. It was very annoying."

I felt a corner of my mouth lift despite myself. Sam's smile had always been infectious. "Pull you away from anything important?"

She stuck her tongue out at me. "You know I can't tell you that." I had no idea where people went when they crossed the line between living and dead, and Sam wasn't allowed to tell me much about it. The one time she'd tried to talk about her death, she'd been blinked away from me.

"I'm sorry about your memories," Sam offered.

I shook my head, trying to find words. "It's not the pain," I said at last. "The memory of physical pain is always terrible, but it's never as bad as the experience itself."

"It was watching them die," Sam said matter-of-factly. "And being helpless."

I stared at her. "You could see that inside my head?"

She gave me a wry smile. "I just know you, babe."

I missed her so much right then; it was like a fresh ache in my stomach. Why did she have to die? Then fresh tears overwhelmed me as I remembered what I'd learned in LA. "You were eaten by a werewolf," I said abruptly.

Sam didn't look the least bit ruffled. "Yes."

"I am so sorry, Sammy. But . . . why did you send me to LA?" I asked, giving voice to the question that had haunted me since I'd found out what really happened to my sister. "Why did you think I needed to know?"

"I thought you had the *right* to know," she corrected me, her face softening. "The Old World keeps secrets, Allie. That's what they do. And I was afraid if you didn't find out the truth for yourself, someone would use it against you later." She winced. "Granted, I didn't realize just how badly the trip would go for you."

I bit my lip. "Was it . . . were *you* in terrible pain?"

Sam leaned back, considering her answer for a long moment. "I was," she said finally. We didn't lie to each other, which was something I loved about my twin. We told it like it was. "It took me a while to die, and pretty much the whole time I knew that I was *going* to die. I was so *angry* . . . and so worried about John and Charlie."

She leaned forward, her hands lifting from her lap, and I could tell she was struggling not to touch me. That wasn't allowed. "But— and this is gonna sound like I'm blowing smoke up your ass, I know, but I swear it's true—as I was fading, and lost the energy for rage or worry, I felt this great sense of peace, because I knew with perfect certainty that you would protect them." Sunlight shone out of her smile. "And I was so right."

"I feel like I'm hanging on by my fingernails," I confessed. "Or like the little Dutch boy, trying to hold back the whole dike with one finger."

Sam shrugged. "Part of that is just what it feels like to love a child," she said, not unkindly.

"But I have no idea what I'm doing," I whispered. "And I don't know how to keep going."

"Well, that's part of loving a child too," she said with a tiny smile, but then gestured at the tattoos that crawled up my arms and to my hands. "Do you know why Anna always said that griffins were your spirit animal?"

I looked down at the designs. Lily had created them, but it was our cousin Anna who'd first suggested the connection. "She just said they symbolized courage and boldness." I shrugged. "I assume it was her way of saying she believed in me."

Sam nodded. "That's true, but first and foremost, griffins were guardians. Protectors of the divine."

My eyes met hers. "If we're going for symbolism, wouldn't a phoenix be more appropriate? You know, with the whole not being able to die thing?"

Sam shook her head hard, suddenly fierce. "No, babe. Boundary magic is what you can *do*, not who you are. When we were kids, you protected me, and then you protected our country, and now you're protecting my daughter."

"Sometimes I think protecting the country was easier," I grumbled, but I couldn't hold back a smile.

She smiled back. "Regardless. *That's* the person you chose to be." Sitting back, she waved a hand dismissively. "The rest of this is logistics."

I raised my eyebrows. *"Logistics?"*

"Okay, maybe it's a *touch* more stressful than logistics," she allowed, "but you know what I mean. You already know what you need to do, babe. You just have to figure out how to do it." She cocked her head for a second, like she was listening to something, and then she smiled again. "Maybe he'll help."

"Who?"

"I need to go, Allie," she said in reply. "But listen. There's one more thing you need to know: not all the werewolves are evil."

"One of them *killed* you," I said, anger rising in my voice. "And I saw what it did to your friend Lizzy. How can you say—"

"Babe, you're gonna have to trust me on this," she interrupted. "Setting aside what Henry Remus did, werewolves are just sort of tormented by what they are. Stop seeing them as demons, and start thinking about what they bring to the table."

"Sammy—"

But of course, she was already gone.

When I opened my eyes, I was curled up in a ball in Sashi Brighton's darkened hotel room.

I could see sunlight peeking through a crack in the curtain, and I was relieved that I hadn't slept through the whole day. I stretched out my limbs, which were still remarkably ache-free, at least compared to how stiff they'd been in the morning. I decided that Sashi was worth every penny of her consultant fee.

My legs felt shaky, but I needed to get moving. Rising, I went over to collect my keys and cell phone from the top of the TV stand where I'd stashed them while Sashi was working on me. To my relief, the clock said 10:45—I'd only been out for a few minutes, though it had felt longer. I turned back to clean up my blanket fort—and almost bumped into a man.

"Aaaah!" I reared back just in time. He just stood there in a suit and tie, giving me a placid look. He was short—roughly my height—and appeared to be in his late forties, with pale thinning hair and a surprisingly calm expression. "Who the hell are you?" I screeched.

The man smiled politely and gave a little bow. "Hugh Mark, hotel manager, at your service, miss."

"Oh," I said, taken aback. Mark hadn't been standing there a moment ago, and I was in between him and the door. That was impossible, unless—

I looked at his suit, but I didn't know anything about men's fashion through the decades. "When did you start working here?" I said carefully.

"I became assistant manager in 1912, and took over as hotel manager in 1917. I have been here ever since." He looked fondly around the old-fashioned room.

I went over to the bed and perched on the edge, feeling completely discombobulated. First the memory dump, then talking to Sam for the first time since my trip to LA, and now a ghost? I was talking to a *ghost*, in broad daylight. In the middle of someone else's hotel room.

In broad daylight.

Maven and Sashi had both mentioned that remnants could only be seen at night. But if magic was all stirred up in the area, maybe it was affecting the remnants themselves?

"And what year is it now, Mr. Mark?" I asked.

His face clouded over with confusion. "Why, it's 1934, of course, but . . ." He trailed off as his eyes landed on the television, my clothes, and Sashi's modern luggage. "I'm sorry, miss, I seem to be a bit muddled at the moment."

Whoops, I'd pushed him too far. Quinn had said most of them were only an echo of themselves, like a little bit of a recording. It seemed as if he could only answer a few simple questions before deferring back to his "can I help you" default. "Don't worry about it, Mr. Mark," I said quickly. "I've been very pleased with the service here."

He brightened. "Is there anything else I can do to help you, miss?"

I thought it over. *Was* there a way this guy could help me? "Can you tell me anything about how I look to you? Do I have the same appearance as the other hotel guests?"

The uncertainty on his face cleared up a little, but doubt lingered around the edges of his features. "Not entirely, miss. If you don't mind me saying, I'd wager that compared to the rest of our guests, you have a sort of veil about you." He frowned. "Only, veils usually *conceal* something. Yours makes you more vibrant."

I considered that for a moment. So, to the remnants, I looked different from other living people. Interesting.

You know what you need to do . . . you just have to figure out how to do it.

"Mr. Mark," I said, "would you mind if I shook your hand?"

The remnant seemed surprised, but he gallantly offered his arm. I reached out and tried to take his hand. It took me a couple of tries, because at first my fingers passed right through him. Then I realized I could rest my fingertips on the back of his hand very lightly, sort of like touching the surface tension of water without sticking your hand all the way in. When my fingertips connected, a startled look bloomed on Mark's face.

"Miss . . ." he said shakily. "What's happening?" He lifted his head and looked around the room again. "I don't . . . this is wrong. This is all wrong."

"Take it easy," I said gently. "Keep your hand still, please. You died, Mr. Mark. Do you remember that?"

A pause, followed by a reluctant nod. "It was at the breakfast table, here at the hotel," he whispered. "I'm a specter, aren't I?"

"I'm afraid so."

He nodded, anguished. "There are a number of us here in the hotel. We see each other sometimes, but we're generally so *unaware*. What has changed?" He looked down at my fingers. "Are you doing this, miss?"

"I think so. Why didn't you cross over?"

"I . . . I was afraid for the hotel, and for my family. They lived here with me, and I worried about what would happen to them when I was no longer manager. I lingered too long . . . and then it was too late."

"I'm sorry, Mr. Mark," I said, meaning it. "That must be awful."

"Thank you, miss." He looked at me hopefully. "Is there—pardon me, miss, but is there anything you can do? Can you send me across?"

Now it was my turn to be surprised. I hadn't even considered the possibility. "I don't know," I confessed. "Hold still a minute."

I closed my eyes, took a breath, and dropped into the mind-space where I could sense life. Humans and witches tended to glow sort of bluish in my mind, and vampires were a dark, rich red. I didn't know if I'd be able to sense Mark at all, but sure enough, he was there: a silver-gray outline, faded, yet undeniably *there*.

Using the same techniques I'd experimented on with mice, I tried to pull at his spirit. Nothing happened. I opened my eyes and looked into Mark's eager gaze.

"I'm sorry," I said. "I don't know how to help you." His face fell. I added, "But I'll try to find out."

I pulled my hand back, and instantly Mark gave me a confused look. "I hope you're enjoying your stay at the Boulderado, miss," he said pleasantly. "Is there anything I can help you with?"

Chapter 31

I went back down through the hotel with my eyes trained on the floor, avoiding looking at any of the people in my path. I didn't want to stop and think about who might be real and who might be a "specter," as Mark had called himself. I couldn't help them, at least not yet, and I needed to find Nellie Evans. I could only hope that whatever was stirring up Boulder's magic would extend to Denver as well, because that meant I wouldn't have to wait until nightfall to talk to her.

My hands were shaking as I put the keys in the ignition. The memories from the war washed over me again, and I had to spend a few minutes with my eyes closed, breathing deeply, as cars whooshed past me on their way to the Pearl Street district. I felt like my brain was fracturing into different people. I'd gone into the army as Allie Luther, but by halfway through my first deployment I had become a different person: harder, more cynical. I'd been that version of myself for the whole deployment. When I finally returned home from the hospital in Germany, it was obvious that Allie was dead, but less obvious who I was supposed to become next. The old Allie was gone, but the soldier Lex felt betrayed by the army. They'd discharged me—honorably—as soon as it became clear that there was something fishy about my medical situation.

Switching identities between soldier and civilian was never an easy thing. The first few weeks home had been rough: I remembered going into stores and being overwhelmed by the crowds of people and the variety of options for every product. I would go to the park or for a bike ride and find myself terrified of the garbage barrels, the trash on the ground.

It was Sam who'd gone to Target to buy toilet paper for me, Sam who'd held my hand at the mall when I absolutely could not go any longer without buying new clothes. My sister had helped me forge another new identity: still Lex, but tempered with enough Allie to keep me securely connected to the people who loved me.

But Sam was dead. And now I felt split in two again, and there was no one to help me with that. There was nothing to do but sit in my car and wait for the wave of anxiety and panic to recede again. It took a while, but it helped that I was more determined than ever to go see Nellie Evans. I sure as hell wasn't going to go through all of this for nothing.

Realizing that I hadn't eaten since a quick drive-thru breakfast hash brown, I stopped at one of Boulder's many coffee shop/lunch cafés and got a veggie sandwich to go and a coffee. The caffeine probably wasn't the *best* idea while I was still a little unsteady, but the cup was warm and comforting in my hand, and having food in my stomach helped the shakes. I stopped at a Target for a few B&E tools, and then followed the navigation app on my phone to Market Street in Denver—specifically the area that used to be the red-light district.

I knew from Quinn's printouts that a hundred years ago this whole neighborhood had been elaborately divided into sections representing different classes of prostitute: the upscale parlor houses, the more "common" brothels, the specific areas reserved for women of color. Now, however, the entire neighborhood had been taken over by trendy businesses that leeched onto the consumer runoff from nearby Coors Field: pricey taverns, steakhouses, and coffee shops with pretentious fonts on their signs.

Nellie Evans's old brothel was only two blocks away from the stadium, and it was the very definition of the word "eyesore"—a dingy gray-brick building that seemed to suck the light out of the clubs on either side. The front door was boarded over, and plywood covered both windows in the front. Glancing around to make sure no one was looking, I ducked down the narrow alley between the brothel and the club next door. The back alley stank of vomit and urine, which wasn't surprising given the building's neighbors. I ignored the club on my right and circled to the back door of Nellie Evans's building, pulling a hand-sized pry bar out of the Target bag I'd brought from the car. There was a large "Keep Out" sign and several boards nailed unceremoniously across the entrance. Just as unceremoniously, I ripped them off with the pry bar and jimmied the door open.

The back entryway led into a grand foyer with a long winding staircase that immediately caught the eye, even in the dim light filtering between the boarded windows. This was normally the kind of entrance one saw at the front of a building, but a brothel would emphasize discretion, meaning customers had probably always come in and out the back entrance.

I clicked on the flashlight I'd brought and shone it around the room. In the harsh white beam, I could see how decrepit and worn-down the interior had become. There were spiderwebs everywhere, and the wooden floors and bannister had turned green with mold. The air reeked of decay and dust, and I shuddered as I imagined trying to live in such a place. It wasn't exactly the Munsters' house, but it was pretty damn unpleasant.

Suddenly a voice pealed from the balcony, streaming down the grand staircase. "Why, hel*lo*!"

Fear sloshing in my stomach, I shifted the light toward the top of the steps, illuminating the figure of a woman. She was in her forties, with a slim waist and an hourglass body, like a 1930s pinup girl. She was dressed like a pinup girl too: I'd expected Victorian clothing, but she wore shorts that barely went past her hips, bright red lipstick, and sky-high heels that strapped around her ankles. Her top was sort of like half a dress shirt, polka-dotted—it tied right under her breasts and ended there. Her stomach was slim but slightly rounded, obviously from a time before women were expected to have abs of steel. Her black hair, just beginning to gray at the temples, was curled in bangs over her forehead and tied up in a high ponytail.

After a moment of posing, she trotted down the stairs, no easy feat in those heels, and rushed down to greet me, pausing a few inches in front of me to look me over. "You're *here*," she exclaimed. "I know what you are. I know you can see me too, so don't go pretending you can't."

"Okay . . ." I said, thrown off by her familiarity. "Um, I'm looking for Nellie Evans."

She whooped victoriously, displaying rotting teeth in a heart-shaped face that must have been downright pretty before it became so weathered. "Well, that's me! You found me!" In response to my confused look, she glanced down at her clothes. "Oh, gracious me. You thought I'd look more like a shady lady, didn't you?" She waved her hand over her body, and her clothes transformed into a Victorian dress with a tight, lower-than-average bodice and an enormous skirt complete with a bustle. It wasn't like a movie costume or an antique in a museum: There were small stains and fraying at the hems, and a slight darkening under her arms. This outfit wasn't a fading relic or a prop, it was her everyday clothing, and Nellie looked comfortable in it. Well, as comfortable as anyone could look in a corset.

She still had the hair and lipstick of a thirties pinup girl, though, which was surprisingly disorienting. "There, now. You see why I'd rather not spend all eternity in this, don't you?" She turned around, showing off the bustle. "My lord, when I think of what we had to go through each day, just to greet the gentlemen! This house was a museum for a while, you know, and one of the displays was about women's clothing. This little box of moving pictures would run through all the different periods, and I had the *best* time trying out styles!"

I just stood there gaping at her. I wasn't sure what I'd expected, exactly, but probably not someone so . . . chatty. "Now, I'm told that modern trollops opt for something more like this"—she waved her hand again, and the elaborate gown vanished, replaced by a tight-fitting, simple black cocktail dress. She still had the ankle-strap pumps. "Why, just think of how many more tricks my girls could have turned each night if they hadn't needed to fuss with panta-loons, stockings, and corsets!" She gave me an elaborate wink.

"Ms. Evans—" I began.

"Please call me Nellie. And, oh! I haven't asked for your name yet; what terrible manners. You'll have to forgive me, I've had no one to talk to for *ever* so long." She looked at me expectantly.

"Lex," I said. "Lex Luther."

I rarely phrase my name that way, but if Nellie had ever heard of Superman's archnemesis, she didn't show it. "Such an unusual name," she exclaimed. "And who are your people? You're a proper witch of the demimonde, I can see it all over you, so you must have a coven."

I blinked, not quite sure how to respond to that. Finally I settled for the truth. "I was adopted, I'm afraid. I don't know my people."

Nellie folded her hands over her heart dramatically. "Well, if that isn't the most tragic thing I've ever heard!" she cried. "You poor thing. I would embrace you, but I'd pass right through, you know, and I'm told it's quite unnerving." A tiny, malevolent smirk appeared on her face and vanished immediately. I remembered all those potential buyers who'd been scared away from the property.

"What does 'demimonde' mean?" I couldn't help but ask.

She gave me a look of genuine surprise. "Why, the half-world, of course. The world beneath the world." Her eyes flashed flinty. "My mother brought me up in the demimonde, and her mother before her. We may not have had much, but there were always those willing to pay for what we could do. Why, when it was fashionable, I ran séances out of that very parlor." She nodded her head toward one of the decrepit doorways. Her smugness faltered a bit as she gave me an admiring once-over. "Then again, on my *best* day I had nothing like the kind of influence you employ. It's a shame you don't know your people; I bet there's a story there for sure."

"Ms. Evans," I started again, trying to get back on track. "I'm here to ask you a question. Some strange things have been happening in Boulder, about thirty miles northwest of here."

Her smile began to change, growing craftier. "Aye, I've felt it my own self. That's how I'm able to appear so clear and strong, you know. Why, I wager you can't even see through me just now." I couldn't get a grip on her speech patterns: it was like she'd come to the country as an immigrant, received an education, and was then exposed to half a dozen different dialects. Which, given her background and the house's museum status, was probably exactly what had happened.

"You're right, I can't. But, ma'am, if you'll pardon my forwardness, you don't seem surprised by it."

"No, 'course not." She looked confused. "Is it not a good thing, then, having your little fragment of the line reawaken?"

"The moon line, you mean?" I asked.

I'd been too eager. Nellie Evans's eyes narrowed with sudden mistrust. "Who sent you to me, then?" she asked suspiciously. "I haven't had a single visitor in near on five—no, six years, and you show up asking questions about the lines? How did you know to find me here?"

"A vampire told me about you," I said. "Do you know that word, vampire?"

Her face darkened. "Aye," she snarled. "The baobhan sith, my ma used to call them. 'Twas one of the very same who put me here. I've no love for the vampires, though they had plenty of love for me."

My thoughts snagged on that phrase, and I simply had to ask. "Were they drawn to you?"

"Yes, that's a good word for it." She gestured around, at the once-grand house. "That is how I was able to build my business so quickly, and compete with the likes of Mattie Silks and her gang . . . well, for a bit, anyway. They paid top dollar for my blood." She glared at me. "Which one sent you, then, hmm?"

Moment of decision. If I told her the truth, would she be more or less likely to give me answers? Less, probably. But if I lied, she might be able to tell, or she might ask me follow-up questions I couldn't answer.

I rolled the dice. "Her name is Maven," I said. "She's the cardinal vampire of the state, meaning she's in charge."

No recognition, but it wasn't like Maven was using the same name. "And what does she look like?" Nellie demanded.

I held up a flat hand. "About this tall, orange hair, pert nose. Very powerful."

She studied me for a moment, thinking that over. "Dresses in layers, does she? All decked out with jewelry and extra petticoats like she's trying to hide?"

"Yes."

"I *knew* it!"

Then Nellie threw a tantrum.

There was really no other word for it. She cursed and stomped, which was odd because her heels made no noise on the wooden floors. She threw her arms up and muttered under her breath about leeches and slaves and retribution. Then she did some further cursing that deeply impressed me, and I have heard some creative expletives in my day. I just stood at ease, waiting her out.

Finally Nellie calmed down enough to whirl around and face me. "Do you have any idea who you're working for?" she demanded. "Pale Jennie, she's the devil herself."

"Tell me more about the moon lines," I said calmly.

"And why would I do that?" she contended. "Why on earth would I help the likes of her?"

"If you don't, people will die."

She snorted. "I don't care about that." She gestured around herself. "Look at me! Look at this place! What concern is it of mine if others suffer the same fate?"

"Well, then, what do you want?"

Another glare. "You're suggestin' you'd *trade* me for the information?"

I shrugged. "Maybe. What do you want?" Remembering Hugh Mark, I ventured, "To cross over the line?"

Instantly, terror erupted on Nellie Evans's leathery face. *"No!* No, please. I don't want to cross over," she blurted. "I like it here."

Interesting. "What, then?"

She thought it over for a few minutes, tapping one toe soundlessly on the floor. "I want one of them motion-picture boxes," she said finally.

"A television?"

She nodded. "I want one set up in here so's I can learn about the world outside these walls." She shot an annoyed look around the brothel.

There was enough room on my credit card for a small TV and some bunny ears, and even if he ever found it, I doubted the owner of the building would much care. "If you answer all my questions, and the information turns out to be good," I said carefully, "I'll come back with a television."

Nellie pursed her lips. "That's not right," she complained. "How do I know you won't just leave and never come back?"

Kind of a fair question. Shaking out my wrist, I removed the small women's Rolex watch I was wearing. My father had given it to Sam as a college graduation gift. Nellie's greedy eyes lit up at the flash of silver. "This watch belonged to my twin sister," I told Nellie. "Her husband gave it to me after she died. I said I would wear it until my niece is old enough to take it. It's the most expensive thing I own, not to mention irreplaceable." I looked around for a moment, then crossed to a decrepit little coat closet and set the watch on the highest shelf. "Now I have to come back. Deal?"

"Deal," Nellie said, looking satisfied.

I went back over to the grand staircase and sat down, giving Nellie my full attention. "Tell me about the lines, please."

Curt nod. "When my ma came to this country," Nellie began, "she met with some of the Indians. They recognized her for what she was, so they treated her with more respect than they did near *anyone* else with a white face. Showed her where her magic was strongest."

"The moon lines?"

"They're not actually *called* 'moon lines,'" Nellie corrected, "that's just the wolves' term for them. To the rest of us, they're called *ley* lines." She shot me a triumphant look, like she'd just solved all my problems for me.

"But what are they?"

Nellie waved a hand toward the closest boarded-up window. "You have electricity that moves through those black ropes, right? The ones that hang on tall poles?"

I nodded. "Power lines."

"Aye, exactly. Ley lines were once the power lines for magic, buried deep, deep underground. The Indians believed the lines fueled *all* magic." She frowned. "Only, as time passed, the ley lines began to fade. This was long before my years walking the earth. It was like a fire dying: one bit cooling at a time, starting on the edges and moving inward until the last glowing ember fades."

There's something wrong with magic. How many times had I heard that phrase from Quinn or Simon? Everyone agreed that the Old World's magic was weaker than it used to be, and it was now much more difficult to change a human into a werewolf or vampire. And according to Simon, there used to be lots of magical creatures, but now most were extinct. "Do the ley lines still . . . um, work? Is that still where magic comes from?"

She shrugged. "Ma said they were sleeping. There's a word for it, something that's out of the picture for years and years, but not really dead . . ."

"Dormant."

Nellie snapped her fingers at me. "Aye. The ley lines are dormant. Not dead, though. That's why there are still places where magic works a little better than others. And your Boulder is one of them."

"But why?" I asked, though I didn't really expect her to have the answer. "I mean, why did they go dormant?"

She hesitated for a moment, like she was about to say something embarrassing. "The Indians may have believed that ley lines fueled *all* the magic, but me ma said different. She claimed *witches* fueled the lines, and the lines in turn fueled the demimonde." She shrugged again. "If she was right, and witch magic alone is what powers those lines, then it's the lack of witch magic that made them fade." She gave me a crafty look. "And witch magic that woke up the line, or at least your little part of it."

The weight of her words settled on my shoulders. *No one* I'd met in the Old World knew why magic was fading, not even Maven—or if she knew, she'd kept the information closely guarded. But Nellie's account could explain a lot. Witches had been targeted by humans since the Inquisition, and many witches had willfully *chosen* to stop practicing magic. Even active clans, like Clan Pellar, needed less and less magic to solve their everyday problems thanks to improvements in technology, transportation, and communication. And the witches in Colorado had stopped using apex magic because of their agreement with Maven.

Simon was definitely going to freak out when I told him.

"My little part of it," I echoed, feeling almost numb with the shock of it. "But it seems so limited to Boulder, and parts of Denver. If the ley lines go on for miles and miles, why is it just this one part?"

She looked around in frustration. "If I could just draw a *map* for you . . ."

"Here." I pulled my phone out of my pocket and pulled up a map of the Boulder-Denver area. "It's small, but it's something."

"Yes, yes." She didn't look too surprised to see the phone, but smart phones had probably been around the last time her house had seen visitors. The former madam sat down on the step and crowded in close to me. My body automatically anticipated the smell of her breath or the closeness of her body heat—*something*—but she was just made out of air.

"There," she said, tracing a line on the phone. The screen didn't react to her finger at all. "The main line in these parts runs northwest and southeast. Boulder to Denver, but extending forever in either direction. But there was another line, southwest and northeast, here." She traced another line that connected to the first right over my hometown.

"Hang on," I said, zooming in on the phone. "Can you show me again?" I asked.

Shrugging, Nellie retraced the lines, and I saw the exact spot where they connected.

Right over Chautauqua.

Chapter 32

"It's a crossroads," I breathed.

"Aye. Or it was, back when the lines were active." Her face was serious now, no more guile or attempts at manipulation. "The crossroads of two ley lines," she said, shaking her head, "now, *that* made for some powerful magic. And someone has found a way to wake up that little fragment."

"Fragment . . . *vestige*," I said aloud, remembering the Unktehila's words to us. The vestige was the sun it revolved around. "Someone is controlling the vestige of the ley line."

"Someone is *powering* it," she corrected, "stirring it up, like hot coals in a fire."

"Power the ley lines, the ley lines power magic," I mumbled. To Nellie, I said, "How would you do that?"

She shrugged. "There must be a specific spell. But it's not *our* kind of magic, so I'm not familiar with it."

Not boundary magic, then. "It *has* to be a witch?" I said, hearing the desperation in my voice. "You're sure?"

"Of course." Her look was a little disdainful now, like I was being intentionally stupid. "Haven't you ever noticed, girl, that of the three remaining demimonde creatures, witches seem the least powerful, on the face of it? The wolves and the vampires, they have all that strength and healing and speed. Doesn't that seem unfair to you?"

Well, it did *now*. Without waiting for my response, she continued,

"It's balance of power, you see? Without witch magic, the ley lines die, and it becomes harder and harder for the vampires and the wolves to reproduce."

My brow furrowed. It was entirely possible that Nellie Evans was messing with me or that she was just plain wrong. But my gut told me she was right. "They don't know," I whispered. "The other witches. Why don't they know?"

Nellie shrugged again, starting to look bored. She reached down and ran her hand over her shoes, changing them to match my own lightweight hiking boots. She wrinkled her nose in disgust and switched them back to the heels. "Even in my time, that knowledge was a rare thing. Without my ma's connections, I wouldn't have known. Most witch clans are like the werewolf packs: They only care about their own members. What is it to them if vampires are having a hard time reproducing? Good riddance, we all thought." A greedy smile. "Plus, the economics. The less access there was to magic, the more in demand it became. And the more we got paid to use it."

Holy shit. It was like goddamned global warming all over again. Suddenly I felt like the pull of gravity on my body had increased, sinking me into the floor with worry. A trades witch had caused *all* of this: the werewolves, the Unktehila, the vampires losing control. It seemed like more than enough to start a war.

"Would the witch have to be in Boulder to do the spell?" I asked, praying the answer was no.

But Nellie nodded. "Aye. The vestige, as you call it, that little bit of ley line, would need direct contact."

I let out a few very unladylike words that made Nellie do a double-take, admiration on her face. There were a number of different witch clans in Colorado, but as far as I knew, only one of them was in Boulder . . . which meant someone in Clan Pellar had done all of this.

But who? Reactivating the ley line vestige had provoked the werewolves, which had technically forced Maven to break her covenant with the witches. Any witch in Colorado had ample motivation to want to break the pact with Maven, especially the ones who were upset about losing their access to apex magic. I trusted Lily and Simon—even though Simon had changed his mind about the covenant, there was no way he'd go on letting the Unktehila kill innocent people—but it could be any one of the other witches. Maybe I could go to Hazel, explain my suspicions, and ask if she would help me identify the spell used to activate the vestige?

Except Hazel might be the one who's doing all this. The realization struck me like a physical slap. Hazel had more motivation than *anyone* to stir shit up in Boulder, because breaking the pact with Maven would pacify the other clans who were still pissed about her deal. And if Hazel couldn't be trusted, neither could Simon and Lily, because if they even suspected one of their family members was involved, they'd close ranks around them, right? That's what family does.

I was so screwed.

By the time I got back in my car, it was twelve thirty. Four and a half hours until sunset. Maven was expecting me to tell her everything I'd learned from Nellie Evans, a conversation that had every possibility of kicking off a war. Whichever side I chose, I would be pitted against someone I cared about.

And that wasn't the only time crunch, I realized. It had now been a full week since the last full moon. That meant the Wyoming werewolves, the pack that occasionally visited Tobias, could change again starting tonight. Would they make another attack on the borders? Hell, for all I knew, they were already in town, just waiting for the sun to set before they changed form.

The one thing I had going for me was that Maven didn't know that ghosts were visible during the day. She wouldn't expect any news from me until an hour or two after sundown, which meant I had until maybe seven p.m. to figure out what the hell to do.

Except I had no idea where to start.

When I was only a couple of miles outside town, Simon called. "Lex? Hey, I'm with Sashi and Grace. We got back to the hotel room and you weren't there anymore." He paused for a second. "Sashi said healing you was kind of rough. Are you . . . okay?"

How the hell did I answer that? My head was still a wasp's nest, the werewolves could be anywhere in the state, and oh yes, an unidentified witch had subtly declared war on my boss. "Not exactly," I summarized. "We need to talk, Simon."

"Yeah, I'm right there with you." Simon's voice was grim. "We gotta figure out what to do about the Unktehila tonight."

I smacked the steering wheel. "Goddammit, I forgot about the Unktehila."

"Are you kidding?" Simon said, incredulous. "You forgot about a people-eating magical worm monster?"

"It's been a rough day."

"Well, time to remember," Simon said unsympathetically. "He needs to feed again tonight, and I doubt he's gonna go back to Chautauqua after we ambushed him there. He might pop up in Iowa, for all we know."

"Oh, I have a hunch he'll stay pretty close to Boulder." I rubbed my eyes, trying to think. My impulse was to tell Simon and Lily everything, but there was no guarantee that the witch responsible for all of this wasn't a member of their family. But Quinn wouldn't be awake for four more hours, and I needed help. Fast. What the hell was I gonna do?

Maybe he can help. At first I'd thought Sam might have been referring to Hugh Mark, but what if I was wrong? What if there was another "he" who could help me?

Stop seeing them as demons, and start thinking about what they can bring to the table.

"Dammit, Sam," I muttered. "You've got to be kidding me."

There might be a way to both avoid war and keep all my friends alive. It would cost me a pretty serious compromise, but what choice did I have, at this point?

"What?" Simon asked. I'd kind of forgotten he was still on the line.

"Sorry, nothing," I replied. "Listen, Simon, is Sashi still on the clock? I mean, does she still work for us even though she already healed me?"

"Hang on, I'll ask." There was some muffled discussion, and Simon returned. "She says we've got her until her flight leaves tomorrow," he reported, "but she'll need someone to take care of Grace if you guys are doing anything too . . . suggestive."

I thought that over for a moment. "Ask her if Grace likes animals."

Another moment of conversation, and then Simon came back on the line and said, "Yes, Grace is into anything cute with fur."

"Great. Tell her to be ready to go in ten. I'm on my way."

I hung up the phone and called my cousin Jake's wife, who was a stay-at-home mom. "Hey, Cara, I need a favor. Could you and Dani use some company today?"

I arranged to meet Simon, Sashi, and Grace at a coffee shop near the Boulderado. As I walked in, I couldn't help but grin at the sight of Simon, who was flushed with health and excitement. He and Sashi were sitting at a table just inside the door, and although their voices were low, he was gesturing wildly, so animated and expressive that he didn't even see me walk in. There was no sign of his cane. While I was—well, "sleeping" is too innocuous a word, but I hadn't technically passed out, so we'll go with that—Sashi had obviously healed his remaining injuries. I looked around for Grace, and saw her leaning against the back wall near the sugar-and-milk bar, talking on Sashi's cell phone. Out of earshot. Good.

Relief crossed Sashi's face when she caught sight of me, but I wasn't sure if it was because I was up and moving or because I was rescuing her from the well-meaning scientist.

"Hey, guys," I greeted them. "Looking good, Simon."

"Feeling good, Lex," he said, a little smug. I remembered how wonderful my whole body had felt after Sashi's treatment, and I didn't blame him one bit.

"You guys ready?" I asked Sashi.

She nodded. "I haven't told Grace about your family yet. Just give me a second."

The thaumaturge witch left the table to join her daughter, and I sat down near Simon. "So. Where are we going?" he asked expectantly.

Oops. I had half of a rather slapdash and implausible plan, but I wasn't ready to deal with the fallout of Simon learning everything right now. "I need her help with someone, kind of a personal thing," I told him. He gave me a quizzical look, and I added, "Meanwhile, I'd like you and Lily to work on figuring out where the Unktehila might turn up next."

He frowned at me. "I'm not an idiot, Lex. You're not telling me something."

I sighed. "No, but it's because I can't yet. Can you just trust me for a few hours? Please?"

Simon gave me a long, measuring look, and then shrugged and glanced at his watch. "Lily's teaching yoga for the next half hour, but then, yeah, we can work on it," he said. "But remember, even if we figure out where it's gonna show up, we'll need some serious firepower to stop it. You got in a direct shot last time, and it only lost a scale."

"Let me worry about that," I told him.

Sashi and I dropped Grace off at Cara's house. I'd arranged for her to ride along to Dani's piano lesson and then join them at Efrain's for Mexican food.

"And they won't say anything about the Old World, right?" Sashi asked me worriedly as we pulled away. She looked tired, and I realized that healing Simon and me must have taken something out of her.

"They can't talk about what they don't know," I assured her. "No one in my family knows about magic. Grace is just having a playdate."

"Oh." Sashi gave me a surprised look. "I guess I just assumed, with you being a boundary witch and all . . ."

I shook my head. "My sister and I were adopted."

"Ah." Sashi smoothed down her pants, seeming to relax a little. "Great, then. And sorry if I'm being a pest . . . Grace and I haven't spent much time apart. She says I'm overprotective."

"My mother was the same way," I said with a grin. "Take it from a former overprotected daughter: there are worse things for mothers to be."

Sashi returned the smile. "Did you eventually grow out of it, then? Your mother was able to let go?"

"Not exactly," I admitted, thinking of how much my own mother still worried about me, especially now that Sam was gone. "But when I joined the army, she kind of learned to do it long distance."

Her smile faded, and I figured we were both thinking of her attempt to heal me that morning. "Listen," I began, "thank you for what you did for me, back at the hotel."

"That's my job," she said, shrugging it off.

"Healing the scar tissue, that was your job. But building me a blanket fort and letting me crash in your hotel room, that was above and beyond."

I glanced over and saw that Sashi was smiling again. "Grace used to have anxiety attacks when she was smaller. Blankets and pillows made her feel safe. At any rate, you're quite welcome." She looked out the window for a moment, admiring the mountains again. "Where exactly are we going?"

I told her, and to my surprise the thaumaturge witch paled. "Lex . . . I don't know if I can do that."

"Because we're farther from Boulder, and the extra boost it gives your magic?"

"Not just that, I have a . . . history." Her voice was almost a whisper. "With them."

"You said you healed them before."

Sashi nodded. "A very long time ago. Grace's father . . . well, let's just say werewolves are the reason I'm raising her alone."

Shit. *Are you sure about this, Sam?* She'd told me to get over my hatred of werewolves, but how could I when everywhere I turned, they were ruining lives—Sashi's, the Pellars', even my own family's?

But I trusted Sam. If she said werewolves were more than psychotic killers, I had to believe her. After all, Keller believed more or less the same thing about me, and I was more than what he saw in me. A lot more.

Now I just had to convince Sashi of that. "You work for Maven, right?" I said abruptly. "I mean, she's paying your bill, so your loyalties are with her?"

Sashi nodded. "She spoke to the accountant who handles my billing," she said uncomfortably, as though afraid I was about to strong-arm her. "My instructions were to help you with whatever you need."

I was a little surprised that Maven had given me that much leeway, but then, this had been my idea in the first place. I pressed on, "So if I told you something, you wouldn't necessarily feel obligated to report it back to the witch clan?"

She looked surprised at the suggestion. "No, of course not. I wasn't raised in a clan system, Lex. I have no loyalty to the Pellars or any other witch family."

"Okay, then." I took a deep breath. "Look, I need your help to prevent a war."

I told her all of it, beginning with what I understood of the were-wolf war. That explanation alone filled up all the time in between our brief stops at a hardware store and a butcher, plus a run out to my cabin. Sashi waited in the car while I let out the dogs, grabbed my homemade ghillie suit, and changed my clothes—I could only fight evil so long without a bra.

By the time we were finally on our way north I had moved on to the sandworm, the vampire uprising, the werewolf attacks, and the meeting with Nellie Evans, which fascinated Sashi. It took almost the entire rest of the drive north.

"Ley lines," Sashi marveled after I finished. "I've heard the term, but I had no idea they actually existed. I thought it was just a silly form of misdirection, like the idea that vampires can't stand holy relics."

"Yeah, well, apparently they're real, and whatever has awakened this particular fragment has stirred up enough magic to essentially force the werewolves to break their promise," I told her. "And if I don't do something, now, *today*, Maven is gonna learn who caused all of this and quite possibly declare war. She'll practically be obliged to attack, if she wants to appear strong enough to hold the state. I have to find the witch who did it and stop him or her before Maven does." I made a face. "Believe me, I have no love for the werewolves, either, but I can't think of any other way to do this."

Sashi absorbed my words quietly for a moment. "I've just . . . I want to help you, but I've seen them get violent before, Lex. And I know you're strong, but these people . . ."

So, probably not a good time to tell her how Sam had died, then. "I brought my silver bullets," I offered.

Her face was still bleak. "That's assuming you get a shot. The werewolves are beyond normal strength . . . normal weapons."

"I know," I said grimly. "But just this once, I'm counting on that."

Chapter 33

Sashi eventually agreed to the plan, even though she was obviously worried about it. I'd been prepared to offer her a bonus, out of my own pocket if necessary, but she didn't even hint that she wanted more money. She seemed to understand I was doing my best to help, and I respected her for that.

We made it up to the wolf preserve around four. The daily feeding tour had already started, which meant one of the staff members was out leading the tour, leaving two more inside. Since Sashi had the phobia about wolves, her job would be to go inside and chat with the employees, making sure they stayed away from the windows. "Don't worry," she said, still looking a little unnerved, but determined. "If I can have a chat with my patients while I heal them, I can certainly manage this."

She dropped me off at the entrance gate and proceeded into the visitors' center on her own. At this elevation, twilight was already starting to fall, and the thick patches of trees made it appear even darker than it was. I was hoping that the fading light and the ghillie suit would conceal me from the guests on the tour, who would have to look through the darkened pens, the trees, and the wolves to spot me.

I remembered the way to Tobias's enclosure, and crept there after I was sure the tour group had already moved past that area. A couple of his neighbors trotted over and growled suspiciously at me, but I threw a couple of extra chunks of shoulder roast at them, and they ignored me to eat the goodies. I had half a vial of doggie painkillers in my pocket from my dog Chip's last surgery, but I was hoping I wouldn't have to use them. I'd be guessing at a dosage, and I didn't actually want to hurt any of the wolves.

At Tobias's pen, there was no sign of the dark wolf, but I was short on time, so I just lifted the massive bolt cutters I'd bought and began cutting the chain links on the outer fence. The snap of each piece of metal sounded so loud to my ears—too loud. The tour was only a couple hundred feet away, and I figured they'd think the first one or two snaps were just twigs breaking, but any more than that was liable to get me in trouble. I paused, not sure what to do.

Before I could decide, my eyes caught movement in the dim light, and I looked up in time to see Tobias creeping toward the interior fence, the back of his dusty brown fur standing up with hostility. When he saw me, his ears flicked back and forth uncertainly. He came right up to the fence, bared his teeth, then dropped his lip, whining and pacing back a few feet as he tried to figure out why I had returned. "Tobias," I whispered, "I need to talk to you. Please shake your fur if you understand what I'm saying."

The brown wolf hesitated for a moment, then stiffened his legs and shook himself hard. I sighed in relief. I'd been half afraid that he would be too far gone, after spending so much time fighting the call of the ley line vestige. Tobias sat down and watched me warily. "Okay," I said. "Listen: I know why the moon lines have been calling you, and I think I can help. In return, I need you to help me stop a war between all the Old World factions. But I've got to break you out of here first."

He gave me a baleful look, giving no indication that he either understood or cared. Crap. I hadn't considered the possibility that Tobias simply wouldn't give a shit. "You remember what it was like when Trask was in charge?" I asked him.

That got his attention. The big wolf bared his canines and growled at me. "I know," I said. "I've been to my own war. But if I don't do something, if *we* don't do something, that's gonna happen again. People are going to die, and some of them will be werewolves."

The wolf looked from me to the bolt cutters. Then the fences. Finally he chuffed unhappily and trotted to the opposite end of his pen, near where the tour group was still circling. Where I certainly couldn't follow.

For a moment I thought that was it—Tobias had refused, and even if I snapped the whole fence apart, I couldn't exactly go in there and drag him out. It would blow his cover, for one thing, and he'd have no choice but to attack me, which meant I'd have no choice but to shoot him.

Then Tobias began howling, which prompted the other wolves to join the chorus. It drew the attention of the tour group members—and made a heck of a racket. Grinning, I lifted the bolt cutters again and quickly snapped off a big circular chunk of fence, large enough to accommodate even a wolf of Tobias's size. I darted through the opening, scrambled the few feet to the interior fence, and repeated the process as quickly as I could. Tobias must have heard or sensed my progress, because he kept the howls going until I was finished. A moment later the howls petered off and Tobias returned. I pulled the chunk of fencing free, he carefully stepped through it, and just like that, we took off for the road.

I texted Sashi to let her know we were ready, and Tobias and I crouched in a ditch while we waited. Between the falling darkness, his brown fur, and my ghillie suit, we really were damned-near invisible. Sashi arrived a moment later, and I opened the back door for Tobias to climb into the vehicle. He was enormous, but the trusty old Subaru had a big backseat, and I was used to hauling canines around. Tobias got busy sniffing the cushions with great enthusiasm. I could see Sashi gripping the wheel tighter when the enormous wolf moved around the seat, but he ignored her, and after a few minutes her shoulders dropped away from her ears.

I directed her to the same secluded spot where I'd pulled over on my last trip. Tobias hopped out and trotted into the woods, while I set out a cheap pair of men's sweat pants, a T-shirt, and a hoodie from the hardware store. They hadn't sold any shoes, and I didn't know his size anyway, so he'd have to go barefoot for now. Then I climbed back into the passenger seat next to Sashi and started stripping off the ghillie suit. I was wearing regular street clothes underneath.

Sashi eyed me. "You're very good at this werewolf jailbreak business," she remarked.

I gave her a wry smile. "Thanks. If Maven fires me for this, maybe I can go pro."

We waited. Five minutes slipped by, and then ten. I texted Cara to check on Grace, and learned that the girl was in the process of eating her weight in Mexican food and was a happy camper. More time passed, and soon the sun dipped below the tree line and disappeared entirely. I started to worry. Maven and Quinn had said the werewolves needed a week to recover in between changes, but how did that work when the werewolf in question spent most of his time in wolf form? Did he still need as much time to recover, and if so, could he get, like, stuck between forms? I hadn't thought of that, either.

Thirty minutes after we'd stopped, I saw movement in the woods, and a moment later Tobias was fumbling with the door to the backseat. He finally got it open and slouched in. Sashi and I twisted around to face him.

"Hope you're happy," he muttered. "Stuck now. Stuck on man side."

"Forever?" I asked Tobias.

He shrugged. "Week. Two." He looked at Sashi and tilted his head. "Don't know this smell."

"Tobias, this is Sashi," I introduced. "She's a witch." He nodded his head, and Sashi gave him a little wave. "We need you to help us find the other werewolves," I said to him. He immediately began to glower at me, and I rushed to add, "No, they're not in any trouble, I promise. But we need their help."

"To prevent war," he said clearly.

That sounded so lucid, I had to work to keep the surprise off my face. "Yes. Can you tell me more about the other werewolves? The name of the alpha, for example?"

He gave me a blank look. "Mary-Cammie-Ryan-Matt-Alex-Jamie," he said.

"Right. Which one of them is the alpha?" I asked. He just shrugged at me. "Do you know any of their last names?" Now he tilted his head in confusion, like last names were some weird, useless human detail like male nipples. "How about what they look like?"

"People," he said promptly. "Wolves, sometimes."

This wasn't getting us anywhere. I looked at Sashi, and she nodded. "Listen, Tobias," I began again, "Sashi has some experience with healing. She's going to try to help you with your . . . um . . ."

"Help clear your head," Sashi volunteered. She still looked a bit shaky, but seemed to be controlling it okay. "Is it okay if I come back there and sit by you?"

Tobias looked a little dubious, but he nodded. Sashi climbed out of the front and got in the backseat by him. I watched him closely, ready to grab the sidearm out of the glove compartment where I'd stashed it, but he only looked at her with mild curiosity.

"I'm going to touch your arm," she said gently. Tobias allowed her to put both her hands on his wrist. He and I watched silently as Sashi closed her eyes, frowning. Her face was concentrated, like she was listening to something, and her brow furrowed even more. Finally her eyes opened. "It's not working."

"What?" Tobias asked.

"My job is to help people by healing their bodies," she explained to him. "Sometimes their minds, too. I can't usually use my magic on other Old World creatures, but I was able to help Lex earlier today, so we thought maybe I'd be able to help you, too."

"Don't need help," Tobias said mournfully. "Need wolf. Food. Den." He shuddered. "Hate man side."

Sashi and I exchanged a look. "We need to be closer to Boulder," I said.

She nodded. "If the ley line is really what's responsible for the boost in magic, I need to be closer to it."

"Moon lines!" Tobias said, bouncing excitedly in his seat. "Go to moon lines!"

I scooted over and started the car. "I guess it's unanimous."

I started south on the highway. At Tobias's request, we went through a Good Times drive-thru in Fort Collins, and he happily munched on French fries and frozen custard and enough burgers to turn my stomach. The food seemed to put him in better spirits, and he listened contentedly as Sashi and I made harmless small talk about the resorts in Vegas.

When we were almost to Longmont, not far from the Pellar farm, I pulled over so Sashi could try again. She repeated the procedure, resting her hands on Tobias's wrist. She closed her eyes, concentrating hard, and this time Tobias's eyes went blank and distant, like he was listening to a song only he could hear. This went on for a while. I'd turned on the car's interior lights, and I watched in fascination as he suddenly squeezed his eyes shut too. When he opened them, tears ran down his cheeks, into his cheap sweatshirt. "Oh," he whispered. "Oh." Sashi opened her eyes and released his arm, and the werewolf popped open his door, bolting into the night.

Sashi and I exchanged a look, and both of us reached for our door handles. Only I grabbed the gun first. I had no idea what to expect, and although I trusted Sam, I couldn't exactly predict the behavior of a werewolf who had been nuts ten minutes ago.

He hadn't moved across the headlights, so both Sashi and I ran around the back of the car. "Tobias!" I yelled, scared that he'd taken off running. But then I made out a figure, illuminated red from my taillights: the werewolf was on his knees a dozen feet away from the car, digging his fingers into the ground and taking huge, ragged breaths. I held back, holding the revolver in both hands, but Sashi went right over and kneeled beside him, touching his shoulder with one hand. "Tobias, are you okay?" she asked. I quietly took a few steps to the right so she wasn't in my line of fire. Just in case.

"You did that?" he asked, meeting her eyes. "You untangled the knots?"

Sashi nodded, and the werewolf abruptly lunged toward her. I had the weapon pointed at him before I realized that he was hugging her, not attacking. He lifted her to her feet and swung her around in a circle, effortlessly. "Thank you, thank you," he cried. "It's like I just woke up after years of sleepwalking. I . . . oh, God, I can't believe it doesn't hurt anymore."

He set her down, still hugging her tight, his face glowing with gratitude. I saw Sashi pat his back, her eyes uncertain. She looked exhausted. A few tears had run down her cheeks too, and I realized that my own eyes had filled.

I didn't want to intrude on his moment of peace, but we were running out of time. "Tobias," I began. "I'm sorry, but we're short on time. I don't know if you remember my question, but I need your help finding the other werewolves, the ones who used to be in your pack. Do you remember their names any better now?"

He nodded, his face tilted up toward me. "But if you want, we can just go see them."

I winced. Maven was going to call me any minute to demand

an update. "I'm not sure we've got enough time to drive back to Wyoming," I told him.

He tilted his head in confusion. "We don't have to," he said. "I can smell them. They're just a few miles that way." He raised his arm, one index finger extended to point southwest.

Right toward Boulder.

Chapter 34

I'd guessed right. The werewolves had already infiltrated Boulder in human form, which wasn't surprising—from what Nellie had said, the whole town was pretty irresistible to all things supernatural right now—but it did complicate the situation. Or rather, it complicated the degree to which I was disobeying Maven. I'd planned to take Tobias with me to talk to her, figuring that although I'd further broken her covenant with the witches by bringing a werewolf into the state, she'd let it slide because it was one guy, who she already knew about, who used to be crazy.

While I was still deciding what to do, Maven called my cell phone. My time was up. I held a finger up to my lips, and both Sashi and Tobias nodded their understanding. "Hello, Maven," I said into the phone.

"Hello. Update, please."

"I was just on my way to debrief in person," I lied. "I'll be there in fifteen minutes."

A pause. "That's acceptable." She hung up.

I breathed a sigh of relief and looked at Sashi and Tobias. "Okay, guys, we gotta change the plan a little."

I dropped both of them off in front of the Boulderado, which wasn't far from Magic Beans. Sashi had been even more helpful than I could have hoped, and the next part was going to be dangerous, so she was going back to the hotel to meet Grace as she returned from dinner. The thaumaturge witch had promised to be on standby, though, in case anyone was injured. I had a scary feeling we might end up needing her.

Meanwhile, Tobias would collect as many of the other werewolves as he could find and call me. He didn't really understand the concept of a prepaid cell phone, but he said he'd just stop into a business and ask to make a local call to my cell. If I didn't answer and/or Maven had flipped out and vowed to kill all the werewolves in Boulder, Tobias would tell them to run as far and fast as they could.

To my surprise, Magic Beans was open that night, and business was thriving. It was hard to believe that life went on outside of the threat posed by the ley lines, but I supposed even Maven couldn't keep the place closed too many nights in a row without causing suspicion. Ryan greeted me at the counter. "Hey," I said. "Working late tonight?"

He smiled. "Just a bit. Go on back to the office; Maven is expecting you."

I went in the big concrete-floored room—completely clean of blood now—but I didn't quite make it to the office door. My attention was drawn by a handful of people who were standing idly around the room. One of them was a college-aged girl sitting on the floor with her back against the wall, squinting up at the back door as if someone had just burst through it, but there was no one there. On the far side of the room was an older woman with a shaved head and a strained expression. She had her hands out like she was pleading for something, but there was no one in front of her. And the third was a homeless guy huddled in the corner nearest me. He had his eyes closed, but something about him set off a red flag in my mind. It wasn't like Maven to let a homeless guy hang out in the coffee shop.

Then I realized that he didn't smell. Not at all.

"Um, Maven?" I called in a shaky voice.

She came to the door of the office and gazed at me for a long moment, reading my face. "I take it the thaumaturge witch was useful, then," she said mildly.

"They're . . . you have *ghosts* in your place?"

She sighed. "Wherever vampires go, we tend to leave remnants."

"That's horrible," I said without thinking.

"These aren't spirits or souls, Lex," she said, her voice harder. "They're not *gjenganger*, either. None of these deaths were violent or horrific enough to leave that big of a psychic imprint."

"What *are* they then?"

She shrugged. "Think of them sort of like . . . a fingerprint left on a wall. They are a tiny, nonsentient impression of what once happened. You'll get used to seeing them wherever you go."

I didn't like that . . . but I had been warned, hadn't I? Sashi had tried to tell me that seeing ghosts everywhere was undesirable at best, but I'd been too focused on my goals to really consider it. Now there was no one to blame but myself.

Well, for seeing the ghosts. But the fact remained that the vampires had killed people in this very room, and now I'd be reminded of that every time I walked in. Then something else occurred to me. "Why isn't Itachi here?" I asked. "Or . . . what was his name, Benton? They both died here. Violently."

"Vampires can't leave ghosts of any kind," she said shortly. "Please come into the office so we can chat." Turning on her heel, she headed back into the office.

I swallowed hard, tearing my eyes away from the remnants, and followed her.

I sat down at the chair in front of her desk. Maven looked so small behind the massive desk, not much bigger than Dani, and I had to remind myself that she was a centuries-old vampire who could snap me in half before my eyes managed to process that she had left her chair. "Where's Quinn?" I asked. The two of us needed to have a serious talk, which he would not in any way enjoy.

"Driving your new friend Clara over to John Wheaton's house so she can keep an eye on the baby. I know things have been . . . difficult in Boulder lately, but I haven't forgotten my promise to protect Charlie. He'll be back soon."

"Thank you," I said, meaning it.

She waved it off. "So. How was Nellie?" she said, the hint of a smile on her lips. "Does she still hold a grudge against me?"

"Oh, yeah. Big-time grudge." I described the decrepit brothel and Nellie's excitement about seeing me, then explained what she'd said about the "vestige" being stirred up.

"Ley lines," Maven said when I was finished. "I should have remembered that. I've heard the theory, of course, but I've also heard about phrenology and osmosis and the idea that witches float rather than drown. It never occurred to me that ley lines were actually real." Her eyes went distant for a moment, as if considering other alternatives, but she shook her head. "I can't think of a single other viable explanation for what's going on, though. One incident, certainly, but not everything we've been seeing." She cocked an eyebrow at me. "If she still holds a grudge, I can't imagine Nellie was very forthcoming with information," she remarked. "How did you get her to talk to you?"

"I promised her a TV."

Maven threw her head back and laughed, a tinkling, musical sound that went on for a couple of minutes and completely flummoxed me. Had I ever heard her laugh, aside from a dry sarcastic chuckle? I didn't think so. "I'm sorry," she said when she recovered. "I was expecting something like 'I threatened her' or maybe some grand manipulation you accomplished. But it's just like Nellie to toss aside the greatest grievance of her afterlife in exchange for worldly goods." The smile dropped off her face. "But she didn't know how this vestige was activated?"

I squirmed in my seat. I'd known this moment was coming, of course, and there was really only one course of action that would keep Charlie safe. But that didn't make it comfortable. "According to Nellie, it's not boundary magic, so she's not familiar with the workings," I said reluctantly. "But it has to have been a witch, and it has to have been in Boulder."

"A witch." Maven's eyes went distant again, and I could see her coming to the same conclusion that I'd needed a lot more time to reach: every witch in Colorado had a motive to activate the vestige, thereby nullifying Maven's covenant with the witches. "I see the problem," Maven mused, and although her expression was placid, her voice was as cold as I'd ever heard it. If this were a movie, she'd have snapped a pencil in her hand or dramatically dropped a glass of water, but instead the room was suddenly filled with the weight of malevolent silence. Her power, the terrible strength that seemed to call to me like a beacon, suddenly felt oppressive. I swallowed, wishing I could raise a hand to brace myself against the wall. I didn't want to show weakness. Not when I needed her to trust me.

"We can still fix this," I said quietly.

"How." It was a statement, not a question, because she didn't think I had a chance in hell of fixing it.

I took a breath. "We find out who did it and punish her. Or him," I amended. "Just that individual. Not the whole clan."

Her eyes finally focused in on me. "You presume a lot—that you can find this person without conflict, that they'll submit to punishment, and that Hazel will allow it."

"Yes, ma'am. But it's better than the alternative." Very softly, praying she wouldn't kill me, I added, "No one can afford a war right now."

Her eyes narrowed, and I got the feeling her anger over the ley lines had just been briefly usurped by anger at me. I stood my ground, because I was right, and she needed to hear it. If she rallied the troops to fight both the witches and werewolves right now, how many of them would even come?

She must have been thinking the same thing, because without conceding anything she said, "What exactly are you proposing?"

"That we prioritize. The Unktehila is probably gonna hunt tonight, which means someone else will die. So tonight we stop the Unktehila, and tomorrow night we confront Hazel about the witches. Quietly. Respectfully."

I couldn't read Maven's expression, but she didn't immediately jump out of her chair and rip open my rib cage, so, bonus. "The Unktehila *is* the more immediate threat," she allowed. "I've seen the papers. The public is already very interested in the man-eating animal that seems to be stalking the city. Any further deaths—and any further evidence—will only cause a greater panic, bringing more attention to all of us."

"Yes, ma'am. I do kind of have a plan for dealing with the Unktehila," I began. "But you're not going to like it."

Her eyebrows quirked, as if to say *Then why would you even mention it?*

Before I could lose my nerve, I told her about Tobias and the werewolves in Boulder, and what I thought we should do with them. "You want to send a pack of stirred-up werewolves to kill this Unktehila, and you want to do it in my name?" she said disbelievingly.

"Um, yeah. And in exchange, they get a pardon for invading the state . . . and for what happened to Allegra and Travis." Her eyes narrowed. "It wasn't their fault, Maven," I added quickly. "Much as I'd love to condemn every werewolf in the country, something else was pulling their strings."

"Did you already promise this?"

"No, but I did float the possibility that you would go for it," I admitted.

She gave me a sour look. "This is *not* how things are done, Lex. I didn't hire you to make your own decisions and follow your own agenda. Our agreement is that you will do things during the day that I can't do myself."

"But that's exactly what I'm doing—things you can't," I argued. "You need a peaceful resolution here, and you can't broker it yourself.

Peace doesn't work when the most powerful player tries to force it on everyone else."

She just continued to stare at me with hooded eyes, like a falcon watching its prey. I tried to soften my voice. "Maven, you said that you didn't want to lead, but you felt responsible. Well, I feel responsible too. I took an oath to defend you, to take care of your interests, and that's exactly what I'm trying to do—even if I couldn't get permission first."

Maven continued to study me for a long, silent moment. I stared back at her, knowing full well that it was something most people couldn't do. My witchblood protected me from being pressed by vampires. I could even have tried to press her into doing what *I* wanted, but I chose life instead. Maven was way out of my league.

"When this is over," she said finally, "you and I are going to have a conversation about the difference between taking initiative and taking control."

I bowed my head, trying to look contrite. "Fine. And in the meantime?"

She sighed. "We kill the Unktehila tonight, *then* deal with the problem of which witch is responsible for activating the vestige."

"Yes, ma'am."

"Tell me more about this plan."

I nodded. "The way I see it, we have two options: We either cut off the sandworm's power supply, which means putting the ley line back to . . . sleep, or whatever, or we figure out where it's going to appear again and kill it the old-fashioned way." I smiled, not in a nice way. "Since we don't know enough about ley line magic, I'd like to pursue the second option, with Simon and Lily's help."

She leaned back in her chair and gave me a measured look. "Are you sure about those two? They're Pellars, after all."

I considered it for a moment. Was I? Was I absolutely certain they weren't involved in waking up the vestige, even tangentially?

"Yeah," I told her. "I'm sure. If I go after the Unktehila tonight, they will help me. Not because of any pact, but because they're my friends."

She sat there for a long moment. Her eyes were pointed more or less in my direction, but they'd gone distant. Finally she said, "Very well, then, Lieutenant. You'll be in charge of killing the Unktehila. I'll send Quinn and Opal with you. They've both proven themselves, and can help keep the situation under wraps. Quinn will also get you whatever he has in the armory that might help." She stood up. "Wait here a moment."

Maven rose and left the room, disappearing into the coffee shop. She was gone for a while, but I didn't dare so much as walk to the office door and peek out. I just waited, feeling like I'd just survived three rounds in the ring with a tiger.

Finally, Maven returned to the office and held out her hand to me. In it was a small container, like an oversized jewelry box.

"What is this?" I asked, accepting the box. She nodded at me to open it. Inside was a large, clear marble made of some kind of translucent glass or stone, just slightly too big for my thumb and forefinger to fit around it. I raised my hand to touch it, but stopped when my fingers were a couple of centimeters away. I decided I didn't want to touch anything that seemed to give off its own heat.

I looked back at Maven. "What is it?" I asked again.

"As you know, thirteen years ago I made a bargain with Hazel and the other witch clans, in exchange for stopping Trask," Maven said. "They had to give up their apex magic, which included the dangerous spells used for combat. This deal would last for a period of two decades." There was a weary smile on her face. "I never dreamed I would want to stay in Colorado longer than that."

None of that explained the bauble in my hand. I raised my eyebrows, lifting the box a little. "I couldn't just rely on a promise," she explained. "I knew of a witch in Portugal who could channel clan magic into crystal or glass, imprisoning it. She went to every clan in the state and siphoned strength into one of these." She nodded toward the bauble. "The one you're now holding contains all of Clan Pellar's apex magic."

"Oh," I said in a small voice.

"If this Unktehila is really as powerful as you say, you're going to need every weapon at your disposal," Maven said soberly. "It would be irresponsible of me to send Simon to fight it without his full power." She nodded at the glass container. "Break it, and Clan Pellar has its apex magic back."

I sucked in a sharp breath. "Are you sure you want to do that? Considering one of the witches in Clan Pellar is responsible for activating the vestige?"

Maven quirked a smile. "That's the least of my concerns at the moment. Besides, no one else in the clan will know the apex magic has been returned to them. Why would you try a spell you didn't think you could use?"

I nodded, thinking that through. I would have to tell Simon that he could use his powerful magic again, and if I was wrong about him being trustworthy . . . he could tell everyone else, and they would have some serious juice to turn against Maven's interests.

It was a test.

Maven saw that line of thought travel over my face. "Yes," she said softly, "a lot depends on the choices you will make tonight." She glanced at the bauble again. "I leave it up to you."

I stared into the depths of the tiny crystal ball for a long moment, feeling its weight in my hand. Then I tightened my grip on the box and jerked it up, tossing the ball in a shimmering arc toward the ground.

Chapter 35

The ball shattered on the concrete office floor with a hard crack, exactly the same sound as when Sam had once dropped my mother's favorite snow globe. Instead of exploding into fragments, however, the bauble instantly dissolved into a violet-hued vapor that rose a few inches off the ground and vanished into the air. A moment later there was no sign that the crystal sphere had ever existed.

"Is that it?" I asked Maven, raising my eyes to her.

"That's it," she assured me. "Good hunting."

I got up and went out into the big auditorium room, doing my best to ignore the three ghosts that still glowed in there. Simon sounded breathless and hyper when he answered his phone. "Lex!" he cried. "I think I figured it out." Lily's voice said something in the background, and he amended, "Okay, *we* figured it out."

"Figured what out?"

"Where the Unktehila's gonna strike! Where are you? We're at the BioLounge, and I can show you everything on the map, but Lily forgot her phone and I think my battery's—"

His voice cut off abruptly, and I checked my own phone. Crap. I didn't have time for science show-and-tell, but I wasn't far from campus, and I'd need to pick them up anyway. I jammed the phone into my pocket and headed out to the car.

I had been taking magic lessons from Simon and Lily since I'd learned about being a witch. Most of the time, one of them came over and we did it at the cabin, but once or twice I'd stopped to pick up Simon after his office hours, which he held in the BioLounge, a sort of makeshift coffee shop that had been set up in the basement of the Henderson Building, underneath the University of Colorado Museum of Natural History. There was kitschy, eclectic furniture; small, interesting exhibits; and best of all, free tea and coffee. It didn't surprise me to learn that many of the associate professors preferred to hold their office hours there, rather than in cramped, windowless offices.

Tobias finally called while I was parking rather illegally outside the Henderson Building. I told him to meet me there with whatever pack members he'd found. Maven would be calling Quinn to tell him about my plan, so I texted him to meet us at the BioLounge too. Might as well get everyone in the same place.

The museum was closed by now, but Lily was waiting by the door to let me in. "Hey," she said as she pushed the heavy door open for me. "Simon ran upstairs to get his phone charger . . . and you should probably know he's had at least three espressos."

I grinned. "I sort of got that impression on the phone."

"Also," Lily began, gesturing for me to follow her down the stairs, "I think I probably owe you an apology."

I blanched for a second. "Oh, because of your sisters?" I waved it off. "I get it. They were just being protective."

She snorted. "I would have used the words 'stuck-up bitches,' but sure. Protective. Anyway, if I had known they were planning to treat you that way, I never would have invited you. Sybil in particular was in rare form."

My rush down the stairs slowed a little. Sybil. Now, if there was any witch with an especially strong motive for wanting Maven deposed and the clan freed from their agreement, it was Sybil. She wasn't her mother's golden child, and she was dying to prove her worth. Wouldn't dissolving Maven's pact with the witches be a great way to do just that?

But I couldn't exactly come out and say that to Lily. "How far do you think she would go?" I asked instead.

Lily paused and turned around to look at me. "To keep us apart? Well, if you get any breakup notes from me, you should probably take a close look at the handwriting." When I didn't laugh, Lily stepped toward me. "Lex? What is it?"

Shit. I really didn't want to accuse her sister of anything, certainly not without serious proof. I backpedaled. "Listen, there's something I need to tell you and Simon. I think we've figured out what's been causing all this unrest in the Old World lately."

"What—" Lily began, but her brother's voice cut her off.

"Lex!" I turned to see Simon bounding down the last few stairs. He was practically bouncing from caffeine and excitement, and it was pretty spectacular to see him this way after weeks of him looking like death. And I would know. "Come on, I gotta show you this." He grabbed my hand and tugged me down the short hallway into the BioLounge, which was deserted except for tables. Most of the tables were covered in large maps and other documents. He pulled me toward the biggest one.

"Simon—" I began, but I was immediately shushed.

"Just hang on a second; this took me all day." We stopped at a large piece of butcher paper with a hand-drawn sketch, sort of like a family tree. The top of the tree was a little stick figure wearing what appeared to be a wizard hat. Below him, in three branches, were crude drawings of a vampire, a witch, and a werewolf. I particularly enjoyed the vampire fangs, which were the approximate size and shape of walrus tusks.

"Why do I feel like *you* drew this and not Lily?" I wondered aloud.

"Shush. See, we already know that witches evolved from the same source as vampires and werewolves," Simon began, pushing his glasses higher on his nose. "Magical conduits. And they were created when magic bonded with one evolutionary strain of the human species."

I nodded. "Yeah, I got that back in Magic 101."

"Magic *also* bonded with certain metals, and a specific family of plants called Solanaceae, commonly known as nightshades." He pointed toward a second sketch lower on the same sheet, of a variety of plant species. "But that's as much as we know about how magic works, right?"

Without waiting for my answer, he reached for the stack of papers on an adjoining table and pulled out a chart that could have been subtitled "Biological Classification for Dummies." It was a colorful pyramid explaining the order of classification I dimly remembered from high school science class: life, domain, kingdom, phylum, class, order, etc., all the way down to species. "This is the chart I show my students," Simon continued. "You can trace every single organism, including Old World organisms, up this pyramid, and the sandworm—the Unktehila—is no different."

"Simon . . . no offense, but can you maybe move on to the point? We've got a time deficit here."

"Yeah, Lex has something important to tell us," Lily said pointedly.

Simon ignored her. "Almost there. I've been examining the scale we found, and comparing both the scale and the physical character-istics of the Unktehila with all known species. I've traced it back to the order Squamata, which is a group of scaled reptiles that includes the green anaconda and the Komodo dragon. When the order began to speciate into multiple families, magic stepped in and formed a new species. The Unktehila."

"Okay . . ." I spotted the scale on a nearby table and picked it up cautiously. I flexed it back and forth for a moment, which was like trying to bend a piece of iron. Damn, that thing was thick. And apparently bulletproof. How the hell were we going to kill this thing?

"Considering its preferred climate and the fact that it's venomous," Simon went on, "I'd guess that it belongs to the same superfamily as the Gila monster and the Komodo: Varanoidea. It simply didn't evolve legs, because it didn't need them."

"That's really interesting, Simon," I said patiently, "but what does it tell us about finding and killing the fucker?"

Shooting me a *be patient* look, Simon held up a finger. "One: I'm guessing it may be semiaquatic, much like the anaconda. Some of the legends about this thing are likely connected to the Native American myth of the water panther. Two: It's definitely cold-blooded, so it's going to seek out heat, which speeds its digestion. The fact that it was able to digest a meal as large as a human body as quickly as it did suggests that it *has* a heat source, which is probably where it goes during the day. It can't be too far from Boulder, though, because whatever's going on with the city's magic seems to be limited to this area. Otherwise there's no reason for the thing to come here at all."

He looked at me expectantly, and I realized I was supposed to put this together. Now it was my turn to roll my eyes. "Stop being such a frickin' teacher, Simon, and tell me . . ." My voice trailed off as all the clues registered. None of that would have meant much in most American states, but this was Colorado.

"The hot springs," I breathed. "It's going to the hot springs."

Simon, the jerk, actually applauded, like I was the star pupil in a class of one. "Exactly."

"But which one? There must be half a dozen in Colorado, and none of them are very close to Boulder."

"There are more than that, actually, but that's not the point. Here, look." He pulled me to another table, where he'd laid out a simple road map of Colorado, the kind you can get at rest stops and gas stations. Simon had circled about thirty different towns with a black marker. "These are the locations of all the natural hot springs near us," he announced.

Two of the black circles were fairly close to Boulder, and the rest all a distance away. I bent forward to examine the map. "So it could be either Idaho Springs or Steamboat Springs, assuming this thing doesn't need to follow the road system."

"Oh, yeah. Where this thing's going, it doesn't need roads," Simon intoned, a manic grin on his face.

"Simon . . ."

"I mentioned the espresso, right?" Lily said dryly.

Simon hurried to add, "But listen, remember the first gastric pellet?"

"The homeless guy?"

He shook his head. "Technically, that was the *second*. The first gastric pellet was the one found in Golden Gate Canyon Park." He pointed at it on the map, and I leaned forward to see.

The park was almost exactly halfway between Boulder and Idaho Springs.

Chapter 36

"This is great, Simon," I said appreciatively. I was finally starting to put together a real plan on how best to use my resources, which was so much better than floundering around putting out fires. "But it's not enough to know the general area; this thing moves too fast. We need a way to lure it out, to herd it to a specific spot where we can kill it," I concluded. "Any ideas?"

Simon hesitated for a long moment, then said reluctantly, "If my theory is right, the Unktehila's sight isn't the greatest, especially in dim lighting. It mostly gets around underground by sensing tremors. Above ground, in an area with a natural heat source, it must mostly rely on smell to hunt." He gestured toward his mouth. "It does the forked tongue thing, like snakes and the Komodo."

I remembered seeing it flick its tongue out, just before it identified me as a boundary witch. It could smell my blood, like vampires. "Okay, so?"

He took a deep breath, pushed it out. "So, it can probably distinguish the smells of individual people, and it does have a particular hatred of me, so . . ."

Lily squeaked as we both understood his meaning. "You want to use yourself as bait?" I said incredulously, at the same time as Lily said, "Si, you *can't*!"

"Remember what it called me?" Simon said, looking at me.

"'Wounded disruptor.' It doesn't know that I've been healed. We can *use* that."

Lily looked back and forth between our faces. "You guys can't be serious. Si, I know you've staked a couple of vampires, but that does *not* make you a badass."

"It's the best way we can draw this thing in, Lil," he told his sister. "Don't worry. Lex will have my back."

Tears rushed to my eyes, and I had to blink rapidly to keep them from falling. Even after what had happened with Atwood, Simon was still willing to count on me in a fight. I just nodded.

"Mom's gonna be pissed," Lily muttered.

"Don't tell her, then."

That reminded me of why I'd really come here, what I had to tell them—not to mention our very serious time crunch: Quinn and the werewolves would arrive any minute. "Guys, there's something else you need to know." As briefly as I could, I told them about werewolves coming into the state and killing Travis and Allegra. Both Pellars were shocked, and more than a little angry.

"There are *werewolves* in Colorado and you're just now getting around to telling us?" Simon snapped.

"Yes," I said simply. "I believed there was an external force pushing them to break the arrangement with Maven, and I wanted to figure out what that was before I told the clan that the pact had been broken."

Simon and Lily exchanged a look, as if telepathically deciding who would respond to that. "We're a lot more than 'the clan,' Lex. We're your friends," Lily pointed out. "You should have said something."

I looked back and forth between the Pellar siblings, who wore identical determined, wounded expressions. "Your father—" I began.

"Was killed by a werewolf? So what?" Simon snapped back. "That was over thirteen years ago, and the werewolf who did it is dead. Assuming that all werewolves are evil because one of them killed our dad is shortsighted at best. It's also bigoted, hateful, and prejudiced."

I felt shame creep over my cheeks. I had assumed Simon and Lily wouldn't be able to set aside their prejudices and see the werewolves as a diverse group, because that was how *I'd* reacted, until Sam had set me straight.

"You're right, and I'm sorry," I told them. "But there's another reason I didn't know if I could tell you. It turns out that the person behind all of this has to be a witch." I told them about ley lines and the recently activated vestige in Boulder. Simon's face got excited as I explained the theory that witches power the lines, but his excitement faded to fear as he absorbed the implications. And then anger, as he followed that line of thought through to the logical end. "You thought it could be one of *us?*" he said, hurt and outrage written all over his features.

"Of course not, dummy," Lily said, giving him a little backhand on his arm. She looked to me for confirmation. "Right?"

I nodded. "Right. I never suspected either of you. Duh. But according to Maven's expert, the witch who did this has to be a member of Clan Pellar. And as far as I know, half the clan is related to you in one way or another." I spread my hands helplessly.

"Oh," Lily said in a small voice.

Simon looked dazed, like I'd suddenly slapped him across the face. They both did. "You're . . . sure?" he said.

"Pretty sure."

The Pellars exchanged a horrified look. "Sybil?" Lily whispered.

"That's what I was thinking too," Simon answered, his voice heavy. "But let's be honest, it could be Mom. Or any of the other witches who've complained about the pact over the last dozen years."

"You're right." Lily looked at me. "Um . . . what do we do?"

"What did *Maven* tell you to do?" Simon added, looking nervous.

"She said we get the Unktehila first, tonight, and *then* worry about who's behind it," I said firmly. "The Unktehila has to take priority."

Simon nodded, looking resolved, but his sister was biting her lower lip nervously. "Si," Lily began, "we gotta tell Mom. She needs to know if one of us is . . . is . . ."

"And if Mom's actually the one who's doing it?" Simon asked her. "What then? We unite against Lex? Or turn the witch over to Maven?"

Lily shot me an uncomfortable look, like this was junior high and I'd just caught them gossiping. "No, but . . ."

Simon shook his head forcefully. "Lex is right. We need to focus on getting this done, and then worry about finding the witch who did it." He squared his shoulders and looked at me. "What do you need from us?"

"I want to put together two teams: one to go to Idaho Springs, and a smaller force to go back to Chautauqua just in case the Unktehila goes back there after all," I explained. "You'll come with me."

"I'm coming too," Lily insisted. "I can help."

Simon snorted. "Now who thinks she's a badass?"

"I need you to stay in Boulder and keep an eye on the clan," I told her. "There's a chance that whatever witch did this will try to interfere with us, or that he or she will stir up even more trouble for Maven and your mom while we're busy dealing with the sandworm. If that happens, I can't promise Maven will have any mercy."

"So you want me to just, what, hang out with a bunch of people who may be responsible for all this without saying anything?" She gave me an indignant look.

"Yes. You can't let anyone know what we're doing, or what's happening with the ley lines."

Lily looked from me to her brother and heaved out a resigned sigh. "Fine. I can do that."

I'm not a touchy-feely person, but Lily is, so I reached over and squeezed her arm. Her answering smile told me she recognized the significance of the gesture. I turned back to Simon, but my attention was caught by something shining in a glass case behind him. "Simon? What's in that exhibit?" I pointed to the display.

"Hmm?" He turned around to see. "Oh, I love this—these are all things that were confiscated by the TSA in the last ten years. That's a two-handed Danish sword from the fifteenth century. There's a complete zebra hide over there too, and—" Turning around again, Simon saw my face and began to glare at me. "Oh, no. No way."

"Simon . . ."

"I can't just take something out of an *exhibit*, Lex!" he said, exasperated.

"You saw the Unktehila, Simon," I wheedled. "The shotgun did nothing against those scales; they're like chain mail. The werewolves have teeth and claws. I need a blade."

"I could lose my job for stealing something from the museum! Let's just go to the hardware store and get a machete or something."

I shook my head. "No time. We gotta move on this if we're gonna make it to the hot springs in time. And besides . . . it's *so* pretty."

It really was. The sword was nearly five feet long, thin and sharp, with a diamond cross section to give it rigidity for thrusts. It was even resting on top of a beautiful leather scabbard with a strap attached halfway down.

Simon still looked unhappy, but he was considering it now, so I added, "Come on, you can have it back in the morning before anyone even knows it was gone. It's a victimless crime, Simon, and it could save lives."

He sighed. "Fine. I'll go get the keys."

My phone buzzed: a text from Quinn to tell me that he was outside with the werewolves. "They're here," I said to the Pellar siblings. "Give me a minute to make sure everyone is friendly."

Outside, Quinn was standing on the sidewalk leading up to the museum, looking as nonchalant as one can while one is flanked by seven restless-looking werewolves. They were currently human, but every last one of them looked as twitchy as a junkie in a jail cell. Tobias was toward the back, still wearing the clothes I'd grabbed for him at the hardware store. He seemed as jumpy as the rest, but he also couldn't stop smiling, and I figured he was still feeling pretty great about having his sanity back.

Behind him were two females, one a brunette coed in a mini-dress, the other a very trim, perfectly made-up Caucasian woman with a buzz cut and a beige sweater set. The three men who ringed them were of varying ages and heights, but they were all dressed in old sweats and ratty T-shirts—clothes you wouldn't mind losing or destroying. I approved.

The man at Quinn's elbow stepped forward. He strode up to me, getting a little too far into my personal space, and held out his hand. "Ryan Dunn," he said abruptly. "Alpha of the Cheyenne pack. The other wolves near the state border fled after the full moon."

I nodded and shook his hand, sizing him up. Dunn was well over six feet tall and barrel-shaped, and if I had to guess, I'd say one of his parents was Hispanic—his skin was light, but he had dark eyes and black hair that was beginning to gray at the temples. He appeared to be in his late forties or early fifties, and had the habit of leaning forward to tower over people.

"I'm Lex," I said. "Quinn and I represent Maven's wishes this evening."

Dunn nodded. "Tobias filled me in on the situation with the ley lines. It's a relief to know we weren't all losing our minds at the same time." I smiled in response, but Dunn didn't, and from the look on the werewolves' faces, I realized it hadn't been intended as a joke. They really had thought they might be going insane, as a group.

"Did Quinn explain the deal to you?" I asked.

There was some shifting of weight and eyes amongst the were-wolves, and Tobias gave a little cringe. "You want us to fight a monster tonight," Dunn said, in the same gruff tone, "and in return,

Maven will overlook our . . . transgressions with the vamp chick in Julesburg."

I glanced over his shoulder at Quinn. His jaw had tightened, and his eyes had gone to their *special* blank place. If I hadn't known him so well, I might not have caught that he was furious.

"Only thing is," Dunn continued, "I can't see as how killing that girl was our fault. We couldn't stay away from Colorado owing to the line, and she came after us that night. We were just defending ourselves." Out of the corner of my eye, I saw the other werewolves nodding their agreement. "I see no cause for us to risk our very lives fighting this thing, to pay for an act we had no control over."

I could have pointed out that life isn't fair and Maven could crush him like a Japanese beetle, but this guy didn't seem like the type who'd back down from threats. He didn't seem like the type to back down, period, and I didn't have time to get Maven over here to kick his ass. I studied him, his upright posture, his arms held out in front of him—one hand holding the opposite wrist. "You were military," I said.

Looking a little surprised, Dunn gave me a grudging nod. "Marines," he grunted. "Until '99, when I was mauled down in Panama." He glared a little. "No medical benefits for shapeshifters. Barely a pension."

I nodded. "Not very fair," I remarked.

"Damn right, it wasn't."

"But if you were a Marine, you understand unfair." Behind him, Tobias tilted his head. They were all listening. "You also understand the greater good. We don't have the time to debate your responsibility for Allegra's death right now, not when this thing is about to take, eat, and kill another human being. In that order."

I paused to let that sink in for a moment, but Dunn's face didn't change, so I went on, "I could try to convince you to help us for that reason alone, because we have a better chance of saving a life tonight than the human cops do. But I don't know you, and I don't know if a moral appeal will do any good. So how about this: After we kill this thing, you can go present your case to Maven. If you can convince her that you deserve it, she'll owe you a favor."

Quinn shot me a look that suggested I was playing with fire, but I ignored it. The only thing I'd really promised was a face-to-face meeting with Maven, and honestly, it couldn't be *that* big a deal.

Meanwhile, Dunn's interest was piqued. "A favor?"

I waved one hand in a circle. "A boon, a marker, a chit. The most powerful vampire in the state, maybe the world, will owe you one."

Dunn considered that for a moment. "And if Maven disagrees? If she turns me down flat?"

"Then *I'll* owe you the favor."

The alpha regarded me with renewed interest. There was some more murmuring and shifting behind Dunn, but the big alpha's eyes were on me. I held his gaze, keeping my chin level: not challenging, not defying, but sure as hell not backing down. "You say it's already killed two?" he said at last.

"That we know of. It ate everything but the clothes and some of the larger bones," I said flatly.

Dunn sighed and held out his hand again. "You've got a deal."

Chapter 37

Lily had texted Hazel and learned that some of the clan members were hanging out at the farmhouse to play cards. She took off after hugging Simon and me and warning us both to be careful. She even told Quinn not to "get more dead." I was still pissed at him, but I had to smile at that.

The campus was still crowded enough that we were exposed, so the rest of us retreated back down to the BioLounge. Quinn carried in three massive duffel bags that were straining at the seams—weapons, I figured.

When everyone was inside, I laid out the plan: Simon and I would take Dunn and two other werewolves with us to the hot springs, while the remaining four went to Chautauqua with the second team. Dunn could choose the wolves himself; he knew his people best. I put Quinn in charge of leading the Chautauqua team. I made a point of not looking at him when I explained that part.

Quinn had laid each of his bags out on a table like some sort of demented sample sale, and as soon as I'd delivered instructions, everyone started to drift over to the weapon stash to check out the gear. Quinn came over and pulled me aside.

"The second team?" he said in a low voice. "I should be with you guys at the hot springs."

"I need a vampire at Chautauqua in case the creature shows up there instead," I said coolly. "You're the best at pressing people"—my voice *may* have gotten a little edgy there—"so it makes sense to put you in the highly populated area."

"But you'll need a vampire in Idaho Springs, too," he argued. "If the hot springs are still open, there will be people there. You'll need to be able to press any human witnesses."

"That's why Opal is picking us up in the Jeep."

"So send *her* to Chautauqua and take me along," Quinn argued.

I lifted my chin. "I'm taking Opal. That's final."

He searched my face. "You know, don't you? About Bryant."

"Damn right I do."

He sighed, but his body language was unapologetic. "I was just trying to protect you. To *help* you."

"Against my wishes?" I countered. "Despite what I specifically told you I wanted for myself? Pressing minds isn't a game, Quinn, and it isn't a get-out-of-jail-free card, either."

"Don't be a child." His face was impassive again, and my fingers clenched into fists. I glanced over at the group of werewolves, who were very pointedly studying the weapons Quinn had brought, the exhibits around us, the ceiling tiles. Oh yeah, they could hear us. Only Simon truly seemed oblivious. He had regular human hearing.

I turned back to Quinn and crossed my arms. "Maven put me in charge of tonight. I'm putting *you* in charge of the second team, because I don't trust you to do what I tell you, rather than what you think is best for me." Quinn's eyes narrowed, but I continued before he could say anything else. "If you have a problem with my plan, you can take it up with Maven. But know that any delay might mean we don't make it there in time to stop this thing." I lifted my eyebrows in a challenge, and his face went blank. But he didn't say anything, and after a moment I turned away from him and walked carefully over to Simon. I did not stomp or flounce away, because I am a grown-ass woman.

I watched as Simon worriedly perused a selection of handguns on one of the tables. The wolves didn't really need to bring weapons—they *were* weapons—but the vampires and I would be bringing some of Quinn's arsenal to the hot springs. There was a really good chance I'd have to fire them, and I didn't want the police to be able to connect the ballistics to my personal weapons. But Simon was terrible with firearms, and he knew it. Luckily, I could help with that.

"So, Simon," I said casually, pretending to study a Sig Sauer on the table. "I broke a little glass ball today at Magic Beans."

He went still for a moment, then it clicked, and he looked at me with wide eyes. "Does that mean . . ."

I nodded, grinning. "Yes!" Simon crowed, and he threw his arms around me. I barely had time to set down the Glock I'd been examining before he hugged me so hard he knocked me backward into a table. I laughed, even though Dunn and the other wolves gave me baffled, *what kind of operation is she running here* looks.

"Sorry, sorry!" Simon exclaimed, but he was doing an honest-to-God happy dance. "This is awesome—oh! I gotta get ready, I—" he looked around for a moment and then dug keys out of his pocket. "One of my dad's journals is up in my office, I can probably figure out a couple of hexes on the way."

I left him to his planning and continued to gather my own weapons. I already had the sword, but I picked up an Israeli .50 caliber Desert Eagle. It was so big that I would be forced to use both hands to shoot it, but it was the only .50 caliber sidearm there that was magazine-fed, and I wanted the extra shots. The Desert Eagle was too big for my Wild West quick-draw holster, so I also grabbed a thigh holster and moved on down Quinn's little blood-shed buffet. I didn't see anything else I thought would help against the Unktehila—until I got to the very last table. "No way," I said disbelievingly.

How in the hell would Quinn get access to fragmentation grenades?

Chapter 38

Quinn and I didn't speak much as the teams split up. He was still angry with my decision, but I was stubborn, and we parted with just a brief nod and a "Good hunting."

My team made a quick stop at a grocery store for steaks, and half an hour later we were crowded into Maven's tricked-out Jeep, headed for Idaho Springs: one vampire, two witches, and three werewolves. It sounded like the beginning of a Halloween picture book.

Dunn had said he was bringing his best two fighters, who turned out to be a lean Australian guy with bleached hair named Jamie, and the brunette woman in the minidress, six-inch heels, and enough makeup to decorate a room full of showgirls. Her name was Mary, and although she looked like she'd just walked out of a Eurotrash nightclub, she was all sharp cheekbones and scary curved fingernails, like the talons of a bird. A predator. Quinn had included a sharpening kit in his weapons cache, and Mary had offered to sharpen the Danish sword for me during the car ride. I didn't hear a word from her the whole way.

I let Opal drive, which freed Simon to study his spells and me to work on the plan for finding the Unktehila. She would also be able to press the minds of any cop who stopped us, although I told her to try to stay within ten miles of the speed limit.

I closed my eyes and reviewed what little I knew about where we were going. Like so many small cities in Colorado, Idaho Springs had sprung to life during the Gold Rush, and then managed to stay alive after the gold dried up by throwing itself headlong into tourism. That in itself wouldn't have kept the town afloat, but luckily Idaho Springs had another big draw: the natural hot springs. The first public bathhouse in town was established during the Civil War, and had been available to the public in some form or another ever since, though it had been through any number of names, owners, and structures.

I'd actually been to the current incarnation, Grizzly Springs and Spa, back in high school, when my aunt Violet had decided to take Sam and me for an educational spa day at the springs. Violet was a high school science teacher, and had spent much of the drive down explaining how the springs worked: underground pockets of magma heated up the water, which then rose, just like any other type of heat, until it reached the surface and bubbled out of the ground. Because the water absorbs minerals from the surrounding rocks, people had long since decided the waters are good for our health.

I wasn't a scientist, but I felt instinctively that Simon was right about us finding the Unktehila there—it was just too perfect a den for an underground snake monster—but the problem was going to be figuring out where the thing would surface. The springs consisted of a big public pool, private baths, a room for "mudding," and geothermal caves, which seemed like perfect entry points for a creature that traveled underground. We needed to draw it out of its den, but our intel was so limited, there was bound to be a certain amount of improvisation. I didn't like that.

It was a little after nine when we arrived in Idaho Springs. The highway dumped us out at the mouth of downtown, which was really just one long street filled with trinket shops and ice cream parlors. I directed Opal to go left toward the hot springs. There was an empty lot just before Grizzly, with a couple of picnic tables and a small abandoned building—probably an old trailhead or some kind of failed tourism business. We parked there, and the werewolves got out of the car and began to strip. Jamie and Dunn left their boxers on out of modesty, but Mary unzipped the minidress with one long arm and shimmied out of it, revealing nothing but smooth, pale skin underneath. She stepped out of the heels and swooped them up gracefully, stalking over to me in her bare feet. "Here," she said, piling the shoes and dress in my arms. She was completely nude, but couldn't be less bothered by it. "Take care of these. They're Christian Louboutin."

The three of them disappeared behind the empty building to shift into wolf form. Opal and Simon waited in the car—Simon still frantically scanning the old journal he'd brought, and Opal drinking a little blood bag she'd brought "as a pre-fight snack." I was too nervous to sit still, so after securing Mary's stuff in the vampire hidey-hole, I got back out and paced in front of the Jeep.

We weren't in Boulder anymore, so who knew how long it would take the werewolves to shift. I berated myself for not having them shift before we'd left. Timewise, we were within the Unktehila's killing window now, and it would be horrible if we found out it was eating someone fifty yards down the road while we were standing around doing nothing. The groaning and whimpering I heard from behind the building made me feel an unexpected jab of sympathy for the werewolves.

Needing something to do to distract myself, I got the sword out of the Jeep and swung it around a bit, getting used to the unusual weight. As long as it was, the whole sword weighed maybe four or five pounds. I knew a little bit about swords: I had taken foil fencing classes in high school, and my cousin Anna had once talked me into doing an eight-week course of tai chi with wooden practice swords. This Danish sword was a completely different animal, though. It was two-handed fighting, with a double-edged blade, and I spent some time attacking one of the picnic tables to get used to the feel of it. I'd seen a demonstration of Western martial arts a few years earlier, and I did my best to mimic those movements. Lucky for me, it didn't have to be pretty or perfect. It just had to be effective.

After ten minutes of me warming up, the three wolves came loping silently around the corner. I was bowled over again by their size: the smallest of the three looked like it could eat Cody and Chip for breakfast. That one was black, with amber-green eyes—Mary. I was able to differentiate the two males by their eye color: the wolf with the white undercoat and black overcoat had sky-blue irises like Australian Jamie, and the biggest wolf, who looked entirely gray on top but white on his legs and tail, had Dunn's dark eyes. They stood there staring expectantly at me, and I led them over to the hood of the Jeep, where I'd left out the steaks. Dunn had told me earlier that each change cost them energy, and it would be hard on everyone if they tried to cooperate with us on empty stomachs. I took out the raw meat and tossed one to each of them, being careful to keep my fingers well away from those teeth.

While they ate, Simon got out of the Jeep and came over to us. "I found it," he said, pleased. "The concealment spell."

"Well, thank God," I said. "I didn't think we could pass all of them off as guide dogs. Is it ready?"

He nodded, looking confident, but his hands clutched the old journal like he was afraid one of us might try to snatch it away. I gestured for him to go ahead.

When they had all finished eating, Simon asked the wolves to sit down, and one by one he approached each of them, carefully touched their heads, and murmured a few words. And that was it. I was watching closely, but I didn't see any difference. I waited until he'd gone all the way down the line before saying, "Um, Simon? Are you sure this worked?"

He smiled, maybe a tiny bit smug. "Oh, it worked. You're just seeing through it because of your witchblood. Magic doesn't work against magic, remember?"

Oh. Duh. I'd gotten so used to things being twisted around in Boulder that I'd forgotten one of the cardinal rules of the Old World. "Besides," he added, "you're expecting to see werewolves. Humans expect to see a guide dog, or a rolling suitcase, or even a small child, so that's what they'll see."

"Okay," I said, deciding to trust him. When he was finished, he came over to me and put the same spell on my extremely conspicuous sword and the Desert Eagle attached to my thigh. "It'll wear off by dawn," he advised, "but that sword will be back in the exhibit way before that anyway, right?" He blinked pointedly.

I nodded and stepped up to address the werewolves, who looked at me with a keen intelligence and maybe a little menace. They looked ready for a fight. It should have felt silly to stand there talking to giant wolves who sat in a patient line, but surprisingly it didn't. It was like talking to soldiers.

"Go into that building," I said slowly, pointing to the spa, which was just across an empty lot, "and look for any sign of this thing." I held out the scale, walking down the line so they could all sniff it. "When you find it, howl." I was about to add that they should come running if they heard one of the others howling, but realized it was pointless. They'd do that no matter what I said. They were a pack.

In response to my nod, the wolves turned and slunk into the shadows, always keeping an eye on their leader. If you really watched them, it was obvious that they were staying a little behind and below him, allowing him to be the biggest. Dunn, for his part, had a relaxed loping swagger that was entirely absent from his human form.

"What about us?" Simon asked, indicating himself and Opal. "Where do you want us?"

I turned to face them. "Opal, you're in charge of crowd control. Go around to any humans who look confused or suspicious, like they might be on to the wolves, and press them. If this all goes to hell, head to the main entrance and press people who are leaving."

She nodded and took a few quick steps backward, disappearing into the shadows.

I turned to Simon. "You and I are going to take a self-guided tour. If you're going to be the bait, we gotta get your smell out there for the Unktehila to find. Come on."

I led the way toward the spa entrance. Inside, there was an old-fashioned wooden reception desk staffed by a bored, overweight teenager. Her eyes were glued to a cell phone in front of her.

"We're closing in forty-five minutes," she said blandly as she heard us approach.

"That's okay," Simon said brightly. "We just wanted to get in a quick soak before bedtime." The teenager looked up. I could see the interest spark in her face as she took in Simon's lean frame and boyish glasses. I was betting the surfer-hippie look worked wonders on his students, too. Simon paid the spa admission fee, chatting amiably with the girl, and then we ducked down a flight of steps into his-and-her dressing rooms. I had no intention of trying to fight the Unktehila in a bathing suit, but we'd agreed to abandon our shoes and roll up our pants, as though we were just there to soak our feet. I figured bare feet would probably fare better on slippery pool tiles than sneakers would anyway.

I had no bars at all down here, so I left my cell phone in the locker too. Like it or not, I figured there was a pretty good chance I was about to get wet.

Simon and I met up outside, where we took a quick walk down to the geothermal caves. It was divided into specific areas by gender, so I checked the women's room and Simon checked the men's. From the title, you'd expected something natural and imposing, but the women's "geothermal cave" was just a big concrete room with low lighting and what looked like a sunken Jacuzzi. It was empty, this late on a weeknight, and I found myself shying away from the murky-looking water. I've never been afraid of clear pools or bathtubs, but I can't stand being in water that isn't transparent. In my defense, though, I did drown in some when I was a teenager.

The adjacent women's mud room was equally unimpressive: it was nearly identical to the geothermal caves, but with an enormous bowl of soupy mud in the middle instead of a hot tub. Two women in their sixties had rubbed some of the mud on their nude bodies and were stretched out on deck chairs chatting. They looked up in confusion when I stepped in wearing my T-shirt and rolled-up jeans—thank God they couldn't see the sword or the massive sidearm—but I just made a show of looking around like I was there to meet someone and ducked back out. To my relief, Simon was just stepping out of the men's area. "Any signs of it?" I asked him. He shook his head. "But remind me to really start working out when I hit fifty," he said gravely.

"Well, let's—"

But I was interrupted by a chorus of terrified voices. It wasn't the wolves, though.

It was screaming.

Chapter 39

Simon and I raced back the way we'd come, following the sounds of shouting people and snarling wolves. It was obviously coming from the main pool of mineral water, about half the size of an Olympic pool. We had to dodge eight or ten fleeing bathers: adults in various stages of undress who pounded past us, hollering about monsters. I hoped Opal was in place at the main entrance, or we were going to have a lot of cops to deal with in the very near future.

Just before a sign marked "Pool Entrance," I spotted a familiar red box on the wall and reached over to pull the fire alarm. It only heightened the pandemonium, but hopefully it would keep any would-be Samaritans from running in to offer their help. With Simon on my heels I burst through the door, grabbing at my weapons as I took in the scene. We were in one long room fringed by rainforest-type plants, with a pool in the middle and a glass skylight taking up half the ceiling. They were going for a tropical theme, which was augmented by the enormous snake monster thrashing around in the water, its attention focused on the far left corner of the pool so its back was to me. The mineral water was tinged with red, and I realized it had already eaten or crushed at least one victim. There was an Unktehila-sized hole in the cheap plaster wall. I didn't know if it had smelled Simon or the werewolves, but something had caused it to burst in looking for a fight.

I had the sword in hand by then, raised to the ceiling like a medieval lance, but I hesitated for a moment, gaping. The lighting was dim in here—probably the spa owners depended mostly on the skylight—but for the first time I was able to take in the sight of the Unktehila's entire body at once. The full size of it was jolting: It was the length of at least one and a half school buses, and it had expanded to its full diameter of about six feet. My brain kept telling me that this was wrong, this was fake, that animals didn't come that big. But the evidence was right there in front of me, paralyzingly scary and *fast*.

I crept forward to see what was making the Unktehila so angry, and realized that all the hissing and thrashing was directed at the werewolves, who were pacing the edges of the pool, in front of the potted trees. No, wait, it wasn't just looking at the wolves—the pool was cordoned off into a little hot tub, and the creature had cornered someone in there. I couldn't see the person behind the leviathan, but he or she must have still been alive, judging by the Unktehila's desperation to get to them.

The wolves were trying to draw away the monster, and it was sort of working—every time it got close to its prey, one of them darted forward, snapping with jaws or swiping with claws, and the Unktehila would get distracted. It kept spitting venom at the wolves, but they were fast enough to jerk away in time to avoid its attacks. I saw Mary, the black wolf, dancing back a little, and I realized she'd stepped in some of the venom. The wolves only had seconds before the floor would be too covered in it for them to move.

The creature's back was still to me, so this was my only shot at a surprise attack. I wanted to aim at its head—the throat, the eyes, something vital—but it would take me too long to run all the way around the pool.

Fuck. I was going to have to get into that water, wasn't I?

Simon was already moving around the pool's edge, so I shouted after him, "Get the people out!" He waved a hand in acknowledgment.

Without letting myself think too much about it, I leaped into the four-foot-deep water, aiming my body straight for the Unktehila's clubbed tail, which was only about as thick as my waist. The tail was thrashing around, but only a little, since most of the upper body was focused on attack right now, not movement. With a bellow, I swung the sword back over my left shoulder like a golfer and sent it straight into the tail, chopping at an angle to go under the scales. I was just trying to get its attention, but to my surprise, I actually severed a chunk off the tail.

Damn, that Mary sure could sharpen a sword.

The Unktehila raised its upper body straight up and screamed, a terrifyingly high-pitched sound that actually sent spiderweb cracks spurting across the glass skylight. The wolves cringed with pain—the sound had to be excruciating to their sensitive ears—and I began backing away from the red blood that was blossoming in the pink water all around me. I tried sloshing toward the side of the pool, but by then the Unktehila had finished its scream and turned on me, its cobra hood unfurling. Behind it, I saw Simon helping someone out of the hot tub—a twenty-something woman holding a toddler. I set my jaw.

You, the Unktehila roared into my head. It hadn't bothered to adjust the frequency for our comfort, and I almost doubled over from the sensation of knives cutting at the inside of my skull. In my peripheral vision I saw that Simon, the woman, and the wailing toddler all did the same, but the wolves didn't seem affected. You dare interfere with me again? I will—

With effort, I straightened up, bending against the wave of pain. "Yeah, yeah," I shouted, waving the sword in front of the thing's ugly snout. "You should have stayed asleep, asshole."

Hissing with rage, the Unktehila reared back, the telltale sign that it was about to spit venom my way. I threw up my free arm in useless defense, ducking, but to my surprise, nothing happened. I looked back at the Unktehila, and we realized at the same time that it was all out of venom. Without giving it time to react, I dove forward, just managing to throw myself out of the pool before a heavy coil of muscle snapped toward me hard enough to break bones. It cracked tiles on the side of the pool instead, sending a splash of bloody mineral water over me. Gross.

On the other side of the pool, Simon had gotten the woman and her child through the emergency exit door. He turned back and threw out his arms, shouting something at the Unktehila. A short lance of fire, like a firework just before it explodes, arced through the air at the sandworm. It struck the creature in the back of the head, not really doing any damage, but it gave me an idea. As the Unktehila turned to deal with the new threat, I skidded along the side of the pool until I was just above the nearest coil, and plunged my sword into the thing's flesh at a sideways angle, wrenching it to dig under the scales. The werewolves must have had the same idea as me, because they split up and began racing toward the coils nearest to them, so that the five of us were spread more or less evenly around the pool.

Seeing this, the Unktehila roared in anger and then screamed something into our minds, not even trying to communicate now, just to destroy. Simon and I both dropped to our knees in agony—I managed to keep my grip on the sword, but it was a near thing—and the Unktehila turned to attack Simon, the most vulnerable of all of us. Before it could get there, though, I saw the nearest werewolf—Jamie—dash forward and actually climb *onto* a wide chunk of the Unktehila's tail. He gouged his two front paws into and beside the scales like he was digging a hole for a bone, and the sandworm shrieked in pain and rage, turning to snap its tremendous jaws at Jamie. I wanted to applaud as the werewolf leaped nimbly off the coil and raced away, skidding a little on the wet surface.

It can't get into the werewolves' minds, I realized, as my ability to think was slowly returned to me. They were on a different frequency.

We resumed the strategy, keeping more or less evenly spaced around the creature and attacking one at a time. When the Unktehila turned on one of us, another would attack all the harder, dividing its attention. This continued for what seemed like twenty minutes but was probably only two, until the Unktehila was worked up into a froth of wild animal rage and pain. At one point, it tried the psychic scream again to break Simon and me, but all three werewolves attacked with such viciousness that the piercing agony only lasted a few seconds this time.

We were winning—but suddenly the Unktehila seemed to realize our goal: to wear it out, or even bleed it out. Simon and one of the wolves were standing between it and the plaster hole it'd created, but its head abruptly ducked underwater with tremendous force. The ground seemed to shift suddenly as the creature rammed into the floor of the pool.

"It's going for the tunnels!" Simon hollered. "It's running!"

"Like hell!" I yelled back. We were never going to have a better chance than this, and we sure as hell couldn't release it into the wild when it was worked into a frenzy.

The Unktehila reared back and shot forward a second time, butting the sharp point of its beak against the same spot on the bottom of the pool, and this time something gave way. I *couldn't* let it escape. So I did the only thing I could do.

I jumped back into the water. Like an idiot.

I pulled the Desert Eagle out of the thigh holster and looked frantically for something to shoot. I did not want a .50-caliber bullet ricocheting off those scales. The water was already beginning to drain from the pool, and the Unktehila was starting to worm his way out through the small hole, contracting to fit it. Inspired, I looked around the bloody water until I located the thrashing stump of its tail—the open wound still oozing blood. Torn red muscle and a little bit of bone could *just* be seen as the stump flicked in and out of the water. I sloshed over as close as I could, watching the movement, and took my shot, putting two of the enormous bullets right into that muscle.

I'd braced with both arms, but the recoil still knocked me backward. If I hadn't been in the water, I would have fallen on my ass. As it was, I staggered back hard enough for my head to go under, and I came up spitting bloody mineral water, trying not to panic because it had gone up my nose. When I wiped at my eyes, I saw that the Unktehila had instinctively wrenched itself backward again, and it was *livid*. The shots must have traveled quite a way into its muscle, maybe hitting some spine, because as it thrashed around, the last twelve feet of its tail no longer seemed to be functioning. Unable to move forward smoothly, it wheeled on me.

I thought we'd worked it into a frenzy before, but the look it gave me, on its not-very-expressive face, was terrifying. It had flipped the tail out of my reach, so I looked around for the sword, only to realize I'd left it on the side of the pool.

Simon and the werewolves chose that exact moment to leap into the water, or what was left of it—the pool was draining through the Unktehila's escape hole—and each of them went for the nearest section of giant snake, attacking however they could. But instead of getting distracted again, the Unktehila continued its beeline straight for me.

I raised the Desert Eagle and took aim for its eye, but the thing was moving too fast, and my next bullet bounced off the scales and buried itself harmlessly in the bottom of the pool. Shit. The head flowed toward me, looking gleeful, but as it pulled back its fangs and prepared to strike there was a shout and a motion to my left, and the Unktehila suddenly staggered back as if it had been cuffed in the side of the head by an invisible force. We both turned to see Simon holding up one hand and shouting at it.

I was looking at the back of the Unktehila's head, but I could see its cobra hood spread again as it rounded on Simon. I made you a promise, interloper. I intend to keep it.

I turned my back for long enough to slog over to my sword, but by the time I'd scooped it up and turned around, the Unktehila was already in motion, seeming to propel itself straight up into the air. It hit the already-cracked skylight, which shattered into a million tiny knives of falling glass. Simon and I both covered our faces as the shards sprinkled down on us, and by the time I lowered my arms and saw the Unktehila's head coming back down, it was about three seconds too late to get a warning out of my mouth.

The Unktehila crashed back down, jaws wide open, mouth unhinged, and its head landed right on top of the exact spot where Simon had been standing.

Chapter 40

"No!" I screamed. The Unktehila's voice was back in my head again, and it was laughing.

Nonononono not again. This could not happen again. I would not allow it.

I lurched sideways toward the nearest coil, which was more or less the halfway point of the thing's body. I drove the sword in at an angle and then down. The Unktehila began to struggle, trying to move away from me with Simon still gripped in its mouth, but I held fast to the handle of the sword and used it to lever my weight up, allowing me to swing up onto the thing's back. I reached into my right pants pocket and pulled out the single grenade I'd grabbed, using my left hand, still holding the sword, to fumble off the safety clip. I pulled the pin and, with the grenade clutched in my other hand, wrenched the sword sideways. Then I jerked it out, letting it crash to the ground, and thrust the grenade into the hole I'd made, pushing it in as deep as my arm could reach. It was so far beyond disgusting that I didn't let my brain think about what my arm was touching.

Bracing myself against the creature's back, I pulled my arm out as far as I could and I threw myself to one side, tumbling into a clumsy roll on the pool tiles. I managed to drag myself to my knees and crawl away, my hands bloody and spiky with splinters of broken glass from the skylight.

Then the grenade exploded.

I was clubbed down by a chunk of meat the size of a basketball. I landed on my face, my cheek pressed against the cool tile, as more chunks of steaming flesh rained down around me. Between the Desert Eagle and the grenade, my hearing was shot, and it seemed like a really good idea to just lie there in the broken glass for a little while. Yes, that was a great idea.

But Simon.

Could Simon still be alive?

I somehow managed to get my bleeding palms underneath me, and then laboriously pushed my body up until my feet were under me, remembering what they were supposed to do. I managed to force my hand around the sword and tottered toward the head of the Unktehila, which had been cut in half by the explosion. Even an immortal snake monster can't survive a full-on bisection. When I reached the head, I saw that the Unktehila's mouth had fallen open slightly. I dragged my body forward and put the tip of the sword in, levering it open farther. Then I repeated the process. Farther. Farther. When I had the two jaws about three feet apart, I saw a bare foot. I clutched at it, trying to pull, but my hands were slippery with blood and pool water and there was no give at all. And Simon hadn't had any air in there. I tried to stand, hoping it would give me more leverage, but my feet slipped on glass and blood. My limbs gave out and when I went down this time, I knew I couldn't drag myself back up. I lay there as my vision began to cloud, knowing that I had failed. I had gotten Simon killed, and I couldn't save him.

Then I saw a slender hand pick up my sword. I watched its point move down the Unktehila, about six feet from where the foot was, and then the sword was thrust in. The last thing I saw before my eyes closed was Mary, gloriously nude, reaching in to dig at the Unktehila's insides.

When I opened my eyes again, I found myself staring directly into the warm brown gaze of Sashi Brighton, who was maybe eighteen inches away from my face. She grinned widely when she realized I was looking at her. "Welcome back," she said in her crisp accent.

I blinked. I was lying on my stomach on a white cot, so why wasn't Sashi's face sideways? Then I got it: she was lying on a cot too. "You hurt?" I managed to say.

She smiled, and I recognized the weariness in her expression. She was too tired to get up. "Just wiped out. Healing isn't as easy as I make it look, you know. You had a hairline fracture in your ankle, about a dozen life-threatening cuts, shrapnel in your back and legs, and just a little bit of internal bleeding. And don't get me started on Simon."

I sat up too fast, and had to clutch the sides of my cot. It hurt, and I realized that under the light bandages I was wearing, my palms still had dozens of tiny abrasions from where I'd touched the broken glass. I was naked and the sheet that had covered me pooled at my waist, but I was too shaky to even try to cover myself. "Is he alive?" I asked Sashi.

She didn't sit up, which told me how drained she really was. "Behind you."

I turned, which hurt—there were a lot of small cuts on my arms and knees, too, but they were too shallow to even warrant a bandage—and saw him lying on the cot behind mine. His expression was peaceful, and he was breathing, but everything else was covered under a sheet.

Then I spotted a huddled figure against the wall behind him and realized where we were: the big back room at Magic Beans. Complete with ghosts. Of course. "Will he recover?" I asked without turning around.

"Yes. Although if you've ever considered getting swallowed by an enormous snake, I wouldn't recommend it. Most of his major bones were broken, and the thing did its damnedest to liquefy his insides." I turned back to the thaumaturge witch, who let out a jaw-cracking yawn. "I did as much as I could tonight and gave him a sedative to let us both rest," she continued. "I'll work on him again tomorrow."

"Grace?"

She smiled briefly. "With your cousin's family again. I hope you don't mind that I called them."

"Of course not."

Her eyes drifted closed. "They're really nice, your family. Sometimes I wish I . . ."

Her voice drifted off as exhaustion overtook her. I let her sleep.

Swinging my legs slowly over the side of the cot, I sat up and took stock of my leftover injuries. I was stiff and achy again, but aside from the dozens of small cuts on my hands, arms, and knees, I seemed to be in okay shape. My feet were still bare, but they were fine. Sashi must have healed the superficial cuts there so I could walk without pain. Smart.

Then I realized that someone must have cut off my shredded clothes, bathed me, and even washed my hair. Ordinarily I'd feel violated by this, but considering what I'd been—quite literally—soaked in at the springs, I was planning to find whoever had done it and kiss their feet in gratitude. Of course, I was also very naked now, which was less than ideal.

"Sashi brought you some clothes. They're in Maven's office."

I jumped, clutching the sheet to my chest, and twisted around to see the back exit, the one that led outdoors. Quinn stood there, leaning against the wall with his hands in his pockets.

"How—how long have you been there?" I stammered.

"Since we brought you back."

"Who's we?"

He pushed off the wall and walked over to sit down at the edge of my cot. I hugged my knees to my chest, both to make more room for him and to cover my nakedness. "Opal called me and Maven as soon as she got the last civilians out of Grizzly Springs. Maven pulled some strings to get the transport helicopter at Memorial to fly down there and bring you and Simon back."

It took me a long moment to absorb all of that. "What time is it?" I'd left my watch at a brothel in Denver.

"Three a.m. Same night," he added, after seeing my confusion.

"The werewolves?" I asked.

"They'd recovered by the time the chopper got there," he assured me. "They brought the Jeep back just a little bit ago. Dunn said it handles like a dream." He looked at Simon for a long moment. His usual impassive expression was clouded by concern. "I was worried about you guys."

"I should have let you come," I said quietly. "I was hurt, and I was being petulant. And once again I almost got Simon killed because I didn't trust you."

"I didn't give you much reason to trust me," he said matter-of-factly. "I shouldn't have pressed the police chief for you without asking." He looked away, hesitating, and I realized that he wasn't finished. "I also realize you could have pressed me to listen to you at any point, and you didn't," he said softly. "I'm sorry, Lex."

"I'm sorry too."

One side of his mouth quirked up. "Did we just have our first fight?"

I rolled my eyes. "Please visualize me hitting you with a pillow," I said tartly, "as I currently lack the strength."

He smiled, but it faded quickly. "How hurt are you?" he asked, and there was an edge to his voice that made me very nervous.

"What happened?" I said.

Quinn froze for a moment, deciding, and then said, "The trip to Chautauqua wasn't a waste. The werewolves have really good noses, and between us, and some detective work . . ."

Why was he drawing this out? "*What*, Quinn?"

"I know who activated the ley line."

Chapter 41

"Are you positive?" I asked for about the fifth time. I believed him, of course. I just didn't want it to be true.

Quinn's voice was still remarkably patient. "Yes. I'm sure. They're sure. And they have no reason to lie to me."

"Right." I swallowed hard. "Does Maven know? Where is she?"

"She knows, and she went to see Hazel first, out of respect."

I shook my head, but then a new thought occurred to me. "Lily?"

"I didn't call her. I couldn't see any reason to tell her now."

"Tell me what?"

I jumped; Quinn just looked briefly vexed. The voice came from the other side of the door that led to the rest of the coffee shop. "Could someone unlock this?" Lily called. "And maybe tell me what the hell is going on?"

"I've got to talk to Maven about soundproofing the doors," Quinn muttered, but he went over to let her in. Lily burst into the room.

"Si!" She rushed over to her brother and started wringing her hands, obviously afraid to touch him.

"He's gonna be fine," I promised her. "He was given a sedative until Sashi can finish healing him tomorrow. He's fine."

Nodding, Lily carefully ruffled her fingers through her brother's hair, then rested a hand on his shoulder. "Stupid nerd cowboy," she grumbled at him, but the worry was still written all over her face.

"What are you doing here?" Quinn asked.

"I called Simon and Lex looking for news. When neither of them answered, I figured you'd be here . . ." She looked between the two of us. "Now tell me what I'm not supposed to know."

Quinn and I exchanged a look, and then Quinn said, "The werewolves picked up a witch scent in Chautauqua, someone who'd been all over there recently, doing magic. We followed the trail back to your sister Sybil's house."

"But I just left her," Lily whispered. "She had three glasses of wine and passed out on my mom's couch."

"She'll be waking up soon," Quinn said soberly. "Maven went to talk to your mother."

"Oh *shit*!" Lily looked anguished, her fingers rising to twist into her dreadlocked hair. "I mean, she's *Sybil*, but she's still a Pellar! I never *really* thought . . ." She paced in a tight circle, then froze, her lovely face paling as she looked back at Quinn. "Is Maven going to kill my sister?"

"I honestly don't know," he said, and his voice was so frank and tired that even Lily believed him.

"I gotta go over there," she cried. "I gotta talk to them, see if I can—"

"No, you don't," Quinn ordered. "They'll figure out what they figure out. It'll only make it worse if you're there."

Lily glared at him, tears running down her face. "She's my sister, you prick!"

"I'm gonna go get dressed," I broke in. I had a feeling I was about to either drive Lily to Hazel's or physically restrain her from leaving, and I wanted to be wearing clothes when that happened. I wrapped the sheet around myself as best I could and left the two of them to their argument, closing the door to Maven's office behind me.

Sashi had brought me a spare outfit from her own suitcase, God love her. There was silk underwear, a wireless silk bra, jeans, and a long-sleeved knit T-shirt in an earthy brown. The jeans were a little tight in the thigh and the bra was a little bigger than strictly necessary, but it was close enough. My shoes, which someone had possessed the presence of mind to snatch out of the locker room at Grizzly Springs, were there too, as was my cell phone. Score. When I picked up the phone, I saw that I'd missed a text message seven minutes earlier. It was from John.

911 come over now. EMERGENCY. Don't tell ANYONE.

I stared at it. And stared at it. Then I called John's cell, but it went straight to voicemail. So I stared at the message some more. Had something happened to Charlie? It couldn't be related to Sybil; Lily had just seen her. And it couldn't have anything to do with the sandworm, obviously, since we'd killed it. What else . . . Keller? Could he have gone to John and persuaded him to lure me over? John wouldn't voluntarily set me up, but I could see Keller tricking him into setting a trap.

Even if it wasn't a trap, John wasn't answering, so there was only one way to find out. I picked up the keys to Maven's Jeep. I didn't know what she'd driven to see Hazel—maybe Quinn's car. It didn't matter.

Back in the main room, Quinn and Lily were still arguing over whether Lily should go to the farmhouse. "I have to leave," I broke in loudly.

Both of them stopped talking to stare at me. "*Now?*" Lily said incredulously.

"It's a family thing," I said apologetically. "I'm sorry, I can't say more."

The two of them shouted for me to stop, but I kept right on walking, all the way out the back door and over to the Jeep. As I turned the key in the ignition, the passenger door jerked open and Lily hopped in.

"Lily, I have—"

"To go, yeah, I get it. Wherever you're going, I'm going with you. I can't sit in there arguing with Quinn for *one more second*. He'll keep an eye on Sashi and Simon." She buckled her seat belt resolutely.

I didn't move. "You can't just invite yourself—"

"It seemed like this was urgent," Lily interrupted me again. "Or at least I'm assuming it was, if you were willing to walk out on me in the middle of a crisis. Do you really have time to argue about it?"

I sighed and put the Jeep in reverse. "No, I don't. But you're staying in the car."

"Fine. Where are we going?"

I told her.

The cul-de-sac was quiet, but I parked a few houses away anyway, and took the keys with me in case Lily had any bright ideas about driving it to the Pellar farm. She pouted at me and held up her cell phone. "Okay, okay. Call me if you need me. I'll be using produce to save the world from a zombie plague. And obsessively calling my mother over and over until she answers."

I tried to run straight inside, but John had installed a new front door since the break-in, and I didn't have the keys. So I pounded on the front door instead, and when I didn't get an immediate reply, I rang the doorbell. About twenty times. Nobody answered.

I had just stepped back, and was scanning the front windows for the best one to break, when the new door finally popped open, revealing a very sleepy-looking John. "Lex?" he said blearily. "What are you doing here?"

"You texted me," I said, panting with adrenaline. "You said '911.' So I came. Where's Charlie?"

His face morphed into utter confusion. "She's in the kitchen with Sarah. She had a bad dream, so we were going to make her some warm milk. What text?"

I stared at him for a second, puzzled. What the fuck was going on?

Without another word, I handed him my cell phone and strode past him into the kitchen. From the hallway I could hear a woman's voice cooing at my niece, and part of me relaxed a little. Was it all a misunderstanding? I hadn't known that John and his girlfriend had progressed to sleepovers, and I didn't love it, but everything sounded okay.

About two steps before I reached the kitchen, though, I realized that I recognized the voice that was humming to Charlie. I rounded the corner and saw her, wearing a pretty white nightgown, rocking back and forth with my niece draped over her shoulder. John's cell phone sat right in front of her.

I started forward, but she held up her free hand. "That's far enough. Let's keep your hands where I can see them, shall we?" I froze, and Simon and Lily's eldest sister smiled at me. "Hello, Lex."

I swallowed hard. "Hello, Morgan."

Chapter 42

"Did you just call her Morgan?" John asked, stepping into the kitchen behind me. "This is Sarah, my girlfriend."

"That's not her name," I said softly.

"Well of course it is," Morgan laughed. "Oh, I'm sorry, I see the confusion. My full name is Morgan Sarah, I just prefer to go by the latter."

"That's probably it then." John went around the kitchen island to peck her on the lips. "How's my girl?"

"She passed out again, of course," Morgan/Sarah said with false good humor. "Right when I had the pan all ready." She took a step to the right so we would both see the cast-iron saucepan full of milk on the stove.

"Of course," John said, picking up an apple from a bowl on the island and shining it on his shirt. He moved it toward his mouth to take a bite.

"John," I said in a low voice. "You need to take Charlie and step away. This woman is not who you think she is."

My brother-in-law's hands went still and he shot me a bewildered look. "Lex, what are you talking about? I saw the message on your phone, but it's just some weird fluke. Charlie is fine."

"This woman has been lying to you," I said desperately. "Please, take Charlie from her. You have to trust me."

His brow furrowed, and he opened his mouth to answer—but then the saucepan of hot milk struck him square on the back of his head.

John's eyes rolled up as he crumpled forward, smacking his forehead on the counter as he went down. "No!" I cried out, starting forward to help him. Morgan held up a warning finger, stopping me in my tracks. Charlie was stirring in her arms. The witch whispered some soothing words to her, and my niece snuggled into her neck.

My fists clenched, and for a moment the only sound in the kitchen was the drip-drip-drip of the spilled milk. At that moment I hated her worse than I'd hated any person in my entire life.

"It was you," I growled. "All this? The ley lines?"

"Calm down, Allison," Morgan said in that same soothing tone. She opened the drawer in front of her and pulled out a 9mm Sig Sauer. "I would hate to have to use this on someone."

The sight of a sidearm that close to Charlie made me go cold. *Stall for time,* I told myself. Just about the only thing I could do was stall for time and hope Lily got bored and came in, or John woke up. If he was still alive. I swallowed my pride and tried to modify my tone to sound awestruck. "How did you activate the ley line?"

Morgan snorted, hard enough to make her perfect cascade of earth-mother hair tremble. "I have you to thank for that. Really, everything that's happened is *your* fault, Allison."

"How do you figure? And stop calling me Allison."

Her eyes hardened. "Of course, I've known for a long time that I would need to be more strict than my mother: her peace-and-love hippie shit was great once upon a time, but the real world is much harsher than that now." She cuddled her head against Charlie's. "Still, I was planning to bide my time until our contract with Maven was up, but when you showed up with your *complete* lack of control and your ridiculous amount of death magic, trying to poison the clan, I had to move up my time line."

"The spells?"

She glowered at me. I'd interrupted her. "I asked around," she snapped. "There's a storage facility in San Diego where we keep the oldest spells, the stuff nobody bothers with anymore." She shrugged. "A full week buried in dusty boxes, but I had to do it. I couldn't risk you hurting someone."

"Me?!" I cried, tilting my head toward John. "I haven't hit anyone with a pan today, Morgan." Sure, I'd killed a giant snake monster, but still.

Morgan shrugged, unruffled. "Sacrifices have always needed to be made for the greater good, *Allison*."

"And is John one of those sacrifices?" I countered.

She looked down at him, like she'd genuinely forgotten he was there. "No. Just a means to an end." She bounced Charlie lightly in her arms. "I needed a contingency plan, just in case the werewolves didn't invade, or you threw a wrench in things, which of course you *have*." She sighed. "Maybe I should have shot you right away in the beginning. Saved everyone the trouble."

"How exactly do you see this going down?" I said quickly. *Keep her talking.* "You kill me, you'll go to jail."

She gave me an annoyed look. "Come on, now. Don't insult my intelligence, not when I'm holding this *cute widdle baby*," she kissed the top of Charlie's head.

I thought my own head might explode when I saw that, but I kept my mouth shut. Seeing that I wouldn't take the bait, Morgan sighed and waved the Sig at the back door. "Bad guys came in, hit John, and shot you. I managed to hide in the bathroom with the baby. End of story." She leveled the weapon at my head.

"And Charlie?" I insisted. "If I'm going to die, at least let me know what's gonna happen to my niece."

She thought for a moment, then set the Sig back down in front of her, bobbing her head in concession. "Fair enough. I'm not a *monster*. You'll be happy to know that I have no real interest in Charlie, and no intention of interfering with her upbringing. After

I shoot you, she and I will just make a quick run to the coffee shop to shoot Maven before we go to the police station." She looked down at her nightie. "Should I change first, do you think, or will this be more sympathetic?" I just stared at her. "Anyway, in a week or two I'll quietly break up with John, and Charlie will go on living her life. Unless I need her again. Of course, there are a number of vampires and witches who know of her existence now; I can't help that. Maybe John can get a security system or something." She shifted Charlie in her arms and picked up the Sig again, pointing it at my head.

"There's just one problem with that plan," said a voice just over my shoulder. "Maven isn't at the coffee shop. She's at the farmhouse accusing Sybil of all your crimes."

Lily. Behind me, she stepped forward out of the shadows, and I silently moved aside to let her in.

Instinctively, Morgan pointed the weapon at the new threat. "You're going to shoot me too, big sister?" Lily snapped. "Am I going to become another casualty in the Morgan Pellar world domination plan?" Her voice was raw with pain.

Morgan wrinkled her nose. "Really?" she said to Lily. "The farmhouse? Drat." Her lips worked a little, like she was trying to get a bad taste out of her mouth. "I had hoped she wouldn't get that far, certainly not this quickly."

"You framed Sybil," Lily said. Tears were running down her face. "You're setting her up to take a fall for you."

"All I did was ask her to do a couple of spells for me," Morgan said airily. "That ley line spell has to be renewed every night, and I have things to do. Anyway, Sybil doesn't know anything, and Maven should be able to smell that on her. I doubt she'll *kill* Sybil."

"What is *wrong* with you?" Lily whispered.

Morgan looked genuinely angry at that. "I am *trying* to take care of you," she hissed, with a little stomp of her foot. "Isn't that what you've always wanted, Lilith? For all of us to take care of you, let you be the free-spirited wild child? You want to go flouncing around teaching *yoga* and following your *passions*, well, this is what it costs." She tilted her head at me. "I'm not going to let her destroy our clan while you're off picking daisies."

"Look at what you're doing right now!" Lily cried. "What would your kids say about this? Your husband?"

Morgan rolled her eyes, but I didn't hear her response. I had a really bad idea. Like, really bad. But it was the only idea I had, so what the fuck, why not run with it? "So shoot me," I said very loudly. The Sig swerved back toward me, as confusion erupted on the faces of both Pellar sisters. "Lily can keep her mouth shut. She knows how to go along with things. I'm close enough to Charlie, it should work. *Just shoot me.*"

"Lex—" Lily cried.

"Shut up, Lily," Morgan snarled. "Okay, fine," she said to me. She thumbed the safety off the weapon. "You asked for—"

There was a blur of motion, and then Clara was there, coldcocking Morgan right on the fucking chin.

She had to slow to human speed when she got close to Charlie, but she still managed to wrench both the Sig and the baby away from Morgan as the witch tumbled to the ground.

Charlie woke up with an annoyed squall, and I rushed forward and scooped her up, hugging her to my chest. "Wek!" she cried, because my name is tough to say when you're not even two. I held out my hand, and Clara handed over the sidearm. I hit the button to release the magazine, letting it fall onto the floor.

"You couldn't have come in a bit earlier?" I said to her.

"Safety was on," she said with a shrug, and this time I heard the slight Eastern European accent. "I know guns. No danger with the safety on."

"She had Charlie!"

"You heard her," Clara contended. "No harm to baby. Baby was fine."

Lily had gone over to check on John right away, which I appreciated. "He's breathing," she reported. "But his pulse is weak. He needs to be in a hospital." She turned around to face her sister, but Morgan was already struggling to her feet. Her nose was pouring blood and she screamed in frustration. "You ruin *everything*!" she yelled at Lily. She took a step toward her little sister, and I moved backward, getting out of the way so Lily could back up.

To my surprise, though, Lily held her ground. In fact, she raised one hand and yelled something, and I saw the same saucepan that had been used to attack John go flying across the room to strike Morgan in the stomach, knocking her backward with such force that the older woman left a dent in the cupboard. Morgan's eyes went huge with surprise. "How . . ." she gasped.

Lily's smile was ice cold. "Apex magic." She reached into her jacket pocket and held up the little journal that Simon had left in the Jeep. "I'd say you should try it sometime, but I'm not sure you'll live that long."

"Bang," Charlie said happily.

Epilogue

On a cold Monday morning, a few days before Thanksgiving, I wrestled a new eighteen-inch television into the boarded-up brothel in Denver. Lily trailed behind me, holding a plastic bag with the new bunny ears.

"Hello?" I yelled after I'd jimmied the door. "Nellie?"

"Is she here?" Lily asked, peering over my shoulder. It was the first time I'd ever seen her wearing plain old everyday blue jeans, but of course she'd paired them with a faux snakeskin jacket. She'd been wearing that particular jacket a lot lately, and I was pretty sure it was meant to poke fun at her brother.

"I guess she's not visible during the day anymore," I said, shrugging. Morgan had confessed that the only way to keep the ley lines active in our low-magic times was to perform a ritual every single night. Once she stopped doing that, the haywire magic in Boulder began to settle back down. Hazel estimated it'd take a couple more weeks to get back to normal.

"That sucks," Lily said, disappointed. "I mean, I know I can't see her, but I had like, a thousand questions for you to translate."

"Too bad," I said. I was a bit relieved, actually: Nellie was undoubtedly a gold mine of knowledge about boundary magic, but we had only just finished cleaning up all the fallout from the last big magic crisis; I wasn't interested in dicking around with my powers right now.

We set up the television in the main entryway. Electricity had been a problem, until I took it to Maven, who somehow arranged for power to be turned back on in the lower floors of the brothel, no questions asked. While I squatted in front of the TV, messing with the bunny ears, Lily stood up and looked around. "It's weird to think that Maven was once a—what did you say they called themselves?"

"Soiled doves," I supplied. "Although there were like a dozen other terms too."

"Right. Soiled dove." I looked up in time to see her plop down on the steps, surveying the boarded-up windows, the miles of spiderwebs. I thought the whole place was creepy as hell, but Lily was looking around like she had special time-travel goggles. "There was a whole world here once," she marveled. "A whole society and system of rules."

"With lots of disease, abuse, and corruption," I put in. "Not to mention corsets." I went back to fidgeting with the bunny ears, balancing on my heels.

"Speaking of corruption," Lily said slyly, "how's vampire sex treating you?"

I lost my balance and toppled over, sending the antennae smacking on the floor behind the TV. Lily whooped. "That good, huh?" Her face went serious. "Or, wait, that *bad*?"

"That's none of your business, *Lilith*," I said severely, but I smiled as I picked myself up and went after the bunny ears. To my surprise, being on the floor actually seemed to help.

"Come on, one detail," she coaxed. "Does he use superspeed during sex? Do vampire superpowers extend to, you know, stamina? Does he drink your blood after? *During*?"

I made a face. "You have put way too much thought into us having sex. How about I'll tell you one thing if you promise never to use the phrase 'vampire sex' again?"

She clapped her hands. "Deal."

I thought it over. Quinn and I had been spending almost every night together over the last couple of weeks. We were just . . . hungry for each other. But I'd taken to leaving his place before dawn. I said it was to take care of the herd, but we both knew I didn't want to be around when he went cold. "He doesn't drink my blood. He says he doesn't want to, but I know he's afraid he wouldn't be able to stop himself," I said quietly.

Lily wrinkled her nose. "I meant, like, a sexy detail, but I'll accept that answer for now."

"Oh, good. What a relief." I finally got the TV channel to come in clearly, and I stood, wiping my hands on my pants. Then I went over to the closet and retrieved my watch, fastening it around my wrist. It felt good to have it on again, like that piece of Sam was back with me. "How's your family doing?" I asked Lily. She'd been awfully quiet on the ride to Denver.

"About like you'd expect. Mom's taking it hard. She's talking about just canceling Thanksgiving this year."

After we'd subdued Morgan, Lily had restrained her while Maven and Hazel had a big sit-down meeting in Maven's office that lasted until dawn, and picked up again the following night. Hazel had eventually persuaded Maven to let her eldest daughter live, but Morgan would be banished from the state of Colorado for the rest of her natural life. One toe over the state line, and Maven would eviscerate her. It was actually pretty generous of Maven to let Morgan go, especially now that she would be able to use apex magic to stir up shit in someone else's territory. But that was some other henchwoman's problem now. I was done with Morgan.

For her part, Hazel had promised not to tell any other members of Clan Pellar about apex magic, or do any in front of them. The other witch clans in Colorado would not be told about it either, and both parties would carry out the terms of their original covenant as closely as possible.

Hazel had done the best she could, but Morgan's crimes and her banishment were creating a lot of drama in the family, considering that her soon-to-be-ex husband lived in town with their children. He was going to have to decide whether to move the kids to wherever Morgan ended up, start driving them to meet her, or withhold custody altogether. Morgan would have to go along with whatever he decided.

"What about your brother-in-law?" Lily asked me. "Have you told him yet?"

I wrinkled my nose unhappily. Clara had helped me rush John to Magic Beans, where Sashi had just enough juice left to heal his head wound. Then Quinn had pressed him into forgetting the whole night and thinking "Sarah" had left town . . . it had been a whole big tap dance, but he'd eventually bought it.

I hated keeping John in the dark, so as a kind of reward for saving her life again, Maven had given me permission to tell John about the Old World and Charlie's place in it. I sighed. "No, and I have no idea when or how. It needs to be soon—he has too many questions I can't answer, but it's just . . ."

"Hard," she finished. "I get it. You love him, you want him to know, but you want to protect him too."

"Exactly."

She shook her head. "These ties among family, they're so strange, aren't they? Like, I hate Morgan. Hate her. But she's my sister and I love her too, and part of me wants good things to happen for her."

"Yup." I rested my chin on my knees, copying Lily's posture. "Family's complicated. Did I tell you that John asked me if Sashi has a boyfriend?"

"What? No!" She considered that for a second, and huffed, "I'm actually a little offended he got over my sister that quickly."

Oh, jeez. I shook my head and leaned back against the steps. "Visualize me hitting you with a pillow . . ." I began.

Acknowledgments

The book you're now holding is arguably the most-researched project I've ever worked on, and it was only possible with a lot of help from a number of pleasant and gracious people. First and foremost, thank you to my Boulder guide, Brieta Bejin, who gave up the better part of a weekend to patiently show me around her city, and answered follow-up questions pretty much until I turned in the final draft. My deepest thanks to Pat Kociolek of the Museum of Natural History at the University of Colorado Boulder, who was willing to humor my bizarre questions about snake monsters, and to all the nice folks at the Boulder Police Department, who were so generous and gracious that now I feel a little bad about Keller. Thank you to the Colorado Wolf and Wildlife Center for giving me the chance to observe real wolves (I really don't think any of them were shapeshifters, but I was very respectful just in case), and to my beta-reading rock star, Elizabeth Kraft. My gratitude also goes out to Sybil Ward (no relation to the fictional Sybil) and Brandon Beaty, who both read through the story for errors in the military references or lingo. Thanks to Brandon, I may never use the word "gun" again.

I found additional insight into the mindset of the female soldier in Helen Thorpe's *Soldier Girls: The Battles of Three Women at Home and at War*, which I highly recommend. For more information on the surprisingly fascinating history of prostitution in Colorado, I urge you to consult *Brothels, Bordellos, and Bad Girls: Prostitution in Colorado, 1860–1930* by Jan Mackell. You can also read all about the Boulderado in *Legend of a Landmark: A History of the Hotel*

Boulderado by Silvia Pettem. Hugh Mark was a real person and by all accounts a lovely man.

A few more random thanks go out to Tracy Tong and Jody Yuan, who somehow knew what a label-obsessed vampire would probably be into, and Matt Ventimiglia, who responded nimbly to my demand of "Quick, gimme a name for a vampire." Thank you to my development editor Angela Polidoro, for being as excited about Sashi's return as I was—and for being patient with me even when we didn't have a lot of time for patience.

And of course, huge, huge thank-yous to my team at 47North: Britt Rogers, Adrienne Lombardo, Ben Smith, and Alex Carr. You guys fought for this series right when I needed it the most, and I'll always appreciate your being my champions.

About the Author

Melissa F. Olson was raised in Chippewa Falls, Wisconsin, and studied film and literature at the University of Southern California in Los Angeles. After a brief stint in the Hollywood studio system, Melissa moved to Madison, Wisconsin, where she eventually acquired a master's degree from the University of Wisconsin–Milwaukee, a husband, a mortgage, a teaching gig, two kids, and two comically oversized dogs, not at all in that order. Learn more about Melissa, her work, and her dog at www.MelissaFOlson.com.